Whispers

Book 4 of the World In-between Series

IE Castellano

Laurel
Highlands
Publishing

Cover by JosDCreations
http://JosDCreations.com

Laurel Highlands Publishing
Mount Pleasant, PA
USA
http://LaurelHighlandsPublishing.com

ISBN-13: 978-1-941087-29-9
ISBN-10: 1-941087-29-9

This book is a work of fiction. Names, characters, places, and incidents either are products of the author's imagination or are used fictitiously. Any resemblance to actual persons, living or dead, events, or locales is entirely coincidental.

Magic is everywhere if one knows how to look

Chapter One

Uninvited

His crimson bowtie sat perfectly against his white shirt collar. His garnet cufflinks glimmered in the mirror. Berty slipped on his tuxedo jacket. As he adjusted his sleeves, he heard a knock on the door. "Come in," he said.

Declan entered, fidgeting in his tuxedo. "Your brother and his family have just arrived," he announced. "Your mother wants to pin flowers on us." Berty had spent the night in his old bedroom down the hall from his parents while Declan stayed in Jon's old room. He stood next to Berty, gazing at their reflections in the full-length mirror. "I look ridiculous in this. Your mother said that I look dashing." He shook his head. "Delyth is going to laugh."

"Don't worry," said Berty with a chuckle, "Jon, Dad, and Matt are all wearing tuxes, too."

"Edwin says everything is secure and Delyth and her mother are preparing the Fairy Ring," Declan said.

Before Berty could answer, Jon strolled into the room with a crimson boutonniere pinned to his lapel. "My big brother is finally getting married. Of course, you have to leave your bedroom first."

"A man's got to look good on his wedding day," Berty joked.

"Yeah, but you can do magic, so it shouldn't take you that long," said Jon.

Berty snapped his fingers. Jon's tuxedo pants turned into a sparkly black tutu. "You mean like that?" He and Declan laughed.

"Very funny," Jon said in a flat voice.

"I think the black socks and dress shoes make it," said Berty.

"When you're done laughing, can you change it back please?"

"Berty Chase!" a woman's voice scolded.

Seeing Teresa in the doorway, Berty returned Jon's pants. "Don't you look lovely in dark red," he said.

Teresa rolled her eyes. "Declan, let's get your boutonniere," she said.

Left alone in his old room with his brother, Berty said, "I'm not the only one with magic in this family. Remember, the Pixie Priestess appeared to both of us in that fire in the Outlands. Magic runs through your blood. You just need to find it."

Jon adjusted his glasses while checking his reflection. "You're still wearing pants," Berty said. "Come on; don't want to be late for my own wedding."

In the living room, Berty stood still as his mother pinned a crimson mum to his lapel. Stepping back, she smiled.

"The limo is here," his father announced. "Kate, are we ready?"

"I think so," she said. His mother sparkled in her claret dress.

The seven of them climbed into the back of the limousine. Sitting between her mother and grandmother in the same color red dress, Hope stared at Berty. He watched his niece's dark brown curls begin to fall while he waited for her question.

The houses of his parents' neighborhood blurred in the tinted window above her head. Finally, she asked, "After you and Silvia marry, will she become an empress again?"

"No," answered Berty. "All the Empress' husbands became Lord Hunter. Silvia will be known as Lady Chase, but to you, she'll be Aunt Silvia." He smiled at her.

"Why not?" Teresa asked. "Why won't she hold the title of Empress?"

"Because only the Scepter can bestow that title," he explained.

"That doesn't seem fair," Teresa said.

Berty shrugged.

Turning her attention to Declan, Teresa asked, "Have you spoken with Julie yet?"

"She sent me a," Declan glanced at Berty, "postcard from Japan. Then last night, she called when she and Matt got back. Hearing her voice through that phone thing was different. She sounds happy. Life on this side of the portal agrees with her, I think."

Smiling, Teresa said, "My brother loved showing her Japan. He's so happy with Julie in his life and being able to be home, now that he's working for Jon."

The limo passed the Victorian Berty called home. It drove until the tree-lined street ended at the beginning of the woods. After Berty, his family, and Declan exited the car, the limo driver cruised back the way it came. Berty led the group into the forest.

Away from the view of the street, an Empire Guard escort waited for them. Surrounded by leather armored men, they continued through the trees.

A Goblin stepped out of the shadows. "Congratulations, my

Lord," it squeaked. Berty gave the Goblin a nod. The gray skinned creature rushed out of sight.

Wedding guests already sat in chairs under an autumnal canopy. More Empire Guards patrolled the ceremony space.

"Is all this security really necessary?" Kate asked.

"Very," Berty replied.

"Everything is as you specified, my Lord," Edwin said into his ear.

"Thank you, Edwin," he said. He watched Hope run over to Obie who sat with Julie and Matt. "You can take your seat with Lark. We're going to start soon." All his Advisors were present except for Alvar. His wife, Hedda, saved him a seat while he escorted Silvia and her family to the forest ceremony. Prince Goscislaw sat near the front with his wife and daughter. High Elf Avery attended alone while Lord Darnell and Chief Miercia arrived together. They wanted to show a strong Goblin-Troll alliance. Unfortunately, Ojore could not attend. He and his father sent a gift that sat in the house with the others waiting to be opened after the ceremony.

"My Lord," said Alvar. "Everyone has arrived. Queen Lida has closed the Fairy Ring."

After giving the Elf a nod, he clapped his brother's shoulder. "It's time."

Jon walked down the aisle between the chairs by himself. He stopped in front of the flower covered canopy. Turning to face the guests, he waited for Alvar and Lida to take their seats. He adjusted his glasses, then said, "I'd like to welcome all of you to the union of my brother, Berty, and the love of his life, Silvia." Flashing a quick smile, he sat next to Teresa.

With his mother on one side and his father on the other, Berty strode down the aisle. His parents left him to stand alone at the entrance to the canopy. He took a breath.

Silvia stood at the end of the aisle, shimmering in a silvery light blue gown. In a tailed tuxedo, Martin held her arm. She glided towards him. All he could do was smile.

Martin kissed his sister on the cheek, then sat next to his wife in the front row. Taking each other's hands, Berty and Silvia stepped under the canopy. In the center of the canopied space, they faced each other while holding hands. Their gazes locked.

"Berty, I willingly take you as my husband," Silvia said.

He could see his life in her brown eyes. "Silvia, I willingly take you as my wife," he said.

"Together," they said in unison, "we will face whatever life brings as equal partners. In this union, two hearts become one, two souls merge." A candle behind them magically lit. "Let our love bind us." His lips found hers.

When they finally turned to their guests, everyone was standing. A line formed behind Martin and his wife, Martha, in the center aisle. "So beautiful. Congratulations," said Martha. She hugged him both.

"Welcome to the family, Berty," Martin said.

Berty's family and Teresa's family gave them hugs, some with happy tears. The Heads of the Empire and their families wished them well next. King Elrick proudly used a cane to walk. Delyth took Telor's place by her parents' side—congratulating them as Princess of Fairyland instead of Historian of the Empire.

Running between Declan and Hatcher, Hope shouted, "People came through the portal with weapons!"

Some of the guests froze while Empire Guards and others ran into position. Berty closed his eyes. Near the portal, a dozen men in dark cloaks waited as more crossed into their forest.

"Anti-imperialists," said Berty.

Silvia nodded. "Martin, are you ready to lead the guests back to the house the back way?"

"Yes."

"Delyth will break the Fairy Ring. Gather everyone."

Under tufts of leaves, people grabbed weapons. Berty found his sword right outside the canopy. His mother stared at the blade in his hand. "You're coming with us," she said.

"We'll be right behind you," he told her. "Get within the property line as quickly as you can. In the garage, you'll find weapons on the second floor. Use them if need be."

"Broken!" Delyth announced.

Silvia raised her right palm. "That should keep them at bay long enough to get a head start."

Carrying a sword, Martin led most of the wedding guests into the forest. Hedda, at Alvar's insistence, was the last to leave with a spear and shield.

Silvia shuddered backwards. "They're fighting my magic."

Firework like explosions rocked the forest. With his eagle eye, Berty saw Obie rolling colored spheres of magic. Wielding a crossbow in each hand, Julie used the trees as cover. Hedda touched a tree, becoming invisible. She surprised an attacker with her spear. Jon pulled Hope away from the fighting. "I wanna help," she protested.

"It's our job to protect the house," said Jon. "And you have to bring people through the portal." Taking her father's hand, she ran.

"I can't hold them any longer." Silvia's arm lowered. She stumbled.

Catching his new wife, Berty helped her take refuge under the canopy. Delyth stared at Silvia collapsing to the ground. "Old Fairy

Dust," she said to Lida. Unfolding their wings, the Fairies leapt into flight.

Even with Empire Guards, Berty felt underprepared for a battle. He removed the magic that returned his and Declan's tuxedos to their usual Empire garb. Edwin's shield blocked an arrow. Swords clanged beyond the ceremony space.

Silvia knelt to recover her strength. With his palm out, Berty's arm crossed in front of his body. The forest reclaimed the chairs. A tree hid Silvia from view.

Arrows whistled through the autumn air while dark cloaks charged between the trees. Empire Guards met the charge. From behind the guards, Declan's arrows pierced the dark line.

Berty's blade struck another's. Blue sparkles rained on dark cloaks from the Fairies. Magical explosions shook the forest. A scream pierced his eardrums.

Fighting paused as a bluish purple shape tumbled out of the sky. The free fall froze feet from the forest floor. Lida, convulsing in pain, gently fell to the earth. Blue oozed from her wing.

A second shape slammed to the ground. Red fed the earth. A male Fairy's crumpled body twitched on the dry, brittle, discarded leaf carpet.

When Berty's foe fell, another took its place. The dark cloaked anti-imperialists outnumbered them. Hedda materialized, viciously stabbing her husband's attackers with her spear. From the side, arrows hit targets. Julie's dual crossbows kept the advance at bay.

Magically, the injured Lida slid behind Berty. Silvia stood at the center of the former ceremonial space. She breathed deeply. When she exhaled, a pulse pushed the attackers back.

A horn called through the woods. Dragging their dead and

wounded, the anti-imperialists retreated.

Delyth landed, running to her mother. "Mom!" she cried. She crouched next to Lida. "Your wings."

Lida held a torn piece of her gown over the gash in her wing. Blue blood streamed through her fingers. "Thank you for stopping my fall, Lady Chase," she said. With the help of her daughter, she stood.

Silvia gave the Fairy Queen a nod. "We need to get inside the house's protection. Follow me."

Weapons still drawn, they followed Silvia through the forest. Even with Delyth's aid, Lida stumbled often. Declan tried to help, but Lida said, "Watch and protect."

The squeaks of an old, rusty swing set carried onto their path. Edwin froze. "What's that noise?" The other Empire Guards shifted their weight while their eyes examined the trees.

"A nearby park," said Silvia. "Stay on the path. We won't be seen." They hurried as quickly as Lida could.

Fallen leaves speckled the backyard. Berty spotted the blue wood siding of the two story garage. Colvin, Avery, and Matt lowered their weapons, then greeted the wedding party.

"Everyone is in the house," said Matt.

"Lida!" Avery said, rushing to help.

Lida raised a hand to stop the Elf. "Only Fairies can help me," she said in a weak voice. "Fairy wing blood is worse than Fairy Dust, especially for an Elf, but I appreciate your concern, Avery."

Matt's eyes scanned the group. "Where's Obie?"

"He came back here with you," said Julie.

"He's not with me. I thought he was with you," Matt said.

"Obie?" Julie said, trying to hide the panic in her voice. She spun, searching. "He could be lost in the woods. We need to look for him."

Hope ran from the garage with her bow. Taking a step outside the property line, she touched a tree. "They took him through the portal."

All feeling left Berty's limbs. Again, they came for Hope. What would happen to Obie when they discover they abducted the wrong child? Instead of a Wood Listener, they got a young Warlock. Berty closed his eyes.

Dark cloaked men surrounded Obie as they marched. He said nothing to his captors. Every so many feet, he would touch a tree in passing. His hand left a glowing mark none of them saw.

When he opened his eyes, he said, "Obie's leaving us a magical trail."

Silvia approached with two cloaks draped over her arm. After handing Declan his purplish-black cloak, she gave Berty his claret cloak. "Good luck." She kissed him on the cheek.

He squeezed his wife's hand, then glanced at Declan and Edwin.

"I'm coming, too," said Hope.

"No," Silvia said before Berty could. "You are able to help Obie in another way. I'll show you."

Hope looked from Berty to Silvia, then stood next to Silvia.

After fastening his cloak, Berty led Declan and Edwin back into the woods the way they came. "I hear someone," said Edwin. He looked behind him while Declan raised his bow.

"Don't shoot," said Matt. He carried the battle staff Julie honed for him.

Berty noticed the gray cloak fastened around his shoulders. If Matt expected an argument, Berty did not oblige. He simply gave him a nod, then continued leading them towards the portal.

In front of the two oak trees, Berty closed his eyes. Two Guardian Trolls laid motionless on the forest floor. Neon blue specks covered the pine grove and the Trolls.

"Cover your faces," he said when he opened his eyes. "Fairy Dust is everywhere."

Edwin threw his cloak over his head.

"Wait," said Matt. "Our eyes, too?"

"Fairy Dust can affect you through your eyes, nose, and mouth," Declan explained.

"How are we going to see?"

"Leave that to me," said Berty. "Grab hold of Declan. Keep your faces covered until I say otherwise."

When he felt Edwin's hand on his shoulder, Berty covered his face with his cloak. With his eyes closed, he saw a shimmering blue disc between the trees. He stepped toward the portal. In the grove of pines, it looked as though a Fairy Dust bomb exploded. He led them past the knocked out Trolls. When he no longer could see neon blue particles, he dropped his cloak from his face. "It's safe," he said.

Declan turned to look at the pine grove. "They expected to be followed. Fairy Dust is everywhere."

"What does Fairy Dust look like?" Matt asked. "I don't see anything."

"I can see its magical residue," explained Declan. He stood at the edge of Perimeter Road. His eyes scanned until he pointed. "There." Walking across the road to a tree, Declan crouched. He extracted his wand from his quiver. "Clever boy."

"What is it?" Matt asked.

"He knew my wand could follow his trail," he said. "And by touching trees… very smart. This way."

Declan's wand directed them through the forest. Sunlight escaped beneath the horizon. The dark forest slowed their search. Berty relied on his eyes adjusting. He did not want to alert anyone to their position.

An eagle called through the night. Stopping, Berty closed his eyes. He saw a camp. Obie sat near the fire, surrounded by men. When he opened his eyes, he whispered, "We're close. And extremely outnumbered."

The trees creaked. Different colored lights floated around the trunks. "Knownots," whispered Edwin. Opening his mouth, the Elf emitted a sound that made the three of them stare.

A blue light flew to Edwin. The tiny winged creature hovered like a hummingbird in front of Edwin's face. It conversed with the Elf using a series of squeaks.

"The Emperor suggests using an area around a nearby campfire for a Knownot party," Edwin whispered. "Just don't touch the boy."

After squeaking, the Knownot flew back to the other waiting lights.

"The trees summoned them here," Edwin told them.

Berty saw Hope standing on the Star Gazing Platform with her arms outstretched. The forest below her pulsed at her command.

They crept closer to the camp, staying in the shadows. Little colored lights converged on the campsite. They lost their glow as they transformed into woodland creatures. Berty thought he heard faint, mischievous giggling. He peeked through a bush.

"Where's my spoon?" one of the men asked.

Tents collapsed. Swords clanged to the ground. Pants dropped as people walked.

A man screamed, "Knownots!" He ran towards the only person who the tiny shape shifters ignored. "This is the boy's doing." Grabbing Obie from behind, he held a blade to his throat. "Stop it now or the boy dies!"

The tricksters froze. An arrow pierced the man's forehead.

Clutching a sword, another snatched Obie. He crouched behind the boy, using him as a shield. Others grabbed weapons as they stared into the trees.

Obie released a magical sphere. It collided with the fire, sending flames shooting into the camp. The scrambling men did not know which way to look.

The trees creaked over the commotion. Berty watched a Knownot exodus of the camp. All the creatures stayed low to the ground. "Get down," Berty said.

The four of them laid on the ground. The camp exploded over their heads in blues and greens. Silence blanketed the forest.

"Uncle Declan?" Obie called.

Jumping off the ground, Declan said, "I'm here."

Obie hugged his uncle. "I thought I saw your arrow."

"Let's get away from here," said Edwin, surveying the scattered bodies.

Declan placed his wand in his opened palm. "We can't go back through the portal."

They followed Declan through the dark forest. "That was some explosion," said Matt.

"I didn't know I could do that," said Obie. "Hope said I could."

"How were you talking to Hope?" Berty asked.

"Through the trees."

Berty and Declan exchanged glances.

"I started touching them, so they thought I was she," Obie explained. "With each touch, I left magic, then Hope spoke to me. I don't know how. She sent the Knownots." He smiled.

They found a well-protected, secluded spot to make camp. Obie sat close to the fire in the sweater and slacks Matt's parents bought him for the wedding. He shivered a little without a body enveloping cloak.

"Take my cloak," Declan said to his nephew.

"I'm okay, Uncle Declan." Obie formed a sphere between his palms. His fingers stretched it wider than his shoulders. With a flick, as if he were shaking a blanket, it grew into a long rectangle, which he threw around him.

Sitting next to Obie, Declan said, "Cloaks made out of magic are useful in a pinch."

"But?" Obie asked.

"Just know that a Watcher can find you while wearing that."

"I thought you approved of my magic."

"I do, Obie. Magic, like everything, has its limitations and its consequences. It's important you learn that, as a Warlock."

Tearing his blue eyes away from his uncle, Obie stared into the dancing flames. "What are the limitations to your magic, Uncle Declan?" he asked finally.

"I don't have any magic of my own," said Declan. "I can only see it."

"But your wand?" implored Obie.

"Detects magic," Declan explained. "If I were to use magic in the way you do with my wand, then I'd have to take it from somewhere."

"I don't understand."

"You, the Emperor, and Hope have true magic. That magic resides within you. I can only conduct the magic surrounding me." He watched Obie digest his words for a moment. "Get some sleep. We'll discuss magic later."

The five of them laid on loosely piled pine needles around the fire for warmth. Lying beside Berty, Matt fidgeted. "You okay, Matt?" Berty asked.

"Just getting comfortable," Matt answered.

They awoke with a cold sun barely touching a cold sky. Matt stood next to the morning fire, rubbing his neck and back. Handing Matt a cup of magically brewed coffee, Berty asked, "Problem?"

Matt sipped the warm coffee before saying, "Sleeping outside on the ground is much more glamorous on tv and in books and movies. The ground is hard and lumpy. I can see my breath. I'm surprised my nose doesn't have frost on the tip."

Berty laughed. "It gets cold in November," he said. "Drink your coffee. We gotta go."

After erasing their fire magically, Berty asked Declan, "Does Delyth still have your locket?"

"No. She gave it back before the wedding," Declan said.

They hiked in the direction Declan's wand steered. Hearing cracks, they stopped. Edwin unsheathed his sword. Declan pointed his wand at Obie. It quickly absorbed the magic cloak.

A dark cloaked man holding a wand approached. "Give us the child," he demanded.

Berty pushed Obie behind him. He could see a few men lurking in the shadows.

Declan flicked his wand towards the other Watcher. A stream of magic shot from the tip. With a quick wrist movement, the Watcher caught the magic, then shot it at Edwin. The Blade of the Golden Flame sliced through the stream. Magic dispersed into the trees.

Berty's hand grazed the hilt of his sword. His fingers plunged into a small velvet pouch. He released the pinch of sparkling Fairy Dust. The Watcher fell.

The lurkers attacked, giving Berty a wide berth. Obie raised his hand, but Berty stopped him. Unsheathing his sword, Berty attached himself to Obie.

He held Obie's hand as he fought. Declan ran from tree to tree, lobbing arrows at men out of Berty's view. Edwin battled two men with his golden sword and shield. Using his battle staff, Matt knocked a man to the ground.

Disarming his opponent, Berty dropped Obie's hand. He gave the boy a slight nod.

With both hands, Obie created a magical disk. It hovered in front of him, growing larger. His hands pulsed. The disk pushed their attackers through the forest.

Berty approached the dusted Watcher. "My Lord," said Edwin, holding out his sword. "To slice his wand and dispel any magic." Taking the Blade of the Golden Flame, he located the wand in the underbrush. He promptly sliced it in two.

They hurried through the forest. "I'm sorry, Uncle Declan," Obie said in a small voice.

"We must learn from our mistakes, Obie," Declan said.

The sun's warmth faded quickly. Declan wrapped his nephew in his cloak. When they lost daylight, they traversed slower. With rumbling stomachs, they emerged from the woods. Berty's weary eyes gazed upon the treed wall of the Sages' Grove. They followed the wall to the gates. A door inside the wooden gates opened, letting them inside the protection of the trees.

When they reached the Empire Tree, they climbed the steps to the Reception Room. Silvia met them at the top of the stairs. Looking at Declan, she said, "The Fairies are still in the house. Freesia will take you through the portal."

After giving his nephew a quick hug, he sprinted up the main staircase.

Julie wrapped her arms around Obie. "I'm so glad you're okay," she breathed. When she unlatched from her nephew, she hugged Matt. "Thank you."

Berty noticed his family sitting with members of the Advisory Council and Heads of the Empire. He took his wife's hand. Together, they approached the table.

"Avery, I assume you arrived with a Warrior escort?" Berty said.

"I did, Emperor."

"I would like you to return with a Fairy of the Containment Unit stationed here," he said. "That Fairy will then reside in Irmingard in case of a Fairy Dust attack."

Alfred smiled at Berty. "That would prove prudent during our travels," said Avery, "but the Dominatrix has activated our moat. It is our ancient defense against Fairy Dust. The Fairy can return once we are within the walls of Irmingard."

"I believe that to be unwise, Avery," said Alfred.

"Grandfather? How else are we to defend ourselves?"

"I am not talking about the moat. I would advise against turning away the Fairy," said Alfred.

Allowing the Elves to discuss, Berty turned his attention. "Miercia," he said, "your Guardian Trolls have been dusted. In fact, the entire portal area is smothered in a layer of Fairy Dust. A Containment Unit will be dispatched shortly. Hope, Jon, and Teresa, come with me." He tugged Silvia's hand lightly to ask her to come with him.

Matt's parents doted on Matt, Obie, and Edwin as Berty climbed the steps with his family. Entering the Roundtable Room, he asked everyone to sit.

"Berty, what's wrong?" Jon asked, sliding in his chair.

He looked directly through his brother's spectacles into his brown eyes. "They abducted Obie, thinking he was Hope."

"How is that possible?" asked Teresa.

His eyes switched focus. "Because they are looking for a child with a specific gift. They just don't know which child has this gift." He looked at Hope sitting on the large chair between her parents. "Hope is a Wood Listener," he said. As soon as the words left his mouth, he felt purged of his final secret between him and his brother.

"What does that mean?" Teresa asked.

"She can communicate with the trees," answered Silvia.

"And this is useful?" continued Teresa.

"Very," said Berty.

"How did she become a Wood Listener?" Jon asked.

"A person is born with magical ability," Silvia said.

"So wackos are after my child because she can talk to the trees? Are they going to be after my other child as well once she's born?" Jon asked.

"I don't know, Jon," said Berty.

Jon said nothing. An uneasy silence filled the room.

"What can Hope do to defend herself?" Teresa asked. "What can we do to protect her?"

"Hope has two weapons. One is her bow. The other is Fairy Dust," said Berty.

"And us?" said Jon.

"Let her," said Berty.

"I can join the archery club at school," said Hope. She bounced on her seat in excitement.

"Daddy and I will talk about it," Teresa told her daughter.

Staring at Berty, Jon asked, "How long have you known about the tree thing?"

"Last Thanksgiving when I gave her the doll."

Jon nodded.

"And what of Obie?" asked Teresa.

"Obie is a Warlock who is joining the Empire Guard," answered Berty.

"A Warlock?"

"A Warlock's magic is more concentrated than say a Mage's," Silvia explained. "His magic mostly manifests as spheres or streams of energy. Warlocks are best suited for defense."

Jon removed his glasses. His hands pressed against his face. "Why didn't you tell us?" he asked.

"You wouldn't have believed me," Berty said.

"You don't know that," Jon snapped.

Berty stared at his brother across the table. Retorts swam in his mind, but did not pass his lips. "Nothing was fully realized until you left her here with me."

"Well, that's not going to happen again."

Hope's brown eyes welled as her shoulders dropped.

"Jon," said Teresa.

"It's this place. Look what it's done to her."

Between her parents, Hope shrank to the back of the chair. She kept her eyes downcast.

"No, Jon." Teresa's soft gaze moved from daughter to husband. "Hope could always do this—talk to trees. We're the ones who didn't listen. Do you remember her imaginary friend who could never come inside the house? It was a tree. She would sit under it and talk to it."

Chapter Two

Family

Jon stared into the reflective tabletop. "I remember," he said softly. His eyes focused on his deflated daughter. He smiled. "You're going to have to come here on the weekends for Fairy Dust and archery lessons," he said to her. "Now, go get ready for dinner. We'll be down shortly."

In fits of giggles, Hope skipped out of the room. Teresa placed her hand on Jon's arm. "I was afraid that archery would make her lose her innocence," she said. "She is more mature than other kids her age, but she has retained an innocence not found in most children anymore." She wistfully glanced at the door. Her misty eyes blinked away the moisture as she focused on Berty and Silvia. "You two have not yet had your wedding reception." She rose from the chair, gently tugging on her husband's hand.

Alone with Silvia for the first time since before their wedding, Berty kissed the back of her hand. "At least we got through the ceremony," he said. "How is Lida?"

"Weak. She lost a lot of blue wing blood. I had them stay on that side of the portal so that time would pass more slowly for her," Silvia said. "Delyth was going to attempt some ancient Fairy magic on her."

"If Hope wears her pendant, she should be able to ask Freesia to give us an update," said Berty.

Opening the door of the Roundtable Room, Berty heard Delyth say, "We could have used the basket, Mother."

"I want to walk, Delyth. I need to walk," Lida's voice replied.

His eyes searched in the direction of the voices. He saw the Fairies and Declan descending towards them. Lida's bluish-purple wings wore bandages. The Fairy Queen leaned on her daughter and Declan for support.

"Lida, how are you?" Silvia asked.

"Hungry," she answered with a wince. "Food should help regain some of my strength."

Silvia nodded. Elrick paused on the landing while his wife hobbled down the steps. Leaning on his cane, he said, "The important thing is that she has her life, although she may never fly again. There are worse things for a Fairy." The Fairy King continued his descent.

Berty met Silvia's gaze. The Fairies had endured much as if they were being punished. Together, they trailed behind the Fairies to the Reception Room.

Estelle greeted them at the bottom of the staircase. "Before we have the reception, you must have your union ceremony on this side. Starjen requests the Advisory Council and your brother, my Lord," she said.

The members of the Advisory Council stood. "You, too, Daddy," Hope said. Jon followed Alvar.

Estelle led them up the stairs. Each level passed until the staircase ended at the Watching Rooms. A cool night breeze caressed them as they climbed out of the Tree.

On the Star Gazing Platform, Estelle motioned for Jon and the Council to stand against the railing. A circle glowed white in the center of the platform. Hand in hand, Berty and Silvia stood inside the circle. Standing with the others, Estelle instructed, "Join hands."

Berty and Silvia faced each other. Their hands interlocked. Out of the corner of his eye, he saw those against the railing take the hand of the person beside them. Berty stared into the brown depths of Silvia's eyes. She returned his stare. They smiled.

A column of white shot through the floor, encasing the two of them. Leaning forward, they kissed. The white diffused into the dark sky. Over the treetops, magic exploded into multiple colored fireworks.

Their foreheads touched while their fingers stayed entwined. After a few breaths, their heads allowed air to flow between them. Berty noticed the Sages' Seal emblazoned on the wooden platform. The colors of the Seal flowed in the outline like fire in an opal.

"At what are you looking?" Silvia asked.

"The Sages' Seal," Berty answered.

"Where?" Her eyes scanned the platform where he looked.

He looked at her then whispered, "You don't see it."

She shook her head.

"Declan?" he called.

"Yes?"

"Do you see something on the platform?"

"Yes."

Berty looked at the others in the circle. "Does anyone else?"

"No," they said.

"Declan, what do you see?"

"The Sages' Seal," Declan answered. "Colors swim in the white fire outline. I've never seen anything like it. It's a beautiful version of the Sages' Seal."

Berty searched into Silvia's warm, brown eyes. "I saw the Fairy Dust, too," he whispered.

Light blue and dark red shot through the floor where they stood. The wind mixed the colors to make a purple that swirled into white. When the light faded, Declan asked, "Did everyone see that or was it just me?"

"I saw that," said Colvin.

"Alfred," said Delyth, "does this mean what I think it means?"

"I believe so," Alfred answered. "We have an Emperor and an Empress."

Berty's and Silvia's brown eyes met. "You haven't touched the Scepter," Berty said.

"I didn't have to. There was no transfer. My Empress-ship has simply been restored," she answered. She glanced at the others around them.

He squeezed her hand, saying, "Let's celebrate."

Hand in hand, Berty and Silvia led everyone into the Reception Room. Berty glanced at the second carved wooden throne on the dais.

"Please stand for the Emperor and the Empress of all that surround us," Alfred announced. The wedding guests stood. Elrick helped Lida to her feet.

"That explains the appearance of the throne," said Elrick.

They took their seats at the long table. Once everyone else found seats, Tenders filled the table with food and drink. Jon raised his glass. "To my brother and new sister-in-law," he said. "First, I want to welcome Silvia into our family. I've never seen Berty so happy. The two of you are embarking on a spectacular new adventure. Together, you will be able to overcome any obstacle. To true partnership, true love, and a bright future."

Glasses clinked. Kate dabbed her eyes. Jon led the sipping of drinks. A joyous atmosphere surrounded the table, melting all that happened prior to dinner for the moment.

Music began to play. Berty and Silvia danced. Happiness filled his heart as he held his wife close. He stared into her loving eyes. Jon was right; they could face anything together.

Finally, Berty and Silvia said goodnight. They ascended the main staircase. When the stairs ended at the Watching Rooms, they stepped through the wall that brought them to their private hallway. With a foot on the bridge connecting the trunk to their chambers, Berty's heart fluttered. "Who's," he began to ask. Reaching the end of the bridge, they faced a large door. The two separate bundles of leafy branches, which used to be his and her respective chambers, grew into one large leafy bundle.

"Interesting," Silvia said. "I wondered about this."

Together, they entered the wide arched doorway. Both of their studies merged into one, yet separate. Each had its own side—Berty's to the right and Silvia's to the left. The dining table bridged the two studies. A curved center staircase beckoned them upstairs.

"Amazing," she remarked. "I've never seen anything like it. The Scepter must sense the encroaching danger."

"What do you mean?" asked Berty. His eyes traced the large, Sages' Seal carved into the shared back wall.

"Emperor and Empress. Even your brother's toast held clues," Silvia said.

His fingers entwined with hers. "Let's not worry about that right now," he said. His eyes searched into warm brown. "Tonight, let's just be Mister and Missus." His other hand reached around her back, pulling her closer. "Let's just be Berty and Silvia Chase."

Everything that transpired and conspired beyond the Empire Tree's branches could wait. The mysteries of the Scepter would not reveal themselves—not yet, if ever. She smiled, but her smile contained worry. Berty lowered her head to hers. Their foreheads touched and noses grazed. "The Scepter spoke through Jon tonight," he said.

"Together, we can overcome any obstacle," Silvia recited.

"Together," he repeated. His lips found hers. "I love you, Silvia Chase," he breathed.

She giggled. "Silvia Chase," she whispered.

He liked her saying that as much as he liked her calling him Berty.

Breathing deeply, she said in an exhale, "I love you so much." She closed her eyes.

His lips grazed her cheek, kissing their way to her lips. Her fingers swam in his hair. He swept her off the floor then carried her up the new staircase.

Berty did not get a good look at the new bedroom until he awoke with Silvia sleeping in his arms. The early morning sunlight streamed onto their bed. The fire in her dark red hair danced in the warm rays. He longed to stroke her cheek, but he did not want to wake her.

Her eyelashes moved. She caught him watching her. "Morning," she said, smiling.

Squeezing her closer, he answered with a kiss. Their bedroom filled with laughter.

"Do you think Theodore can bring us breakfast?" he asked.

She laughed. "We need to make an appearance at breakfast."

Groaning, he said, "Do we have to?"

"It's tradition," she said, then kissed him softly.

"But I spent the night before on the cold ground without my wife." His lips brushed against her cheek.

"A shower will make you feel better."

Berty shook his head. "Nope. Spending the day in here with you will do that." He kissed her neck, traveling to her exposed shoulder.

"Berty!" she squealed.

His head snapped away from her arm. Hovering over her, he said, "What?"

She rolled her eyes then pushed on his chest. "We can come back."

"Promises, promises," he mumbled. He flashed her a mischievous grin then slid out of their warm bed. His eyes reluctantly shifted from her smiling face to their bedroom.

The double room housed Silvia's dressing table, two wardrobes, two doors leading to bathrooms, and the Hunter family's tapestry. Berty guessed that his bathroom was on the same side as his study. He took a few steps then stopped when Silvia's fingers grazed his back. The tips of her fingers encircled his Empire Mark.

"It hasn't changed," she said.

"Should it have?"

"I wasn't sure how this works." She stood in front of her mirror. Her silk robe slid off her back. Over her shoulder, she studied her Empire Mark.

Her brownish-charcoal monochromatic Sages' Seal breathed with the life of an Empress. He quickly peeked at his pastel colored Mark. Although their union made them one, their Empire Marks told a different story.

"We're still different families," he said.

"No," she said. Her brown eyes blazed into his. "*We* are family. Different lineages. When our heir stewards the Empire, one of the lineages will be chosen. Or he or she will carry a new Empire Mark."

Berty slipped his hands around her waist, then nuzzled his face next to hers. They stared at themselves in her mirror. "We should get to breakfast. See how Lida is doing this morning and Obie," he said.

She smiled. Turning her face towards his, she gave him a kiss. They entered their respective bathrooms.

The hot water soothed any remaining aching muscles. Alone, he could not stop smiling, knowing that he and Silvia were husband and wife.

As he pulled his shirt with its gold trimmed sleeves over his head, he watched Silvia magically button the back of her dress. Gold trimmed her garnet gown. She spun, catching him peering with a smile.

Downstairs, he helped her with her light blue cloak. Donning his dark red one, they crossed to the trunk. Together, they descended their private staircase. Emerging from behind the Sages' Seal, they stepped off the dais into the Reception Room.

The wedding guests stood. "My Lord, my Lady, good morning," Alfred greeted.

"Good morning," they answered. He and Silvia took their seats at the table with everyone.

"Lida, how are you this morning?" Berty asked.

She smiled weakly. "What Declan gave me is working to dull the pain," Lida stated. "I am afraid I'll be spending the next few days resting."

"Oh, Lida. I'm so sorry," said Silvia.

"Fighting for the Empire has been the greatest honor," the Fairy Queen replied. "You saved my life, Empress. I will never forget that. Even if I never take to the skies after this, I will be able to see my son again." Her eyes glistened.

They passed food around the table after Berty and Silvia took theirs. "Now that we have an Emperor and an Empress," Hatcher asked, "what happens to the Advisory Council?"

Berty and Silvia exchanged a glance. "Nothing," replied Silvia.

"There can only be one of each of your positions," explained Berty.

"And you are all the best at what you do," Silvia added. "We see no reason to make any changes."

After breakfast, Berty and Silvia bid farewell to Chief Miercia, Lord Darnell, High Elf Avery, and Prince Goscislaw and his family. "Brana will return in two days to start her training," Goscislaw growled to Alvar before descending below the floor.

"Berty," Matt whispered, "can I have a word?"

Hating to leave Silvia's side, he ushered Matt up the stairs and into the Roundtable Room. He stood near his chair, waiting for him to continue.

"I want to go to Boudon," Matt began. "Declan said that I had to ask for your permission to go."

"It takes five days to get to Boudon from here—on horseback," said Berty.

"I'm going to marry Julie. Now that the portals aren't closing, I want to do things the right way according to her family," Matt explained.

"That means your family must go to hers," Berty said. "Are your parents up for that?"

Matt's gaze got lost in the reflective tabletop. "I don't know," he said finally. "But, I don't feel right not meeting her parents when I have the opportunity to do so."

Berty sighed. "We're on the brink of war, Matt. However, I understand. Why don't we discuss this with both yours and Julie's families?"

"Julie doesn't know," Matt said. "I was going to surprise her with the news. That's why I was talking to Declan."

Nodding, Berty said, "Tell her now and surprise her. I'll send her up. Then, we'll all talk about it."

Matt's smile spread across his face. He slapped Berty's arm.

After Berty sent Julie to the Roundtable Room, he whispered Matt's intentions to Silvia. "Either just the two of them on horseback or everyone in a carriage," she suggested.

Matt wandered down the stairs, holding Julie's hand. He nodded to Berty. Turning to his brother, Berty said, "Bring Mom, Dad, Teresa, and her parents to the Roundtable Room."

Lida bowed her head to Berty and Silvia as Elrick and Delyth helped her to her chambers. "We must be getting back," Martin said as he approached with Martha.

Silvia hugged her brother and sister-in-law. "Thank you for coming," she said. "And Martha, thank you for understanding."

"I never knew my husband could still use a sword," Martha said. "How manly is that?" She laughed.

Martin blushed.

"Hope," Silvia asked, "could you bring us through the portal please?"

"I'll wait," said Berty.

"Nonsense. I'll meet you in there."

He watched the four of them ascend the stairs before entering the Roundtable Room with Declan.

"Is it safe for them to travel?" Lillian asked as soon as she caught sight of Berty.

He understood her concerns, especially after Jon and Teresa had been kidnapped months ago. "Please, everyone, have a seat," he said. Once they were seated around the Roundtable, he explained, "It is customary here for the man and his family to go to the woman's family. At her family's home is where the nuptials officially begin."

Lillian looked at Julie sitting between Matt and Declan. She then glanced at Robert who gave her a nod. "Then we will go, too," she said. "Tradition must be upheld. We want to respect the ways of Julie's family so that she may be part of ours."

"She was willing to give up everything she knew to live on our side of the portal. We can do this for her," added Robert.

Matt beamed as he squeezed Julie's hand. "What about Teresa and Jon, Hope and Obie?" he asked.

"No," said Lillian before Teresa could speak. "Just us and Declan."

"I'm afraid Obie will disagree," Declan said.

"But you just rescued him," protested Lillian.

"All the more reason why he should go," Silvia said as she entered the room. The men stood. After taking her seat, she continued, "Obie is joining the Empire Guard. He won't be able to go home for years. He should not miss his aunt's nuptials. It would be safer if we all went via carriage. Including, Hope, Obie, and Freesia."

"No Empire Guard?" Declan asked. "My Lady," he quickly added.

"It won't be necessary," Silvia answered. "No one is going to attack Boudon again. If we use magic, we can arrive in less than three days. I suggest we leave this afternoon. We'll return in time for

Thanksgiving and Wassail."

"Kate, George, are you two coming?" said Robert.

Berty's parents looked at one another then smiled. "We'd love to," said Kate.

"What should we bring?" asked Teresa.

"Ask the wardrobes in your chambers for traveling clothes," Silvia said. "Theodore will provide us with everything else."

"But we should bring some sort of gift," Lillian said.

Smiling, Silvia nodded. "Come with me," she told Lillian and Robert.

His family began to leave while he called for Theodore. When Theodore arrived, he told the Dwarf their plans. "And, Theodore," he said quietly, "make sure there are extra weapons in the carriage. Just in case." With a bow, the Head Tender disappeared.

Silvia already began packing a bag when Berty entered their bedroom. "Robert and Lillian went home for a few things," she said. "I think they want to bring them a gift from the other side."

Nodding, Berty packed alongside his wife.

Dressed in traveling clothes and cloaks, they met in the Reception Room. "Are you sure I should not go with you?" asked Edwin.

"We'll be fine, Edwin," Silvia assured.

Edwin's mouth moved in silent protest. "Yes, my Lady," he said finally.

"I had Theodore load everything for us in the carriage house," Silvia told Berty. "We're going to leave from there."

Berty felt her emanating strength as he gazed at her.

"What?" she asked.

"You never cease to amaze me," he answered. Hope stood next to her parents with her bow and Fairy Stone pendant. "Are we all ready?" he asked.

His cloaked family collectively said, "Yes."

"Follow me," Silvia said. She led them across the bridges that spanned over the Sages' Grove.

Walking behind everyone else, Declan said to Berty, "It's smart to have both Hope and Obie come. I'm glad we're all going. I didn't like the idea of Julie and Matt going alone."

"I'm only sorry that we can't alert your family to our arrival," Berty said.

Declan's eyes landed on his sister. "It's nice to see that love can prosper during what I fear will be a terrible war."

Chapter Three

Convergence

The RV-sized, dark green carriage had two doors on the one side, flanking a Sages' Seal. At Silvia's touch, the green darkened to brown, covering the seal. "Get in. Sit wherever you'd like," she said. Her hand touched the wall of the carriage house. It pulsed a shimmer.

"What are you doing?" Berty asked.

"We're leaving through the wall instead of the gates," she answered.

She, Berty, and Declan entered the carriage last. The families sat on the cushioned couch that wrapped around sides of the carriage and down the middle. Declan and Berty secured the doors while Silvia kept the curtains drawn over the windows. Taking her seat next to Berty, she said, "Hold on tight. We're going to be going quite fast."

With a touch of her finger, the carriage lurched forward. At automobile speed, they sped down the road to Boudon.

"This is better than our last carriage ride, Uncle Berty," Hope said.

Chuckling, Berty said, "That's because your Aunt Silvia wasn't with us that time."

After hours of traveling, Silvia asked Hope, "I know it's dark, but is it safe to stop for a little while?"

Hope waited for a moment as if she were listening, then nodded.

The carriage slowed. "We're going to stop to eat," Silvia said.

When they stopped, they stepped into the dark woods. Berty lit a campfire using magic. No one spoke much while eating. The dark forest intimated those not used to it. As everyone climbed back inside the carriage, Berty and Declan cleared the campsite. "How long have you been able to see?" Declan asked quietly.

"Since restoring the Scepter," Berty answered. "It's especially strong when I close my eyes."

Nodding, Declan glanced around. "I wouldn't tell anyone beyond the Empress," he whispered. "I can train you so you know what you're seeing."

"What do you mean?"

"Each type of magic has its own properties. And it all looks different," explained Declan.

"Okay," said Berty. They entered the carriage, making sure the doors closed securely. The carriage raced through the dark forest.

They slept on the couches and pull down berths while the carriage continued its journey. After only two days of traveling, the carriage stopped under the houses and bridges of Boudon. Julie and Declan exited first, so the lookouts knew not to shoot them. Berty's family marveled at the village in the trees.

"We should split into three groups to go up the lift," Julie suggested. The fire in her light eyes burned brighter.

Matt and his parents joined Julie in the first ride. Obie took

Hope, Jon, Teresa, and Freesia. Berty, Silvia, and his parents rode up with Declan.

Boudonians glanced as they passed. At the Firth family home, Obie ran inside, calling, "Daddy!"

"Obie." Cecil sounded surprised and a bit worried. "What are you doing here? What's wrong?"

"Nothing," said Obie. "I'm here with Aunt Julie."

"Mom, Dad," greeted Julie as she entered. "Sorry we couldn't give forewarning. I want to introduce you to Matt and his family."

Berty stayed on the balcony with Silvia, his parents, Freesia, and Declan. The others squeezed next to the doorway. He could not see inside the house, but he heard everything.

"Mister and Missus Firth, it is a pleasure to meet you," said Matt. "I am here to ask for your daughter's hand—your blessing."

"Mister Firth—Leon, please," said Julie's father. Footsteps crossed the room. "After Julie's letter, we are so glad to be able to get this chance. My wife, Geraldine. Julie's brothers, Cecil and Vander."

"My father and mother," Matt began.

"Robert," Robert introduced himself, "and this is my wife, Lillian. Matt's sister, Teresa, her husband, Jon, and their daughter, Hope."

"Oh, yes, we've met Hope," said Geraldine. "Did you happen to bring your brother, by any chance, Julie?"

"Out here, Mom," said Declan.

"Come in here," she said. Peering out the doorway, she added, "All of you, come, come."

They crammed into the massive wooden room. Julie and Matt continued their introductions. "And, of course, you remember the Emperor," she said, "but you have not met the Empress."

Standing against the far wall, Vander's jaw dropped a little.

"We understand why you couldn't tell us you were coming," said Leon.

"Please, sit." Geraldine gestured to the long, central, plank table. She looked at Matt and beamed, then took stock of the others. "Where is your little Fairy friend?" she asked Declan.

"Taking care of her mother." Declan answered.

Freesia had Hope and Obie sit on a bench along the wall with her. The rest of them swarmed around the table.

"So, Matt," Leon began. "What is it that you do?"

"I'm a financial analyst," Matt answered. When he saw the blank expressions on Julie's family's faces, he reworked his answer. "I work for the Emperor's brother as a Vice President of Chase Technologies."

"The other side of the portal... Is it a good life?" Cecil asked like an overprotective older brother.

"It's different. I like it over there," answered Julie.

"What about your dreams?" asked Vander.

Declan gave his brother a look that questioned if Vander could care about things like dreams.

"King Elrick and Queen Lida of the Fairies would very much like me to be Fairyland's Woodsmith," Julie countered. "However, Fairyland has been taken by the enemy. We have been discussing a workshop on the other side of the portal."

"You and the Fairy King and Queen?" Vander asked.

Julie laughed. "Me, Matt, and his parents." She glared at her brothers. "Just because you're older than me, doesn't mean I need your blessing."

Laughing, Declan almost fell over in his chair.

"We're allowed to worry about you, too, Julie," Cecil defended.

"We just want to make sure you're not getting into something like—" Vander did not finish. Berty knew he wanted to say *with Owen*—Julie's abusive ex-husband.

After watching everyone's reactions to the unspoken name, Leon smiled. He reached for his wife's hand. Geraldine squeezed it with a smile. She gave him a small nod. "Geraldine and I very much bless this union of our daughter, Julie, to Matt Regnik from the other side of the portal."

Matt and Julie could not stop smiling. Berty grabbed Silvia's hand. Coming to Boudon was the right thing to do.

"Let's have a family dinner this evening," said Geraldine. "We'll make the public announcement tomorrow."

During dinner, Julie and Matt's family explained life on the other side of the portal. Afterwards, they sat around the fire while Leon poured amber colored liquid into goblets and glasses. Vander handed one to everyone.

"What is it?" Teresa asked.

"Spiced whiskey. Mom's own recipe," he replied.

"Oh. Sorry, but I can't have any, but thank you."

"Water?"

"Yes, please."

Once everyone had a glass, Leon raised his glass and said, "To Julie and Matt."

Berty happily sipped his cordial while relaxing next to Silvia. From their seats along the wall, they observed the families interact.

"Are you learning a lot from your Uncle Declan about healing?" Cecil asked his son.

"Tons of stuff," said Obie. "We identify plants and make healing concoctions. Sometimes, I'll watch Alina, too. But I can't do everything she can."

"Who's Alina?" asked Cecil.

"Future Witch of Rowan," Declan answered quietly.

Cecil nodded. Turning back to Obie, he continued, "So, you're going to be a Healer in the Empire Guard."

Obie shook his head.

"He's going to fight?" Cecil asked Declan.

"Dad, don't get made," Obie said. "It's different."

Cecil looked at his son. "What's different?"

Swallowing, Obie glanced at Declan who gave him a nod. "I'm..." He sighed. "I'm going in as a Warlock."

"A Warlock?" Cecil turned to Declan for an answer. "How?"

"What did you do?" Vander accused his brother. All talking in the room stopped.

"Nothing," said Declan. "A person can't acquire or develop magical skill. One must be born with it."

"How do you know?" Vander said.

"I've studied," answered Declan. "There are these things called books. You open them and read the information on the pages."

"And reading a few books makes you an expert?"

"Enough, the two of you," Leon scolded.

Declan smiled nostalgically. "Why don't you give us a demonstration, Obie?" he said.

Obie's light eyes glanced at his family. He turned his left palm to the ceiling. A yellow sphere floated above his head. Geraldine gasped. Turning his right hand, a blue sphere hovered. After a moment, he clapped the spheres into his hands.

"Does your Uncle Declan help you with that, too?" Cecil asked hesitantly.

"No," replied Obie. "Captain Alvar has Lieutenant Edwin and

Mister Colvin training me in the large cavern under the Empire Tree. Then, the scholar, Alfred, and Princess Delyth will work with me in the vaults. And Head Tender Theodore and I practice in the Watching Rooms."

Laughing, Declan said, "So, that's what you're up to when you're not with me."

"Well, I have lessons with Freesia and, sometimes, I'll read Hope's books from the other side," admitted Obie.

"Guess you're learning a lot," Cecil said with a smile.

"And," Obie said with a fire in his eyes, "Ojore, the son of the Chief of the Ghost Tribe in the Outlands, taught me how to use a spear. And, he gave me a bone dagger. Wanna see it, Dad?"

As Obie showed off his gift, Jon chuckled. "These kids have seen much," he said to Berty. "Is there any place Hope hasn't been?"

Berty laughed. "I'm sure."

Cecil and Vander gave up their rooms for Berty's and Matt's parents. Julie, Declan, and Obie slept in the house while the rest of them slept in the carriage.

After breakfast in the Firth home, Leon and Geraldine called the village onto the bridges and balconies. "We'd like to announce the engagement of our daughter, Julie, to Matt, a man of a good family," said Leon.

"We invite you all to the nuptial commencement tonight," Geraldine said.

Robert and Lillian brought the Firths a gift from their collection. The Firths placed the vintage music box on a side table. It played a song they had never heard and depicted the city skyline from the 1920s in a glass-encased globe. Geraldine marveled at its beauty and song. Robert showed Leon how it worked with George describing all the finer details.

Some of the villagers lowered tables and chairs to the forest floor. Others cooked for a feast. Everyone helped with tasks like building and tending fires, placing lanterns, setting the tables, or filling the centers with fall flowers and berries. The children tied sprigs of honeysuckle to the backs of the chairs. By the time dusk approached, every seat around the extremely long table had an occupant. Small fires surrounding the table provided light and warmth. Lanterns and candles illuminated the spread of food pouring into every bare spot.

At the very center, Matt and Julie stood in front of their chairs. "Does anyone oppose this union?" asked one of the village elders.

"I do," said a voice in the shadows.

"Your opposition means nothing, Owen," another elder said.

He stepped into the edge of the firelight. "I know. I'm just making my piece heard," Owen said. His eyes held onto shadow while he leered at Matt. After glancing at Julie, he turned from the merriment.

The third village elder stood. "Let your union be strong like the trees, rooted deep with love, and last like the forest forever," she said. Matt and Julie kissed. The elder raised her glass and the other two followed suit. "To the happy couple," she toasted. Villagers sipped from their glasses. Julie and Matt sat while the food passed from person to person.

Robert discreetly dabbed the corners of his eyes with a handkerchief. Laughter, food, and drink flowed freely.

As the fires died, the villagers returned to their tree houses without their tables and chairs. Entering the carriage, Matt asked, "What happens next?"

"Dancing. Lots of it. All day," answered Declan. "You'll need your sleep." Laughing, he strode to the lift.

Matt sat on the edge of his bunk. "Berty, Silvia, thanks for doing this, especially on the heels of your own wedding," he said.

"You're welcome, Matt," said Berty.

"We don't mind. It was the right thing to do," Silvia added.

In the morning, the villagers hoisted some of the tables back into the trees. The remaining tables and chairs were arranged into an oblong. Matt and his parents waited in the center of the oblong. Julie and her parents descended in the central lift. The family members and villagers watched from the edges of the oblong.

Her parents walked Julie to Matt and his parents. Matt and Julie joined hands. Geraldine and Lillian wove a ribbon around their children's hands.

"Matt, do you promise to love Julie through everything?" Leon asked.

"Yes, I do," said Matt. His gaze never left Julie's.

"Julie, do you promise to love Matt through everything?" Robert asked.

Julie smile widened. "Yes," she said.

The sets of parents hugged each other, then joined the others at the edges.

Matt and Julie laughed. Hands still bound, they danced around the oblong. After two revolutions, Leon and Lillian and Robert and Geraldine joined. Then Cecil and Teresa danced. Finally, Obie and Hope danced within the oblong.

"If Fiona was still alive, she would dance with Jon," Declan said to Berty. "A total melding of the families."

Vander took his turn dancing with Teresa followed by Declan.

"What would have happened if Matt didn't have a sister?" Berty asked. Silvia chuckled.

Being the youngest of the brothers, Declan handed Teresa off to Jon as others joined the dance floor.

"Hey," Vander said to Declan. "I'm working my way up to dance with Heather. I know you don't have a dance partner, so just anyone but her."

"He doesn't have to worry about that."

Declan and Vander turned. "Delyth, you made it. How's your mother?" Declan asked.

"She's doing well. She's resting," Delyth said. She looked up at Vander. "If you want to dance with this woman, Heather, go and dance with her before someone else beats you to it."

Vander took a deep breath, then strolled towards another part of the oblong.

"I think we can dance now without taking the spotlight," Berty whispered to Silvia. She took his hand as he guided her between the dancing couples. He saw his parents dancing with a new life. The forest suited them. Declan swept Delyth across the dance floor. Seeing his friend so happy made him laugh.

"What?" Silvia asked.

His head nodded toward Declan and Delyth. Smiling, Silvia nuzzled closer to him.

Once the ribbon had slid off their hands, the dance finished. The remaining tables and chairs rose into the trees. The now joined families returned to the Firth house. They had lunch while resting their weary feet.

The Firths joined them at the carriage to say good-bye. Lots of hugging preceded anyone entering the carriage. Matt and Julie were the last to say good-bye to Julie's family. Stepping into the carriage, Matt screamed in agony. He clutched his right shoulder and stumbled backwards. "Matt!" shrieked Julie.

The opening of the second door flooded the carriage with light. A gunshot echoed through the forest. Berty ran outside. Vander struggled to hold Matt. A dark shape crashed to the forest floor. Sunlight glistened off the round barrel of a revolver.

"Obie, grab my bag," Declan bellowed. He extracted an arrow out of Matt's shoulder. Berty tried to shut out Matt's groans.

Cocking the hammer of the pistol, Robert approached the shape on the ground.

Declan pulled a vial from his bag. "This is going to burn," he warned. As he poured, Matt screamed.

"Drink this, now," ordered Declan.

Matt swallowed whatever Declan gave him.

The shape did not move. Robert's bullet and several arrows pierced Owen's broken body. Blood spread across the matted leaves and pine needles.

"What did you give him?" Lillian asked.

"The antidote," answered Declan. "I've carried it on me ever since…"

"Antidote? He was poisoned?" Lillian said.

Declan nodded. "We should get him to Alina as quickly as possible."

"Robert, we need to go," Berty said quietly. As he tugged on Robert's arm, Vander and Cecil carried Matt into the carriage.

Silvia touched the carriage wall. It began to race towards the Sages' Grove.

Robert and George kept Matt upright per Declan's instructions.

While Matt fluttered in and out of consciousness, tears streamed down Julie's face. Berty could see Silvia push her magic to make them go faster.

"How did you know what kind of poison Owen used?" Julie asked finally. Her puffy eyes found her brother.

"We were best friends," Declan answered with a sigh. "I always feared he'd use that poison on me one day."

"So, you always carried the antidote," Kate said.

Declan nodded.

"How... how do you know that he hadn't changed the formula?" asked Jon.

"I don't," admitted Declan. "That's why we need to take Matt to Alina."

"Alina... Alina... Hope's friend, Alina?" Robert asked.

"Yes."

"A young girl?"

"A very powerful young girl," said Declan.

"I don't understand," said Lillian, finally breaking her calm stoniness. "What can she do that you can't?"

Declan looked from Robert to Lillian. "Magic."

Without stopping, they reached the Sages' Grove in the early morning. "Go," Silvia insisted. "I need to recoup."

Berty kissed her cheek, then said, "Hope, Obie, quietly wake Alina. Tell her we're coming."

Opening the carriage doors, the kids ran between the white cob buildings. "Come on, Matt," said Berty. "Time to go." With Jon's and Declan's help, they maneuvered a weak and partially unconscious Matt out of the carriage. Julie, Robert, Lillian, and Teresa followed closely.

The opened door of the Rowan house spilled a welcoming light onto the dirt path. "What happened?" Alina asked before they reached the threshold. Her voice sounded years beyond her young age.

"Poison," Declan answered.

Alina nodded. "Place him on the table."

Her father, Cal, helped them lay Matt on their wooden table. Alina wafted smoking herbs in front of Matt's nose, saying some incantation. His eyes snapped open. She placed a little hand on his forehead. After a moment, she disappeared into her Witch Room. When she returned, she spooned something into his mouth.

Matt coughed and sputtered. He sat up. Standing on a bench, she peered at the wound on his shoulder. "Burn the shirt and the cloak," she instructed. "I'll prepare a dressing."

They helped Matt remove his cloak and shirt. Alina had him sit on a stool so she could reach his shoulder properly. She spread something over the wound, then bandaged it. "Leave it on for a day," she said.

Berty threw his cloak around Matt's bare shoulders. "Thank you, Alina," he said, handing her four lids.

Glancing at the gold coins, she said, "My Lord?"

"You should get paid for your work. It is only fair," Berty told her.

"But, I'm not a full Witch yet."

He smiled. "I know. Although no price can be placed on a life, you still saved a man."

Alina smiled back. She was so young, yet so wise.

Turning to her parents who stood near the steps, Berty said, "Cal, Natalie, thank you for opening your door to us at this hour."

"It's the least we can do, my Lord," said Cal.

Berty and Declan helped Matt navigate the bridges to the Empire

Tree. In the Reception Room, Edwin paced in his dressing gown. Seeing them, he took over for Berty.

Berty joined his parents at the table while Edwin and Declan half carried Matt to the bridge. "Where's Silvia?" he asked.

"The carriage ride took a lot out of her," said George.

"She went to bed," Kate said. "Matt will be fine?"

"Yeah. He, too, needs rest."

Jon kept Hope and Obie from following Matt's parents to his chambers. "Give Uncle Matt time to heal. Let's get you two ready for bed." As Jon ushered them to their rooms with Freesia, Berty stepped into his private staircase.

Silvia slept soundly in their bed. Berty tiptoed to his wardrobe. Gingerly getting into bed, he noticed that she clutched a stick. He whispered, "Goodnight, my love," not wanting to wake her.

"No goodnight kiss?" she asked with her eyes closed.

"I didn't want to disturb you."

She smiled. "I find that pushing my magic drains me. Holding onto this," she shook the stick, "helps me regain my strength faster. It is what became of the walking stick I used while Elder."

"Interesting. Perhaps you should carry it with you."

"Perhaps I should." One of her brown eyes peeked at Berty.

Planting his lips on hers, he softly kissed her. She placed the stick on her nightstand, then snuggled into his chest.

Berty eventually woke around noon. From the bed, he watched Silvia spin in her gown. "Morning," she said. "I know Matt will be okay. How are you?"

"Exhausted."

Silvia nodded. "I'll wait for you downstairs."

After washing and dressing, Berty paused on the steps to watch Silvia browse the newly joined structures. He smiled, thinking about her being his wife. Hearing the wind chimes, he descended into the study. Silvia gave him a little nod, then said, "Come in."

"My Lord, my Lady," said Alvar with a bow, "I don't mean to intrude. I have news of Fairyland."

"Do King Elrick and Queen Lida know?" she asked.

"No. I thought it best to report directly to you first."

Silvia looked at the furniture on either side of the room. The couches from her side and the club chairs from his arranged themselves in the center of their combined study. She motioned for the Elf to sit.

Berty and Silvia sat next to each other while Alvar chose a seat across from them. "We've observed explosions in Fairyland. The anti-Imperialists have been scouring buildings and digging," Alvar reported. "We believe they are searching for something."

Berty remembered his vision of Telor removing a stone from the tower. "They won't find it. It's not there," he said.

"You know for what they search, my Lord?" asked Alvar.

"I know of it. I won't pretend to understand it," said Berty. "Leif covets it more than the Staff of Lightning."

Silvia's nose wrinkled at the mention of Leif's name. "We need to tell the Fairies," she said.

"They already know," said Berty. "What if," he looked from Alvar to Silvia, "we attack them while they're busy searching? They'll figure out sooner or later that it's not in Fairyland."

"And when that happens, what will they do?" said Silvia.

"They'll start attacking every village and hamlet," Alvar reasoned.

"Most likely," agreed Berty.

"We can't protect every village," Silvia said. "And we only have one functioning outpost."

"We're going to need as much might as possible to free Fairyland," said Berty.

Silvia nodded in agreement.

"How do we stop them from scattering?" asked Alvar.

"We can't," said Berty.

"But Leif and Millicent must not be allowed to get away," Silvia said with bite in her voice. "Gather the Advisory Council."

Alvar bowed his head, then left.

"They must be searching for something connected with the Fairy's power," she said to Berty.

"It's a stone," he explained. "I overheard Delyth and Lida describe its power as only second to the crystal of the Scepter. Telor escaped Fairyland with it."

Silvia stared at the wall for a moment. "So, they plan on using it to attack the Empire Tree."

"Along with everything else they've gathered along the way," Berty said.

She nodded, closing her eyes. "I fear we are not prepared for this, Berty."

He caressed her hand. "I know. I know."

The Advisory Council stood when Berty and Silvia entered from their private staircase. They sat on equal chairs between Alfred and Declan. "An opportunity to free Fairyland has presented itself," Silvia announced.

"But winter is approaching," Colvin said.

"Yes," said Berty, "and we may not get another chance."

"They're searching for the stone, aren't they?" asked Delyth.

"Yes," answered Silvia.

"Then winter is precisely the time to attack," said Delyth.

"Why is that?" Alvar asked the Fairy.

Delyth took a deep breath. "The stone breathes with the seasons. Come spring, if one is armed with the right tools, then one could divine its location."

Berty and Silvia exchanged a glance. "Perhaps, your parents should be here to discuss strategy, if they are able," he suggested.

"I will fetch them at once," said Delyth. She ran out of the room.

The Fairies arrived in the Roundtable Room before Berty could think of an inkling of a plan. They sat in the extra chairs that appeared beside Delyth's seat. "I am afraid that we won't be able to fight, but we will assist in any way we can," said Elrick.

"That will be plenty. Thank you, Elrick and Lida," said Silvia.

Lida stared into the reflective tabletop. "How many are there?" she asked quietly. When no one answered, she raised her voice a little. "How many anti-imperialists trudge in my city?"

"Our best estimate is over five hundred," Alvar answered.

The Queen did not flinch. "Fairyland's weakness is the inability to be a self-sustaining city. We rely heavily on outside trade for food, medicine, fuel for heat, and practically everything else." She looked at Alvar, then at Silvia and Berty. "Lay siege to the Fairyland and everyone in it."

Elrick stared at his wife for a moment. "Yes, of course," he said slowly. "It would use a lot less resources to disrupt supply lines and weaken them."

"For the entire winter?" Delyth asked.

"You said yourself that the stone is best protected by ancient magic," Lida told her daughter. "Trust in it."

Delyth nodded.

"Does anyone see a problem laying siege to Fairyland?" asked Silvia. "Estelle?"

"Starjen will align for us right after the final day of Wassail," Estelle said.

Since no one objected, Silvia said, "Good. Let's prepare to take back Fairyland."

Chapter Four

Whisperer

Alvar asked the Fairies to draw a map of Fairyland and its surrounding lands. Berty and Silvia gave them the use of the Roundtable. While Delyth spread paper over the tabletop, Berty and Silvia met with his and Matt's families in the Reception Room.

"How's Matt?" Silvia asked.

"Well. Resting," answered Julie.

"We began planning a small ceremony when the portals were supposed to close," said Lillian. "Since Julie already has her dress, Robert and I can call in some favors at the country club. We will only need a few days. That should give Matt and us enough time to recoup." She smiled, placing a hand on Silvia's arm. "You will come, won't you? And, of course, Julie's brother, nephew, and Declan's girlfriend."

"We would be delighted," said Silvia. "It may be best if Matt stays here for another day while you make preparations."

"Oh, that's a great idea," Kate said. "The men just show up any-way." The two mothers laughed.

"Silvia and I will see you through the portal," said Berty.

"Wonderful," Lillian beamed. She gathered her and Kate's hus-bands, their children, and grandchild.

With their bags, they assembled in Hope's chambers. Matt, De-clan, and Obie followed them through the portal to say farewell. During the hugging, Berty overheard Julie tell Declan, "I really like her. Make sure she comes. You guys are really good together, you know."

"Julie," Declan complained.

"Everything will work out, you'll see," Julie said with a smile. She got in the car with Matt's parents.

They waved from the porch as the cars drove away. "Julie seems to be adjusting well to life on this side," observed Silvia. "She will always have a foot on both sides." She turned to Matt. "And now, so do you."

The men followed Silvia back inside the house. "How do I ever repay you for saving my life?" Matt asked Declan.

"Treat my sister well and keep her happy," replied Declan. "We're family. That's what we do."

"Uncle Declan," Obie said as they climbed the steps, "when are you going to marry Princess Delyth?"

Declan stopped.

"You two love each other, don't you, Uncle Declan?"

Sighing, Declan explained, "It's not always that simple."

"Sure it is."

"Tell you what," said Declan. "For you, it can be. Just make sure when you fall in love, she's neither a Fairy nor a princess."

"I can do that," said Obie.

Rustling Obie's blond hair, Declan said, "Come on. It's almost time for dinner."

The five of them stepped through the tapestry. "It's probably best I'm staying here," Matt said while they walked through the Tree. "Especially with all of us living in the same house and I'm not allowed to see Julie's dress. Makes everything so much easier. I'm so exhausted."

"You're going to be," said Declan. "A good meal should help."

When they reached the Reception Room for dinner, only the Fairies were absent. Halfway through dinner, the Fairies finally descended from the Roundtable Room. "The map may take us a few days," said Elrick.

"But it will be thorough," Lida added.

"The room will always be open for you," said Berty. He watched Declan steal a glance at Delyth before taking Obie for Healer lessons.

"Thank you, my Lord," said Delyth. She smiled as her eyes followed Declan and Obie up the stairs.

Lida glanced from Delyth to the hem of Declan's cloak. Without saying a word, she took a bite of her food.

"Is everything okay, Matt?" Estelle asked from across the table.

Matt jumped a little. "I," he began. "It just hit me that Julie is not here."

Smiling, Estelle said, "You'll be back together soon. I'm going for my evening stroll. Would you like to come?"

"Sure," he answered. He rose from the table like out of a daze.

Silvia's hand slid onto Berty's arm. Together, they disappeared into their private staircase. "What's on your mind?" he asked her.

Stopping at the top of the stairs, Silvia said, "A siege, I fear, will only slow them. We need to be able to defeat them. Join me in the vaults?"

Her words felt censored. He wondered who could possibly be listening to them in their own private area of the Empire Tree.

The hatch in the floor of Silvia's side of the study still took them to the Vault Room antechamber. Silvia touched the picture of the scroll. The Library Vault's rock door slid open. Entering with Silvia, he waited for her to explain.

"They're using magic we haven't seen in centuries," she said. "We are at a great disadvantage."

"And we don't have a way to protect against it," he said.

"Surrounding Fairyland we are exposed." Silvia peered at the shelves. "Hlyvinsa," she said to the room. A few books and scrolls flew across the Library.

"Why Whisperer?" asked Berty.

Silvia watched the books pile on the table. "We can't stop Whispers, but someone, somewhere, is a Whisperer." Scrolls outnumbered books on the wood. As they sat, Berty's pocket vibrated. He opened the large, gold Watcher's locket.

"Declan's brothers just arrived from Boudon," he said.

She smiled at him. "That was nice. They must be tired. You go greet them."

"Would you like Alfred to help you?" he asked.

"No. I'll be fine." She practically pushed him away from the table. "I'll see you later."

After giving her a kiss, he ascended into their study. He traipsed through their private areas of the tree to the Reception Room.

Emerging from behind the Sages' Seal, Berty decided not to greet them on the dais. The heavy purple drapes hid Berty from view as he walked down the few steps on the side. He heard Vander's voice say, "She's an attractive woman. There's no harm in acknowledging that."

"Show some respect," said Cecil in hushed tones.

Berty strolled beside the dais to where they stood in the center of the room. "Cecil, Vander, welcome to the Empire Tree," he greeted.

"My Lord," Cecil said with a bow of his head. "We came to see how Matt fared."

Matt sat at a table while Estelle asked Tenders to bring tea. Behind Matt, Declan wore a strange smile.

"Please, have a seat," Berty said, gesturing to the table.

The brothers sat. Vander watched Tenders set some food and drink near him. With a smile, Estelle said, "It was very nice meeting you both. I must be off. Goodnight."

"Thank you, Estelle," said Matt.

She gave him a nod, then turned. Vander's eyes tried not to follow her up the stairs.

Declan chuckled silently. "I'll get Obie," she said to Cecil.

Joining them, Berty sat next to Matt. "Julie is not here?" Cecil asked.

"She crossed through the portal earlier today," answered Berty.

"You must come to our wedding," said Matt. "Julie would be so delighted."

"On the other side of the portal?" asked Vander.

Obie ran down the steps to greet his father. Slowly, Declan followed.

"Stay as our guests," Berty told the brothers. "You can send a letter to your parents in the morning. Just be careful of what you put in writing." Rising, he gave Declan a nod then returned to his private staircase.

In his and Silvia's study, Berty found the trap door still open. He climbed into the vaults. Silvia turned a page of one of the books. She glowed as she read. Watching her work, he could forget the word outside the Library Vault.

"Julie's letter must have passed them," Silvia said. She knew Berty stood in the antechamber without looking away from her book.

He smiled. "I think they followed just in case," he said as he entered the Library. "Anything useful?"

She glanced at the small stack of books. "Some of the scrolls are written in languages I don't recognize," she began. "However, from what I could read, it seems that Whisperers are the rarest of all magical abilities."

Sitting next to her, he said, "And they just *happened* to find one?"

"That's what I thought, too," she continued. "Until I read that the majority of Whisperers are Pixies. Pixies tend not to leave Pixisle often, if at all." She looked at Berty. "The Pixie Priestess was here—in the Empire Tree."

"To deliver the prophecy."

"Yes."

"Which Leif heard."

"And saw," Silvia added. "She arrived with an entourage. They stayed the night right outside the wall before journeying back to their ship."

"Do you think one of them stayed behind?" he asked her.

"I don't know. They could have been followed. One doesn't just come across Pixisle."

"But Millicent didn't become Historian until after the prophecy," he argued.

"I know. That's what disturbs me." Her tired eyes rested on the scrolls she could not read.

"Perhaps they are written in ancient Fairy or Elf," Berty suggested.

Silvia shook her head. "I've seen those languages, even if I can't read them," she said. "They have to be in a Pixie language of some sort."

"And no one can read Pixie?"

Sighing, Silvia said, "The Dominatrix might."

"A weapons expert?"

"Who is well versed in antiquity," she said. "After Julie and Matt's wedding, we will travel to Irmingard with Declan and Edwin." She gathered the scroll off the table. "I cannot do anymore tonight."

Berty closed the door of the Library Vault, then followed Silvia up the ladder. She stored the scrolls in a box on one of her shelves. When she returned to Berty's side, they climbed the steps to their bedroom.

With Silvia sleeping next to him, Berty watched the first rays of morning sunlight pour through the window. He wondered about the Whisperer and what type of relationship the Elves and the Pixies had, at least at one time.

"You're in deep thought," Silvia said.

"Wouldn't Alfred know?" he asked with his eyes following the rising sun. "He was High Elf."

"Alfred knows many things," agreed Silvia. "I'm sure the Elves and the Pixies have a history. We should probably ask him in private."

The word *private* made him ask, "What is it you believe is listening to us?"

Sitting up, she faced Berty, shielding the window from his view. "Not listening, per se. Observing. It's just a feeling I have. Nothing has penetrated the Sages' Grove magical barrier, according to Declan and the other Watchers. However, it could hide just beyond the barrier. When the Watchers do an outer perimeter patrol, nothing is ever there."

Berty caressed her shoulder. "Leif?"

"I don't know." She glanced at the window, then leaned towards him. "I think it's best to feign ignorance, yet be careful—for now."

He gave her a slight nod. His hand pulled her closer. After a long kiss, he said, "Good morning." They would not discuss the entity further. His lips nuzzled her skin. They needed to rely on the magical protection the Scepter afforded.

At breakfast in the Reception Room, Berty and Silvia greeted Declan's brothers. Vander and Cecil sat in awe of everyone to whom they had been introduced.

"Lieutenant Edwin," said Obie, "can my dad watch me practice today?"

Edwin gave Obie a knowing look. "Of course he can."

"Teresa," called Matt.

Turning, Berty saw his sister-in-law descend the main staircase.

"Is something wrong?" Matt asked.

"No," she answered with a smile. "Everything is ready for your wedding tomorrow."

"Join us for breakfast," said Silvia.

"Thank you, but it's later in the day on the other side."

Rising from his chair, Matt approached his sister. "Come with me to see Alina," he said.

"Okay."

When those at breakfast began to disperse, Vander watched Cecil head down the steps with his son and Edwin. "Come on," said Declan. "Bring your bow." With a smile, Vander jumped out of his chair.

"Alfred," said Silvia, "do you have anything pressing?"

"Not at all, Empress."

She smiled at the elderly Elf. He walked with Silvia and Berty up the staircase. Once they reached their shared study, Berty offered Alfred a seat. Sitting, the Elf waited.

Silvia kept her eyes on the Scholar while she sat across from him, a coffee table separating them. "Tell us about the Elves and the Pixies." Her commanding presence emanated from her.

Alfred sighed. "I wish I could," he said. "I know that the Elves and the Pixies have a history, but that history predates Irmingard. Very few know the actual details. As High Elf, my first duty was to preserve Irmingard. The Scrollist should know where this information would be. Many clan histories were preserved in our library after Irmingard was founded. To persevere as a people united, we dissolved the clans. Why ask me about the Pixies? Did the Priestess speak again?"

"Because Whispers are usually Elves," Silvia explained, "and Whisperers are usually Pixies."

Alfred glanced from Silvia to Berty with understanding. "You will have to travel to Irmingard," he said. "I will compose a note in the ancient Elf language for you to give to the Scrollist."

"Thank you Alfred," Silvia said. "We will leave the day after tomorrow."

"If I may," Alfred began.

Berty nodded for him to continue.

"The trip should be under the guise of speaking with the High Elf and his Commander," advised Alfred. "Unfortunately, Irmingard is riddled with busybodies. By seeking Avery, everyone will assume you are discussing the state of the Empire. My grandson will bring you to the Scrollist."

After Alfred left, Berty turned to his wife. "What isn't he telling us?"

"The Elves are not as united as they lead others to believe," she answered. "I would suspect that dissolved ancient Elf clans are still very much alive."

"That might explain the animosity former Warrior Commander Marshall has against Edwin," said Berty.

She nodded. "He probably has allies, even spies, within Irmingard."

"For the anti-imperialists?" he asked.

"I don't know. He might be more anti-Irmingard than anti-Empire," Silvia replied.

"Either way, I'm sure Avery and Wystan are his enemies," added Berty.

"Yes, but we can't rule out that there might be more than one opposing group of Elves."

Berty stared at the empty chair Alfred had previously occupied. "Do you think," he began, "that the Vindalf who fought in Boudon with the Firewalker crossed the tree line of their own free will?"

"Consciously choosing to tear their own souls away from their bodies?" asked Silvia in return. "I can't imagine anyone actually choosing that path. To give up everything to become a Vindalf."

"I know," agreed Berty. "Someone had to expose that Elf secret. Makes me wonder if we can trust this Scrollist."

"That's why I want to speak with the Dominatrix," Silvia said.

They strolled on the bridges that crossed over the Sages' Grove.

Vander and Declan shot arrows at practice targets. While Vander was an excellent archer, he did not have the same smooth fluidity of his younger brother. Declan patted his brother on the shoulder before they retrieved their arrows. Walking further, they noticed Edwin train Obie and a young Elf recruit, slightly older than Obie, in swordsmanship. Cecil smiled every time Edwin praised his son.

On the other side of the Tree, Berty spied Teresa and Matt emerging from the Rowan house. His sister-in-law would leave soon. They returned to the Empire Tree.

Berty and Silvia met them in the Reception Room. "Thanks, Berty, Silvia," said Matt. "I'm heading home with Teresa. Alina says I'm fully recovered. I'll be right back."

After Matt left, Berty asked Teresa, "How are you?"

"Doing well." She smiled while her hand automatically rubbed her abdomen.

Once Matt returned with his bag, Silvia said, "We'll walk with you." As they climbed the steps, she continued, "I don't recall hearing the doorbell before you arrived, Teresa."

"I didn't have to ring it," Teresa answered. "The front door opened when I crossed the porch."

A strange smile swept across Silvia's face. "Then you crossed the portal by yourself?"

"Yes," said Teresa. "Was that wrong?"

Silvia said nothing until they entered Hope's chambers. "The portals between the Tree and the house only permit certain people to cross without an escort," she explained. "Your child gives you access." Silvia smiled as Teresa touched her belly.

"What does this mean?" asked Teresa.

"Your child has quite a bit of magic," Silvia said.

"Guess the Shaman was right," Teresa replied.

"We'll see you both tomorrow," said Berty. "Could you have my parents come tomorrow? They're going to have to bring either Declan or his brothers. My car only has so much room."

"Sure thing, Berty," said Teresa, giving him a hug. Taking her brother's arm, she pulled him through the tapestry.

Berty walked down the steps with Silvia. "Can anyone with magic go through the portals?" he asked.

"I believe it has to do with the magic in your bloodline," she answered. "But to be sure, we'll have Obie test it this evening when we return to the house."

Still inside Hope's chambers, they called for Theodore. They asked him to have provisions ready for their trip to Irmingard.

"Everything will be ready," Theodore said with a bow to both of them. "Will you need horses for your journey?"

"Horses would be very welcome, Theodore. Thank you," Silvia replied.

After the Head Tender left them, Berty asked, "Would horses be noisy?"

"Cuts our travel time by half," said Silvia. "Besides, we're not exactly hiding our trip, just our reason."

"And the lack of a formal escort is prudent in these times."

"Exactly." She smiled. "Let's pack before we are expected at lunch in the Reception Room." He followed his wife across the bridge to their chambers.

After preparing for their post-wedding Irmingard visit, they descended to the Reception Room. "Emperor, Empress," called Elrick. "We have finished."

"Then, we head to the Roundtable after we eat," said Silvia.

Once they had finished eating, the Fairies led Berty, Silvia, and the Advisory Council up the stairs. A colorful mound covered the reflective surface. As Berty reached his chair, he gawked at the three-dimensional representation of Fairyland and the surrounding area. The blue castle and its colorful walled city sat at the center of the map with farmland and forest spreading to the edges.

"Your Majesties," Alvar commented, "your map is spectacular. May I ask how we take this into battle?"

"A little ancient Fairy magic will allow us to fold it for portability," answered Delyth.

Alvar nodded.

"Every entry point of which we know is marked," said Lida. "We have included all drains and airshafts, even if not accessible by a person."

While Elrick described other aspects, Berty realized how similar the "map" was to the miniature Sages' Grove, now residing in magical item storage. "Delyth," Berty interrupted, "does this have the same qualities as what was in the Watching Rooms?"

Delyth's violet eyes flashed with understanding. "I don't know, my Lord."

"That may require being within Fairyland," suggested Silvia. "I do not think it wise to attempt such magic here."

Confused looks swept around the table. Only a few of them knew of the miniature's ability to show the Sages' Grove in motion.

"No," agreed Delyth. "Because Fairy magic is connected to the Scepter and to the foundations of Fairyland itself, we cannot take the chance that conjuring would open in multiple locations, possibly exposing not only ourselves, but Telor and the refugees as well."

"I don't understand. What would the magic do?" asked Colvin.

"Track movement, in real time, of everyone within Fairyland," Silvia explained.

Colvin's eyes widened. "That would be useful."

"Not if it tells them our movements," said Berty, "or Telor's."

"Very old magic," Alfred said. "Best to leave it be."

"We will celebrate Wassail sooner rather than later," said Silvia. "Alvar, you and your top men need to strategize with King Elrick and Queen Lida's guidance immediately. Hatcher, Wassail will continue as if we plan for nothing. Do what you need to do for the gates. Colvin, you will prepare for the Light of Life Tree as normal directly following Wassail. Alfred, Estelle, and Declan, you three are tasked, in your own ways, with finding out about Whispers and Whisperers. A single piece of information can give us the advantage."

"The Empress and I will be heading to Irmingard with Declan and Edwin to discuss the impending war and their part," said Berty. "Alvar, you will have Edwin tonight and tomorrow before he joins us. Let's not waste any more time. Declan and Delyth, gather what you need for the portal crossing and your family, Declan, and meet us in Hope's chambers."

As the room emptied, a Tender answered Alvar's summons. While the Captain stayed to study the map and ask questions of the Fairies, the Tender fetched his top Lieutenants in the Sages' Grove.

Berty and Silvia waited for the Firths and Delyth in Hope's chambers. Once they all assembled, Silvia had Obie try passing through the portal by himself. He stepped towards the tapestry. The owl scene fluttered as he hit the wall. Satisfied, Berty had everyone grab hold of one another. He led them through the tapestry.

Chapter Five

Love Always Finds a Way

Gaslight sconces illuminated the dark hallway. Hesitantly, Cecil and Vander followed Declan and Obie. The Firth men placed their bags into the two bedrooms with the connecting bathroom. Delyth entered the remaining guest bedroom across the hall. Berty showed Declan's brothers downstairs, giving them a quick tour. Vander froze in awe while the kitchen made dinner per Silvia's instructions. Cecil tugged Vander's shoulder.

"But the," was all Vander managed to say.

Declan laughed at his brother's bewildered expression when they entered the front sitting room with Berty. While accepting a drink from Declan, Vander asked, "Does everything on this side have magic?"

"No," said Berty. "Magic rarely exists on this side. This house is the exception."

Sitting next to Berty, Silvia announced, "Dinner should be ready soon."

"I suppose you don't stay here long enough to warrant having Tenders," said Delyth.

Silvia shook her head. "Cecil, Vander, and even Delyth, tomorrow, we will be interacting with people who know nothing of the world from which we come," she began. "And we aim to keep it that way. With that said, there are things we should explain about life on this side."

They discussed cars, electricity, and wedding customs during dinner. "Since Declan has ridden in a car before," said Berty, "he and Delyth will ride with my parents. Cecil, Vander, and Obie will ride with us."

Obie smiled as he helped clear the dining room table. "Are you looking forward to riding in the car thing?" Vander asked him.

Shrugging, Obie replied, "Sure."

"You look excited," Vander said, following him through the swinging door.

"I get to see Hope tomorrow." Obie placed the plates in the sink.

Smiling, Vander said, "You like her?"

"Uncle Vander," Obie complained with a roll of his eyes. He walked out of the kitchen.

Vander stared at the swinging door then turned to Declan and Berty near the sink. "What did I say?"

Laughing, Declan said, "Obie and Hope are best friends."

"How am I supposed to know these things?" Vander asked.

Berty magically activated the sink to clean, then ushered the brothers out of the kitchen. In the back sitting room, Obie played with Hope's games until Cecil declared his bedtime. "But, Dad," he protested.

"No arguments," Cecil told his son. When Obie reluctantly put away the game, Cecil smiled. With an arm on Obie's shoulder, father and son walked out of the room.

Berty wanted to talk about Whispers and find out what Declan had learned, but no Empire discussions could take place in front of Vander and Cecil. Returning, Cecil sat on a chair with his elbows on his knees. He stared at Declan. "Obie told me about his kidnapping and how you rescued him," Cecil said.

Declan waited for his brother to continue.

"From what I've seen today, Obie is progressing with a sword, skilled with a dagger, and very good with magic. I have no doubt that this was the best path for him. He will become an extremely skilled man." Cecil studied the arm of his chair for a moment. "He needs to be able to make it to manhood. If they weren't after him, why was he taken?"

Declan glanced at Berty who gave him a nod. "They know there is a child who possesses a magical ability they want to exploit. However, they don't know who the child is," explained Declan. "Obie was taken by mistake because he was in the wrong place at the wrong time."

"I don't want that to happen again," said Cecil.

"It won't," said Berty. Both Cecil and Declan looked at him for an explanation. "They will know by now that he's not the one they want."

"Whispers," said Declan.

Berty nodded.

Cecil's head turned from Berty to Declan. "What does that mean?"

"It means they won't be coming after Obie unless they need another Warlock," Declan answered. His brow scrunched.

"What?" said Delyth.

"How are they controlling the Whispers?" pondered Declan. "They are supposed to be independent entities. Elves are the main transformers and transformees, but the Elves don't own them."

"Those books you read cloud your senses," said Vander.

Shaking his head, Declan said, "Be glad you don't know what I'm talking about."

"Why?" Vander immediately wanted to know.

"Imagine an unknown, unseen entity watching your every move, listening to your every word," said Declan, "then reporting it to someone else. And that someone having the power to covet and grab anything and everything you have, including you, or perhaps, have you slain because someone feels that you pose a threat."

"Great. Now, I won't be able to sleep," Vander said, sounding disgusted.

"There aren't any Whispers on this side of the portal," Delyth said. "You don't have to worry."

"Not tonight. Just every night and day after," Vander muttered.

"The only Whisper that would be remotely interested in watching you is Grandpa," Declan said quietly.

Both his brothers' eyes fixed on him.

"I was with him when he...." Declan could not finish his thought.

Vander opened his mouth to speak, but Cecil cut him off. "Vander. Stop being difficult," he scolded. "Declan didn't have the time with him like we did." He shook his head at him.

Lowering his head, Vander's hair drew a dark blond curtain across his face. After a breath, the curtain parted. "Sorry, Declan. Would I know if Grandpa was near?"

"No," Declan answered. "Only Watchers can see Whispers and

Whisperers can hear them."

Vander nodded as if he understood. "Well, I'm going to get some sleep. See you all in the morning." Declan watched his brother leave the room.

Looking at the remaining occupants, Cecil shifted in his chair. "I'm glad I had this opportunity to see Obie in his new life," he said. "Fiona would be proud." He smiled as his gaze flickered from Silvia to Delyth.

Declan finished his drink. "Julie will be thrilled to see you tomorrow," he said to his brother.

"And I am curious to see this land where she will be living," said Cecil. "Don't know if I'll sleep, but I should go up and try."

Once Cecil left them, Silvia said softly, "Hopefully, the Elves will be able to answer our questions and fill in the holes." She stared at Declan until he nodded. Tugging on Berty's hand, she encouraged him to retire to their bedroom, leaving Declan and Delyth alone in the back sitting room.

Trying to find appropriate clothes for Declan's brothers filled most of the morning. Finally, all the men wore suits to attend a late afternoon wedding. Delyth donned a modified modern dress complete with a shrug that hid her folded wings. When Berty's parents arrived, he had them park in the back next to his car so they could all leave together. While they buttoned their coats, George said, "The official story is that Julie, and therefore all of you, are from Canada. Your family are loggers in Northern Canada."

"Canada," repeated Vander.

"It's a country directly north of the United States—where we are now," explained Kate.

"Don't worry about it," said George. "There will only be a few outside people attending."

Grabbing his car keys and cell phone from the cabinet, Berty said, "Okay, Dad, I'll be right behind you."

Cecil and Vander followed their brother to the cars. After opening the door for Silvia, Berty showed Declan's brothers how to open theirs. Sitting in the middle, Obie helped his father and uncle fasten their seat belts. They jumped a little when the car started. "That's the engine," said Obie. "Matt said that he'll teach me to drive when I'm old enough." Cecil smiled at his son, then returned his gaze to the world outside the window. The brothers rode in silence while modernity displayed its plumage.

The burgundy car Berty followed turned. A sign saying, *The Greenbrooke Country Club*, welcomed their cars onto painstakingly manicured grounds. Berty stopped behind his father's car under the portico of a white and stone multistory building. Young valets rushed to open the car doors. Berty handed the car keys to one, then walked through the double doors with the group.

A man at the reception desk greeted Berty's father. "Last name, please."

"Chase and Firth," said George.

"For the wedding," the man replied. "Take the hall to the left. Crystal ballroom."

"Thank you." George led them down the hall.

White ballroom chairs formed rows on either side of a center aisle. A smattering of guests already filled Matt's side. "Save us seats near the aisle," George said to Berty.

"We're going to check on the bride," said Kate.

Berty had the Firth men fill the front row. Delyth sat on the end next to Declan. Keeping two seats free, Berty and Silvia sat in the second row. He nodded a greeting to his brother who sat by himself on the other side.

Chamber music played while the last of the guests filed into the rows. Kate slipped into the saved seat next to Berty. An older man holding a small book took his spot in the center of the front. The guests turned when Matt strolled down the aisle in his tuxedo. His parents walked in stride with him. While they moved to the front row, Matt stood at the end of the aisle. His eyes scanned the rows of guests.

Berty missed Matt's childhood friend make his way to Matt's side as his best man. Teresa strode down the aisle next, holding a petite array of purple and cream roses. She stood across from her brother as matron of honor. The guests awed as Hope paraded down the aisle, throwing purple and cream petals.

The music changed. The guests stood. On George's arm, Julie floated down the aisle. Her cream lace gown brushed the petal-studded runner as she stepped. Pearls secured her long, light brown trusses to her head. The flowers she carried paled in the brightness of her smile. Her gaze only broke from Matt when she noticed her brothers. Tears escaped as she hugged each of them. Reaching Matt, she passed her bouquet to Teresa, then took his hand. George rushed to his wife's side as the guests sat.

"We are gathered here today to witness the union between Julie Firth and Matthew Regnik," the officiant began. Berty pulled Silvia's hand into his. "Do you, Julie, take this man as your lawfully wedded husband in sickness and in health, for richer or for poorer, 'til death do you part?"

"I do," said Julie.

"Do you, Matt—"

"I do," said Matt.

Everyone laughed.

The officiant finished the vow.

"I do," Matt repeated.

They exchanged rings. "I now pronounce you husband and wife. You may kiss the bride." Matt did not need prompting. When Matt and Julie turned to face family and friends, the officiant continued, "I present Mister and Missus Matthew Regnik."

Country Club staff removed the screens that divided the ballroom. Berty migrated with the other guests to the dining area. Staff whisked away the rows of chairs and aisle runner, revealing the dance floor.

Cream tablecloths covered each of the four circular tables, one being the couple's table. Low floral rich vases crowded the centers. Simple name cards rested on plain white plates dressed with cream napkins and elegant silverware. Berty found his seat between *Silvia Chase* and *Delyth Fairland*. He chuckled at the surname they gave the Princess of Fairyland. Delyth did not seem to notice. Her violet eyes absorbed her surroundings.

The officiant joined them as the tenth seat at their table. "Ah, you must be Judge Mitchell," George said, extending his hand.

"Jim," the judge introduced himself. He turned to Julie's brothers. "It's so nice to meet the bride's family," he said. "Must be difficult to get away. But I guess with the onset of winter, you're not going to be felling any trees."

"No. Winter is mainly spent processing the wood," Cecil explained.

All conversation hushed once the newlyweds entered. They visited each of the guests' tables, making sure they spoke with every person. When they sat at their private table, servers brought the food.

Music began to play as Matt led Julie onto the wooden dance floor. They glided to the music, never taking their eyes off one another. Julie then danced with each of her brothers, in turn, while Matt danced with his mother and sister. Other couples soon joined them.

The dancing paused for the cutting of the wedding cake. Matt and Julie sliced into a three tiered cream colored cake dotted with purple sugar paste flowers. They gently plunked a piece in each other's mouths. The happy couple sat while the rest of the cake was served.

Vander devoured his piece of cake while Cecil laid down his fork after a couple of bites. "Are you not eating that?" Vander asked him. Shaking his head, Cecil pushed the plate to his brother. After quickly finishing his cake, Obie ran to Hope's table.

The reception continued on the dance floor. Eventually, Matt and Julie said their good-byes before heading on their honeymoon. "I'm so glad you guys were here," she said to Cecil and Vander.

"We are, too," said Cecil.

"Write often," added Vander.

"I will." She gave them both hugs. "Matt's dad is going to send pictures of the wedding to Mom and Dad." Vander gave her a confused look. "You'll understand when you see them," she assured. She hugged them again.

"Declan," she said, "thank you. Thank you for coming home." As she hugged him, she whispered something Berty could not hear.

Embracing Delyth, Julie said, "I know you have bigger things on your mind. Thank you for taking the time to come."

"If we can't take the time to celebrate love, then nothing in this world is worth fighting for," said Delyth. The Fairy smiled. "I wish you all the best. I know you and Matt will be very happy."

"My Lord, my Lady," Julie said quietly, "none of this would be

72

possible if not for you."

"Love always finds you," Silvia said with a quick glance at Berty. "You can come to our house anytime you wish to cross the portal."

"Send any letters to your family there as well," said Berty. "They will reach their destination."

Julie's eyes brimmed with tears. "I hope you and Matt will be able to join us for Wassail," Silvia continued.

With a smile, Julie hugged them both. She then turned to Berty's parents.

After everyone was hugged at least once, Matt and Julie departed. The guests began to take their leave. Robert and Lillian thanked everyone for coming.

Watching the room, Berty found Jon standing next to him. "So, the new normal," Jon said. "Anyway, don't forget Thanksgiving is next week."

"Why would I forget?" asked Berty.

"Being Emperor and all."

"I was Emperor last Thanksgiving, too," Berty whispered.

"It's at our house again," Jon continued. "Matt and Julie will be back for it. Declan, Delyth, and Obie are invited as well." He lowered his voice. "I don't want Teresa making too much herself. She's insisting on hosting Thanksgiving although her mom wanted to. Please come early. Maybe Silvia can talk some sense into her."

"Okay," said Berty. "I'm sure Mom will do as much as she can."

"Yeah, but still." Jon paused. He stared as their wives laughing together. "After all the problems she's had… Do you think I'm being too…?" He looked at his brother without finishing.

"Perhaps," Berty answered. His eyes migrated to Teresa then to Silvia. "But you're a husband madly in love with his wife and a father who loves his daughter and his daughter yet to be born."

Jon's hand rested on Berty's shoulder.

Hope and Obie ran past in fits of giggles. The brothers laughed. "Well, Jon," said Cecil, strolling paces behind his son, "I'm glad we met. I have a feeling you're going to be seeing a lot of my son."

Jon chuckled. "I believe you're right, Cecil."

Tuning out their conversation, Berty studied the room again. Declan and Vander chatted with Matt's best man who lingered. Delyth kept company with Kate and Lillian. George and Robert shared a drink with Judge Mitchell. Sure they discussed he and Jon, he watched Teresa and Silvia gab like they were old friends. On this side of the portal, no one prepared for war.

"Berty," called Robert. His usual strong voice was quiet. "I've been thinking about how to repay you."

"Repay me?"

"You've saved both my children's lives," he explained. "I know they're grown adults, but—"

"I didn't—"

"Berty, you've always been modest and humble," said Robert. "I won't forget what you've done for my family. Lillian and I will find a way to thank you properly. We're glad you could make it and bring Julie's brothers. It's a shame her parents couldn't be here, but we knew that going in." He smiled as the country club turned on all the lights. "We'll see you and your wife soon." After shaking Berty's hand, he approached Julie's brothers.

"Can Obie stay over tonight?" Berty heard Hope ask.

"No," said Jon.

"Daddy, please?" begged Hope.

"Not tonight. Obie's father is leaving tomorrow. But your mother and I will discuss having him stay for Thanksgiving," Jon said.

Smiling, Hope hugged her father.

At Berty's side, Silvia said, "What a lovely wedding." His hand found hers.

"Ready?" he asked.

She scanned the room. "Yes."

Silvia gathered Delyth and the Firths while Berty approached his father. "Dad, we should get going," he said.

"So soon?" said Judge Mitchell. "We're taking this party to the clubhouse."

Berty gave the judge a forced smile. "As great as that sounds, we have an early morning departure."

"That's too bad. I was hoping you'd tell me how you managed to sneak Teresa and Jon back into the States from their ordeal in Africa."

Berty's muscles tensed, freezing the smile on his face. Relaxing, he lowered his voice. "Well, I'm not allowed to disclose this, but we had a little *help*." He raised his eyebrows knowingly.

"Say no more," Judge Mitchell said, waving his glass. "It was nice meeting you. Safe journeys."

Under the country club's portico, the valet handed Berty the keys to his car. When everyone had gotten into the cars, Berty followed his father out of the country club's long drive. The car ride lulled Obie to rest his head on his father's arm. "This side is bright at night," Cecil mentioned. "I don't know how Julie will sleep."

Berty chuckled. He never really noticed the little differences. George pulled to the side to allow Berty into the driveway first. Cecil woke Obie when the car stopped.

Inside the house, Kate and George began making a pot of tea while everyone else changed. Berty and Silvia were the first to join his parents in the kitchen. While tea poured into cups, the door opened. Obie walked over to them. "Excuse me, my Lady, my dad thanks you for the clothes and would like to know what he and Uncle Vander should do with them."

"Place the clothes on the bed. The house will take care of them," Silvia said.

Obie ran out of the kitchen. "Sorry, Your Highness," he said in the hall.

Delyth entered the kitchen with a smile. "We are returning tonight?" she asked.

"Yes," replied Silvia.

"We leave for Irmingard first thing in the morning," said Berty.

"I think my brothers should travel with us," said Declan from the doorway, "at least until our paths split."

Berty nodded.

"You will be home in time for Thanksgiving," said Kate.

"We should only be there two days at most," said Silvia.

Once Vander poked his head next to Declan's, they left the kitchen. Kate and George accompanied them to the tapestry to say goodbye. Linking arms, they crossed the portal to the Empire Tree.

Freesia entered Hope's chambers as Berty led the group downstairs. "I didn't mean to intrude, my Lord," she said.

"No intrusions," said Berty. "Hope will be returning for Wassail."

"Everything will be ready," she said before climbing the steps to her bedroom.

"Theodore will have provisions waiting in the Reception Room," said Silvia. "See you in the morning." Exiting Hope's chambers, Berty and Silvia crossed the bridge to theirs while the others crossed to the trunk. Berty followed his wife's lead in checking their packs before heading to bed.

Waking in the dark, early morning, Berty envied Matt. Matt would be spending days with his new wife uninterrupted. He could hear Silvia breathing next to him. At least they were together and would be traveling together. His lips met her cheek in a soft kiss.

"What was that for?" she asked.

"I love you," he said.

He could feel her smile.

They awoke when light edged the horizon. Their traveling clothes matched with hints of gold threads in their shirts and plain brown pants. Bags in tow, they met Edwin, Declan, and his brothers at breakfast. Obie gave his father a long hug good-bye, then followed them to the horses. Cecil dug into his pocket to pay the stable hand for boarding his and Vander's horses, but the boy refused. "It's already been paid," he said. Cecil glanced at Declan who gave him a quick smile.

On their horses, they rode out of the Sages' Grove with the morning traffic. After galloping for hours, they rested for a short break. "It's time for us to take the northern road," said Cecil.

"Safe travels," Declan said. "Give my best to Mom and Dad."

"We will." Cecil gave him a one armed hug.

After mounting their horses, Declan's brothers split from the group. Edwin led the rest of them on the road to Irmingard. They kept their quick, almost racing pace.

Riding beside Berty, Declan shot an arrow. It whizzed past the Elf's ear. At Declan's encouragement, the arrow made a U-turn in front of Edwin, then returned to the quiver.

Chapter Six

Irmingard

Heeding the warning, Edwin slowed. Declan shot three arrows at once. Berty could not see Declan's target until the empty space ahead shimmered where the arrows pierced. A fourth arrow landed in the path.

Edwin dismounted. He unsheathed the Blade of the Golden Flame. Starting at Declan's fourth arrow, the Elf sliced the air. Shimmering curtains parted on either side of the path. "Center only," said Declan. He took the lead.

Going forward, the horses neighed in protest. Berty swore he noticed movement in the trees. Edwin's arrows started to fly. "Ambush!" he yelled.

Dark cloaked men sprang from the forest on both sides of the road. As they rode, Edwin and Declan fired arrows. Berty used his magic to push the men back and block oncoming arrows. Swordsmen surged towards them. They dropped before reaching the road. From behind the dark line, Cecil and Vander shot a path through the forest.

"I spotted more up ahead," reported Vander when the brothers reached the road.

"We're immensely outnumbered," Berty said, still making men fly through the air.

"They're going to use magic against us. We won't be able to defend ourselves," said Silvia. "Weapons away. Ride as fast as we can. My magic will hold them at bay for as long as possible."

They raced. Berty willed the horses to go faster. Silvia's barrier surrounded them. It rippled when something or someone hit it.

A clouded night settled over the forest. "They're using magic against me," Silvia said.

"Keep pushing," Edwin called over the sound of hooves hitting dirt. "Not much further now."

Silvia waivered on her horse. "I can hold it," she said to Berty. "I'm going to give them a hard push, then we'll be exposed.

"No slowing down," said Berty.

He heard projectiles whistle when Silvia's barricade broke. His body tingled. Closing his eyes, he looked behind them. Four different colored spheres flew towards them. His hand automatically snapped open, whipping to his shoulder. The spheres exploded, momentarily lighting the road and surrounding forest. When he opened his eyes, Irmingard glowed white in the distance. The glow grew to white ramparts sitting across a moat.

"Slow down or we will make you," yelled a voice from the bridge.

"We are a delegation from the Empire Tree. We are being pursued," Edwin yelled in response. "Let us pass and drop the bridge."

"Do not come any further," the voice yelled. Berty was sure a half dozen arrows were trained on them.

"Let them through," demanded a new voice. "Do as the Lieutenant commands."

Horse hooves finally reached the wooden bridge. Once they passed halfway, wood crashed into rock. They slowed to pass under the gate. Stopping, they turned to look behind them. Half the bridge had collapsed into the wall on the other side of the moat.

"Lieutenant Edwin, accept our deepest apologies for not recognizing you straightaway," said an Elf Warrior Berty remembered, but could not recall his name. "Raise the other half until daylight," he ordered.

Edwin nodded. "We need to see High Elf Avery and Commander Wystan at once," he said. "If you could have someone awaken them, Garik, we would appreciate it."

Garik's eyes swept over the group. "They'll be waiting for you." He gave Berty a respectful bow of his head.

With Edwin in the lead, they rode at a slower pace through the empty streets of the Elf stronghold. No light illuminated the pavement. Berty could not see much beyond the dim white city walls.

An olive green cloaked Elf waited for them on the steps to a large domed building. "This way," said the Elf. Other Elves took their horses while they followed the Elf inside.

Wearing plain clothes, Wystan greeted them in the white marble colonnade. "Edwin," he said.

"Wystan," Edwin greeted his brother.

"I'll escort them to the High Elf," Wystan said to the other Elf.

"Yes, Commander," he said with a small bow.

"Wish the hour was better," Edwin said.

"Couldn't be helped," said Wystan. "Did anyone sustain injuries?"

"No. Just sore from the ride," Edwin answered. His brother nodded knowingly as he led them through a series of marble lined hallways.

Wystan knocked twice on a door. After a second, he opened it. Through the tall doorway, Berty saw a cozy room with plenty of cushioned furniture. A robed Elf rose to greet them. "Emperor, Empress, do come in," he said.

"Avery," said Silvia, walking inside first, "good of you to see us on such short notice."

Declan nudged his uncertain brothers into the room with them.

"Please, everyone, take a seat," said Avery. The cushions relaxed Berty's sore backside. "Anti-imperialists hiding on the road between the Sages' Grove and Irmingard," said Avery. "Why haven't our scouts found them?" he asked Wystan.

"I don't know," said Wystan. "Clean reports come across my desk every morning."

Avery stared at the Commander, but his face revealed no emotion or thought. He turned his attention to Berty and Silvia. "I'm having rooms prepared for you in my residence as we speak," he said.

"Thank you, Avery," said Berty. "We have come for a specific reason. However, right now, we need to discuss the sheer number of men across the moat from us." He glanced at Edwin to continue.

"These were not the same men we battled in Boudon," Edwin explained. "They were well organized and well trained. If I had to guess, I'd say they were planning on attacking Irmingard."

Wystan's eyes widened.

"Our journey interrupted their plan," said Silvia, "but did not stop it."

"Probably hastened their time table," Wystan agreed. "I will need a full assessment."

"Declan, his brothers, and I will report what we saw," said Edwin.

Wystan looked to Avery.

"Do what you need, Commander," Avery said.

Rising, Wystan gave the High Elf a bow. He quickly ushered his brother and the Firths out of the room.

"Now," said Avery after the door closed, "why are both Emperor and Empress sitting with me in Irmingard?"

"We need information," said Berty.

"Your grandfather directed us to see the Scrollist," Silvia added. "But he also warned us to be discreet about it."

Looking from Silvia to Berty, the Elf nodded. "Of course. Why don't both of you rest from your harrowing journey. In the morning, you can speak with the Commander and the Dominatrix. I will personally take you on a tour of the library in the afternoon."

Silvia gave him a tired smile. "We will bid you goodnight then."

"I'll have someone show you to your room," he said.

After navigating cozier marble halls, they entered a plush bedroom. "Well, that was interesting," Berty said.

"Very," agreed Silvia. She checked through her bag. "It looks as though we can trust Avery's staff. Irmingard is in worse shape than Alfred admitted."

"Dissention within the Warriors," Berty said. "Has the former Commander trained the anti-imperialists? Does he have allies in the Warriors that will help bring down Irmingard?"

Silvia sighed. She looked from the door to the windows. "Magically locked," she whispered. Berty nodded as he readied for a short sleep.

Knocking at the door roused Berty. Silvia opened her eyes. Clutching his sword, he tiptoed to the door. "Who is it?" he asked.

"Declan. Can I come in?"

Silvia wrapped a robe around her, then gave Berty a nod. He quickly granted Declan entrance.

"Sorry for waking you so early," said Declan. "I wanted to talk before we *mingled*."

Berty motioned for him to sit in one of the chairs that surrounded a small table. Silvia joined the men. "Having the Bow of the Moon does not exactly endear me to some of the Elves," he said. "With that said, I believe both Edwin and Wystan have enemies here. Whether they the are all the same enemies, I do not know."

"Irmingard is not maintaining its delicate balance," said Silvia. "As outsiders, your brothers are the most neutral party here."

"How did your brothers manage to come to our aid?" asked Berty.

"Vander stopped to collect some feathers," explained Declan. "Cecil spotted men in dark cloaks—like Obie described. He followed. When he realized what they were doing, he and Vander went after them." He shook his head. "Probably allowed Cecil to feel like he was getting back at them for kidnapping Obie."

"Hopefully, he excised that from his system," Silvia said. "I don't think any of us will be safe outside this complex. And I am doubting our safety inside."

Nodding, Declan said, "See you for our morning charade."

When Berty and Silvia arrived at breakfast, everyone stood except one Elf. Glancing around the table, Berty noticed that only their companions, Avery, and the sitting Elf occupied chairs. "Empress, Emperor," said Avery, "an honor to have you both in Irmingard. Forgive my mother for not standing. She lost the use of her legs when she was a child."

Silvia smiled, while Berty said, "Please sit. We are honored you could receive us without a formal notice."

Once seated, Avery said, "Allow me to introduce you to my mother, Rane."

With pride in her eyes, Rane's mouth moved, but undiscernible words escaped.

"She is very pleased to meet you," Avery interpreted.

Rane spoke more unformed words.

"Mother, it is not—"

She cut him off with an insistent tone in her voice.

Avery let out a small sigh. "My mother would like you to know," he began, "that her incapacities in both speech and movement were due to an accident."

Rane protested politely.

"An accident my mother believes was contrived," continued Avery. "It can be suggested that the accident was supposed to end the line of High Elf. My mother should have assumed the role years ago. However, both she and my grandfather thought it best for me to be the next High Elf. So, my grandfather held the position until he deemed me old enough. There are those who believe that my mother is mentally incapacitated as well as physically. Because of these rumors, I have often been dubbed a miracle child. Elves have a deep reverence for magic, and therefore, some believe that I am High Elf for a higher purpose."

"And what of your father, Avery?" asked Silvia.

"He is no longer with us," Avery replied.

"We're sorry to hear that," Silvia said.

"Thank you, my Lady."

"Rane," continued Silvia, "you believe the forces in play now are the same ones that caused your accident."

Rane nodded.

"From what I know of Low Elf Kael, he is a good man," said Avery. "Probably not as good as Wystan, but Wystan had to give up the Low Elf position to become Commander. He makes an excellent Commander. Irmingard politics demand the Low Elf have more say in military decisions than I. For that reason, Low Elves are usually chosen from Warriors. Kael is not a Warrior, but he is good with people. The votes between he and Wystan were very close. While the four of you are in conference, my mother has arranged for Cecil and Vander to have a guide around Irmingard. After your meeting, my Lord and Lady, I will take you on a tour of our library."

A door on the side opened. Two female Elves entered. "Ah, just in time," said Avery. "May I present Katell and Jordis." The women bowed their braided heads. "Katell is apprenticing for the Dominatrix and Jordis is my mother's main caretaker."

"My Lord, my Lady, Lieutenant, Your Grace," said Katell, "allow me to escort you to the War Room."

Berty and the others rose. As he followed the Elf out of the room, he heard Jordis ask, "How may I address the brothers of the Duke?"

"I'm Vander. My brother, Cecil."

Grinning, Berty walked in step with Silvia down the marble corridor. A labyrinth separated the High Elf's residence from the War Room. Katell opened an iron door to a dark stone room. Light from the marble corridors spilled in only to die on the dull surfaces. Around a table stood Wystan in his Commander's uniform, the Dominatrix in the leather Berty saw her wear when Edwin and Declan met her for the first time, and a frail, short for his kind, young Elf in a dark green robe.

The Elf, who could only be Low Elf Kael, studied them. "My

Lord, my Lady, it is an honor to be in your presence," he said with a bow.

Berty found him too flattering.

"I am Low Elf Kael," he continued. "You, of course, already know Commander Wystan. I do not believe you have met the Dominatrix."

"We wish we could meet you in better circumstances, Low Elf," said Berty. "Lieutenant Edwin and Advisor Declan, the Duke of Fairyland."

"Now," said the Dominatrix impatiently, "our moat keeps out most. Unfortunately, it also keeps us in. We have catapults and our archers are the best in the land, save for present company." She gave Declan a respectful nod.

"Are you saying attack them before they attack us?" Kael asked.

"Do propose a better idea?" she asked in return.

"How do we know they will attack? We should wait. Find out what they want," suggested Kael.

"Smiles and rhetoric may win elections," retorted the Dominatrix, "but they do not win wars."

"I sent a scout last night after speaking with Lieutenant Edwin and Advisor Declan," mentioned Wystan.

"Without notifying me?" Kael almost accused.

"Technically, you don't need to be notified for a scout, Kael," reprimanded Wystan. "Besides, no Elf was sent."

Kael's eyes narrowed.

"With the Emperor's blessing, the High Elf accepted a Fairy," Wystan said. "Under the charge of His Grace and with an order from my direct superior, the Fairy left and returned under the cover of darkness."

"What was his report, Commander?" asked Declan.

"Over two hundred wait out there," said Wystan. "Mostly Humans, Fairies, and Elves."

"Elves," Kael repeated quietly.

"Probably Vindalf," dismissed Wystan.

"Mostly?' asked Declan. "What else did he see?"

"He's not sure," Wystan replied. "Creatures of some sort en mass. He's never seen anything like them. He was able to confiscate some old Fairy Dust as well."

"Do you believe him?" Kael asked.

Wystan gave him a look.

"Well, he is a *Fairy*," said Kael.

"Harbor old prejudices, Kael?" asked Edwin.

Kael's jaw moved, then his eyes studied the table.

"Can you see them?" Silvia whispered to Berty.

He knew what she asked, but he never tried anything like that. His eyes unfocused on the dark stone. His eagle eyes saw the moat and the raised bridge. Delving into the trees beyond, he saw the men in dark cloaks. "Yes," he whispered.

"Hold on to that," she breathed. Her hand touched his. The War Room transformed into a forest. A mist encircled the area of the War Room. Anti-imperialists moved on the other side of the mist.

"Where are we?" Kael asked. He took a couple of steps towards the mist. "Can they see us?" he asked in a panicked tone. "Can they hear us?" he whispered. "We need to hide."

The stone table around which they stood appeared. Silvia's hand rested on it. The forest faded into the dark stone walls. When the room returned to its normal state, Silvia said, "Low Elf Kael, you are either with us or against us. There is no in-between. Next time, I will leave you to the mercy of those men."

Fear washed over his face. Berty noticed the Dominatrix crack a smile.

"I—I am with you," Kael finally said.

"Good," said Silvia. "I would hate to see Irmingard go the way of Fairyland."

Kael swallowed. Straightening his shoulders, he said, "I don't want that either." He stared at Silvia. In a soft voice, he said, "I am not a Warrior. I have never held a weapon in my hands. My only skill is speech. I am too weak for everything else."

"Speech's strength can be used as effectively as any weapon," said Silvia. "Words alone may not defeat the enemy, but they can be used to rally the people to defend their homes."

With resolution, Kael gave Silvia a nod.

"So far, they are using all the same tactics," said Berty. "Old Fairy Dust, Vindalf, other magic, and creatures of some sort. Only now, they've had a chance to organize and train. Will the moat be able to stop the old Fairy Dust?"

"That has not been tested," the Dominatrix answered.

"We are in possession of some. Perhaps there is an inconspicuous place to test it," said Berty.

"I believe there is," she said. "His Grace's Watcher skills could hasten analyzing."

"Of course," said Declan.

"The catapults and archers should stand ready for a counter attack," said Wystan. "We do not strike first unless they intend to trap us here."

"Trap us in Irmingard?" said Kael. "We'd outlast them in a siege."

"Yes," the Dominatrix agreed. "But they do not have to overtake us to stop us."

"To stop us from what?" asked Kael.

"Helping the Empire," said Edwin. "If Irmingard Warriors fought alongside the Empire Guard, we would be an unstoppable force."

"Or," said the Dominatrix, "perhaps they knew you were coming." She looked from Berty to Silvia. "The Empire Guard would be sent to facilitate your return. They would be forced to fight on two fronts. They would never win, however, wining this battle is not their goal."

"A different force would attack a weakened Sages' Grove," said Berty.

"Precisely."

"So, what do we do?" asked Kael.

"We protect the Empire at all costs," the Dominatrix replied. "The fall of the Empire Tree is detrimental to all of us."

Kael nodded. "I will speak with the Ørgranden," he said. "Commander, I know you will defend Irmingard well. The people trust you. I will leave you to your preparations while I do my own." After bowing to Berty and Silvia, he strode out of the room.

"Much of our defenses will hinge on how well we can combat old Fairy Dust," the Dominatrix said. "I would like to test it right away. My Lord and Lady, may I seek an audience with you later today?"

"You may indeed," Silvia replied.

The Dominatrix bowed her head. "If His Grace would follow me," she said.

"I must begin reinforcing our defenses," said Wystan. "Edwin and I will then plan an escape route for the six of you."

"Very well," said Berty.

Outside the War Room, Katell waited for them. Berty and Silvia walked in silence behind the Elf. He knew her mind turned and she waited for privacy. Finally, Katell knocked on a door.

"Come in," said Avery's voice.

The three of them entered what looked like Avery's study. He sat behind a handsomely decorated wooden desk. "High Elf Avery," Katell said with a bow, "the Dominatrix would like a conference later."

"Yes, of course. She knows where to find me," said Avery. Katell closed the door upon leaving. Standing, Avery walked around his desk to the upholstered chairs grouped in front of it. He motioned for them to sit. As they sat, the room felt familiar to Berty, yet he was unsure why.

"Please know that whatever we say here is private," said Avery. "No magic can enter or leave this room." A memory of seeing Delyth discussing Vindalf with Avery in this room flashed in Berty's mind. "I am going to advise that we hunker down for a long fight. You and your party will be safe within this residence."

"Avery," said Silvia, "they knew we were coming."

"So it seems," he agreed. "And Irmingard will soon be fighting a civil war."

"What if I use magic to send us back?" said Berty. "I've sent items different places before."

"Things, yes, but people?" said Silvia. "It might be too dangerous."

Avery shook his head. "Wouldn't matter. The moat is active. No magic can go in or out with an active moat. The stages of deactivation will take too much time and leave us vulnerable. I'm sure they have a Watcher."

The ground beneath Berty shook. He grabbed hold of the arm of his chair as to not fall on the floor.

"Berty?" asked Silvia.

"You didn't feel that?"

Both Silvia and Avery shook their heads.

"I thought you said magic couldn't enter this room," he said to Avery.

"It can't."

"They must be testing the moat with the old Fairy Dust," said Berty.

"Ah," said Avery. "That would make sense. The moat's magic is ancient and so are the magical bindings of this room. Somehow, the ancient magic is connected. Your magical sense is very powerful, Emperor."

Berty merely nodded in response.

"There is a way to get you out," Avery said. "Be packed. But first, the Scrollist." The Elf rose. Crossing to a bookshelf behind him, he turned a decorative horn about thirty degrees. "This way. My direct route to the library."

Berty and Silvia followed Avery through the doorway behind the books. Rose quartz lined the walls and floor of the corridor. "When our war with the Fairies ended," Avery explained, "we entered a new war of sorts. A war of knowledge gathering. The Fairies succeeded in surpassing us in most areas. Hence, their reputation as storytellers and securing the position of Empire Historian for ages. However, besides securing Elf history, we have an extensive collection on weaponry, the healing arts, and magic."

When they turned down another hallway the rose gave way to green. "For a people so connected with the trees, you surround yourself with a lot of stone," Silvia observed.

"I suppose we have," Avery said as they stepped between tall shelves crowded with books. They emerged into a hallway where wooden bookshelves lined in rows on either side. "This way." Avery led them to the left. The continuous lines of bookshelves paused for tables. A spiral staircase hid in a corner. "Up here."

They climbed until they reached a plain wooden door. After a single knock, the door opened. Avery preceded them into the domed room above the library.

A woman in a long, dark blue robe approached. "High Elf," she said with a slight accent. Silver streaked her dark braided bowed head. "How may I assist the Empress and Emperor of all that surrounds us?" Her head stayed low.

"Are you the Scrollist?" asked Silvia.

The Elf raised her head. "I am, my Lady."

Silvia handed the Scrollist the note Alfred wrote.

Opening it, the Scrollist said, "The ancient Elf script." She smiled. "Have a seat. I will explain all."

Four chairs materialized in the center of the room. Once they sat, the Scrollist began, "Irmingard, in its heyday, was *the* center for culture and learning. The Pixies were one of our greatest allies. The Priestess of the time would send her best to train here. The Pixies received a well-rounded education in art, healing, and fighting. In return, they granted us access to rare ore and herbs that are only available on Pixisle. The Sprite Conflict ended our relationship with the Pixies. You see, the Elves have always been friends with the Wood Sprites. Elves who became Whispers helped the Wood Sprites tend to the forest and keep the magic flowing. After the petrifaction of the Wood Sprites, the Mother Wood Sprite went to live on Pixisle for the protection the island's remoteness afforded. Without any more Wood Sprites, the Whispers had no guidance. The Mother Wood Sprite made select Pixies Whisperers to guide Whispers so the forest and its magic would not fade. This angered the Water Sprites. They, in turn, sank Pixie ships, keeping them marooned on their own island. The Water Sprites allow the Pixie Priestess passage only during every third blue moon to the mainland. The Mother Wood Sprite is not allowed to leave Pixisle—ever. When the Pixie Priestess comes ashore, her crew must stay on the boat. She can have two protectors to escort her to her destination and back. All Pixies must return to Pixisle."

"Then how is a Whisperer on the main land?" asked Silvia.

"I wish I knew, my Lady. My knowledge is limited to what the library has procured or what visitors such as yourselves have told me personally. The Water Sprites will permit your passage to Pixisle as long as you travel without an Elf."

"Can you tell us anything about Whispers themselves?" Silvia enquired further.

"The transformation uses ancient Elf magic and conducted by the Dominatrix. The knowledge is passed from Dominatrix to Dominatrix."

"Thank you," said Silvia.

"War might be coming, Scrollist. Prepare," Avery said.

"Internal or external?" she asked.

"Perhaps both."

The Scrollist gave him a nod. "Beware, High Elf. Your line must not be unseated," she continued. "According to records, you have no heir apparent. If history tells us anything, there are two other lines who covet your seat. The ancient magic of Albrecht runs through your blood and your blood only. As long as your line lives, so does Irmingard and Elves everywhere. It is part of the covenant Albrecht made with the trees." Her gaze locked with Avery's. "I have answered all asked of me. If there is nothing more, please leave me to prepare.

Lockdown begins tonight."

"Thank you, Scrollist," said Avery.

The Scrollist rose out of her chair first. As they walked towards the door, she said, "May the horn's call always be with you, Avery." The three of them turned. She was gone.

"Magic," Avery muttered. He led them back to his study. Once he closed the bookshelf door, Avery said, "We must not speak of her to protect her. She has been an asset to Irmingard for centuries. As our honored guests, we are to have a meal with the Raðþing. A warning: they will ask about everything. Answer however you see fit."

When they returned to their room to freshen up, Berty said, "A meal with Irmingard's entire legislative body? I would rather not have to be with so many people at one time." He flopped into a chair. "Can this trip get any worse?"

Soft knocking interrupted his complaints.

"Come in," Silvia said.

"I hope I'm not intruding," said the Dominatrix. "I want to speak with you both before dinner."

"Not at all," Silvia assured. "We're just relaxing." She walked the Dominatrix to the sitting area.

"You'll need it. These Raðþing meals can be arduous," the Dominatrix said. "At least one Whisper had to know of your plans."

"Whispers cannot enter the Sages' Grove," said Berty.

"I know. That is what disturbs me."

"What can you tell us about Whispers?" asked Silvia.

She sighed a little. "They are not supposed to be used as spies. They are needed to keep magic flowing in this world." Her dark eyes moved between them. "Anyone can become a Whisper, not just Elves."

"Like Declan's grandfather," said Berty.

"Yes. It is a one way transformation," the Dominatrix continued. "The newly transformed will have a stronger hold on their pre-Whisper identities. Over time, that is lost. They become part of the collective magic."

"If you control that collective magic, you can control the Whispers?" asked Berty.

The Dominatrix stared at him for a moment. "Perhaps... Of course. It makes perfect sense." She sat a little straighter. "When I oversee the transformation, I wear white. Irmingard is a city of white. Warriors wear white metal armor. Why didn't I see this before? Whispers cannot process white. The anti-imperialists will have the upper hand if we don't start bleaching all our cloaks." She smiled. "We can win and we can get you out without being seen."

"White," Silvia murmured. "While you are here," she said, "I came across some scrolls written in a language that I cannot read. Maybe you can." She handed the scrolls to the Dominatrix

The Elf affixed glasses to her nose, then rolled open a scroll. "This is a caution list of people who should never become Whispers," she said. "Empress, their kin, Sages and their kin, Listeners, and Watchers." Opening the next scroll, her eyes studied it. "This is not a language with which I am familiar. My guess would be some form of an old Pixie language. Besides the ancient and common tongue, I can read two Pixies languages, ancient Fairy, and ancient Elf." She opened the third scroll. Her face fell. "Huh. This one is a completely separate language than the other two. The first two are definitely of Pixie origin. This one, however, I cannot place." She placed the opened scroll on the table between the others. Her head swung as she studied the letters. "I first thought that it could be the same list written in three different languages. But why write it in two different forms of Pixie?" She tapped the old Pixie scroll. "One of these words might be wood, but I am not sure what comes after."

Berty peered at the angular lettering of the third scroll. "Could it be a Dwarf language?"

"It's not two forms of Pixie," the Dominatrix said. "Of course, my Lord. The middle scroll could originate from the Dwarves. This other scroll might be written in Trollian."

"Are you sure?" asked Silvia.

"Yes. Trollian is, for all purposes, a dead language. The Troll Chief herself may not even know it. There is a chance the Reducer would. Most race specific magic still uses race specific language. Trolls would have written about Whispers since Whispers cannot cross a portal. Though, I am not sure why Dwarves would be concerned with Whispers."

"What about the Goblins?" asked Berty.

"No," answered the Dominatrix. "I know Goblish when I see it. They use distinct glyphs in their written language. Probably easier to see in the dark."

"Thank you for your counsel," Silvia said.

"It is an honor. The Empire will prevail." The Dominatrix removed her glasses. "I have faith."

Rising with her, Berty saw her out of the room. When he turned around, he spied Silvia gathering the scrolls off the table. "Ready to go?" she asked him.

"At a moment's notice," he replied.

With their cloaks secured like red and blue capes, they left for the dining hall.

Waiting outside closed double doors, Berty could hear someone announcing him and Silvia. The doors opened. Elves stood around a long table. Two empty chairs in the center of the table faced each other. Berty had to sit across from his wife. Separating from her to walk on opposite sides of the table, he felt short. Even the Elf women were at least as tall as he. He noticed that Low Elf Kael got to sit next to Silvia. Probably so he could feel tall—for once.

Seated, he finally browsed the faces around the table. He sat between Avery and Wystan. The Dominatrix sat on the other side of Silvia. Declan had a seat next to Edwin's father, Ryker, while Edwin sat across from his mother, Femke. None of the other Elves looked familiar to him. Berty was not surprised that Cecil, Vander, and Rane were absent.

The Elves paid no attention to the food. Dinner was about the conversation. Political jostling passed from Elf to Elf. Each one tried to position to speak to Berty or Silvia from his or her chair. After Avery's warm welcome toast, Edwin said, "My Lord, you remember my parents from my nuptials."

"Of course," said Berty.

Edwin smiled. "My Lady," he said, "I am honored to present to you, my mother, Femke," she nodded to Silvia, "and, my father, Ryker," who also gave her a respectful nod, "both of whom are esteemed members of the Ørgranden."

The other Elves carefully watched the exchange.

"A pleasure to meet you both," said Silvia. "Your sons bring a great deal of honor to your family. The Emperor and I work very closely with Lieutenant Edwin. Our Advisors rely heavily on him as well." She faced Berty. "We should make Edwin an honorary Advisor upon our return to the Empire Tree."

"I agree," said Berty. "We should." He and Silvia smiled at each other as the Elves exchanged glances.

"My Lord and Lady," Ryker said, "allow me to introduce the other members of the Ørgranden. Oda, Malte, Alland, Haldis, and Erland." The Elves nodded their heads as Ryker called their names. The Ørgranden sat scattered with the other four Elves Berty did not know.

Kael introduced the remaining Elves. "Irmingard's Varlǫgen are Maren, Hagen, and Jaga. Nash is the Lastóm," he said.

Nodding, Berty relied on his red stoned pinky ring to translate. The Varlǫgen kept the laws while the Lastóm was some sort of devil's advocate.

"Malte," said one of the Elves with a hand to his chest. "Emperor, Empress, how are you finding Irmingard thus far?"

"Unfortunately, we have not been able to see much of it," answered Berty.

"That is a shame," said another Elf. "Haldis," she said, "placing a hand to her chest. "Irmingard is quite lovely in the weeks preceding Wassail."

"Did you find our library suitable?" another asked. "Oda." She introduced herself with a smile.

"I love libraries," confessed Silvia. "I spent quite some time admiring the library in Fairyland."

Berty caught Malte shift in his seat while Oda kept her smiled plastered.

"When High Elf Avery told us about your library, I just had to see it," Silvia said sweetly. "There is just something... magical," she smiled wider, "about the old leather bindings and hand copied pages. Don't you agree, Oda?"

"I do, my Lady, I do," Oda said. "How does Irmingard's library compare to Fairyland's? I have never made the journey up there myself."

Silvia took a long sip of her wine—or pretended to—before answering. "The libraries are not comparable. Fairyland has a breadth of knowledge stores that go unmatched in the Empire. Irmingard, on the other hand, holds a depth of knowledge that can feed the fountain for a very long time. I highly recommend seeing Fairyland's for yourself. Once it is liberated, of course. I do hope the books survive."

All small chatter ceased. Oda's smile froze. Berty marveled at Silvia's maneuvering.

"And that brings us to more pressing matters." An Elf broke the silence. "The name is Erland." His hand did not rest on his chest. "Will Irmingard retain its loveliness while it's being attacked? Will the library still retain its tomes after battle?" he mocked. "Those may be some of my peers concerns. Personally, I have been contemplating whether or not there will be an Irmingard left to legislate. How many Elves will remain to stroll our lovely streets or browse the shelves of our vast library? Forgive me for being blunt, but I am new to the Ørgranden. I have yet to perfect the savvy art of pandering and shoveling smelly piles of you know what to where everyone can step in them."

"We never had this problem with Ferran," someone whispered.

"Oh, no, you had a completely different problem with Ferran from what I understand," said Declan loud enough for the entire table to hear.

Suppressing a smile, Berty knew that many in Irmingard would be glad to be rid of them. He wondered if they stoked a wasp's nest.

"This coming from the Duke who is also a thief," muttered Malte.

"Excuse me?" Declan said even louder. "If you are speaking about the Bow of the Moon, it *chose* me."

Silence overtook the Elves.

"Anyone else have issues?" asked Declan. He glanced around the table. "No? Good. Because if you all don't come together to the same side, you'll never defeat the horde just across the moat."

"Forgive me, Advisor," said a female Elf at the end of the table, "but you…." She paused. "First, you are not an Elf. Second, you are an advisor without military experience."

Declan smiled. "And third, I am the Duke of Fairyland. Tell me…?"

"Maren," she said.

"Maren," repeated Declan, "how much military experience do you have?"

"I received Warrior training like everyone else," she replied.

"And you have fought against…? Thieves? Bandits? Criminals of some sort? Ogres, perhaps?" he asked her.

"No." She looked around the table. "With the exception of the Commander and the Dominatrix, none of us have."

The Dominatrix wore a calculating smile. "His Grace has been trained as a Boudonian Archer," just happened to escape her lips.

Some of the Elves gasped.

"How does a tree dweller—someone from Boudon—become a Duke, especially of Fairyland?" an Elf who had been observing asked.

"Nash," someone reprimanded.

"It's fine," said Declan. "The question is legitimate. The title was bestowed upon me for my service to the King and Queen of Fairyland."

"Oh, Declan, you're being too modest," said Silvia. "He single-handedly killed a Fairy Eater, journeyed beyond the trees to the land of the Frost Giants, and rescued the Crown Prince from Ogres all in the name of King Elrick and Queen Lida."

Nash had nothing more to say.

Silvia met Berty's gaze. She placed her knife and fork together on the plate, angled at four o'clock. A subtle eyebrow raise told him that it was his turn.

"High Elf Avery, Low Elf Kael," said Berty, "we graciously appreciate your hospitality. Our journey to Irmingard has left us a bit worse for wear this evening. It has been enlightening meeting all of you. If you will excuse us, the Empress, the Duke, the Lieutenant, and I will retire now."

"Of course," said Avery.

"We completely understand. It has been an honor," Kael added.

Berty and Silvia stood. Declan and Edwin took their cues and rose a split second after. The Elves quickly stood out of respect. The four of them left through the double door in which they entered.

When they returned to the residence's hallways, Declan said, "What a disaster. Thanks for getting us out of there."

"That was brilliant," Edwin said.

"Whatever that was was no dinner," said Berty. "I'm hungry."

Silvia laughed a little.

"Pardon me." Jordis met them in the hallway. "Rane wanted to let you know that you are all welcome to join her in the dining room." She bowed her head.

Raising an eyebrow, Silvia glanced at Berty. He gave her a small nod. They followed Jordis into a casual dining room where Rane entertained Declan's brothers.

Seeing them enter, Cecil started to stand. Berty gestured to stop him. "Don't," he said. "I can do without all the protocol for a while."

Rane laughed. She said something which Jordis translated. "Avery should be following soon. Please, sit. Help yourselves."

"Thank you, Rane," said Silvia. They filled their plates with food.

"Was it that bad?" asked Vander.

"You know when you've been keeping watch in a tree all day and everything cramps and you can't feel your fingers?" said Declan.

Vander grimaced.

"Dinner made me long for those days," Declan snapped.

Vander grunted in disgust while watching Jordis sit next to Rane.

"How was your day in Irmingard?" Edwin asked them.

"Fiona would have found it beautiful," Cecil said with a sad smile.

Looking up from his plate, Declan stared at his brother.

Cecil sighed. "I miss her every day. Some days more than others."

Wiping a tear from her cheek, Rane said her sounds.

"Your wife lives through your son," Jordis said. "Just like Rane's husband is with her through hers."

Rane rolled her wheelchair over to Cecil. Placing a hand on his arm, she said very slowly and carefully, "Yo no a-lone. Luh-ve wiit yo."

He rested his hand on the Elf's. After taking a deep breath, he said, "Thank you."

Her hand slipped away. To everyone, she said something incoherent.

"Goodnight, everyone," Jordis translated. "Eat well. Sleep well." She wheeled Rane out of the room.

Edwin stared at the door for a few minutes before saying, "I think we need to be prepared for anything. All of us." He looked from Cecil to Vander until they both nodded.

Avery had not joined them by the time they finished eating. Tired, they returned to their respective rooms. Berty and Silvia laid out their clothes before sleeping in their undergarments.

Berty opened his eyes in the dark night. A constant soft knock rapped on the door. "Silvia," he whispered.

"I hear it, too," she whispered.

Berty slipped on his pants, then snatched his sword. Opening the door a crack, he peeked at Rane. She stood in the dim hall with the aid of crutches. "Time to go," she said quietly. Her words slurred slowly, but he easily understood.

He admitted her into their room. She securely closed the door. Silvia was mostly dressed as Berty pulled his shirt over his head.

"We are meeting the others," Rane slurred. Once Silvia and Berty gathered their belongings, she continued, "Follow me." She quickly hobbled into the fireplace. Her hand reached into the chimney. A side wall opened. She pointed her crutch to the opening. Silvia and Berty ducked under the stone into the dark space between the rooms. Rane followed, then closed the wall. Berty could see nothing. "Do you have light?" Rane asked. Berty released a sphere. "Thank you." Rane took the lead. "The crutches make carrying lanterns difficult." As they walked, the only direction Berty was sure they traveled was down.

"What happened?" asked Silvia.

"Irmingard's a mess," answered Rane. "Not safe to be here for you. Jordis is leading the others. We will meet her soon. Forgive my ruse, my speech is not great, I know, and I cannot walk without these. However, we allow people to believe it is much worse."

"Where are we going?" asked Berty.

"Leaving Irmingard," Rane answered. "There is a secret portal so the High Elf can escape. Under the moat. Only the family knows its location."

A light pierced through the darkness ahead of them. "Rane?" Jordis called.

"Here," she replied.

They met Jordis leading Edwin, Declan, and his brothers. Rane turned down another dark hallway. They continued further down—well under Irmingard. Finally, she stopped in front of carved rock. "This is your exit," said Rane.

"Are you sure you won't need me here?" Jordis asked.

"We need you on the outside," Rane slurred. "Go with them."

Tears rolled down Jordis' cheeks. "Stay safe." She hugged Rane.

Rane wiped Jordis' face. "I raised you for this moment, Jordis."

"Do you need a lantern?" asked Jordis.

"The dark doesn't slow me down. Extinguish your lanterns before crossing so you are not seen," Rane instructed.

"Wait," said Silvia. She extracted the stick that used to be her staff when she was Elder. Touching it to Edwin's cloak, his green cloak turned white. "So the Whispers can't see us. Berty and my cloaks will restore." She touched her wand to theirs. "Declan, Vander, Cecil, and Jordis, yours may not."

"Fine with me," said Vander.

"Me, too," Cecil said.

"Please," said Jordis.

"I'd rather not be tracked," Declan said.

Her wand like stick turned all their cloaks white with a single touch. With the lanterns off, Berty's light sphere made the white cloaks glow.

"The portal is one-way," said Rane. "Good luck."

"Thank you," Silvia said. They raised their hoods.

Raising his bow, Declan stepped through the portal first. Edwin followed. Then Cecil, Vander, Jordis, and Silvia crossed the portal. Berty gave Rane a smile and a nod. After absorbing his sphere, he walked into the blue disc.

Chapter Seven

Rane's Plan

Light blinded him. When his eyes adjusted, he saw vertical wood walls, white cloaks, and muscular Elves holding lanterns and a variety of weapons pointed at them.

An older Elf entered the hut. He pushed through the Elf perimeter. His eyes scanned the group. They inventoried Declan's bow before falling on Edwin. "You're not the High Elf," he said.

"No," said Edwin, "he sent us."

"Who are you?"

"Lieutenant Edwin of the Empire Guard."

"Ryker's son?"

Edwin nodded.

"White cloaks," the Elf said. He sighed. "Weapons away, men."

"But, he drew on us," one protested, pointing to Declan.

"Don't give him a reason to use it. The Bow of the Moon never misses. I am Vidor. Welcome," he said to Edwin and the others. "If you are here, then Irmingard is in trouble. Come." He raised a white hood, then led them out of the hut. They descended wooden steps to the forest floor.

In the soft darkness, Berty barely made out wooden A-frame houses on stilts, which raised the houses at least twelve feet off the ground. Vidor brought them to one of the larger houses. Inside, the Elf had them gather around a central open fire. "Does the High Elf have a message?" he asked.

"Through his mother, Rane," said Jordis.

Vidor studied Jordis in the firelight. "And you are who to Rane?"

"After my parents died, Rane raised me alongside Avery," Jordis explained.

He gave her a half smile. "What did Rane say?"

"There is talk of insurrection within Irmingard," said Jordis. "They are going to be using the anti-imperialist presence as cover. However, some are scared after tonight's dinner. There are those who are afraid of angering the Empire. But, that doesn't mean a coup won't be attempted. If Avery needs to escape, he will do so with an escort. Most likely Commander Wystan and the Dominatrix."

"Thank you." He looked at her.

"Jordis, sir."

Turning his attention to Edwin, Vidor said, "If you are of the Empire Guard, then your charge is an Empire delegation."

Edwin nodded.

"We are a rogue community charged with protecting the portal. This was an Elf settlement in ancient times—prior to Irmingard," Vidor told them. "You will be safe here. We also wear white cloaks for obvious reasons. We have a dormitory upstairs where you can stay."

"Thank you, Vidor. We will speak more in the morning," said Edwin.

The dormitory's ceiling sloped steeply with the roof. Single beds lined the short walls. A railing enclosed the opening in the floor for the fire from below. After choosing their beds, they slept in their clothes.

The smell of food cooking woke them. Donning their cloaks over their weapons, they descended into the main room. At the table, Vidor smiled at them. "I hope you slept well," he said. "Haf, bring food for our guests."

A diminutive woman with Elf features ladled porridge into bowls. "Haf is half Elf and half Fairy," explained Vidor.

"How does," Declan began delicately, "how does Fairy Dust affect you?"

Haf blushed. She said, "It doesn't. I am immune. Can't even use it. My father tried to teach me. He is a Fairy. I never grew wings either though I have a Fairy's lightness."

"What about a connection with the trees?" Edwin asked.

"Oh, yes. I can become invisible," she answered.

After she left, Vidor said, "Like I said before, we are a rogue community."

"We are not judging," said Silvia. "But we do need to get back to the Sages' Grove. How far away are we?"

"It's a week's journey to Irmingard," Vidor answered.

"In relation to Boudon?" asked Declan.

"Three days north."

"We're not leaving you to get attacked," protested Vander.

"If we can get to Boudon," said Declan, "the road to the Sages' Grove should be safer."

"The outpost," said Edwin.

"Of course," said Silvia. "Jordis, do we have enough provisions for all of us to make it to Boudon?"

"Yes," she answered. "I am to go with you?"

"Absolutely. Vidor, if and when the High Elf and his party escape Irmingard, have them travel to Boudon. From there, they will receive further instructions," Silvia said.

"Pardon me, ma'am, but the High Elf's safety is my duty," Vidor objected.

Nodding, Silvia smiled. "You're Avery's father."

Vidor stiffened. "No one is supposed to know," he whispered.

"To save your son's life, he must reach Boudon," urged Silvia. "Rane has never stopped loving you, Vidor. She trusts you implicitly. Trust her. She sent us here, knowing we would meet. If the time comes, she will evacuate. Avery will need the protection he can only find in Boudon. You can go to Boudon with him. What if they're followed? What if someone finds the portal? There will be a blood-bath."

Vidor said nothing for a minute or two. "We will need to familiarize ourselves with the way to Boudon," he said. "You will want to leave right away. Let me ready my best to travel with you." He walked out of the hut.

Turning to Silvia, Berty said, "The Dwarves will just be finishing the outpost."

"Exactly," Silvia said with a wry smile.

Berty returned her smile. They were headed to Grunnan via Boudon.

After retrieving their belongings from the dormitory, Vidor met them at the central fire pit with four Elves. "You have already met

Haf," he said. "These are our best trackers. Signe, Lunt, and Hesketh."

Hesketh raised his hood. After checking his hefty sword, he walked to the door. "Thank you for the hospitality, Vidor," said Edwin.

Hesketh led the group north out of the village. They walked at a good pace in silence. Haf scouted a place to make camp when they lost the sun. She, Lunt, and Edwin took first watch.

"Shouldn't we cover up these white cloaks?" Vander asked. "They glow against the trees. Without snow, we'll be seen too easily."

"In theory, that is true," said Signe. "Haf chose this site, because we will see them before they ever spot us. We have never had a problem being seen in white. But, we are Elves. One touch of a tree and we're invisible."

"Unless you're trying to hide from a Watcher," Declan mentioned.

The Elf narrowed her eyes at him.

"Watchers can still see you while you're invoking the magic of the trees."

She turned away without saying a word.

After choosing who would next watch, they turned in early.

Avery turned to look back. His hand touched a wooden wall. "Mother," he said softly.

"Who are you?" a stern voice asked.

He faced the lantern light. Katell stood beside him, cloaked in white. "Are you Vidor?" Avery asked the lantern.

"I am." A large Elf stepped into the light.

Avery's eyes scanned the Elf. "We're the last to come unless things go badly," he said.

"Say no more. Raise your hoods. Come with me," Vidor instructed. He led the two young Elves out of the manned hut. Two other Elves wearing white cloaks joined them. Avery barely glanced at the raised hut village before they hiked into the woods beyond.

"Where are we headed?" Katell asked.

"Change of plans," Vidor answered without stopping.

Katell drew a sword. "He is to be protected," she said.

The other two Elves unsheathed theirs.

Vidor faced the tip of Katell's sword. "We are."

"By bringing him out into the open?"

"The Human woman who came before you," Vidor began.

Katell slid her sword into her scabbard. "This is her plan," she said. "Then we should move more quickly."

Berty woke beside a dying fire. "What is it?" Declan asked.

"She sent him," answered Berty.

"Alone?"

"No. One other."

Hesketh watched the exchange. "Lunt," he called. The Elf emerged from the shadows. "Go back. He is coming. Make sure he gets here. We will keep moving."

Lunt disappeared.

At first light, Hesketh had everyone well on the move. Haf periodically scouted ahead. While they trekked, Berty cryptically whispered what he saw to Silvia.

They found a sheltered area to spend the night. Edwin and Declan would not allow either Berty or Silvia to a take a turn at watch. Hesketh's eyes darted during their discussion, but he said nothing. In the morning, they left Signe at the campsite. She was to wait for Avery.

"We're close," said Cecil. "If we hurry, we can make it by night-fall."

Spying the Woodsmith's cottage, Haf disappeared up a tree. Hesketh accompanied them into the village's forest floor. Cecil found the hidden lift easily in the dark. "We won't all fit," he said.

An arrow thumped into the side of the lift. He backed away. Repelling from a tree, a man said, "Oh, it's you."

"And my brothers and our friends," said Cecil. "If you don't mind, we'd like to go home."

"Sorry." He rose into the trees.

Cecil ushered Berty, Silvia, and Hesketh into the lift with him. On the bridge, they waited for the others. Once they all joined them, Cecil led them across the platforms and bridges.

Opening the door to his family's home, Cecil said, "Hey, Mom, Dad, we're home."

Geraldine watched the eight of them file into her house. "What's wrong? Is it Julie? Matt?"

"They're fine, Geraldine," Berty said right away. "We're just passing though and accompanied Cecil and Vander home."

"Looks as though you've been traveling all day," said Leon. "Please, have a seat."

They set down their packs and removed their cloaks. Geraldine placed some bread and cheese on the table for them. After they began eating, Leon asked, "What is this really about?"

"Irmingard is under attack," explained Silvia. Hesketh's eyes dashed from Leon to Silvia. "The High Elf and his guard are a day behind us. Hesketh, you will make sure that he enters the woodshop. He and his protectors will rendezvous with Vander, who will bring them here."

"He would be better protected where we were," Hesketh said.

"To keep him alive, no one can know the entire plan," said Silvia.

"I do not expect you to understand, madam."

Geraldine gasped. Silvia simply smiled. "I understand more than you know. Vidor trusts me. You trust him. Know that this is not ours nor his final destination."

The Elf said nothing.

"Leon and Geraldine, may we impose on your hospitality tonight? We will be leaving in the morning," Silvia said.

"Or course," she answered. "It is such an honor to have the both of you in our home again."

Silvia and Jordis stayed in Julie's old room. Berty bunked with Declan while Edwin kept an eye on Hesketh in Vander's room.

"First Fairyland and now Irmingard," said Declan.

"The Elves have an advantage," Berty said, laying in the bottom bunk.

"That only helps if they can put aside their little power struggle," said Declan. He extinguished the lantern, then climbed to the top bunk.

"Rane has a plan," Berty said. "We're playing our part."

Geraldine would not let them leave without a hearty breakfast. Vander saw Hesketh to the woodshop. "Cecil, you and Vander will bring them where we're going right now," Silvia said. "Come."

After saying good-bye to Declan's parents, they headed through the busy village. Soon after descending to the forest floor, they reached the still under construction outpost. The stone outer walls loomed in the forest. Most of the outside building was finished.

The guard immediately allowed them entrance. One of the Romans they rescued from God Mountain greeted them. "Lieutenant

Manius," said Edwin.

"Lieutenant Edwin," Manius replied. "My Lord, my Lady, how can I be of service?"

"We were hoping to see how construction was progressing," said Berty.

"Of course, my Lord. This way."

Their white cloaks did not go unnoticed by the Empire Guards they passed. In the center of the outpost, Dwarves moved materials to the different projects. "As you can see, everything is on schedule," Manius said.

"Very good," said Silvia. She had Jordis follow her to where the Dwarves worked.

"Manius," Berty said quietly.

"Yes, my Lord."

"This is the Duke's brother, Cecil," he said. "He and his other brother will be accompanying a small delegation of Elves tomorrow. I want you to personally lead them to this very spot."

Rejoining them, Silvia said, "Jordis will be awaiting them. She will stay the night in the outpost and must be notified at once when they arrive. Once the Elves make it here, she will take them off your hands." She finished with something in Latin.

"I understand," said Manius.

"Cecil, you know what to do," Silvia told him.

After bowing his head, Cecil bade his brother farewell.

"If all goes well, we'll see you tomorrow, Jordis," said Silvia.

The Elf stood aside.

"Keep up the good work, Lieutenant," said Edwin. He clapped Manius on the shoulder. The Roman's green cloak turned white. Manius stared at his cloak, then at Edwin.

"Camouflage against Whispers," Silvia said softly. "Empire Tree magic."

Manius nodded. "Good luck," he said to them. Turning to Jordis, he said, "Come. Let's get you situated."

Silvia led them to the Dwarf Foreman. "We are ready," she told him.

The Dwarf brought them down a series of ladders to what looked like newly dug tunnels. Opening the door to a seated mine cart, he said, "This will take you directly to Grunnan. I will do the same with the party behind you."

"Thank you," said Silvia. She and Berty sat in the front while Edwin and Declan got in the back. When the Dwarf closed the door, the cart began to move. It ran along the tracks in dark tunnels. The smell of damp earth overwhelmed Berty. He did not want to know how close the walls or ceiling were.

His stomach rumbled, but the cart showed no signs of slowing down. A roaring rumble reached his ears. The tunnel ended. Water sprayed them briefly before they entered another tunnel.

Hungry and drained, Berty shifted in his seat. After days of walking, he did not know if he could sit for so long. Finally, his eyes registered light. Edwin breathed a sigh of relief. Grunnan glowed softly somewhere up ahead.

The cart stopped at the base of the steps to a golden pyramid. A Dwarf hurried down the steps to greet them. "Three Humans, one Elf," she said, taking inventory. Reaching the bottom step, she said, "You have arrived without a Dwarf escort. I take it you were sent by a Foreman." She smiled. "What is the nature of your visit to Grunnan this evening?"

"We seek an audience with Prince Goscislaw," Berty said.

"And who may I say is calling?"

"A delegation from the Empire Tree. Urgent business," answered Silvia.

"Oh," the Dwarf said. She opened the cart door. "Right this way, sirs and ma'am." Halfway up the stairs, they entered a golden doorway. Their white cloaks reflected the golden hue of the corridor through which they walked.

When the corridor ended in a golden plaza, the Dwarf said, "I can take you as far as the welcoming room of the palace." Smiling, she led them up another set of stairs off the plaza.

Royal Battalion flanked massive double doors. Just inside, a lavishly dressed Dwarf met them. "Empire Tree delegation," their guide said. She turned and bounced out of the room.

The palace Dwarf stroked his beard. "Empire Tree delegation," he said. "Do you have credentials?"

"Lieutenant Edwin of the Empire Guard," said Edwin. "My breastplate is the only credential you'll need."

The Dwarf stared at the Sages' Seal embossed on Edwin's hard leather armor. "Yes," he said. "One moment."

Berty looked at Silvia. She shrugged. The Dwarf's footsteps echoed off the metal covered stone.

Minutes later, a door opened. A young redheaded Dwarf stood on the other side. She smiled. "Welcome back to Grunnan, my Lord. My Lady, I believe this is your first visit. My father would love for you to join us. We were just about to sit down for dinner. Allow me to show you through the palace," she said.

"Thank you, Brana," said Berty.

The Dwarf blushed. "We apologize for any mistreatment. They did not know who you were." The four of them followed the Princess though the golden palace.

"It's quite all right," said Silvia. "We did not fully announce our-selves."

"That's why father sent me," Brana said. She opened the door to a quaint dining room. Prince Goscislaw and his wife, Leosia, stood in front of their chairs.

After everyone had a seat, Goscislaw asked, "What has happened?"

Silvia and Berty explained their trip to Irmingard and their escape from it. "Elves will be arriving within the next day," said Silvia. "One of which will be Avery."

"Their discreet arrival here will be arranged," growled Goscislaw. He carefully selected the food off his plate. "It is time. After Avery arrives, we will pause construction for winter. By Wassail, our defens-es will be full."

"Gos?" said Leosia.

"I've been running Grunnan like it's still a state within a larger Kingdom of Dwarves," he said. "We're all that's left. It's about time we acted like it. Tomorrow, the Royal Battalion becomes Grunnan's Battalion."

After finishing dinner discussing Irmingard and Fairyland, Leosia escorted them to their rooms. "We have limited accommodations for non-Dwarves," she said. "Do you happen to know how many Elves we will be receiving?"

"Four," said Berty. "Two males and two females." Somehow, he knew that to be correct.

"We won't impose on you for long," said Silvia. "Just until Avery arrives."

"It is not an imposition, my Lady," Leosia said. She opened the doors to Berty and Silvia's room. "Sleep well."

While relieving themselves of their packs and cloaks, Berty said, "I think we're going to miss Thanksgiving."

Nodding, Silvia sat on the bed. "Do you think locket communication is safe?" she asked him.

He extracted the hefty, golden locket from the pocket of his pants. Holding it symbol side up, he sat next to Silvia. "There are five of these," he said. "I don't know if it's as safe in Delyth's hands as it is in Declan's. After Irmingard, I don't know if we can be too careful." Without opening the locket, he slipped off the bed. He crossed to his pack, then slipped it inside. When he returned to Silvia's side, he kissed her goodnight. The soft pillow cradled his head as he closed his eyes.

White cloaked Elves sat around a small fire. "I don't know why you're following orders from some Human. From the Empire Tree or not, it's not like you, Vidor." Berty recognized Hesketh's rarely used voice.

"She's not just any Human," Vidor said. "She was sent to us for a reason—to keep him safe."

"He'd be safer in the village," contested Hesketh.

"I've heard enough from you, Hesketh."

"My mother knows how to play the game," Avery said from his bedroll.

"You need your rest. Sleep. We're sorry we woke you," Vidor apologized.

Avery sat up. "No. You all need to understand something," he said to the Elves. "Irmingard will be fighting two fronts. My mother will orchestrate the battle within while Commander Wystan will try to battle the anti-imperialists on the other side of the moat. I was sent away for my own safety and for the future of not only Irmingard, but all Elves. By me leaving that village of yours, it frees up all of you—an elite force of fighters, loyal to me and to Irmingard. Once I am safely where the Empress wants me to be, what will you do?"

The Elves looked at each other. "Co-ordinate on attack on the anti-imperialists parked outside of Irmingard," said Signe.

Avery smiled. "Since we are meeting with Vander, he can provide you with additional information regarding that force," he said. "He and his brothers fought them. Plan well." Without allowing them to answer, he returned to his bedroll to sleep.

Opening his eyes in the darkness, Berty told Silvia what he had seen.

Breakfast was brought to their room in the morning. They sat on cushions at a small table to eat. "Berty, where are you?" a voice said.

"Jon?" Berty called to the empty room.

"Berty?" said Jon's voice.

"I hear you, but I don't see you," said Berty.

"Okay. This is odd," said Jon. "I'm at home. Where are you?"

"Grunnan."

"I take it you're not coming to Thanksgiving dinner," said Jon.

Berty sighed. "We ran into some trouble. We're fine." He turned to Silvia. "Can you hear him?"

"I can, but can he hear me?" asked Silvia.

"Hello, Silvia. I can indeed hear you. I hope I'm not interrupting anything," said Jon. "I don't exactly know how I did this."

Chuckling, Silvia said, "Just breakfast. This is very interesting."

"Just because we can't make it, Jon," said Berty, "doesn't mean someone can't pick up Obie and perhaps Delyth, if she wants to go. Tell everyone we're sorry. We'll explain when we get back."

"Okay," said Jon. "Um... I'm... I'm not sure I can do this again.

Nor am I sure how to stop this. I'll be right there, Teresa. Did you hear her?"

"No."

"Hmmmm… Well, good luck with what you're doing," said Jon. "See you guys soon."

"Bye, Jon. Have a good Thanksgiving."

Berty heard no reply.

"Looks like you brother found his magic," Silvia said.

Focusing on Jon, Berty closed his eyes.

"What were you doing?" asked Teresa. She placed food on the kitchen island.

"Talking to Berty," Jon answered.

Teresa smiled. "You finally reached him."

"In a manner of speaking."

"When are they getting here?"

Jon adjusted his glasses. "Only Obie and Delyth can make it, if someone goes to get them. He and Silvia, and Declan, I think, have been delayed."

"Delayed?" Teresa placed her hands on her hips, accentuating her growing belly.

"He didn't elaborate."

"How did you talk to him, exactly?"

"I don't know."

"Daddy used magic," Hope exclaimed, running into the kitchen.

Jon collapsed into a chair at the kitchen table. "I don't have magic," he mumbled.

"Our mothers will be here soon," Teresa changed the subject. "I believe they're bringing Julie."

"I'm going to Berty's," Jon said. "I'll take Hope with me. As soon as they get here."

Smiling, he opened his eyes. "He's coming to the Empire Tree for answers," Berty said. "He'll probably talk to Alfred."

"Jon's magic seems similar to yours," Silvia observed. "Alfred will be a good resource for him. Where is Avery now?"

"With Vander." He could see Vander leading the Elves up the spiral staircase inside the tree that connects the woodshop to the Firth's house.

"He should be here tonight. That gives us time to ask," she said.

Berty and Silvia found Goscislaw in the throne room, growling at other Dwarves. Leosia greeted them quietly. "Can I help you with anything?"

After surveying the room, Silvia's eyes fell onto their hostess. "Yes. Is there somewhere we can speak? I do not wish to interrupt the Prince's business."

Leosia smiled. "Right this way." She brought them to a Dwarf sized office off the main hall. The three of them sat on red and purple round ottomans, which threatened to invade the office. "What can I do for you?"

Unrolling a scroll, Silvia said, "We need this language identified and translated." She handed it to the Dwarf.

Leosia merely glanced at the scroll before handing it back. "I can't help you, but I know someone who might," she said. "Wait here. I'll be right back."

She returned wearing a rich brown cloak. "All ready. Come with me." They left the office to find Declan standing in the hall. "It will be quicker if a Watcher accompanies us," she explained. She hurried them down a side hall.

They exited the palace pyramid through a side door. "I hope you don't mind walking a ways," said Leosia. "There are no tracks that go where we're headed."

"Where are we headed?" asked Berty.

Leosia glanced around her. Raising her hood, she said, "Outside Grunnan."

They trekked along the outskirts of the golden pyramids. Taking a deep breath, Leosia led them away from the soft glow of the Dwarf city.

The cavern grew darker. Eventually, the light behind them faded. Leosia lit a small, golden lantern. The flameless light produced a soft glow, which illuminated only a few feet in all directions. Berty resisted the temptation to conjure spheres of light.

Stopping, Leosia said, "Watcher, what do you see?"

"A small cottage," said Declan.

Berty only saw darkness.

"Is there a light in the window?" she asked.

"Yes."

"Good. He's home."

"He who?" asked Berty.

Leosia ignored Berty's question. "There should be magical tests or traps that would be best avoided," she said. "Our goal is to make it to the cabin's front door. Is it safe to continue on this path?"

Declan surveyed the darkness. "Yes. We seemed to be standing before a small opening in an encompassing magical field."

Curious, Berty stepped beside Declan. Leaning towards his friend, Berty saw grass and trees and a stone cottage through a crack in the darkness. "Huh," he said. He could tell that Declan wanted to talk about what each of them could see. However, Declan kept his thoughts to himself.

"We should enter single file behind me," Declan instructed.

Leosia quickly stood in back of the Watcher. Berty allowed Silvia in front of him. Once they stepped through the crack, the view of the cottage disappeared. Declan stopped. After a moment, he led them forward. Berty caught glimpses of the cottage every now and then as if an opening revolved around it. They stopped five more times before reaching the cottage's door.

"You should be the one to knock," Leosia said to Silvia.

Silvia's knuckles rapped on the door twice.

"Go away," snapped an agitated voice from within. "No one's home."

"We know you're there, Faxon," Leosia said.

The door opened. A white haired Dwarf held onto the doorknob. "Her Royalness has left the palace," he almost yelled. "And she comes to visit an old codger like me." The light caught a few orange strands in his long, white hair. "And ya bring Humans."

"Are you going to let us in?" asked Leosia.

The Dwarf's toe-touching beard twitched. "Fine." He stepped aside. After they entered, he said, "My spells, charms, and potions have the best prices in all the Land of Sages."

"We're not here for your trinkets and tricks, Faxon," said Leosia.

"No?" said Faxon. "Then, why are ya here?" He looked at Silvia.

"We need your help," said Leosia.

The Dwarf crossed his arms. "No."

"What's your price?" asked Berty.

"See? This is why I like Humans better than Dwarves," Faxon stated. "Price depends on whatcha be needin'."

"A translation of an unknown language," Silvia said.

Faxon buried his hands in his white beard. "A wand," he said finally. "I want a wand."

"A wand?" Leosia asked.

"My price is a wand." Faxon's already loud voice increased in volume.

Berty, Declan, and Silvia looked at each other. Who would part with a wand? The Dwarf sat in a chair and crossed his arms. Berty stepped outside the cottage. He gravitated to a tree. When he touched a branch, it fell off in his hand. He brought it inside.

"That's not a wand," the Dwarf said. "That's a twig."

With one glance at Silvia, Berty tossed the twig in the air. Grasping her Empire Tree "wand," she froze the twig midflight. The old Dwarf's eyes widened. The twig spun with a slight glow. It stopped in reach of the Dwarf.

"Now, that's a wand," Faxon said. He snatched it from the air. "Show me that document."

Silvia unrolled the scroll for the Dwarf.

After perusing the scroll for a moment, Faxon looked up, saying, "That explains the white cloaks." He turned his attention to the words on the paper. "Our ancestors who built Grunnan discovered that Whispers could flow through the cracks in the earth. Whispers brought with them magic—tree magic. Grunnan uses earth magic. However, the mixing of the magics makes it even stronger. So strong, in fact, that wherever the sunlight touched the ground within the caverns, something green would grow. Generations later, Dwarves were being born with hybrid magic. The King would bring his Queen here often, in hopes of having a child with this magic. After many unsuccessful attempts, he took himself a Grunnan woman. She escaped topside. Some say she was sheltered by the Elves, others by the Pixies. Either way, she became the first and only Dwarf Whisper. The scroll says she had a son while in exile. Her line was to be the Dwarf contribution to Whispers. Her son was never found." Faxon gazed at the four of them. "If ya've noticed, nothing green grows in Grunnan anymore. Dwarf Whispers were supposed to keep the magic flowing. There be a problem with the Whispers. But I don't need to tell *you* that, do I? If ya're looking for someone to blame, blame the Pixies. Ya can't trust a Pixie."

"Faxon!" Leosia reprimanded.

"Ya can't. They're all devious, little schemers," Faxon said to Leosia's raised eyebrows. "They are. And nothing ya can say will make it different."

"Is that all the scroll says?" Silvia asked.

"Beware the screaming Whisper," Faxon added.

"How can a Whisper scream?" Declan said quietly.

"How indeed. How indeed," said Faxon. He turned his body to Silvia. "There is nothing more on this scroll. If you're thinking about traveling to Pixisle, think again." The whiskers around his mouth bristled. "Use a woman sailor. The Water Sprites are treacherous and lead many a man astray. And bring the child. The Pixies will not touch her and by proxy her guard, which would be you." He spun his new wand in his stubby fingers. "It is a fine wand. Touched with Empire Tree magic."

Berty thought he saw the Dwarf smile under the bushy white. Leosia began to usher them out of the cottage.

"Keeper," Faxon called. "The answers to riddle are all within your grasp, but the timing is not quite right. As in the beginning, so in the end." As he tested his wand, Declan closed the cottage's door behind him.

Declan stepped onto the path. "Wait," said Leosia. "The white cloaks."

After explaining, Silvia touched her wand to Leosia's cloak. Brown transformed to white. The Dwarf allowed Declan to lead them away from Faxon's cottage.

Leosia guided them as if she knew all the ways in and out of Grunnan without being seen and regularly sneaked out of lesser known palace doors. They followed her into a corridor when they heard, "Mother!" Brana entered the same corridor with Elves on her heels.

"Avery, you're safe," Leosia said. "We were worried. Come, Goscislaw should have dinner waiting."

Mother and daughter led the way to the dining room. Berty noticed Edwin walking behind Jordis and Vidor. Katell stayed at Avery's side. In the dining room, Goscislaw sipped from a goblet. He looked up, then hastily stood. "High Elf Avery, welcome to Grunnan. Please, all of you, have a seat."

"Thank you, Prince Goscislaw," said Avery. They took seats around the table. "Empress, Emperor, thank you for arranging this for me." Vidor's eyes snapped to Berty and Silvia. The Elf grinned.

They discussed the fate of Irmingard during dinner. "After Irmingard is secure," Avery said, "the Elves will go to Fairyland. We will fight."

"What is next?" asked Vidor.

"We need to head elsewhere," said Silvia.

"You are not returning to the Empire Tree?" Goscislaw asked.

"Not yet. And neither should Avery," Silvia answered. "Grunnan is a fortress disguised as golden pyramids."

"This is true," growled Goscislaw. "Stay here until you can return home."

"Perhaps, they can be here under the guise of training the Battalion in proper combat," Brana suggested. "No one needs to know Avery is the High Elf or even here for that matter."

"We can do that," said Vidor. "Gives us a purpose."

"You can learn something, Jordis," Katell jibed.

"Jordis should return to Boudon," said Silvia.

"My Lady?" said Jordis.

"Stay in the outpost, but make regular visits to the Firth house. Keep your ears open. When the time is right, you will return for Avery," said Silvia.

"I will send Baldur with her," said Goscislaw. "He can stay at the outpost and return with her."

"Good. We leave tomorrow," said Silvia.

As they left the dining room, Declan said, "Jordis, can I have a word?"

"Of course, Your Grace," Jordis replied.

"Why send Jordis away?" Avery asked Silvia.

"Everyone has a strength. Hers is information gathering."

Avery nodded. "My mother knew what she was doing."

"Your mother would have made an excellent High Elf," Vidor said.

"Yes, Vidor," agreed Avery. "My mother always has a plan. Sometimes, you can't even see it until you're so deeply in it. And then, you must follow it through."

"I believe Rane has a greater plan that we haven't even begun to find the end," Vidor said.

"You knew my mother," said Avery.

"I knew her very well once," Vidor said, flashing a rare smile. "I haven't seen her since you were little."

"Were you Commander?" asked Avery.

"No. I have always been a Blóvǫr," Vidor explained. "We are underground protectors. Working in the shadows, we protect the High Elf bloodline."

Avery walked a few steps without saying anything. "My mother never mentioned you to me until right before pushing me through the portal."

"I've known your mother since childhood," Vidor elaborated. "We were friends. That's how the Blóvǫr works. Like how you grew up with Jordis. I wasn't with your mother the day of her accident—the day your grandmother died. We were only children, but I always blamed myself." Vidor stared into Avery's eyes. "She didn't. You mother has always been special, Avery. I have missed her all these years."

Avery's eyes registered an understanding, but he said nothing.

Chapter Eight

Carts and Tunnels

Vidor's and Avery's rooms were near Berty and Silvia's in the forgotten guest wing of the palace. Berty and Silvia bid the Elves a goodnight before entering their room.

"These scrolls," Berty began, "there's not much to them."

"Not really," said Silvia, "but it's what's not in them that's most interesting."

"And you're hoping the Trolls will give us anther snippet to help with the Pixies?" Berty climbed into bed.

Pulling back the covers, Silvia said, "It's the only way to stop the Whisperer." She slid next to her husband.

"Perhaps we should research Pixies in the Library Vault," he suggested.

"There's nothing about them there."

"Nothing?" That's strange," he said.

Silvia's gaze found his in the darkness. "That is strange," she repeated. "There has to be magic that prevents it from flying off the shelves when called."

"A task to tackle when we get home," he said.

"Which needs to be before Wassail," Silvia stressed. "We will be missed."

Berty's hand caressed her shoulder before pulling her close. "We'll make it," he breathed. He gave her a comforting kiss.

In the morning, Goscislaw accompanied the breakfast trays. "I apologize for the morning intrusion," he growled as servants set down the food. "Baldur and Jordis have already left for the outpost."

"Excellent," said Berty. He sipped a goblet of juice.

"Can I ask where you're headed? Perhaps I can give some directions on how to get there from here," the Dwarf said.

"Bridgetown," said Silvia. "We wish to keep this knowledge to ourselves."

Goscislaw nodded. "There's a mine shaft that takes you right to the entrance," he said. "I will send Brana with you. She can control the mine cart. It will be much quicker than on foot."

Berty and Silvia looked at one another. They both nodded. "We leave within the hour," said Berty.

"Very well. I'll leave you to your breakfast," the Dwarf said.

Servants who collected the trays brought provisions. Berty and Silvia finished packing with the door open. When Declan and Edwin joined them in the room, Berty said, "Brana will be joining us soon."

"Sorry to keep you waiting," Brana said from the doorway. Her rich brown cloak covered a thick short sword. She carried two large packs in each hand in addition to the one on her back.

"Are you expecting trouble on the way, Princess?" Declan asked. Both he and Edwin offered to carry a pack.

"One cannot be too careful," she replied. "You each have a weapon. And I have been training with the Empire Guard ever since what happened in Fairyland."

"If you're ready, Brana, lead the way," said Silvia.

She took them through empty golden corridors. "My mother told me about the white cloaks," she stated. "As I am traveling with you, would it be strange that I don't have one? Should I exchange mine with my mother's?"

"That won't be necessary," said Silvia. She touched her wand to Brana's cloak, turning it white.

"Thank you, Empress," she said.

She brought them to an expansive, golden room where a beautiful maze of tracks crisscrossed the floor. "We must hurry to our cart. Father has only guaranteed an empty Track Room for a little while." Choosing a cart, she opened its insignia embossed door. "If you two would be good enough to place those packs under the front bench, then sit."

Declan and Edwin did as asked. After Berty and Silvia were seated, Brana entered, then closed the door. She barely settled into her seat when the cart started to move. Once the cart rode free of the Track Room, Brana released a breath. The cart dashed into a tunnel, speeding away from Grunnan.

The sounds of metal wheels rolling on metal tracks, poured into the tunnel. Brana mumbled something under her breath. The cart switched tracks. The noise disappeared behind them.

As Berty's body began to cramp, Brana lit a lantern. After studying a map, she slowed the cart. A flip of a lever switched their track to a side niche. The cart stopped. "A rest stop," Brana said, opening the cart door. "These have facilities, beds, a stove, and the like. We should take the chance to eat and stretch our legs. We still have a ways to go." She led them into carved out rooms. "Mind your heads. These rest areas are made for Dwarves."

The three men ducked under a doorway into a spartan kitchen. Brana washed her hands in a metal tub like sink after starting a fire in the large metal stove. "Through there is everything else," she said, pointing at another doorway. "I'll be here, getting food ready."

They walked past a long table into a sitting area. Berty pushed a light sphere through a dark doorway. Bunk beds filled the room. Silvia magically lit torch sconces in the sitting area and adjacent bathrooms.

Metal clanged in the kitchen. "I'm going to see if Brana needs any help," said Edwin.

"I want to do a little checking," said Declan. He lifted a torch out of its sconce holder.

"Don't get lost," said Berty.

"Keep the light," Declan said, glancing at the sphere. "I'll find you."

Berty gave Declan a nod. While Silvia disappeared to wash her face, Berty strolled around the room. He was not ready to sit down yet. When Silvia re-emerged, they followed the sound of laughter to the kitchen.

"I'm not exactly practiced," Brana said to Edwin. "Thank you for your help."

"I doubt you've had the need," said Edwin.

"No, but I do know that when riding in these carts for over long periods of time, you need to take longer breaks," she said. Noticing Berty and Silvia, she said, "Shall we wait for His Grace?"

"I'm here," said Declan, entering.

"I think its best that while on the road, we not use our titles," said Silvia.

"Then how should we address each other?" asked Brana.

"Edwin, Declan, Brana," Silvia paused to look at Berty, "Berty, and Silvia."

Brana's eyes widened. "First names? Like equals?"

"That's what other travelers would do," reasoned Berty.

Nodding, Silvia said, "Here, especially, we are equals. Remember, Brana, your ancestor was one of the Seven High Sages. There are those who resent that linage. That resentment fuels the problems with Fairyland and Irmingard and the Empire as a whole. Sometimes, it is best not to stoke the flames."

Understanding crept into Brana's emerald eyes. They sat at the long, plank table with plates of food.

"I found a large workshop back there," said Declan.

"Every rest stop has one to fix tools," Brana explained. "Some are massive with trade stalls, providing everything one needs. Many of the larger ones are permanently settled. We will not come across any of those. The chances we see anyone else dwindles the closer to Bridge-town we get. Guardian Trolls can be quite intimidating to a Dwarf."

"They're intimidating to everyone," said Declan.

After cleaning Brana's supplies and making sure the stove's fire extinguished, they piled back inside the mine cart. Once the cart began to roll, Brana said, "At the next stop, we will sleep."

"How many stops are there between here and there?" Berty asked.

"Two more," she answered. The cart picked up speed.

Vibrations of the speeding wheels coursed through Berty. Traveling through the dark tunnels, his other senses took over. The coolness reeked of earth and metal. Rushing air muffled the sounds of metal rolling against metal.

Berty no longer felt his body by the time the cart began to slow or maybe he imagined it slowing. The cart finally stopped in another niche.

They entered a large gathering room with many doorways leading somewhere. "This is one of the larger ones," Brana said. Finding the kitchen, they decided to eat around the small table there instead of the communal dining table in the other room.

Declan helped Brana with the food. Turning to face a doorway, he raised his bow. A Dwarf inched into the doorway with his opened palms raised in front of him. "I didn't mean to startle. I was in the workroom. I didn't know anyone was here," he said.

"There is no other cart outside," Declan said, holding his aim steady.

"I'm a lone traveler. I walk," the Dwarf replied.

"Do you have a name?" asked Brana.

"Grover. My name is Grover."

"Are you hungry, Grover?" Brana continued. "Please, join us."

"Thank you, but I'll be out of your way in a minute," he said.

"I insist," said Brana.

The forcefulness in her tone caused Grover to stare at her.

"How long have you been staying here?" asked Edwin.

The Dwarf's dark eyes moved to the Elf. "A few days. Resting," answered Grover.

"We'll be gone before you know it and you can get back to resting in solitude," said Berty kindly. "You are very welcome to join us, Grover, but we understand if you want to keep to yourself."

Declan lowered his bow. Letting out a breath, Grover nodded.

"Thank you." When he stepped into the well-lit kitchen, Grover emanated disheveledness. His black hair desperately needed a comb. His threadbare clothes were well made at one time. Berty supposed they were the only ones he owned. He rolled up his dirty cuffs and washed his hands before he sat at the table with them.

Once Declan and Brana joined the table, Silvia said to Grover, "You are not surprised to see Humans and an Elf in these tunnels?"

Grover smelled the warm food. "No."

"From where do you hail, Grover?" asked Brana. "You are not from Grunnan. Not with that short beard."

His hand ran over his black beard that appeared to be about two weeks of growth. He sighed. "No," he admitted. "My family are jewelers. Were jewelers." When no one said anything, he continued, "Our business was destroyed. My parents were killed and my sisters were taken. I'm just trying to survive and I'm doing a poor job of that. They took everything that my parents...." He stared at the table, not touching his food for a moment. "I have nothing left to steal, just in case you were wondering."

"Steal? We would never—" One look from Silvia stopped Brana's protest.

"We are sorry for your loss, Grover," said Silvia. "As Brana says, we are not a band of thieves, merely travelers using the Dwarf tunnels to get from one place to another."

"We are also aware that you could be telling us a sob story to get us to pity or trust you," said Declan. "Distrust goes both ways."

"I barely escaped Calledin with my life!" Grover shouted. "Then I came down here," he shook his head.

"What did Manfred do?" asked Silvia.

Looking at Silvia, Grover said, "You know him?"

"Of him."

Grover nodded. "The Dwarves of Calledin were always left to ourselves. We were the blacksmiths, the jewelers, the bankers," he explained. "A few months ago, everything changed. My sisters, along with other young women, were invited to the castle. When they didn't return, the families tried to contact them, but couldn't. Then they wouldn't allow Dwarves to travel. I escaped the night they raided us. I had to have had help. Just don't know from whom."

"What about the Elves? Were they raided as well?" asked Edwin.

"Not as I know. I think they fear Elves," Grover said.

"My wife has family in Calledin," mentioned Edwin.

"If you ever get word to them, they should probably leave for their own safety," Grover suggested. They finished dinner in relative silence.

Because the area had multiple bunkrooms, they chose one separate from Grover. Before unrolling his bedroll, Berty opened his Watcher's locket. He sent Delyth a message. Only Brana could sleep in a bunk. The rest of them made sleeping arrangements on the floor. As Berty laid close to Silvia, his locket vibrated. He relayed Delyth's message. "What Grover says is true. Lark's family has been helping Dwarves escape unseen. The Elves are untouched so far. They are planning a rescue with some Humans. Delyth will keep us posted."

"Thank you," said Edwin. Berty could tell that he wanted to say, "My Lord," but refrained.

Declan spied Grover in the workroom when they woke. "He's working on something," he told them while cooking breakfast. "Probably a way of coping."

They ate without talking about much of anything. Grover entered the gathering room as they readied to leave. "Going so soon?" he said.

"It was nice meeting you. Safe journey."

"There's a jeweler's guild in Grunnan," Brana told him.

"Thank you, but you need to know someone just to be allowed inside the door," said Grover.

"Someone must know your family," she said.

Grover gave her a weak smile. "They'd be long dead by now."

"Can we drop you off at the next rest area?" she asked.

"That is kind," he said. "But, I am going to stay here for a few more days. Allow me to help you with your bags as a thank you for dinner." Grover carried Brana's packs to the cart. He waved as the cart rolled away.

"I think you have an admirer, Brana," said Declan.

Brana waved away the notion as they plunged into darkness.

They rode in seemingly endless tunnel after tunnel. Every now and then, Berty thought he heard squealing or squeaking. The dark tunnels, however, revealed nothing.

Finally, they found what Brana promised was their last rest stop. As they filed out of the cart, they heard, "Wait!" Grover approached frantically pumping a hand powered flatbed.

Brana unsheathed her sword as the flatbed stopped. She held it to Grover's neck. "Why are you following us? Explain yourself or I spill your blood."

Freezing, Grover breathed slowly. "This was the next logical stop," he whimpered. "It's the only one before the surface. And I had to warn you."

"Warn us?" Brana asked, keeping her sword to his throat.

"This is where I encountered the thieves who took my stuff," he said. "They hide in there, waiting."

"Where did you get the hand cart? You said you walked," she accused.

"I found it. I was fixing it."

She lowered her sword. "They're illegal."

"I saw lots of Dwarves with them," he countered. "I didn't know."

"You're coming with us," demanded Brana.

Hanging his head, Grover followed. Silvia looked at the cart before they headed through the entrance. Shimmers incased it.

The doorway led to a grand hall with empty stalls ready for trade. Another doorway waited for them on the other side of the room. As they crossed the hall, a Dwarf called to them. "Good day to you, sirs and madams. What will you be needing today?"

"Just stretching our legs," answered Berty.

"Ah. Of course," said the Dwarf. "I'm afraid you can't go any further than this room."

"And why is that?" asked Brana.

"You have to pay to use anything here," he answered.

Berty spied Grover ducking behind a stall. "How much?" Declan asked.

"Five cops for the kitchen, three for the privies, a ron for the work room, and ten rons for a bed—each. Though I don't think we have any beds your size."

"No one pays to use these stops," said Brana. "How dare you."

Silvia tried to catch Brana's eye, but the fiery Dwarf only had eyes for the gatekeeper.

"We can do whatever we want here, little missy. If you don't have the coin, we can always find other ways for you to pay." The Dwarf ogled her from head to toe.

Drawing her sword, she said, "You! Will! Not!"

The man merely laughed. "What are you going to do, Girly?" He laughed some more.

Grover sprinted through a side door, carrying a bag.

"Stop him!" someone yelled. Dwarves poured into the room.

"It's my stuff," Grover said. He ran for the door to the carts.

"Time to go," Silvia breathed. She placed a hand on Brana's shoulder.

Edwin caught up to Grover in a few strides. He grabbed him by his shirt collar.

"Thank you for stopping the thief," said a Dwarf who chased after Grover.

"Let me go," said Grover. "It's my stuff. They stole it from me."

Edwin pointed his long, golden blade at the pursuing Dwarf. Every Dwarf stepped back. "This one's mine," he said.

Berty pulled the group to where Edwin stood. "Cart, now," he ordered in a whisper.

With one hand clutching Grover and the other brandishing the Blade of the Golden Flame, Edwin backed out of the rest area behind Berty. As they rushed into their waiting mine cart, Edwin pushed Grover into the front with his bag. Brana started the cart, then latched the door. Grover covered his face with his hands. The cart raced into the darkness.

The line ended near a walkable shaft. They climbed out of the cart confident that they were not followed. With their bags and Grover in tow, they ascended out of the mines to the surface.

The shaft entrance spit them into a dark forest. Camp had a hidden view of the shaft and road. "So," swallowed Grover, "what are you going to do with me?" He sat as close to the fire as possible with his arms wrapped around himself.

"Don't you have a bedroll or a cloak in that pack?" asked Declan. Grover shook his head. "Lost them."

Reaching into his bag, Declan pulled out his old brown cloak. It turned white before he handed it to the Dwarf. "Here, wrap this around you," he said. "It'll be too long for you, but it will keep you warm through the night."

He took it from Declan. "Thank you." Declan's old cloak bundled him.

"As to what we're going to do with you," Berty began. "You will eventually get to Grunnan. For now, however, you stick with us. Going back into the mines will only bring you trouble."

"You're right about that," Grover said. "I retrieved my tools and family heirlooms, but they took my clothes. Well, most of them anyway."

"They're probably wearing them and saved the rest for trading," said Declan.

"I'll take first watch," said Edwin. They laid around the fire while Edwin chose a tree in which to perch.

Shaking woke Berty. "We have company," whispered Declan. Grabbing his sword, Berty saw an arrow sticking in the ground near the head of Declan's bedroll—Edwin's warning.

He and Declan crouched by bushy evergreens. A cluster of Dwarves scoured the dirt near the mineshaft. "Think they'll find us?" Berty whispered.

"Edwin has tracks leading everywhere. They're not using magic," said Declan.

"Maybe we should," Berty replied. "We don't know how many are waiting in the mine shaft. I'll wake Silvia." He tiptoed back to the campfire to find Silvia sitting up.

"What is it?" she asked.

"Dwarves searching for us," he said.

"Then let's make sure they don't find us," Silvia said. "I see Declan. Where's Edwin?"

Berty looked in the trees. He knew Edwin would be invisible, but his magic would leave a trace. His eyes roamed. Berty was not sure for what he was searching. Approaching, Declan pointed. "There. Edwin's there," he said. Berty followed Declan's finger. He thought he saw a faint green shimmer.

"Elves are hard to spot," Declan said. "You have to know what you're looking at. They tend to blend with the magic moving through the branches."

Berty nodded as he helped Silvia to her feet. Her eyes unfocused while her hand clutched her wand. Wooden figures moved through the forest, encircling the Dwarves. The wind blew around the stick figures as they stepped closer. The Dwarves' only exit was back into the mine.

A high pitched shrill of fear cut through the wind.

"Shut him up," one of the Dwarves said.

"This place is haunted," another yelled.

"No, it isn't."

The figures rustled underbrush. A few allowed the moonlight to form a dark silhouette around them.

"Run. Back in the mine," ordered the levelheaded one. Fear shook his voice.

The wind rested, but the figures stayed. "They'll keep watch," Silvia said. "Though they won't be back. Let's get some sleep."

Landing on the ground, Edwin appeared. "They're like the crystal guards when Sean…."

Silvia nodded.

"What about?" Declan looked at Grover.

"He'll be fine," she said. She returned to her bedroll, still holding her wand.

Going back to sleep, Berty was confident that Silvia's conjured protectors would keep everything at bay.

When Berty woke, he noticed Grover rocking himself in front of the fire. Declan's old cloak wrapped around the Dwarf like a straitjacket. Every so often, Grover mumbled.

"Ran into the uh," Declan just smiled. "Almost makes me miss traveling with Sean. Almost."

Laughing, Berty took a hot cup of root infusion that he magically turned into coffee.

After a warming breakfast, they packed the campsite. "Grover, we're leaving," Brana said.

He shook his head vehemently. "I'm not going anywhere," he said. "Not with," he lowered his voice, "*those things*," he raised it, "out there."

"So, you'd rather stay here, all alone, with *those things*?" said Brana.

His dark eyes widened. "On second thought, I'm coming with you," he replied.

Brana rolled her eyes.

"You didn't see them staring at you," he whispered to her.

Walking over to Silvia, Berty said, "Do you know the way from here?"

"Brana does," she answered.

He looked at Brana and Grover. "Are they gone?" he asked her.

"The Wood Guard?" Silvia said. "Not exactly. The wand keeps them going. They will be on the perimeter, keeping watch."

Brana led them through the woods, checking her map periodically. "I thought Guides were only needed in the tunnels," Grover said.

"I am not a Guide," said Brana.

"You know, I know nothing about you people," mentioned Grover.

"All you need to know about me is my name," she quipped. "And that I am well trained with my sword."

Grover said nothing. He adjusted the cloak wrapped around him so that it would not trip him. After a while, he asked, "Do you have any siblings?"

Her head turned to face him so quickly she almost stumbled.

"Just trying to get to know you," he said meekly.

She blushed. "We're here," she said to everyone.

The path brought them to a narrow, stone bridge that disappeared into fog.

Chapter Nine

Into the Fog

"Where is here?" asked Grover.

"Do we just cross?" asked Berty.

Edwin looked around. "Aren't there supposed to be Guardian Trolls?"

"Declan, what do you see?" Silvia asked.

"Just bridge and fog," he answered.

"Large, dark shape," said Berty. "Possibly a Guardian Troll."

"Guardian Troll?" mouthed Grover.

"It's probably waiting for us to step on the bridge," said Silvia. She took the first step into the stone.

A gargantuan, club wielding Troll exited the fog. "You no pass," it said.

"We seek an audience with Chief Miercia," said Silvia.

A normal sized Troll ran between Silvia and the Guardian Troll. "Do you have an appointment, ma'am?" it asked.

"No," Silvia answered. "We are from the Empire Tree. She will want to see us right away."

"It matters not where you are from or who you are. Without a Troll escort, you cannot pass without correctly answering my riddle," said the Troll.

Silvia nodded.

"What has lightning without a storm, a branch without a tree, a crystal without a staff, a key without a lock, wings without a body, an eagle without a nest, and a deer who knows the way?" the Troll asked.

"How can one thing have all that?" mumbled Grover.

Flashes of carved wood and painted stone ran through Berty's mind.

"The Sages' Seal," answered Silvia.

The Troll smiled. "You are who you say you are. Welcome to Bridgetown."

They followed the Troll into the fog. The stone bridge cut through the thick white cloud. Sunlight danced at the other edge of the bridge. Green grass edged a stone road. The fog parted, revealing flat islands peppered with stone buildings. A web of stone bridges connected each island. Fog floated under the bridges. Through the patches of fog, Berty saw sheer cliffs. The islands were columns of dirt and stone.

Crossing over many bridges, the Troll brought them to a central island with one island filling stone building. The stones fit together perfectly without any mortar. They walked through an arched stone doorway into a tall, stone room topped with multicolored stained glass. Under the soft glow, a Troll with loose blonde curls flowing from her head and chin sat on cushions.

"Visitors, Chief Miercia," said the Troll who met them on the bridge.

Miercia stood. "Emperor, Empress, an honor," she said. "Please, sit."

Each of them chose a jewel colored overstuffed pillow on which to sit. Grover tried to hide his surprise.

"You did not arrive with Hatcher," Miercia said. "Is there something wrong?"

"We have not come directly from the Empire Tree," Silvia answered. "This trip was unplanned."

"I understand," the Troll replied. "You are welcome to join us for our midday meal. Rooms are being prepared as we speak so you may freshen up from your travels."

"Thank you," said Berty.

"In the meantime," Miercia started.

"We escaped Irmingard before the attack," Silvia interjected.

"I heard about Irmingard," she said. "The anti-imperialists are being decimated by the force in white cloaks—Elves, Humans, and a Fairy. Bridgetown is putting together a force. The Trolls will join the fight. We will speak after our meal. Your rooms are ready." She gestured to a handful of Trolls standing off to the side.

"We will," said Berty. He stood, then offered his hand to Silvia.

Grover mimicked Berty with Brana. Taking his hand, Brana rose. "Chief Miercia, I would like to send a message to my father," she requested.

"One of Prince Goscislaw's birds will be sent to your room, Princess," the Troll stated.

"Thank you, Chief," Brana said with a bow of her head.

Grover's entire body deflated.

Servants led them up a stone staircase. The Dwarves were separated from them down a different hallway. Berty, Silvia, Declan, and

Edwin entered a multi-room suite. "Will you be needing anything else, my Lord and Lady?" a servant asked.

Noticing a small spread of food and drink on the table, Berty said, "No, thank you."

With a bow, the servants left.

"I'm guessing we're all staying here," said Declan.

Edwin checked the other rooms. "Three bedrooms. One has a long bed," he said.

"Shall we change for dinner?" said Silvia, entering one of the bedrooms. Berty followed her while Edwin and Declan chose their own bedrooms.

Donning the same clothes they wore for the formal dinner in Irmingard, they waited in the sitting room of their suite for someone to collect them. "Do you think the Goblins will join the fight?" asked Edwin.

"It's hard to say," said Silvia. "They usually don't get involved. They like to stay on the sidelines, watching."

"But they were framed for a Troll's death," Berty said.

"And the Trolls will fight," added Declan.

"Which adds to the uncertainty," Silvia said.

A servant knocked on the door. The Troll walked them through the stone edifice to the dining room. Ornately decorated metal doors opened to a room that would rival the Hall of Mirrors in Versailles. The garish gilded trimmings gave the opposite effect of the soothing gold walls of Grunnan. Between the statues, Trolls in fine clothes mingled while an elaborately set table waited for diners in the center of the room. Long, curly beards clung to pointed chins of both male and female Trolls, resting neatly on the scooped necks of their long gowns. Looking from Troll to Troll, Berty hoped he would not offend any

Trolls when he could not tell the difference between them.

Chief Miercia silenced the crowd. "We are honored to have the Emperor and Empress of all that surrounds us in Bridgetown along with their Advisor, the Duke of Fairyland, and the heir to the Princedom of Grunnan," she said. "We also welcome their travel companions, the First Lieutenant of the Empire Guard and the Honorable von Dorsiki of the Seventh State of the Kingdom of the Dwarves."

While Grover shifted in his clean clothes, Berty and Declan exchanged glances.

With the Chief's permission, Trolls introduced themselves. A barrage of names struck Berty, but even after repeating them, they did not stick. A bell rang. Everyone retreated to the stiff, colorful cushions masquerading as seats around the table. Berty could barely see Declan across from him through the centerpieces. The Trolls and Dwarves had no such issue. Many small courses graced the table in neverending succession. The Trolls savored every morsel, speaking and laughing between bites. Feeling full, Berty watched his hosts devour more and more. He intermittently took little bites of food and smiled. Slowly, the Trolls exited one or two at a time.

When only Miercia sat at the table with them, she said, "We rarely have visitors to share in our customs. Troll society has no nobility, only prominent figures of the time. We tend to enjoy our version of pomp and circumstance." She smiled. "Anyway, to the matters at hand. Ever since our wars with the Goblins, we train and prepare for war. If it is possible, the Head Troll would like to coordinate with the Empire."

"Plans have been on-going during our trip," said Berty. "However, Lieutenant Edwin," he looked through the centerpiece at Edwin.

"I will be happy to assist in any way I can, Chief Miercia," Edwin said. "When I return to the Empire Tree, I will assign a sergeant to fully coordinate with the Troll army."

"The Head Troll will be pleased. Will it be possible to meet with him this afternoon?"

"Of course," Edwin answered.

"One more thing, Miercia," said Silvia. "We have something of a more sensitive nature to discuss with you."

Miercia nodded. "Bridgetown can be confusing to outsiders. Someone will take you to the Head Troll, Lieutenant. Please, wait here. The rest of you are free to explore. I will have guides show you around town. Do not cross any bridges without one. Emperor, Empress, if you would follow me."

Berty felt too full to move. He rocked back and forth on the cushion, working up momentum. Stifling a groan, he struggled to his feet. Silvia stood without his help. He threw her a confused look, not knowing how she moved so nimbly after that feast. Silvia gave him a silent little laugh.

Opening a door off a stone hall, Miercia had Berty and Silvia enter a round room. "This is modeled after your Roundtable." Following them in, she motioned for them to sit on lower cushions than in the dining room.

The cushion looked impossibly out of reach. How could he make it back down to the floor? His legs barely worked. Imitating a weeble wobble, he sat. Already perched on an orange cushion, Silvia unrolled one of the scrolls. "We found this in our research about Whispers and Whisperers," she said to Miercia. "No one thus far has been able to translate it. Perhaps you can."

Taking it from Silvia, Miercia gasped. "Trollian," she said. "I can only recognize our ancient language from a few carvings on the old stones. No actual writings survive. I am sorry, Empress, I cannot read it."

stones. No actual writings survive. I am sorry, Empress, I cannot read it."

"Is there anyone who can?" asked Silvia. "Perhaps someone who uses ancient magic."

"Wait here," Miercia said. She popped off her cushion, then left the room.

"How can you move? Aren't you full?" Berty asked Silvia.

"Small bites," said Silvia.

"I took small bites," Berty mumbled.

Ignoring him, she said, "If we leave early enough, we'll make it home for Wassail."

"Meaning, change and go," he said.

"There is time before it gets dark. Besides, my watchmen would still be with us."

Miercia returned with a young Troll in tow. "I would like for you to meet the Reducer," she said to Silvia and Berty. "She is the only one who still speaks Trollian."

The Reducer bowed to them, then took a seat once Miercia sat. "I do speak our ancient tongue. However, I was taught verbally by my predecessor. Reducement is an oral tradition. I promised Chief Miercia that I would try." Looking at the scroll, tears formed in her eyes.

"What is it?" asked Miercia.

"I never thought that I would see it in its written form like this," the Reducer said. "It's so beautiful."

Miercia placed a hand on her arm.

"Unfortunately, my Lady and Lord, I cannot tell you what this means," she said. Her clear eyes looked at the two of them. "Thank you for granting me such a privilege."

After the Reducer left, Miercia said, "I am sorry we could not be of more help."

"Perhaps you can," said Silvia. "What do you know of Whispers?"

"Our magical fog and portals do not permit them to enter Bridge-town, though I don't know why we forbid them," explained Miercia. "Many of our ways or at least the reasons behind our ways were lost during and after the wars. We simply maintain what has already been established. Only small changes are ever made." She looked past them. "During one of the many wars with the Goblins, we burned all our writings and never wrote anything down again. Only the line of Chiefs and Empire Gatekeepers learn to read and write in the modern tongue. Trollian was abandoned for better Empire incorporation. We kept it only where necessary, like with the Reducers." Returning her focus to Silvia and Berty, she continued, "There is something in the magic that keeps Whispers at bay. Strangely, the same magic that works against Whispers also works against Knownots."

"But Knownots can cross portals," said Silvia.

"Yes and no. Knownots have a physical body, so they can go through whereas Whispers get absorbed by the portal. But a single Knownot cannot pass through a portal on its own. A Knownot needs a carrier or they need to combine themselves in such a way, they pretty much become one entity. Knownots have not tried that to go through portals in centuries."

"Thank you, Miercia," said Silvia.

"There is a portal that will bring you just outside the Sages' Grove," said Miercia. "I'll have someone escort you when you're ready. Wassail should not start without the Emperor and Empress."

Berty smiled at the Troll. "Of course it shouldn't. We will change into our traveling clothes and be on our way. Thank you for hospitality."

"The honor has been mine, my Lord," said Miercia.

Returning to their suite, they found Declan sitting, facing the door. "A young Troll approached me about a scroll," he said. "Apparently, literacy is a secret."

Berty raised his eyebrows. "What did the Reducer tell you?" Silvia asked.

"Ancient magic. Whispers should not exist. Pixie punishment. Whispers are the reason the Wood Listener crossed the portal, never to return," Declan said.

"What?" said Berty.

"That's all she said, then just walked away," said Declan.

"We need to return to the Empire Tree," Silvia said.

Edwin entered the suite while they packed. "Did you tell the Head Troll about using white?" Silvia asked him.

"Yes."

"Does anyone know if Brana and Grover are ready?" asked Berty.

"I believe they're meeting us in the Great Hall," said Edwin.

Wearing their white cloaks, they descended the stone steps. Grover stood next to Brana, looking unsure if he should be there. A new brown cloak draped his frame. They said their good-byes to Miercia. Turning to follow an assigned Troll escort, Declan placed his hand on Grover's shoulder.

"I have the cloak you lent me in my bag, Your Grace," Grover said.

"It's not that," said Declan. He watched Grover's cloak turn white. "To travel with us, your cloak must be white. It may return to its original color one day."

Grover nodded.

After leaving the central island, they crossed multiple bridges, hopping from one hamlet filled island to another. Finally, their Troll guide stopped in front of a stone bridge that disappeared into fog. "Safe journey," the Troll said with a bow.

Raising their hoods, they stepped across the bridge. When Berty walked out of the fog, he saw a faint path cutting through the woods. "Where's the bridge on this side?" Brana asked. Turning, Berty saw a pulsing blue disc—a portal. He knew that, except for Declan, the others saw nothing.

"Just a portal," said Declan. "You probably need to be a Troll to find it." He extracted his wand. Laying it on his open palm, he waited for it to point a direction. "This way." He led them off the path.

"Why did you tell them that?" Grover asked Brana, keeping pace with her.

"Tell them what?" she asked.

"The stuff about the Seventh State."

"Is your family name not von Dorsiki?"

"Yes, but—"

Brana stopped to look at Grover. "You don't know who you are." She continued walking with Grover by her side. "Your family name is one of the thirteen noble families of Warseen—the Seventh State of the Kingdom of the Dwarves. I saw your family crest when you were going through your bag before. I wasn't sure if the title falls to you or not, so I introduced you as the Honorable as opposed to Count von Dorsiki."

"Count?"

"That is what your family crest displayed," Brana said. "When we return to Grunnan, you can research your family. As the last Dwarf

State, we have as many histories as we could collect when the Kingdom fell."

Grover wiped under his eye with his cuff. Berty turned his attention away from the Dwarf. "How far are we?" he asked Declan.

"We'll reach it after dark," Declan answered.

Looking at Silvia, he could see her mind turn behind her brown eyes. Berty wanted to ask her about what she mulled, but he knew that it could not be discussed in the open. His right hand rested on the hilt of his sword. His eyes searched the trees. Edwin unsheathed his sword. Declan's arrows flew. Touching a tree, Edwin became a faint shimmer of green.

Berty and Silvia drew their swords. Sword in hand, Brana pushed Grover to the center of them. Silvia clutched her wand in her other hand.

Dark cloaked figures emerged from behind the trees. Berty swiped his free hand. Two soared into trees with thuds. His sword clanged against another's.

Anti-imperialists soon outnumbered them. Armed with a dagger, Grover teamed with Brana. Edwin fought while flashing visibility. Silvia joined the fight beside Berty. She used only her sword while Berty used both magic and his weapon.

Attackers swarmed. His sword felt heavy in his hand. Movement labored. Fatigue set in his muscles.

"Berty! Behind you!" yelled Declan.

Spinning, Berty slashed through the leather armor behind a dark cloak. Silvia's wooden guardsmen marched on their attackers. An anti-imperialist fell with an arrow in his chest. Through the trees, Berty saw white cloaks approach. He willed adrenaline to pump through his veins.

Chapter Ten

The Smoky Time

Whenthe last attacker fell, Berty counted eight white cloaks who came to their aid. An Empire Guard cloaked in white bowed to him. "My Lord," the guard said.

"Good work," Berty praised. "See if anyone is injured." He turned. "Silvia?"

"I'm fine," she answered. "We should find a place to camp."

After the bodies were checked, the wooden protectors led them away from the battlefield. The eight new additions followed them. "Declan," one called.

"Cecil?" said Declan. "Where's Vander?"

"Bringing Jordis to Boudon," Cecil answered. "We've been hunting escaping anti-imperialists."

"Then, it's over in Irmingard?" asked Declan.

"Yes."

"But?"

"The High Elf's mother," began Cecil. "She is gravely injured. Their healers are attending to her."

Arriving at a campsite, they began building a fire. Berty extracted his Watcher's locket. "What are you doing?" Silvia asked. Her wood figures stood as sentries around the campsite.

"Messaging Delyth. She needs to fly to Irmingard with Alina."

"Alina's not a Witch yet. She might not be able to...."

"But maybe... Until Avery and Alfred arrive," he said.

Silvia's moist eyes stared at the locket. She nodded.

Berty sent: "Rane hurt. Fly Alina to Irmingard. Alfred needs Guard escort."

Delyth immediately replied, "On our way."

Around the fire, they shared their food. The eight "hunters" consisted of a mix of Blóvǫr and Empire Guard. Cecil was the only one who was neither. Berty recognized Signe and Lunt from their trek to Boudon. The Empire Guards were stationed at the Outpost. Declan tended to injuries. Watching Declan, Cecil said, "I know why Obie wanted to learn the healing arts."

Declan gave his brother a small smile. "Obie is good at it. I'm going to introduce him to my contacts in the Witch's Trade. It'll be helpful."

"Berty," Silvia said quietly, "can you see the forest from here to there?"

He nodded. "Declan, the direction of home?"

Declan's wand pointed the way to the Empire Tree.

"Hold it a minute," he whispered. Berty closed his eyes. He saw Declan's wand. Like a bird, his view soared in the treetops. The almost bare branches obscured nothing. An empty forest stretched from their campsite to the Sages' Grove. Circling, he saw Alfred and his Empire Guard escorts racing on horseback to Irmingard.   He opened his eyes.   "All clear," he told Silvia.

"Let's keep going," Silvia said.

After extinguishing the fire, all of them followed Declan through the forest.   They navigated using moonlight.   Seeing the treed wall of the Sages' Grove gave Berty renewed energy to walk through its gates.

Down the path to the center of the village, builders worked to finish constructing the kettlebarre for Wassail.   As they approached the Tree, Berty nodded to Edwin.   Turning to the "hunters," Edwin said, "Let's get you a good night's sleep, a hot meal, and resupply your provisions."

"Cecil," said Declan, "your son is upstairs."

His brother walked with him while the rest followed Edwin to the barracks.   Brana pulled Grover next to her as they entered the Empire Tree.

Upstairs, Berty called Theodore.   The Dwarf bowed to his princess.   While the Head Tender readied rooms for their guests, Estelle descended the steps.   "My Lord," she said, "I have found the midwife.   Should I send for her?"

Everyone's eyes landed on Estelle.   "Teresa and my brother should be here for Wassail.   They'll probably want to meet the midwife then," Berty said.   "Thank you, Estelle."

"Your brother as well, my Lord?   Why does a father want to meet the midwife?" asked Estelle.

"Because that's the kind of marriage Jon and Teresa have," he answered.

Estelle blinked, then smiled.   Her navy gown sparkled as she spun to leave.   Declan shook his head.   "Let's go see Obie," he said to his brother.

When Theodore reappeared, Berty said to Brana and Grover, "Theodore will show you to your rooms. I will speak with Colvin in the morning to arrange an escort for your return to Grunnan."

"Thank you, my Lord," said Brana.

Alone with Silvia in the Reception Room, he took her hand. "The first day of Wassail is tomorrow. Are you ready?" she asked.

"I will be," he replied. They entered their private staircase behind the Sages' Seal.

After breakfast in their chambers, Berty and Silvia descended their private staircase. In the Reception Room, they greeted the Cider Master, officially beginning Wassail. They played their parts in front of the kettlebarrel—watching, clapping, and tasting. Neither Delyth nor Alfred were present. Brana and Edwin took their places. Inside the Empire Tree, Berty spoke with Colvin about the Dwarves' return to Grunnan.

Quick footsteps echoed down the main staircase. Delyth rushed into the Reception Room with tears dried on her cheeks. "The High Elf's mother has died," she announced.

"Did Avery?" Silvia asked without finishing her question.

"Yes," replied Delyth. "Avery, Alfred, and another man and woman were with her."

"Where's Alina?" asked Berty.

"With Edwin's parents. She has been tending to others." She blinked back budding tears. "An invitation has been extended to everyone."

"Theodore," said Silvia, "have the carriage ready. Edwin, you know who to bring for the escort."

"I will return and let them know you're coming," said Delyth.

"Wait, Delyth," said Silvia. She touched the Fairy's dark purple cloak with her wand. Delyth stood while her cloak turned white. "No one leaves the Sages' Grove without a white cloak."

"I will personally escort Princess Brana to Grunnan," said Colvin. "We will relay the news to Prince Goscislaw."

Berty gave the Dwarf a nod. "Elrick, Lida, will you be able to travel?"

"Yes," said Lida. "It's important we show our solidarity."

"Are we all going?" asked Hatcher.

"We must," said Berty.

"Then who...?" Hatcher asked tentatively.

Berty and Silvia stared at each other. As if she knew what he wanted to say, she nodded. "My brother, Jon, with Theodore as an Empire Tree consultant," he said.

Accepting his answer, people began to scramble to their chambers. On the platform in front of their bundle of colored leaves, Silvia said, "Make your phone call. I'll pack for the both of us."

He squeezed her arm, then ran to Hope's chambers. Lifting the receiver of the white and brass rotary phone, he dialed.

Ringing.

"Hello?"

"Jon, it's Berty."

"What's wrong?" Jon asked.

"I need to attend a funeral in Irmingard," said Berty. "And, it's Wassail."

"You need someone there," said Jon.

"Yes. Obie will be staying and Freesia. Theodore can explain everything that needs further clarification." Berty paused for a moment. "Bring Mom and Dad, too. Even Matt and Julie and Lillian and Robert, if they'd like."

"When do you need us?"

"As soon as you can. We're leaving soon."

"Okay, Berty. Can't guarantee we'll get there before you leave, but we'll be there."

"Thanks, Jon."

Berty popped into his chambers. "Did you get them?" Silvia asked. He nodded. "Then, we should go." She handed him his pack.

He secured his sword as they returned to the Reception Room. Using her wand, Silvia whitened everyone's cloaks. In the Receiving Room, Brana and Grover followed Colvin into the elevator. Stepping outside, Silvia touched her wand to the dark green carriage. The carriage, the horses, and the reins turned white.

The "hunters" already mounted their horses. Alvar and Cecil claimed horses of their own. After stuffing a bag inside the carriage, Declan, too, climbed into a saddle. "You're a Duke," Lida reminded Declan.

"I'm also a Watcher," Declan said quietly. "I want to see them before they see us."

Smiling to herself, Lida entered the carriage. Elrick followed his wife. As Estelle and Hatcher stepped inside, Silvia said to Alvar, "Ride hard. The carriage can make it."

Alvar gave her a nod. The door closed behind Berty. His bottom barely touched the seat before the carriage began to move. They rode well into the night. When they stopped, they made a fire around which they crowded. Fed and rested, they continued.

Daylight shone through the carriage windows when Berty awoke to the sound of the wheels riding over wood. Peeking behind the curtain, he saw the sparkling white walls of Irmingard. "We're here," he said.

The carriage rolled through the city streets until finally stopping at the domed building they entered over a week ago. Once inside, Declan joined his fellow Advisors.

An Elf brought them to the Garden. In the midst of the flowering plants and fluttering butterflies, Elves spoke in hushed tones. Berty spotted Alfred sitting next to a padded marble slab. On it laid his daughter dressed in pink. Alfred's stoic face stared at the surrounding vegetation. Berty could not begin to imagine his pain.

With reddened skin around his eyes and the tip of his nose, Avery approached them. "Thank you all for coming," he said, his voice raw. "The remaining Ørgranden are here, the Dominatrix, and the Commander."

"Remaining," Silvia breathed.

They strolled with purpose through the Garden. Many of the Ørgranden looked battered and battle fatigued. Low Elf Kael winced on a chair with his arm in a sling.

"Alfred," said Silvia. His eyes found them. "Rane was strong."

"Your children are supposed to outlive you," Alfred said. Tears stained his cheeks.

"The Emperor and I are honored to have known her," said Silvia.

He looked at her still body. "Thank you." The aged Elf forced himself to look at Estelle.

"The honor she brought to Irmingard is written in the stars," Estelle said.

New tears rolled off his chin. He closed his eyes for a moment. "Thank you, child."

Berty and Silvia stepped away to allow others to offer condolences. Searching the marble columned conservatory, Berty began to count.

"Five are dead, one is in prison," said the Dominatrix quietly. "And that's just the Ørgranden. Houses—families—turned on each other."

"How did it end?" asked Berty.

"The Blóvǫr and the others in the white cloaks won the battle on the outside. They fought their way across the moat. Because of the civil wars between houses, we were losing. The battle bubbled onto the doorstep of the High Elf's residence. The Ørgranden combatted each other. Even Low Elf Kael took up arms to defend Irmingard. He... Words are his best weapon. Oda easily disarmed and cornered him. I tried to help him, but I had my own... I'm not as young as I used to be. Rane charged out of nowhere. Her axe raised over her head. She struck Oda with a single blow. All fighting ceased to watch this woman, who they thought to be frail and helpless, save the Low Elf. The only blur of movement...," her eyes welled. "Malte pierced Rane from behind. She fell onto the marble steps, staining them with her blood. Weapons lowered. People rushed to her aid. They seized Malte.

"Every Elf knows Rane's story—her childhood accident, the difficult birth of her son, and the *death* of her husband. Her heroism will be retold for generations." She glanced at the slab, tears threatening to spill. "Every Elf, whether they could walk, be carried, or wheeled, came to pay respects." She swallowed. "She saved Irmingard." Wiping her cheeks, she walked away.

From the butterfly bush next to which he and Silvia stood, Berty watched the room. Vidor mostly kept to Avery's side. Elrick and Lida sat with some of the members of the Ørgranden. Avery greeted Goscislaw, Leosia, Brana, and Colvin.

Someone mentioned that it was time for non-family to depart. Before Berty followed the crowd, he heard Avery say, "Chief Miercia, good of you to come."

"May she be the star that guides your way," Miercia said. The Troll walked to where Rane lay. "Alfred, if you need anything."

The Elf answered by placing a hand on the Troll's shoulder.

Miercia walked with the group out of the Garden. Their footsteps echoed off the marble. They entered a hall-like room with long, bare wood tables and benches. The mix of peoples stood, waiting and speaking softly.

"The last time I was here," said Miercia, "was for Alfred's wife's funeral."

"My father attended the funeral," Goscislaw mentioned.

"If we survive the war, I will make it a point to visit on a happier occasion," she said.

Some, who were not in the Garden with them, entered the room. Delyth and Alina followed a well-poised female Elf with dark braids. The Elf strode to Wystan. Delyth steered Alina to where Delyth's parents stood. Lida called Declan over with them.

When the main doors opened, silence spread throughout the room. Avery and Alfred walked over the threshold with Vidor and Jordis close. The four of them processed between the tables to the front of the room. All eyes rested on Avery, who stood flanked by Alfred and Vidor. Jordis stayed on Vidor's other side.

"Elves, Fairies, Dwarves, Trolls, and Humans, we thank each of you for your support, for your kind words," Avery began. "Nothing would have made my mother happier than to see all of us together. Today marks a new beginning for Irmingard and all of Elfdom. Rane had a vision. A vision of what could be. I will live up to that vision and I challenge each of you to do the same. We have, over the centuries, lost sight of why the families united to build Irmingard. We did not do it to win wars. We united for the betterment of all. To pool our resources. To work with one another. To bring out the best in each other. My mother understood that. She was the best in us. Her life was a testament that hardship can be overcome. Let her death forge a new path—not just for Irmingard, but for all Elves everywhere.

"Join me, my grandfather, my father, and my sister in celebrating Rane—a mother, a daughter, a wife, and a friend."

Servants in white placed food, buffet style, on tables that lined the room. Pitchers and goblets dotted the central long tables. Choosing food and seats, everyone intermingled around the tables. The servants sat at the tables with Ørgranden who sat with Warriors and the Heads of the Empire. All who lived in, worked in, stayed in, or visited the High Elf's residence and adjoining buildings ate around those tables.

Berty found himself sitting with Elves he did not know. Farther down the table, he saw Vidor and Elrick. Silvia sat at the table behind him. Those who knew Rane told stories of her life. They spoke about her kindness and her laughter. Berty mostly listened, knowing that she would be missed by all whose lives she touched.

After only drops remained in the pitchers and only crumbs lined the tables, someone in white showed them to their rooms. "From what I understand," said Silvia as she readied for bed, "meals like that occurred all over Irmingard tonight. More died in the civil battles than fighting the anti-imperialists. The pyres will be lit tomorrow throughout the city, starting with Rane's."

Berty wrapped his arms around her waist.

"I understand what she did," she continued. "I did it, too."

"She was well loved," said Berty. "They're treating her as if she were High Elf."

"As they should." Silvia pulled him into bed with his arms still around her.

In the early morning, Berty and Silvia processed arm in arm behind Avery, Alfred, Vidor, and Jordis. Elrick, Lida, Goscislaw, and Miercia followed with the Empire Advisors and Irmingard's remaining Ørgranden. The procession formed a semicircle on the marble steps of the High Elf's residence.

Rane's body rested on a pyre halfway down the steps. Elves crowded the streets. Jordis stepped down to the pyre. Her hand raised to eye level. She placed a flower on her body. After a moment, she turned. Her hand covered her heart. Vidor laid his flower next. He touched her hand, then rejoined Avery. Alfred slowly descended to his daughter's side as if he were not sure his legs could get him there. His flower found its way onto her body. He stood there for a minute or two before using all his strength to return to his grandson's side. Every eye watched Avery step to where his mother lay. He set his flower with the others. His head bowed. He climbed the stairs to where his family stood. Facing the crowd, he spread his arms.

"*Ba da ee sa, frun ma gon,*" escaped Avery's mouth. The pyre ignited. "With this fire, we release you from this world, Rane, descendent of Albrecht. Let your fire release all who need it today." He motioned Elves holding unlit torches forward. The Elves lighted their torches with the pyre fire. Raising the torches high, they disappeared into the streets of Irmingard. Some of the crowd followed the torchbearers to other funeral pyres.

The flames reached for the open blue sky. When the fire engulfed his mother's body, Avery turned. He drew a breath, then re-entered the building. The procession followed.

Inside, breakfast waited. Avery invited all of them to join him if they had no other funerals to attend. Wystan and the Dominatrix left to be present at Warriors' funerals. Most of the Ørgranden had friends or family to whom they needed to support in the smoky time, as they called it. Many of the Empire Guards wanted to pay their respects to their fallen Elf brethren.

"I've made a decision," Avery said once the ones who stayed had food at the long table at which they ate the previous night. "Father, I understand why you needed to fake your death. I understand why Mother sent only me and Katell through that portal. I wish to install the Blóvǫr at the residence and you to be their Captain."

"Will you still call them by the old word?" asked Alfred.

"Yes," said Avery. "Although we no longer use Jaralf or Firalf for High and Low Elf or Vápkann for the Dominatrix, we have kept the old words for other things. Like our magic. I spoke in Efino today. Most Elves do not understand the old languages. It is safer to use the old word instead of calling them Bloodguard—what they truly are."

Alfred studied his grandson, then smiled.

"It's probably best to install your guard, High Elf, before we replace the... fallen," said Femke.

Ryker nodded. "The war is not over. Just this battle," he said. "The opposing houses feel guilty for Rane's death."

"And that will pass in time," agreed Avery.

"I will speak with Kael to declare an official mourning period," Femke said. "That should afford you enough time."

"Thank you, Femke," said Avery.

After eating, Vidor signaled to Lunt and Signe to follow him. They quickly conversed in a corner of the room. Vidor left them to approach Jordis at the table. "Jordis," he said, "you were the only Blóvǫr in residence. I know Rane's death may change things, but we need you. Will you join us?"

Jordis sighed. "I need some time to figure out what I want to do with my life. However, no one knows this place like I do. I will help them get familiar until the official mourning is over. After that... I don't know."

"That will be perfect," Vidor said.

She watched Vidor join his guard, then looked at Vander and Cecil. "Will you two be returning to Boudon?"

"Yes," said Cecil. "Woodsmen prepare for the next season during winter."

"I'm moving into Grandpa's cottage," said Vander. "It's time I devoted my life to the Woodshop."

"I'll make sure to replace your horses," Avery told the brothers. "It's the least I can do."

Berty caught Jordis smiling. When she rose, she placed a hand on Avery's shoulder. "Thank you for including me as your sister," she said.

"That's how I think of you. Even if we're not blood," he said.

"I'll always think of you as family," she told him. "And you." She kissed Alfred on the cheek.

Vidor watched her leave the room with Lunt and Signe as he sat next to Avery. "If Rane wanted you to marry her, I don't think it worked," he said to his son.

"We were raised more like brother and sister," Avery said. "We were not meant to marry."

"Well then, as your sister, Jordis will vet any woman you intend to marry," said Vidor. Smiling, he muttered, "That plan has revealed itself. What more do you have in store?" With a nod to his son, he walked out of the room.

"My Lord and Lady," said Alfred. "I will not be leaving with you this afternoon."

"Take all the time you need, Alfred," said Berty.

"The Empire Guard who escorted me can return with you," Alfred said.

"I'm sure a few Blóvǫr would be honored to ride with you," said Silvia.

"Yes." The Elf's eyes rested on Berty. "Your brother came to see me."

"I thought he would," Berty said.

Alfred nodded. "Could you tell him for me?"

"Of course."

"How are you doing, Alina?" Declan asked.

"Tired," she admitted.

"Princess Delyth will make sure you sleep during the carriage ride home," said Declan.

"I get to ride in the carriage?" Her eyes sparkled.

Everyone laughed. "Can I join you on your final rounds to see your patients?" he asked her. She nodded.

"Femke and I will take you," said Ryker.

"I need to visit the families of the fallen," Avery announced.

"Take Vidor and Jordis with you," suggested Alfred, "and whoever else Vidor says."

"Yes, Grandfather."

The breakfast guests dispersed. Berty and Silvia found themselves on a balcony with Lida and Elrick. The white city spilled out beneath them. Pyre smoke drifted into the sky. "I miss home," said Elrick. Lida squeezed his hand. Berty knew "home" meant Telor.

"You'll both be there soon," growled Goscislaw, walking onto the balcony with his wife.

Leosia placed both hands on the railing. "What do you think

about the noble from Warseen?" she asked.

"Is he?" asked Berty.

"His family line indicates such," answered Leosia.

"He seems of good character," said Berty. "A bit lost and feeling helpless."

"Can't we do anything about that Calledin?" asked Goscislaw.

Silvia sighed. "Not exactly. Each area within the Land of Sages, and beyond, is autonomous. The Empire cannot intervene in what is considered internal affairs, no matter how dastardly or tragic. Unless something happens whilst an agent of the Empire is present, we need to be asked in order to take action by either the governing body or citizens. And even then, our action is limited."

"But those people," protested Goscislaw.

"I know," said Silvia, "but just because the Empire cannot do anything does not mean others cannot."

"Our new Grunnan Battalion is eradicating scoundrels in the tunnels," said Goscislaw. "They should make sure that none of those scoundrels escape topside."

Silvia smiled at the Dwarf.

"What if, on their hunt, they come across evidence of terrible things?" Leosia asked.

"That evidence can be brought to the Empire's attention," Silvia explained. "A council of surrounding areas will be convened and an investigation will open." She looked from the Dwarves to the Fairies. "We are stewards of the Empire. And we take our stewardship very seriously."

"The pyre grows dim," said Estelle from the corner of the balcony. "Such a beautiful city. I'd like to return someday."

"We would be happy to have you back," Avery said from behind them. "The Duke and the Witch-to-be have returned. You are all welcomed to stay, but I know Wassail has begun elsewhere. Irmingard's Wassail will begin after the mourning." He looked at them all, but Berty knew that he did not really see them. Avery needed time to mourn in private.

Shaking Avery's hand, Berty said, "Good luck, Avery."

Avery and Jordis accompanied the funeral guests to the carriage. The Dwarves' carriage looked like an overgrown, covered mine cart fitted with wagon wheels. No horses pulled it. After saying good-bye, the three Dwarves entered their carriage with Battalion escorts.

An Elf brought two horses to Cecil and Vander. They, too, said good-bye. Berty thought Jordis' hands lingered in Vander's. As the brothers mounted, Alina and the Advisory Council piled into the carriage. Declan and Alvar still rode on horseback surrounding the carriage. Elrick and Lida climbed in before Berty and Silvia. Alfred's Empire Guard escort replaced the Blóvǫr. A Dwarf, a Fairy, and a child heavier, the carriage took a slower pace through the forest.

With a larger traveling party, they stopped for the night. The Empire Guards took a rotating watch, although Silvia's wooden protectors staked a perimeter. "How long do you think peace will hold?" Elrick asked while they kept warm around a fire.

"Who knows," said Silvia.

"They have the chance for peace," said Estelle. "It depends on who replaces the fallen and imprisoned. Starjen shows multiple paths." Her ice blue eyes reflected the fire. "I have told the High Elf and Alfred what I read over their skies."

It took them forever to reach the treed wall of the Sages' Grove. Berty felt cramped inside the confines of the carriage. He ached to be home. To sleep in his own bed, at least for one night.

Chapter Eleven

Magic Is As Magic Does

Berty's family strolled on the path when the carriage finally stopped in front of the Empire Tree. "Hope!" squealed Alina, opening the carriage door. "I was in Irmingard," she breathed.

"Can I go with Alina back to her house, Mommy and Daddy?" Hope asked.

"Go on," said Jon.

The girls ran down the path, giggling.

When Berty stepped out of the carriage, Jon hugged him. "You didn't tell me I had to taste stuff," he said into his ear.

Laughing Berty said, "Where's the fun in that?" He looked at Jon and Teresa. "Thanks for coming."

"Julie is super excited for Wassail," said Teresa. She hugged both him and Silvia. "She's been explaining the process to us."

"Theodore has been super helpful, too," said Jon as they entered through the tree's double doors. "Strange being here without you though," he mentioned quietly to Berty.

In the Reception Room, Declan asked, "Where's Obie?"

"Training with a sword," Julie said. "He's usually back for lunch. Is anything wrong?"

"No. I had an idea on the ride home from Irmingard," said Declan. "And it involves Obie."

"I sent him to train with Tacitus," Edwin said.

"Tacitus," said Berty. He gave Silvia a look that said he had a plan. "When they're finished for today, have Tacitus come to the Roundtable Room. I wish to speak with him."

"Of course, my Lord," said Edwin.

Berty had Silvia, Alvar, the Fairies, and Declan join him in the Roundtable Room. "We need to let Telor know our plans," he said. "The best way to do that is to send him someone he knows and will be loyal to him."

"Telor saved Tacitus' life in that gorge," said Silvia.

"Once Tacitus leaves, he cannot return here until after," Alvar said.

"I am hoping Tong likes Tacitus," Berty continued. "This will be a perfect opportunity to give something to Telor." He looked at the Fairies.

"Thank you, my Lord," said Lida.

"When should Tacitus leave?" asked Alvar.

"At night, so no one notices the Dragon," said Berty.

"He'll need his cloak whitened," said Silvia. "We should start whitening all the cloaks of the Empire Guard, all our tents— everything so we're not noticed."

Edwin knocked on the door, then brought both Tacitus and Obie into the room.

After Berty informed Tacitus of his plan, the former Roman said,

"I owe the Prince my life. It will be an honor to work off my debt to him."

"You'll leave after the feast," said Berty. "Pack everything you can't live without."

Silvia touched her wand to his dark green cloak. "Anyone's cloak you touch while wearing this will turn white," she said. "Before you leave, you will help Captain Alvar and Lieutenant Edwin turn the Empire Guards' cloaks white. You will also turn all of the Fairies' cloaks white."

"I will, my Lady," he said.

After Tacitus left, Obie asked, "What about my cloak? Does it need to be white, too?"

"Declan will take care of that," said Silvia.

"Speaking of taking care of things," Declan began. "I need your help, Obie."

"My help? With healing?"

"With magic," Declan admitted. "I'm not as well practiced with my wand as I should be. In this war, I think it will be prudent that I learn how to use magic."

"What made you come to this decision?" asked Delyth.

"I always believed that me—Watchers—using the magic around us was wrong. That it was a perversion, an abuse, of our skills," he explained. "I studied theory. I learned to distinguish different magic with both seeing it and tracking it. However, I can't do anything if it's used against me. And my wand is capable of absorbing and redistributing magic. They will be using magic against us. I should be able to defend us."

"Wouldn't the Watcher's Guild help you with that?" asked Alvar.

"Um," said Declan. He glanced at everyone in the room. "I'd rather they not know. We've encountered a lot of Watchers. Beyond my order, I don't know who in the Guild I can trust."

"Sounds like a good idea, Declan," said Berty. "Prepare what you want to give Tacitus. Don't forget we need to be seen anticipating the Wassail feast."

As they rose from their chairs, Edwin said to Declan, "Why don't you come down with Obie and me when we do Warlock stuff?"

"Great."

Berty and Silvia retreated to their chambers before heading to lunch. "I'm going to do some research in the Library Vault," Silvia told him.

"You need help?"

"I was hoping to enlist Estelle," she said. "Your help is always welcome." She smiled. "You may need to assist in acclimating your family first."

He laughed. They joined everyone for lunch in the Reception Room.

"I don't see Alfred," said Jon. "Is he okay?"

"He's staying in Irmingard for a little while," Berty answered.

"We're sorry we had to miss Thanksgiving," said Silvia.

"We understand, dear," said Kate. "Obie was able to join us."

Julie talked about all the new foods she tried. "And I'm learning how to use all these e-leck-trick-cal things," she said. "A lot of them are extremely loud."

Smiling, Berty tuned her out. "Is there anything we can do?" George asked.

"Enjoy Wassail," replied Berty.

"So far, so good," said George.

After lunch, the gathered crowd disappeared. "See you later," Silvia said, pecking his cheek. She and Estelle ascended while Declan, Edwin, and Obie descended with the crowd.

"Hope," called Delyth, "can you assist me?"

Nodding enthusiastically, Hope followed Delyth down the steps.

"Can we talk?" Jon asked Berty quietly.

Nodding, he led his brother onto the bridge system. "What's up?"

"I've been meeting with Alfred about the magic," Jon began.

"And?"

"He's says it's a version of Eagle Eye. Some sort of magical communication. I haven't tried it since. He said he'd look into for me. See what it's all about. He also suggested I ask Declan," said Jon.

"Very wise. Declan knows lots about magic."

"But," said Jon. He stopped on a bridge and gazed down at the village. "How do I control it?"

"Practice."

Jon sighed.

"Silvia will know the best place to do that," Berty said. They continued walking.

After a moment of silence, Jon said, "What about, um, learning how to use a sword?"

"That's a little easier. We have a training room in the Tree."

"Good."

They found themselves off the bridges, strolling through the village. Residents received visitors. Children laughed, weaving around passers-by. When they arrived at the kettlebarrel, Jon said, "This thing is huge."

Berty chuckled. "Wanna see the training room?"

Jon nodded. As they walked on the path to the Empire Tree's

main entrance, many greeted Berty with a head bow and a, "My Lord."

"How do you get used to that?" Jon whispered.

"Carefully," Berty answered while they entered the Tree. In the back of the Receiving Room, Declan and Delyth stumbled out of the door to the vaults. Delyth struggled to keep Declan upright. Berty and Jon ran to the back of the room.

Getting under Declan's arm, Berty asked, "What happened?"

"Ah ba daaa fada," said Declan. Berty held on tighter.

"Fairy Dust mishap," Delyth mentioned.

Jon got under his other side.

"Ta dooo da," muttered Declan.

"Don't try to speak," Delyth said. "Can you help get him to his chambers? He needs to lie down."

Declan's feet did not want to work. They slipped and slid on the floor and steps as if it were ice.

"Edwin's watching the children," said Delyth, leading them through the Tree. "He'll bring them up soon."

"Come on, Declan," said Berty as they practically dragged him across the bridge. "We're almost there. Just a little further."

"La la la la la la la laaaa la," Declan answered.

When they reached his door, Delyth placed his hand on the stick that unlocked his door. In Declan's sparse study, Berty glanced at the spiral staircase that led to the bedroom. "This will be interesting."

"You pull. I'll push," said Jon. Delyth ran up the stairs ahead of them. Berty tried to slump Declan over his back while he climbed the steps, round and round.

At the top, Declan slid onto Jon. "He doesn't look too good," said Delyth.

"Bathroom," said Berty. He and Jon dropped Declan in front of the toilet. Giving him some privacy, they heard retching.

"So, that's what happens to people on Fairy Dust," said Jon.

"Actually, no," said Delyth. "Granted, he didn't ingest much, but, how I used it, any amount would have knocked him out. The quantity used determines for how long."

The water ran in the sink. "You need help, Declan?" Berty asked.

Declan leaned against the doorframe, drying his face with a towel. "Someone rethink spiral," he said.

"I've never heard of this before," said Delyth. "You must have some level of immunity."

He pressed the towel over his eyes. "Room spin."

"Lay down," urged Delyth.

Berty and Jon helped Declan to the bed. They removed the Bow of the Moon and its quiver from his back. After hanging them where he indicated, they unlaced his armbands and placed his nightclothes beside him. Delyth turned around while Declan slowly dressed for bed.

Once Declan's head hit the pillow, Berty asked, "Do you need anything?"

"I'll have our Tenders bring us everything," said Delyth. "I'm going to monitor him."

Berty nodded. "I will tell Theodore to send both your Tenders here."

"Thank you, my Lord." Delyth stared at Declan who rested with his eyes closed.

"How did he come in contact with Fairy Dust?" Berty asked her.

"He and Obie were working with magic in the large cavern," Delyth explained. "Hope and I were working with Fairy Dust in an adjacent, secluded cavern. When we finished, we had to walk through their cavern to return to the surface. We stopped to watch. No matter where Obie threw his magic, Declan's wand absorbed it. Then, Declan shot some back, which Obie deflected or destroyed. Declan joked about wanting more of a challenge." Her fingers covered her lips. She shook her head. "I tossed a very small pinch of Fairy Dust. Declan stumbled. Hope froze the remaining Fairy Dust in midair. I cleaned the area of Dust. Edwin caught Declan before he fell, but if he had fallen, it would have been because he was unsteady. He helped Declan to the lift, then returned to finish Obie's lesson. I insisted."

Berty gave her a one-armed squeeze. "He'll be fine," he told her.

"It's just his reaction is so unusual," she said. "I wish I had access to Fairyland's library to research it."

"Perhaps our Library Vault has something."

"I'd like to look once it's clear of him." She sat on the chest at the foot of his bed.

Berty and Jon left Delyth watching Declan sleep. Outside Declan's chambers, Berty called for Theodore. The Dwarf disappeared with his instructions. Obie and Hope sprinted towards them.

"Where do you think you two are going?" Jon asked.

"To see Declan," Hope answered.

"Declan's sleeping," said Jon. "You can visit him later." The kids stopped.

"Will he be okay, Mister Chase?" asked Obie.

Berty saw Edwin standing near the bridge. "He just needs rest. Delyth is with him," he answered.

"Why don't you and Obie go find your mother and grandparents," Jon suggested.

"Hope, Obie," said Berty before they turned, "what happened with the Fairy Dust was an accident. Don't go around telling everyone about this."

"Like about riding Dragons, Uncle Berty?" asked Hope.

"Exactly like that."

"Okay." She took Obie's hand. "Come on, Obie. We'll come back after dinner."

Taking a deep breath, Obie let Hope take him back into the trunk.

Berty and Jon met Edwin on the Circle. They assured him Declan was fine. "I expected him to collapse where he stood," said Edwin. "Perhaps the Bow of the Moon's magic protected him somewhat. It can't be because he's a Watcher. You've dusted Watchers without fail."

"Interesting possibility," said Berty. "Make sure you tell Delyth."

"I will," said Edwin.

Berty and Jon parted with Edwin as they climbed the main staircase. "Why didn't you use magic to carry Declan through the Tree?" asked Jon. "You can use magic for that, can you not?"

Sighing, Berty answered, "It's not that simple. I can, yes, but when Fairy Dust is involved.... When Hope uses Fairy Dust she loses her gift."

"Oh," Jon said in a small voice.

"My magic could have made Declan worse. I didn't want to take that chance."

They crossed the next landing in silence. "Is magic always this confusing?" Jon asked.

"Only because we don't know everything," said Berty. "And when you think you know something, you don't."

When the stairs ended, Berty brought Jon to an arched door. Opening it, Berty said, "This is the train—Dad!"

"Robert and I were just poking around," said George. Robert waved from the other side of the room. "Why is there a dummy just lying on the floor?"

"I cut it down by accident," Berty explained. "It has to stay in the sparring circle to work. I think. I haven't tried it since we renewed the Scepter."

"You mean it's magical?" asked Jon.

"How about a demonstration?" Robert asked.

"Later," said Berty.

"Can Matt practice his... whatever he calls it in here?" asked Robert.

"Sure. The dummies are on cranks."

"What about the magical one?" Robert said. He walked around the lifeless beige lump.

"Not without a working knowledge of magic and a buddy," said Berty. "That dummy is unyielding. Anyway, I think it's almost time for dinner. Why don't we all go?" He ushered them from the room.

At dinner, he asked Silvia, "How does it go?"

"Slow," she answered. "I could use more eyes to go through it manually. If the writings were in English, I'd ask your family." She smiled. "Where's Delyth and Declan?"

"Fairy Dust accident. Tell you later," Berty said. He caught Robert watching him. Robert smiled, then said something to Lillian. "I'm going to join you tonight. I want to look up something."

Berty descended into the Vaults with Silvia and Estelle. He told them about Declan's accident. "It was a good idea," said Estelle. "Wands deal with magic. Fairy Dust is magic."

"Delyth thinks he might have some sort of immunity?" Silvia said. "It could be because of the Bow of the Moon or because he's the Duke of Fairyland."

"Does the Scepter's magic make you two immune?" asked Estelle.

"I don't think the Bow's magic works that way," said Berty.

They walked through the shelves. "Is that what you're looking for?" asked Silvia.

"No. Delyth will like to look that up herself," said Berty. "I'll keep my eyes peeled for Pixie related books." After browsing the shelves for a while, he brought a book about rare magical abilities to the table. He turned the pages to *Eagle Eye*. It referred to sight only. Nowhere did it mention any auditory abilities. Looking up from the page, he mumbled, "But I can hear when I see."

"What?" said Silvia, looking up from her book.

Estelle set a couple of books on the table. "I need to prepare for tonight's gaze," she said. "It's easier to see through the Cider Master's magic at a certain time of the evening."

"Thank you for your help," said Silvia.

"I'll be back tomorrow." Smiling, Estelle crossed to the ladder.

"The trip to Irmingard affected her," said Berty, "for the better, I think."

"We'll see. Now, what were you saying?" said Silvia.

"I'm trying to research Jon's magic. So, I started with Eagle Eye. Eagle Eye is just being able to see. A person with Eagle Eye can only see, not hear or interact in any way."

"Which means Jon doesn't have Eagle Eye."

"That's just it. Neither do I."

Silvia sat up straighter.

"I can see and hear what is going on. I was even able to press my parents' doorbell," said Berty. "And ever since what we did with the Scepter, I have been able to see magic. Is that part of it?"

A gasp escaped her lips. "Do you think that whoever wrote all this down did not know?" she asked. "Even Declan's abilities go beyond what is typically thought of Watchers."

"I don't know. I'd like to bring Jon down here tomorrow for some practice."

"That's a good idea." Silvia closed the book she was reading. "The more I read or don't read about Pixies, the more I think we need to travel to Pixisle. Mostly everything written about Pixies has a prophecy from the Priestess. Some of them came to pass. Some did not. What I have found about the Pixies themselves is already common knowledge." He could see the frustration in her face.

"Remember that trunk in the attic?" he asked.

"With the books we couldn't read?" she said.

"Yeah. What is the whole truth of everything was hidden in there? What if they thought people couldn't handle all the knowledge and stored it where someone other than you or me could access it."

She stared into the depths of the library. I'm going into the backroom tomorrow," she said. "I think you may be right. What we need to know will not be found on these shelves."

Leaving the books on the table, they closed the Library Vault, then ascended to their chambers.

In the morning, Berty and Silvia gathered in the Roundtable Room with their Advisors. Seeing Declan, Berty asked, "How are you this morning?"

"Better, thanks," Declan answered. "Delyth and I had a long talk about Fairy Dust last night. After the room stopped spinning."

"Where is Delyth?" asked Silvia.

Declan glanced around the room. "Oh, she said something about talking with her parents before breakfast."

"Then, she'll probably go to breakfast with them," she said. "Let's go down."

The long table on the dais filled quickly with Advisors and family. "Is it my imagination, or is there less food?" asked George.

"Not your imagination," Colvin said. "The closer we get to the Wassail feast, the more we starve."

"Every year, you complain, and, yet, every year, you don't starve," said Hatcher. "In fact, I think you add a little more," he poked his own belly.

"What exactly are you saying?" Colvin accused.

"You know," said Hatcher. "I'm talking about your pudge."

"What pudge?" asked Colvin. His fiery whiskers bristled.

Watching the two old friends, Berty laughed. He could not help it. The whole table began to laugh, even Colvin and Hatcher. Built up tension dissolved, at least for the moment.

After breakfast, they meandered down to the kettlebarrel. A crowd formed around the large cider making vessel. The Cider Master performed his sniffing, adding, and stirring routine. As the crowd dispersed, Lillian asked, "What is he adding?"

"A little of this. A little of that. No one really knows except the Cider Master," said Delyth.

"And, it changes every year," added Colvin. "Or so they say."

"It would have to because the apple harvest is different every year," Hatcher reasoned.

Inside the Tree, Berty's family climbed the steps. "I like those rooms at the top of the Tree," said Kate. "Is it okay we're up there?"

"Of course," said Silvia.

"Are we going to get that demonstration today, Berty?" Robert asked.

"Well, I promised Jon a lesson later today," said Berty. "It would have to be then."

"Sounds good." Robert stared through the Scepter Room's doorway for a moment before heading up the stairs to the next level.

"Jon, do you have a minute?" Berty asked.

"Sure." Jon returned to Berty's side. They crossed the bridge to Hope's chambers. "Are we going back?" asked Jon.

"No. We're going to my chambers," Berty told him.

When they entered, Silvia opened the hatch in the floor. "Go ahead," she told Estelle. "Close the hatch behind you, Berty. Declan and Delyth are meeting us down there." She climbed in after Estelle.

"Where are we going?" asked Jon.

"You'll see. Just climb down the ladder and head into the large room," Berty instructed. After Jon's head and hands were clear, Berty stepped into the hole in the floor. He grabbed the metal ring of the door. The light from the study disappeared as the floor reclaimed the hatch. He found his brother in the antechamber, gawking at the drawings on the rock walls. Silvia opened the door to the outer vaults. Elrick and Lida waited with Declan and Delyth.

"We want to research Declan's possible immunity to Fairy Dust," said Lida.

"I thought you might," said Silvia.

Berty opened the door to the Library. "So, why am I down here?" asked Jon.

"You'll see. Declan," he called. Watching the others enter the Library, he continued, "Jon's magic manifested while we were in Grunnan. Can you watch?"

Declan nodded.

"I don't understand," said Jon.

"Because Declan can see magic, he can help assess yours," Berty explained.

"First, what magic did you do?" asked Declan.

"I spoke to Berty and Silvia while they were in Grunnan and I was home."

"From the other side of the portal?" Declan asked.

"Yeah. It was the morning of Thanksgiving," Jon explained.

"I've never heard of magic being able to cross the portals without an elemental boost, like with the lockets, or direct access—touching or standing near one," said Declan.

"Really?" said Berty. "I do it all the time."

Declan stared at the brothers with his jaw dropped a little. "Both of you can use cross portal magic. Maybe that's what key magic is. The eye—it sees everything."

"So, Jon might have a version of it?" Berty asked.

"Perhaps." Declan looked from brother to brother. "Hope is in the large training cavern with Edwin and Obie. Can you speak with her?"

"I… I'm not sure how," Jon admitted.

"I find it easiest if I close my eyes and focus on the person," said Berty. "Like this." He closed his eyes. He saw Hope shooting arrows at a wooden target while Obie sparred a dummy. Edwin supervised. When he opened his eyes, he said to Jon, "Your turn."

Jon closed his eyes. "Now what?" he asked.

"Think about Hope and only Hope," Berty said.

"Okay." After a moment, Jon said, "Hope?" He paused as if he were listening. "I'm with Uncle Berty and Declan."

Berty smiled.

"Wait," said Jon, "you can see me?"

Berty and Declan looked at each other. Berty closed his eyes. "Can you see me, Daddy?" asked Hope. She faced Jon who stood with his eyes closed.

"Open your eyes, Jon," Berty said.

Jon opened his eyes. "There you are. How's practice going?" he asked.

Hope's head cocked to the side. "How are you doing this?"

"I'm experimenting," he said.

"Are you really here?" she asked.

"It's magic," he explained.

"Just because something is magic doesn't mean it isn't real," she said in a small voice.

His arm reached for her. "That's not what I meant," he said. "I am standing next to your uncle. I may be just a projection here." He opened his hand. "Can you touch me?"

She moved to grab her father's hand. Hers went through it. "No," she said.

"Okay. This concludes our experiment," he said. "You get back to practicing and I'll see you back in the Tree in a little bit."

"Okay, Daddy." She waved with a smile.

Jon disappeared. Berty opened his eyes.

"I was there. She saw me," he said to Berty and Declan. "Now what?"

"I heard every word you said," said Declan. "Maybe practice speaking as the projection while not actually talking."

"Is this part of the eye?" asked Berty.

"No. This is something different," said Declan.

"How come I could project myself now, but not before?" Jon asked.

"With the Scepter whole, magic is less difficult while under its magical field," explained Declan. "Magic will flourish within the Sages' Grove."

"So, it's better I practice here?" Jon asked.

Nodding, Declan said, "Also why I've agreed to manipulate Fairy Dust with my wand within the confines of my study. That way, it's not such a far trip."

"Is Delyth going to be throwing Fairy Dust at you in your study?" asked Berty.

"No," said Delyth. "If you three would join us at the table."

They followed Delyth into the Library. Jon walked timidly as if he were intruding. Estelle sat at one end of the table while they joined Elrick, Lida, and Silvia at the other.

"Your reaction to Fairy Dust is unheard of, Declan," said Elrick. "The title of Duke of Fairyland carries no magic. In the eyes of Fairy Dust, it does not make you a Fairy like Fairystone does."

"Since we have no access to Fairystone here," said Lida, "we would like you to borrow Hope's pendant, with her father's permission, of course."

"That should not be a problem," said Jon.

"No," said Declan. "I don't want to use Fairystone, even for a little while. I want to see if my wand can control Fairy Dust without help."

"Are you sure?" Delyth asked.

"Yes. I need to know my limits." Declan looked from Fairy to Fairy. "Just place a little pile of Fairy Dust on the desk and see what I do with it."

"You'll need to be monitored at all times while Fairy Dust is loose," Lida said.

"I understand."

"Between the three of us, you can get a lot of practice," said Delyth. "There is one other thing. We have confiscated old Fairy Dust without being able to deposit it in its proper place. I would like permission to work with it—to understand it better—with Hope. Yesterday, we found a secluded area to work. She has an intuitive understanding of the ancient commands. May we, while she is here for Wassail?" She looked to Jon for an answer.

Jon's mouth opened then closed.

"I thought old Fairy Dust was volatile and unpredictable," said Berty.

"It is... for the average user," explained Delyth. "Most Fairies have no understanding of the ancient ways. Hope is different. She can work ancient Fairy magic without wearing Fairystone."

"Can she get hurt?" Jon asked.

Delyth looked Jon in the eye for a beat before answering. "There will be no ingestion of the Fairy Dust. Manipulation will be kept at a safe distance. We will also be working with containment."

"I know Hope will want to do it," said Jon. "I don't have a problem with it, but you need to also ask Teresa."

"Thank you. I will."

"You will want to ask before the midwife arrives," Estelle chirped. "She should be here today."

"I think Teresa is in one of the Watching Rooms," said Berty. "I'll bring you up."

"In the meantime, we're going to do some more research on your possible immunity," said Elrick.

"We met someone with Fairy Dust immunity," said Declan. "She was half Elf and half Fairy. The Fairy was on her father's side."

"Hmmm," was all Lida said.

Standing, Silvia said, "Shall we?"

Elrick and Lida rose. They walked with Silvia towards the back of the Library.

"See you at lunch, Estelle," Berty said as he led Jon, Declan, and Delyth to the ladder.

In the study, Berty closed the hatch. "I wish I had one of those in my study," said Declan. "Much more convenient."

"Maybe you do," said Berty. "Just have to look for it."

Declan studied the seamless floor as if he were trying to figure out where a ladder to the vaults would hide.

Chapter Twelve

Accident Training

Acool breeze hugged their cloaks to their bodies as they crossed the narrow bridge to the trunk. Jon looked at the descending stairs to the left when they followed the hallway to the right. "What is this?" he asked.

"Mine and Silvia's private access," Berty answered. He decided not to mention the Sorcery Room they passed.

When the hallway ended at the door, Berty took Jon's arm. He glanced at Delyth and Declan. Declan held Delyth's hand while she linked her other arm in Jon's. They stepped through the door into the wide, Watching Room hallway.

"Why not just open the door?" asked Jon.

"Don't know what that does," said Berty. They followed the sound of laughter to a Watching Room. Teresa, Lillian, and Kate sat on chairs near a window. Robert inspected an empty table.

"How's the view?" Jon asked. Berty watched Jon approach his wife. For the first time, Berty noticed Teresa's protruding belly. Kate and Lillian left when Jon called Delyth over.

"Berty," Robert said. "What used to be on this table?"

Looking at the empty table, Berty said, "Oh, a miniature Sages' Grove."

"Where is it now?" he asked.

Declan took a step towards the table. "It broke," Berty said.

"That's a nice piece you got there, Robert," said Declan, saving Berty from having to elaborate.

Robert flashed a silver flask Berty had not seen. "Thanks. There's great workmanship here," he said.

"Won't argue with you there," said Declan with a smile. "Where did you get it? I've been looking for a quality flask myself."

Berty wanted to question Declan's sudden interest in flasks, but thought he was just striking up a friendly conversation with his sister's father-in-law. He turned his attention to his brother. "Thanks, Teresa," said Delyth as if they were old friends. Walking over to Declan, she said, "Ready?"

Declan shook Robert's hand before leaving with Delyth. "They make a cute couple," Robert said, stepping closer to Berty. "What are you boys doing?"

Smiling, Berty said, "A little surprise for Jon." He ushered his brother out of the room.

"A surprise?" Jon said in the hall.

"I figured you didn't want anyone else around for this." Berty opened the door to the training room. Once inside, he closed the door behind them.

"You're teaching me how to use a sword?" asked Jon.

"I'm showing you how to put on your training armor," said Berty. Opening a trunk, he pulled out breathable clothing and pads.

Jon picked up a body pad and held it to his chest. "You've got to be kidding."

"Unless you want bruised ribs for a few weeks or worse," Berty motioned for him to wear it.

After the brothers changed, Jon stood in the room, saying, "Now what?"

"Now, you get to hold my training sword," said Berty. He held it hilt out to his brother.

Jon's fingers wrapped around the hilt. "I must be mad," he muttered. The training sword slid out of its holder.

"Edwin told us—"

"Us?"

"Me and Delyth."

"Delyth can use a sword?"

Nodding, Berty said, "She's very adept."

Jon breathed deeply.

Berty continued, "Edwin said that your weapon is an extension of your arm. It moves with you—as one."

"Zen swordsmanship," said Jon. He turned the blade to look at it.

"Perhaps a demonstration. Step outside the training circle." Once Jon moved to the side, Berty said to the heaped dummy, "Begin."

Jon gasped as it rose from the floor. It attacked Berty. He blocked. Berty and the dummy sparred for a minute. "Done," said Berty. The dummy attacked. "We're finished," Berty said mid-block. It attacked again.

"Berty?" Jon said.

"Whatever you do, do not enter this circle," warned Berty. He dodged another attack. "End!" he yelled. The dummy advanced. He lost sight of Jon while focusing on the unrelenting dummy. Their swords clanged. He tried to push it back with magic. It moved only a few inches. He backed out of the circle. The dummy followed. Eyes widening, he attempted disarming.

Another sword entered the fray. Berty glanced at Alvar trying to distract the dummy from keeping Berty in its sights. The dummy ignored the Elf.

"Get behind it," Berty ordered. "We're going to have to cut this thing up."

Alvar moved as instructed. His blade sliced through the dummy's fighting arm. The stuffed arm stayed attached.

Knowing his brother was still in the room somewhere, Berty said, "We need Edwin. Jon, tell him to hurry. I don't know how much longer I can keep this up."

Sweat rolled down the side of his head. He heard Jon say, "Edwin. Edwin. Training room. Now. Berty needs you. He's on his way, Berty."

Berty pushed the dummy back a step. Alvar blocked the next attack. The two of them took turns battling the dummy.

The stuffed monster swiped its sword. Berty backed away, but not without a gash in his padding.

"Emperor!" Alvar exclaimed.

"Keep fighting," said Berty. He ignored the stinging in his chest. Clanging metal rang in his ears. Black edged his vision.

Bounding into the room, Edwin sliced the dummy in two. It collapsed lifeless to the floor. Berty stumbled backwards. His sword slipped from his hand. "He was struck," Alvar told Edwin. "We'll take him to his chambers. Get Declan."

Jon caught his brother. "Declan's in his study," Jon said. Alvar grabbed Berty on his other side. "Where's the passage?"

A chilling breeze encircled Berty. The wide hallway closed around him. He blinked. "A few more feet on the right," he managed.

They passed through the wall. "Grab his legs. I've got his torso," said Alvar.

The bridge swung or perhaps he swung over the bridge. Berty glanced at bare branches waiting for winter. A white cloaked figure stepped out of a basket. "Get him inside. On the table."

Round glasses framed brown eyes. Dark leather filled his view. "Take off the padding."

He heard Declan, but could not see him. "Declan?"

"I'm here," assured Declan's voice. "Get his things from the training room and lock it."

Air nipped at his chest. Heavy footsteps faded. Cold wiped below his pectorals. He shuttered.

"Just cleaning the wound," Declan told him. "It's not deep. The padding took the brunt of it."

"Why's the room coming down on me?"

"Magic is in the wound. I'm going to get it out," said Declan. "Can you see it?"

Berty closed his eyes. A hay colored substance coursed through his body. "Yes," he breathed.

"Can you push it out?" suggested Declan. "Through the wound."

The substance began to gather at the tip of Declan's wand. Berty inhaled deeply. With each exhale, he forced the foreign magic back the way it came.

No longer seeing the magic in his body, he opened his eyes. The walls returned to their places. Jon stood at his one side; Silvia stood on the other. She squeezed his hand.

"Ready, Edwin?" asked Declan.

"Ready," said Edwin.

Magic escaped Declan's wand. Edwin's sword cut through it.

Lifting his head, Berty spotted goop smeared through his chest hair. Declan approached the table. "All the magic is gone," he said. "Let me get a bandage on that and then you can sit up." Declan gently pressed layers of gauze across his chest.

Once he rose from the table, he looked around the room. Alvar, Edwin, Declan, Jon, and Silvia stood around the study. "Let's talk about what happened," she said. She motioned for everyone to sit on the couches and chairs. After slipping into the shirt Jon handed him, he carefully sat on a club chair.

"If anyone asks, it was just a little mishap—a sword slipped," Berty said. "Say nothing of the magic nor the dummy."

"Why?" Jon asked.

"That dummy was tampered with," replied Berty.

"What?" Edwin said.

"By whom?" asked Alvar.

"I think I know," said Declan. "I want permission to bring Delyth in on this. I will need her help."

"Do we have another Kayla on our hands?" Alvar inquired further.

"I don't want to accuse anyone until I have proof," Declan said.

"Fair enough," said Alvar.

"You can tell Delyth," said Berty. He sighed. "Well, Jon, I don't think I'm going to be helping you to learn how to use a sword after all."

"I can teach your brother, my Lord," said Edwin.

Berty nodded. "Is it time for lunch yet?"

"Until the culprit is found, will you be keeping to your chambers, my Lord?" asked Alvar. It was more of a suggestion than a question.

"No," said Silvia. "The Emperor is fine and must appear that way. He might not be doing anything vigorous, but lunch is important to attend."

"What if he or she strikes again?" Alvar asked.

"We are his first defense," Silvia reassured. "Declan, tell Delyth privately before lunch. Be sure you cannot be overheard."

"And what about you, my Lady?" asked Alvar.

"No one would be foolish enough to make an attempt on my life again," she stated. She looked at Berty, saying, "I don't know if this was an attempt on his life either." Her eyes flicked to the others. "This could have been a test or distraction. That's why it is important that this just be a training accident."

"Good thing my father-in-law wasn't with us," said Jon. He glanced at Silvia's raised eyebrows. "He's been very chatty lately. Not to mention, he kept pestering for a demonstration."

"I'll be here after lunch in case anyone finds anything," said Berty. "My mother is going to want to fuss over me."

"Fuss," Jon repeated with a chuckle.

"Declan and Alvar, return to where you were and head to lunch from there," Silvia commanded. "Jon and Edwin will go to lunch with us."

After Declan and Alvar left, Berty brought Jon upstairs to change back into their regular clothes. Bending to pull on his pants, Berty winced.

"Does it hurt?" Jon asked.

"Let's just say certain movement is awkward," he said.

"I feel responsible in a way," said Jon.

"It's not your fault. Besides, if you didn't get Edwin, I'd still be fighting it." Berty lifted his leg to tie his shoes. "How did Alvar know to be there?"

"I found him in the Rounctable Room," said Jon. "I was useless against it, so I ran to see if there was someone more qualified nearby."

"Thanks."

"I called for Silvia while you were," Jon did not finish his thought.

When they returned to the study, Silvia asked, "How are you feeling? Any problems?"

"I'm okay. It's just sore. Standing or sitting up straight helps," he said.

Taking Berty's arm, she led the men through the private corridors to the Roundtable Room. "My Lord," said Colvin, standing, "is everything all right?"

"Yes. My recent travels have made me more exhausted than I realized," said Berty. "Shall we see if there's any food left for us?"

Colvin smiled. "Empress," he said, "on last year's Light of Life Tree, we added red decorations to the usual gold." He walked a step behind Silvia as they descendec to the Reception Room. "This year, I would like to add light blue. Your thoughts, my Lady?"

"What's a—" whispered Jon.

"Think Christmas Tree," explained Berty.

"Very appropriate, Colvin," said Silvia.

Colvin beamed with pride as he sat at the table in the noisy Reception Rom. Declan, Delyth, and Alvar were filling their plates with food.

"Berty," said George, taking a seat across from him, "you're moving gingerly."

"Accident. What have you been up to?" Berty asked his father.

George scanned the room. "Avoiding Robert."

"Why?" asked Jon.

"I feel like I'm on the wrong side of the Spanish Inquisition," said George.

Declan stared at George. "The what?"

Berty shook his head at Declan to say, "You don't want to know."

"There was a right side to the Spanish Inquisition?" Jon asked.

"His incessant questions drove me nuts," said George.

"*You* had a problem with questions?" Berty said, leaning forward. He immediately leaned back and placed his arm over his wound. "Forgot I can't do that."

"There you are, George," said Kate. She approached the table with Lillian, Robert, and Teresa.

"How was your fresh air, George?" asked Robert.

"Watching the workers at the kettlebarrel is fascinating," said George, "and quiet."

Berty and Jon gave each other a look and smile.

"So, Berty," began Robert, "are we going to be privy to your surprise for Jon?"

"Oh. Lieutenant Edwin is going to teach Jon how to use a sword," said Berty.

"That is exciting," said Robert. "In that room George and I found?"

"I don't think so," Berty said. "The Lieutenant has his preferred training areas."

Robert frowned. "That's too bad. What are you doing after lunch, Berty?" he asked.

"Taking a nap," he answered.

"Is something wrong? Are you okay?" Kate asked in fast succession.

"I'm just tired," he replied. "You can come check on me in a little bit."

Saying nothing, Kate glanced from Berty to Jon to Declan to Silvia as if she were trying to discern the truth.

The midwife arrived as they finished eating. Silvia greeted her and introduced Glenda to Berty, Jon, and Teresa. In the after lunch commotion, only Hope and Obie noticed Berty slip behind the dark purple drape. He smiled at them before disappearing behind the Sages' Seal.

Crossing the bridge to his chambers, he saw Hope and Obie watch him. He sighed gently.

"Is everything okay, Uncle Berty?" Hope asked once he reached the platform.

"Come in, guys."

"We were with Edwin when Daddy called for him," Hope said further. Hope sat in one of his club chairs.

Lifting his shirt, Berty showed off his bandage.

"Ouch," said Obie.

"Yeah," agreed Berty. "Declan's taking care of it. It needs to heal. So, I need some rest."

"Can we do anything to help?" Hope asked.

Smiling, Berty answered, "Pile some pillows on the bed for me so I can sit up, but not bend. I will change."

She jumped off the chair. "Okay." The kids ran up the stairs ahead of him.

"Other side of the bed," Berty said when he reached his bedroom. "And make sure you leave a pillow for Aunt Silvia." Grabbing pajamas, he went into his bathroom. After taking off his shoes and changing out of his pants, he removed his shirt. Bright red blood stained his bandage. Opening the bathroom door, he called for Obie.

"Yes, Unc—my Lord," Obie said, running to the door.

Berty chuckled. "You might as well call me Uncle Berty, too. I think I moved too much. It's bleeding through the bandage." He showed Obie his chest. Downstairs, in a pocket of my cloak, is a locket like Declan has. Can you get it for me?"

Obie nodded, then scampered.

"Hope, how are the pillows?"

"All done, Uncle Berty," she said.

"Great." He covered his chest with his shirt, then walked out to examine their handiwork.

Obie returned with Berty's locket. "Here you go, Uncle Berty," he said with a smile.

"Thanks, Obie." He opened the locket. "Can I ask the two of you to put my clothes in the wardrobe for me? I shouldn't bend over anymore." He messaged Declan to come by at his first chance. Afraid the lockets were not entirely private, he did not disclose the bleeding.

He placed the locket on the nightstand, then carefully got into bed. Hope stood next to the bed. "What's the matter?" he asked her.

She looked him in the eyes and said, "I think there's something wrong with Grandpa."

"Grandpa Robert?" asked Berty.

Hope nodded. "No one believes me," she said in a small voice. "But, you do, Uncle Berty. Don't you?"

"He's been acting strange," he agreed. "Obie, what do you think?"

"He asks a lot of questions about magic," said Obie. "I've been avoiding him so I don't have to lie to him."

"Lie?"

Obie nodded. His fingers fidgeted with his shirt. "I just," he sighed. "It doesn't feel right."

"To discuss magic with him in the way he wants to talk about it," Berty finished.

"Yeah. Is that wrong?"

"Not at all, Obie," consoled Berty. "If you feel something is wrong, then you heed it." Berty smiled at him.

"Berty?" called Silvia from below.

"Up here," he said.

Silvia entered their bedroom with Declan, Kate, and George. "Hope, Delyth is waiting for you in the Roundtable Room," she said.

Hope hugged Berty around the neck. "Feel better, Uncle Berty," she said. "Can you fix Grandpa?" she asked quietly.

"We'll do our best," he said, giving her a smile. After Hope left, he removed the shirt. "Declan?"

"*Tired*, Berty?" said Kate.

"You're spending the rest of the day in here," said Declan. "Obie, you can help."

"Sorry, Mom, I didn't want to say anything at the table," he said.

Kate sat while watching Declan and Obie re-bandage her son's wound.

"Let me guess... swordplay?" Kate said. "And now, you're teaching your brother how to cut himself, too."

"Defend himself and his family," corrected Berty. "This is more complicated than mere swordplay."

"Explain," said Kate.

"I'm afraid we can't," said Silvia. "Restoring the Scepter should have restored the magic to everything. There is no conclusive explanation for what happened."

"Magic was restored," said George. "I think there has been an infiltration."

Declan lifted his head. "What makes you say that?" He pressed a new bandage across Berty's chest.

"The Scepter's magic has a certain frequency," George explained. "Probably has to do with its crystalline structure. Anyway, there's a different frequency around. I've been playing with my gadgets."

"And you've detected this magic?" Declan asked.

"Its residue," said George.

Looking at Declan, Berty asked, "What are you thinking?"

"I would like George to bring his... magic reader thing to a few places I found," said Declan. "Then, we need to examine the room and the dummy before you dispose of it. Edwin would have to be with us, of course, and when no one else is around."

"I'd be happy to help, Declan," said George.

"Can I help, too, Uncle Declan?" asked Obie.

"Of course you can," Declan replied. He turned to Berty. "Limit movement. If you need anything, you know how to reach me." He left with George and Obie.

Berty' hand stretched for Silvia's. "Go, do your research," he told her. He caressed her hand. "I'll be here. Just laying on the bed. Doing nothing."

She laughed. "You're going to watch them. Fine. I'll have Theodore bring us dinner tonight." She kissed his forehead.

"Mom," Berty said, "you don't have to stay with me."

"Silvia only agreed to leave, because she knows I will stay," said Kate.

Silvia smiled at the two of them before disappearing down the steps.

"Mom, I'm fine."

"Is Jon the one who—?"

"No. Jon alerted the right people to save me. He didn't even touch a real sword," he said.

"Well, I don't know why he has to. You, I understand, but Jon?" Kate sighed.

"It's his choice, Mom."

Kate nodded. "I know. Although you're both grown men now, he still looks up to his big brother." She smiled. "I'll be downstairs. Call if you need anything."

"Okay, Mom." Hearing his mother descend the steps, he closed his eyes.

Declan had turned George's and Obie's cloaks white. The three of them strolled around the village. George held a reader under his cloak while Declan held his wand under his. "There's a slight change here," George said.

"I can feel that," said Declan. He tuned slightly. "There's a trail. Let's follow it."

The trail meandered through the village to a cart selling metal trinkets. Declan tucked his wand into his cloak. He smiled as he greeted the cart vendor. "Nice metalwork," he said. "Pewter?"

"Yes," said the man. "Did you have something special in mind?"

Declan examined the items for sale. "I wanted to get something nice for Mom," he said to George. "What do you think, Dad?"

"She does like her boxes," George said.

"Hmmm," said Declan as he peered over the selection.

"If you don't find something that pops out at you, you can have something commissioned. I do custom work as well," the seller said.

"I think Grandma would like something to take with her when she travels," Obie offered.

"I craft flasks, bottles, and other travel containers," said the vendor.

"And what kinds of designs can I get on them?" asked Declan.

With a wide smile, the seller showed Declan samples of floral and other feminine designs.

Hope came running over to the cart. "Daddy," she said to Declan, "Mommy's looking for you."

Declan smiled at her for a moment. "Tell her I'll be right there."

"Okay," said Hope before running away.

"You've given me a lot to consider, sir," Declan told the man. "How long will you be here?"

"I leave the day after the Wassail feast," he answered.

"Great. Thank you for your time." Declan ushered Obie and George through the village. When they met up with Hope and Delyth, he asked, "How did you know?"

Hope rolled her eyes. "You know me better than that, Un—"

Berty chuckled at Hope wanting to call Declan, uncle.

"Let's go up," Declan suggested.

Berty opened his eyes. He looked around his room. A few chairs dotted the bedroom. He waited. He wanted to leave his bed. He wanted to do something. Antsiness made his muscles twitch. His wind chimes rang. His mother said, "Come in." He heard footsteps on the stairs.

"How are you feeling?" asked Declan. Delyth, George, Kate, Hope, and Obie followed him into the room.

"Like I want to move—go everywhere I can't right now," Berty answered. "What did you find out?" He motioned for everyone to sit.

Declan pulled a chair near the bed. "Your father and I sneaked into the training room. The dummy has no magical residue or signature whatsoever. The Blade of the Golden Flame got rid of all of it.

However, there are traces in other parts of the room that match what we found in the Sages' Grove." He closed his eyes for a moment. "And there is a worse part. There's this cart selling metal wares. I believe the seller crafted Robert's flask. It holds some sort of magic and I'm not sure if it's the same magic we've been detecting. I will need to re-examine that flask. However, I see no other way that magic got where it did in the Empire Tree. George said that he found Robert in the Training Room poking around."

"That was the day you and Jon found us in there," said George.

Kate covered her mouth with her hand. "Why would Robert?"

"I don't think he is—not intentionally," said Declan. "I think he's under an enchantment."

"Can you fix him?" Hope asked quietly.

"The enchantment must be broken," said Declan. "And there's only one way to do that without the original magic that I know of." He looked at Delyth.

The Fairy nodded.

"Then the item must be taken from him," Declan finished.

"We'll do it after dinner," said Silvia from the top of the stairs. "We will have a little family gathering in here since Berty and I will miss dinner. Edwin should be here just in case, but he'll hide upstairs. No one outside of this room can know." Everyone nodded. "Declan, I need your help looking for something in the vault."

"How do we make sure he'll bring the flask?" asked Kate.

"Tell him we want to discuss Wassail Steins," said Berty. "Declan and Delyth can bring theirs to show."

"A sound plan," said Silvia. "Shall we, Declan?" She and Declan descended the steps.

"I have a question," George began. "Well, two, actually. Who 'gave' Robert the flask? And how did this person know Robert's propensity for a dash of liquor in his after dinner coffee?"

Berty's insides dropped. "The answer to your first question is Leif. The second... If we don't think he could have gleaned that information while Robert's been here or from others talking about him, then we must surmise that we're being watched on the other side of the portal," he said.

The room fell quiet.

"Guards will arrest the vendor as well," Berty eventually said.

"Hope, Obie," called Delyth. She waved for them to join her as she walked to the steps. "See you after dinner, my Lord." The children followed her out of the room.

"We'll be downstairs if you need us," Kate told her son. She and George left him.

He closed his eyes. Silvia and Declan searched the vault where the magical items were stored. "What exactly am I looking for?" asked Declan. "I can't read over half of the name plates."

"In order for the magic to have bespelled Robert," Silvia explained, "he had to either touch the flask or drink from it."

"So whoever touches the flask could be at risk," said Declan.

"Correct. We need something to barricade us from that."

Declan stopped. He examined the room from where he stood. Every item held some sort of magic, although Berty could not distinguish one type of magic from the next. He knew Declan looked for a specific magic. Eventually, he took a few steps in one direction.

"Do you see something?" asked Silvia.

"Maybe." He walked towards a pedestal with a dark pair of gloves upon it. He backed up. "Oh, no. I think this takes magic."

Silvia stood next to him, reading the plaque on the pedestal. "Yes.

It imbues the wearer with magical powers of whatever it touches. Confiscated from… The name's been scratched off."

"Why don't we use leather scraps from the Empire Guard armor. They can withstand some magic," Declan suggested.

"Have Edwin or Alvar go with you. They'll obtain some much more quickly with far less questions," said Silvia.

Opening his eyes, Berty waited for dinner.

"Going stir crazy yet?" Silvia's voice asked.

Berty opened his eyes to see his wife sitting on the bed. "I think I took a nap," he admitted.

"I'm sure you needed it. Theodore is setting the table for dinner for us. Your parents are on their way to the Reception Room."

"Won't we be missed?" he asked.

"Already covered," she said. "You had some bruising from your accident and Declan prescribed some bed rest for you to heal."

He carefully slid out of bed without bending his body.

"You okay?"

"Yeah. I'm just trying not to… I want it to heal quickly." Slipping his feet into his slippers, he said, "I hope you don't mind if I eat in my jammies."

She laughed a little.

He sighed. "I don't want to do this to him."

"We don't have a choice."

"I know."

Downstairs, Theodore bowed when he saw them. "I hope you are feeling better, my Lord."

"I will soon. Thank you, Theodore."

Not wanting to bend too much, he ate slowly. Silvia answered the wind chimes.

"I don't mean to interrupt," said Edwin.

Berty said, "Eh. I'll probably still be eating when everyone else gets here."

"You have the leather?" Silvia asked.

"Yes."

"Good. Hopefully, that's all we'll have to use," said Silvia.

The wind chimes rang again. Edwin hurried up the steps.

"Come in," said Berty.

Jon and Teresa entered. "How are you feeling, Berty?" Jon asked.

"A little better, thanks. Where's Hope?"

"She and Obie are playing some game with Freesia," Teresa said.

Silvia and Teresa sat on the couch while Jon sat with Berty at the table. "Any leads?" asked Jon.

"We'll find out soon," said Berty. He pushed away his plate. "I can't eat another bite right now." The brothers joined their wives in the sitting area.

Soon, people filled their study. Declan's and Delyth's Wassail Steins passed from one pair of hands to another. Delyth's stein glittered in the lantern light. The multitude of stones mesmerized. By contrast, Declan's looked as though he carved it himself. The smooth wood was cherished. Berty noticed a small Watcher's Symbol carved on one side.

"What does this mean?" Matt asked, studying Declan's stein.

"My Guild's symbol," answered Declan.

"Can I use my flask?" Robert asked. He flashed it for everyone to see.

"Unfortunately, the opening won't accommodate the spigot," said Declan.

"So, are you carrying that everywhere you go?" Berty asked.

"Isn't that what you're supposed to do with a flask?" Robert answered.

Berty smiled. "I meant have you used it yet?"

Laughing, Robert said, "I had to try it."

"Of course you did," said Berty.

"Did you know about the magic or was that just a bonus?" Declan asked.

"Magic?" said Robert quietly. His hands automatically began to wring the flask.

"Robert, set the flask on the table and we can talk about the magic," Declan said in a calm, even tone.

Shaking his head, Robert said, "I can't. I can't let go of the flask." His grip tightened.

"Dad," pleaded Matt.

"Yes, you can, Robert," cooed Lillian. "Just place it on the coffee table. They only want to look at it."

"No." Robert's gaze swung wildly around the room. "No," he repeated. He clutched the flask close to his chest. His feet shuffled. "No!" He bolted off his chair, knocking it to the floor. Delyth flicked her wrist. Robert collapsed half on the chair. The flask clanged to the floor.

Matt reached for it. "No," Silvia warned. "Don't touch it." She turned her head to the staircase. "Edwin," she called.

Lillian buried her face in her hands. Stepping into the study, Edwin used the leather to pick up the fallen flask. He followed Silvia into the hole in the floor.

Raising her head, Lillian asked, "What does this mean?"

"Robert was under a spell from the magic imbued into the flask,"

Berty explained. "The Fairy Dust should break it. He'll be out for a while."

"When he comes to, he's going to be awfully sore," said George. "Let's lay him on the couch." Matt, Declan, and Jon carried him to the yellow couch. Teresa placed a pillow under his head.

When Silvia and Edwin emerged, she said, "It's in a safe place." To Edwin, she said, "Take Obie with you to identify him. He is to be interrogated right away."

"Yes, my Lady," said Edwin with a bow.

"Declan, Alvar will conduct the questioning, but I want you there. Stay out of sight. Only intervene in case of magic," ordered Silvia.

Declan gave Silvia a nod, then followed Edwin out the door.

"I'm so sorry," said Lillian. She looked at Berty and Silvia with fearful eyes.

"Lillian, this is Leif's doing," said Berty. "There was no way we could have prevented Robert from obtaining that flask."

She stared at her unconscious husband. Her fingers covered her lips. "His stupid collection!" she said with tears forming.

"Mom," said Teresa. She sat on the arm of her mother's chair and rubbed her back.

"We need to learn to be more careful," said Lillian. "Especially with you and your…" She weakly gestured in front of Teresa's belly.

Teresa closed her eyes.

"How long will he be out?" Lillian asked.

"An hour or two," answered Delyth. "I didn't use much, but each person reacts differently. When he does wake, make sure he drinks plenty of water to completely flush any lingering Dust."

Lillian stared nowhere. A small tick of her head acknowledged Delyth's words.

"Come, why don't we get some tea?" said Julie, standing. "Just us ladies." She looked at Silvia and Delyth. "Will you join us, Empress, Princess?"

Silvia gave a sweet smile. "That would be lovely. Thank you."

The women left the men sitting around Robert. "Am I the only one here who didn't know?" asked Matt.

"What do you mean?" Jon asked in return.

"You and your father were not shocked," said Matt.

"Yes," answered George. "You did not know, Matt."

"To be fair, I didn't know about your father and the flask," said Jon. "But I was with Berty when it happened."

Matt sighed. "I think I prefer my boring, non-magical life," he said.

"Well, don't wake up one day being able to use magic," Jon advised with a smirk.

Shaking his hands in front of him, Matt said, "No."

Berty glanced at Robert. "It's not like you get a choice," he said under his breath.

"Do you think it hurts?" Matt asked, watching his father.

"Magic?" asked Jon.

"Getting hit with Fairy Dust," Matt clarified.

"Hope uses Fairy Dust all the time," said Jon.

"At home?" Berty asked.

"She practices ancient Fairy magic," said Jon. "In the basement."

The wind chimes rang. "Come in," said Berty. Alvar and Declan entered. The Elf glanced at Robert. "Have a seat." His Advisors obeyed. "What did he say?"

"The man claims to know nothing of magic," reported Alvar. "He said he was commissioned to craft the flask for Robert."

"How did he know to give it to Robert?" asked Berty.

"He was given a sketch. Some guy in a dark cloak supposedly paid him a lot to make and deliver it," said Alvar.

"When did he say it was commissioned?" asked Berty.

"Last year. Right after Wassail."

Berty's insides dropped further. He was glad he did not eat much dinner. How could someone have known? His eyebrows furrowed. "Someone must have been following me," he muttered. "None of my family knew then. How would someone know that Robert, the only one who would want a flask, would be here for Wassail this year? The only reason Robert and Lillian even know about here is because—"

"Teresa and I were abducted in Africa," finished Jon.

"But the abduction was an inside job," said Matt.

"I'm beginning to have my doubts," said Berty. "Were you able to confiscate the sketch?"

"We have not yet found it, but we have his cart and guards are searching his room at White Star Inn," answered Alvar.

"Let me know what they find. Keep him in the dungeon until further notice," said Berty. "If he's not an associate, I'm sure he's being watched."

"Yes, my Lord."

"Do you think he could use magic?" Berty asked Declan.

"I don't know. He kept complaining about being identified by a child," said Declan. "I'm thinking about watching him, but I don't really want to be noticed."

"We can put you on guard duty," suggested Alvar. "Dress you like an Empire Guard. Gives you an excuse to watch him."

Nodding, Declan said, "I'll take the next shift."

"We better get you dressed," said Alvar.

"If there's nothing else," Berty said. He motioned to the door.

"I'm going to have Sergeant Tacitus move into the Tree for added security," said Alvar. Rising, he led Declan out of the room.

Berty desperately wanted to be alone with his thoughts, but his father, brother, and Matt stayed in silence.

"Do you think you were being watched before you became Emperor?" asked George finally.

"It's possible," said Berty. "But I only crossed the portal once after my first visit and before becoming Emperor. Plus, I didn't have contact with anyone."

"Before you ever crossed the portal the first time," George said.

Chapter Thirteen

Tactical Magic

Staring at his father, Berty said nothing.

"How can that be?" Jon asked.

"Berty worked for Martin's newspaper for years before Martin gave him the assignment to meet Silvia," George continued.

"Someone has been watching Martin, which led to me," said Berty.

"Precisely," said George.

"But who?" said Jon.

"Leif was Scholar a long time. He would have known Martin as a child," Berty said. "I need to tell Silvia."

"All in good time. She'll be back soon enough. You need to not reopen your wound," said George.

"What wound?" Robert asked in a groggy voice. He rested his hand on his forehead. "What happened? I feel like I drank too much."

"You had a magical misadventure," George told him. "You boys help him sit up. I'll get him a glass of water."

Berty watched Jon and Matt lift Robert into a sitting position. George placed a glass of water on the coffee table in front of him.

"Thanks. I am super thirsty," said Robert, lifting the glass to his lips. After a few gulps, he said, "Berty, when did you guys get back?" He looked around the room. "Where are we?"

"Berty's study. Dad, when did we get here?" asked Matt.

"Yesterday."

"I'm afraid it's been longer than that," said Berty. "It's almost time for the feast."

Robert's face scrunched. He gulped more water. "Did I hit my head? Do I have amnesia? Last thing I remember is looking at items on this cart."

The four of them explained what happened and filled in the missing time.

"Are you sure I didn't hit my head?" asked Robert. "It's throbbing."

"Fairy Dust side effect," said Berty.

When Robert finished the glass, George filled it again. After taking another drink, Robert sighed. "Will I not be able to buy anything in the village?" he asked.

"Sure you can. With Declan. He'll make sure you're not buying anything magical," said Berty.

"Fair enough," said Robert. He stared at Berty. "I'm sorry, Berty. I'd never hurt you."

"I know."

When the women returned, Lillian shrieked, "Robert, you're awake!" She threw her arms around him.

"Mind the head. It hurts," said Robert.

After Delyth examined Robert, she allowed him to go back to his room with Lillian. "I'll have a Tender make sure you always have water, and get me if anything changes."

"We will," said Lillian.

Everyone left Berty and Silvia alone. "There's something we discussed while you were gone," he said. He relayed all his suspicions.

"I'll be back," she said. "I need to call Martin."

"I'll be here, awaiting your return," he said, then blew her a kiss. With his eyes closed, he followed her to Hope's chambers.

Silvia picked up the receiver of the white and brass rotary phone and dialed. "Martin," she said. "I apologize for the hour. I didn't mean to wake you." She paused. "Something has come to light and I need you to not react." A quick pause. "You're being watched. I don't know by whom exactly or how. They may be listening to you as well. I'm not sure if it extends to all your family or just you. Somehow, it connects to Leif." She paused a little longer. "Maybe years." Another pause. "You and Martha should join us for Wassail." Pause. "Great. I'll meet you at the house tomorrow." She paused again. "Until then." She hung up.

Returning, she helped Berty off the couch and then into bed without every pillow in the room.

Before breakfast, Declan yawned into their chambers, still wearing borrowed Empire Guard leather, to check Berty's wound. Berty studied the hard leather armor as Declan examined his torso. "It doesn't suit you."

"I don't know how Edwin moves in this thing," Declan said. He stifled a yawn. "You're healing nicely." He began spreading a thick paste across Berty's chest. "I'm going to leave the jar of salve here. Apply it after bathing for the next few days." Replacing the stopper, he placed the small jar on the coffee table. He sat in a chair, holding his head up with his hands.

"How did guard duty go?" Silvia asked.

"He didn't use any magic nor did he have any magical items on him," Declan reported. "I can't wait to get this heavy stuff off, eat breakfast, and sleep."

"Thanks, Declan. We'll see you downstairs," said Silvia.

Declan gave a weak nod as Berty lowered his shirt. Once he left, Silvia asked, "Do you have the dual watch?"

Berty nodded. "It's in the small box on the shelf."

"Martin and Martha are coming over at seven tonight—their time," she said. "I think Declan should watch them arrive."

Agreeing with his wife, Berty carefully stepped down their private staircase with her to the Reception Room.

Declan joined them at the table half asleep. Berty magically transformed his root infusion to coffee. Squinting at his cup, he stared at it for a moment. He then looked across at Berty. Taking a sip, he grimaced.

"Help you stay awake through breakfast," Berty told him quietly.

"A bit strong," mumbled Declan. Chuckling, Berty lifted his cup of black coffee to him. Declan took another drink.

After breakfast, they all walked to the kettlebarrel where the Cider Master made more additions. Robert, having no memory of the prior days, marveled at the spectacle. Before they parted, Silvia spoke to Declan. He nodded, then bid her a good day.

A year ago, Berty spent the days before the Wassail feast reading about the Empire and watching Silvia using his eagle eye magic. While walking through the Empire Tree with Silvia, he could feel the creamy-gel-like medicine on his chest. The ointment reminded him that he needed to limit his movement. He wondered if that meant not descending the ladder to the vaults.

"The ladder should be okay if you take it slow," Silvia said in their study. "It's certainly better than taking the carts."

He waited for her to descend before he attempted. Each step down did not bother him. When he reached the bottom, he found Silvia already in the library. "Are you still researching Pixies?" he asked.

She looked up from the book she was reading. "Last book I can find," she told him. "I wanted to finish before I whiten everything the Empire Guard uses. Alvar has decided to send a scouting party out with the crowd. Their tents need to be white as well. And bleaching is taking too long. What did you want to read?"

"Eagle Eye magic."

"Thought you might." Her gaze lingered before returning to the page.

Berty browsed the shelves. *A Brief History of Magic* emblazed a four inch spine. He kept moving. Eventually, he chose a small stack of books to bring back to the table.

Halfway through his first book, Silvia closed hers. When he looked up, she said, "I'm finished here." She smiled. "Don't read through lunch. And don't carry too many at one time." She gave him a quick kiss before leaving the library.

When he had read about a third of the stack, he took a break. He walked around the table a few times before returning to his seat. So far, he read nothing new. He felt as if someone deliberately kept him ignorant. Picking up the next book, he flipped through the pages.

"What if," he said aloud, his eyes scanning the library, "what if you're nothing but a ruse? What if you're purposefully holding back knowledge? What is so dangerous that even the Sages' descendants can't know?"

The Library Vault revealed nothing. Not that Berty expected anything. He climbed the ladder to go to lunch.

Sitting with his family, he looked at the faces around the table. "Where's Declan?" he asked.

"Haven't seen him since breakfast," said George.

"Obie, can you go check on your uncle, please?" asked Berty.

As Obie jumped off his chair, Declan wandered over to the table. "Just got up," he said. He grabbed a seat next to George. "How's the chest?" he asked while tearing off a chunk of bread.

Berty said, "Fine." He watched Declan stuff a hunk of ripe, soft cheese in the bread.

Nodding, Declan chewed.

"You should probably check it anyway, just in case," Berty said. He did not know if Declan was awake enough to gather his meaning.

Still chewing, Declan nodded again.

After lunch, Alvar requested to see the Fairies, Berty, Silvia, and Edwin in the Roundtable Room. "I'll wait out here or by your chambers," Declan told Berty.

"Come in, Declan," said Alvar. "Didn't want to bother you if you were going to nap."

"I'll nap tonight," said Declan.

They sat around the Roundtable. Declan shifted in his chair, trying not to slump. "Tacitus moved into the Empire Tree this morning," began Alvar. "Any correspondence shall be sealed in this pouch." He set a white leather pouch with an embossed Sages' Seal on the table. "If you have anything ready at this time, please place it inside. Final collection will be after dinner. The Sergeant's bags will be packed tonight. There will be no opportunity to give him anything tomorrow."

219

"His bags will then be kept in a secret location," said Silvia. "Neither he nor anyone else will have access to them until he leaves."

"Since only I can arrange his transport, only I will see his departure," said Berty.

Reaching for the white pouch, Delyth slipped a document sealed with purple wax inside. "There will be nothing more from me," she said.

"Elrick and I will have something for you after dinner," said Lida. The Fairies took their leave.

"We found nothing out of the ordinary in the man's room at the inn," said Alvar. "We believe he burned the sketch in the fireplace. There were paper ashes with the logs. What shall we do with him?"

"Make sure he gets some Wassail," said Berty. "I don't want him seeing anyone leave. Perhaps it would be best to release him the day after Wassail and have him followed."

"See what he does and who he meets," said Alvar.

"Exactly."

Leaving the Roundtable Room, he and Declan walked to his chambers. In his study, he motioned for Declan to sit. "Martin and Martha are coming in," he opened his dual pocket watch, "about five hours from now. We want you in the house watching them arrive. Choose whichever window gives you the best view."

Declan nodded. "I'm just going to rest until then," he said. "Not sleep." He rubbed his neck. "Can't stay up like I used to."

"Rest here," said Berty. "I want to talk about magic in the meantime."

The men discussed magical half-truths without getting any closer to a full truth. "I'm coming to doubt just about everything I've ever learned as a Watcher," said Declan. "The Guild doesn't seem to know much more. Unless, because of my abysmal ability to learn the ancient tongue, I can't know more—I just can't read it." He laughed with bitterness. "And none of them will translate everything for me. The old Guild Master believed in learning. He tried to teach me the ancient tongue so I could read the older works on my own. I was a hopeless case. My reading is limited and I can't speak it at all. And to think Delyth has been teasing me lately about me learning ancient Fairy." He rolled his eyes. "We should get to dinner."

Berty's injury saved him from having to eat the petite meal like everyone else. He got to eat a decent portion of meat and vegetables.

"Next year, I'm having an accident," said Colvin. "That way, I get to eat. I hate starving."

"You're not starving," said Hatcher. "Not with that physique."

"Are you saying I'm pudgy again?" asked Colvin. His orangey beard bristled.

"I'm saying that you're a healthy Dwarf who won't starve," said Hatcher. The Troll took another bite of his food.

"What are you implying with *healthy*?" the Dwarf said, making air quotes.

Hatcher's hand paused in midair with food dangling from his fork. "I'm not doing this," he said. "Every year, the diminishing food makes you cranky. You're absolutely unbearable until the feast."

"Then don't talk to me."

"I still have to sit in the same room with you," Hatcher retorted.

"I can't believe I had to miss this last year," said Declan.

Edwin laughed into his plate.

"You're lucky your lovely wife is here," Colvin said to the Elf, "or I'd be forced to give you what for."

"Now, Colvin," Lark cooed.

Colvin's face matched the color of his beard.

Lark watched a little brown bird fly through a doorway. She held her hand for it to perch. "A Dwarf force has reached Calledin," she relayed. "They've brought much needed supplies. They'll send word again when they can." She gave the bird a piece of her crust. It flew outside.

"If you weren't going to eat that," Colvin began. Seeing the concern on her face, he said nothing more.

"Is everything okay, Lark?" Julie asked.

"I'm just worried about my family," said Lark. "Violet, my sister, just learned she's with child."

Teresa placed a hand on the Elf's arm. "We pregnant women are tougher than we look," she said with a smile. "You'll know someday."

After dinner, Silvia, Berty, and Declan crossed the portal in the bedroom. Declan looked through the front bedroom windows, then went up to the third floor. Berty checked his pocket watch. Almost seven. He and Silvia headed downstairs.

Watching from the dining room window, they saw headlights slow down. A dark car stopped in front of the house. After the headlights turned off, car doors opened and shut. Two figures walked up the sidewalk.

Silvia and Berty stepped into the foyer. The doorbell rang. Berty opened the door. Hugging warmed the cool air that entered with Martin and Martha.

When the door closed, Martin asked, "Now, what's this all about?"

Martha looked from husband to Silvia and back. "We're not here for Wassail?"

"Of course you are," said Silvia.

Declan walked down the steps. "What's in your coat?" he asked

Martin, tapping his chest.

Martin removed a rectangle from his breast pocket. "My phone," he answered. "How'd you know?"

"In the cabinet, Martin," said Silvia. "You know the rules." He walked towards the kitchen, then opened a panel of the wall. "Anything else?" she asked Declan.

He motioned for both to turn around. "No."

"Shall we?" said Silvia.

Martin chewed his lower lip while he ushered his wife up the stairs.

When Silvia brought them into the bedroom, Martha's head turned in every direction. "I don't..." Her gaze landed on Silvia standing between the wing chairs.

"Take my hand," Silvia said. The three of them disappeared into the fireplace.

"Anything?" Berty asked Declan.

Declan shook his head. "Unless it was in the carriage. Car," he corrected himself. "I have a hard time distinguishing between magic and electrics."

Taking Declan by the elbow, Berty brought him through the fireplace.

Silvia and her family sat on the couches in the study. Saying goodbye, Declan left the four of them to discuss.

"How long have you had your eye on Berty?" asked Silvia. "Before you sent him to me."

Martin stared at his sister. "I thought I was being watched?" Martha's head snapped to look at her husband.

"Yes. And we need to know for how long," said Silvia.

His gaze shifted from Silvia to Berty. Color drained from his face. "What happened?"

"We can't tell you the specifics," she said.

Martin nodded. "You caught my eye when you were in college," he said to Berty. "I ran a background check on your family. My word got you that internship which landed you that first job. Then, I hired you. While waiting for you to be ready, I kept you effectively stagnant at the paper. I'm so sorry, Berty."

"Did you look into my father's company? My brother? His family?" Berty asked.

"No," said Martin. "I had no need."

"Since college, there has been plenty of time for someone to investigate all of that," said Berty.

"Leif had both time and access," said Silvia.

"Leif," Martin repeated. "He knows I am a Matchmaker. He wanted me to record my matches in a journal, then give him that journal. Said it was to research my magic." He shook his head in disbelief.

"You keep a journal," said Martha.

"Yes. It was a good idea," Martin conceded. "I just wasn't going to give it to him."

"And you wrote Berty in that journal?" asked Silvia.

"On my... I have been so stupid." His hand covered his mouth. "I found that journal on the platform outside my chambers. It was wrapped with my name on it." He looked at Silvia. "The night before I left for college."

"Declan will look at the journal after Wassail," said Silvia. "In the meantime, you two should get settled in your chambers."

"I left the journal home," Martin said.

"No matter. Enjoy Wassail while you're here. You'll find white cloaks hanging in your chambers. Wear them everywhere," said Silvia.

Martin gave her a little nod. He and his wife left Berty and Silvia alone.

"We're dealing with decades of planning," said Berty. "It's no wonder they're fifteen steps ahead of us. Do you think they'll be expecting our white army?"

Silvia stared at the Sages' Seal before answering. "It doesn't matter. We must take back Fairyland. I don't want to think about what happens if we don't."

In the morning, Silvia applied the salve to Berty's chest. Movement became easier, but he still used caution. They joined the Advisory Council in the Roundtable Room with their Wassail steins to wait.

Every so many minutes, Colvin grabbed his stein, held it for a few moments, then set it back on the table. Hatcher teetered on his chair, ready to spring. Smiling and silently giggling to herself, Estelle admired her dark sapphire speckled silver stein.

Glad that Estelle was enjoying her first Wassail, Berty glanced at the stoic Elf beside her. Clearly, Alvar's thoughts carried him elsewhere. Berty knew where Silvia stashed Tacitus' bag while he slept. The scouts were ready to leave with the crowd the following day.

Three different scout parties would head out at different times, wearing regular clothes and cloaks. Out of sight of others, they would change into the white cloaks. Between Wassail and Yule, the scouts would gather the intelligence needed to choke Fairyland.

Declan and Delyth sat relaxed, happily waiting. Beside Berty, Silvia studied the stag on her stein. He wished he knew what she thought.

A bluebird flew onto the tabletop. Everyone stared as it opened its mouth to speak. "Emperor, Empress, it is time." The bird flew out of the room.

Clutching his copper Wassail stein, Colvin began the singing. Berty had not learned the words over the past year, so he hummed at Silvia's side. In the Reception Room, the other inhabitants of the Empire Tree and guests stood when they arrived. They joined in the singing, or humming in Berty's family's case, and followed the Advisory Council down the steps and out the door.

The entire village sang as people emerged from their homes. The singing stopped once the Cider Master raised his arms in front of the kettlebarrel in welcome. Bowing his head, the Cider Master cupped his open palms, asking for the first stein.

Together, Berty and Silvia approached the Cider Master. Two steins, one spigot. One of them had to be filled first. Berty gave his wife a smile. Silvia stepped forward. The Elf filled her stein, then Berty's. They toasted before Delyth and the rest of the Advisory Council followed. Then Elrick and Lida, Edwin, Berty's and Silvia's families, and the rest of Tree's inhabitants had their steins filled. Theodore headed the Tenders' line. While the villagers formed a line behind the Rowan family, Berty and Silvia returned to the Reception Room.

Their thrones sat at the center of a long table around which their Council, families, and friends joined. Tables crammed into the round room. Chairs cluttered around the tables. More and more people occupied the seats. Laughter and chatter ceased when Theodore stood on a stool. Once the Head Tender started the feast, steins clanked.

"It was rumored that the Elves in Calledin still celebrated Wassail, though no one called it that," said Estelle between bites of food. "I never imagined it would be like this." Smiling, she dipped her fork into a heap of mashed turnips.

"We never celebrated like this," said Lark. "My parents cooked the birds and either boar or venison. Others brought the bounties of their gardens. And the brewers would craft a special cider." She sipped from her stein. "It tasted nothing like this."

"Teresa!" scolded Lillian. Teresa froze with her stein over the table. "It is alcohol."

"The midwife said to drink what the Cider Master gave me," explained Teresa. "This little amount won't hurt me or the baby. She insisted. Little sips with my food."

"Stop worrying, Lily," said Robert. Leaning towards his wife, he said something Berty could not hear.

Merriment flowed around the Reception Room. Night settled early outside. The tiny bit of Wassail Hope drunk made her sleepy. Obie and even Alina fared better, but they were used to Wassail. After saying goodnight to Hope and Obie, Alina descended the steps with her family.

Soon after, Hope napped on Obie's shoulder. "It's okay, Freesia," he said.

Placing her stein on the table, Freesia smiled at him. "I'll take her to her chambers," she said to Jon and Teresa. The Fairy scooped Hope off of Obie's arm. His eyes followed Hope and Freesia up the steps.

"I don't know how she does it," Jon said. Laughing, Jon's lips returned to his stein. All the members of Berty's family used silver steins embossed with the Chase family crest—a bird of prey soaring over the trees. His stein depicted an intricate, stein-filling scene.

The raucous laughter died down as the people exited the Reception Room. Both food and Wassail dwindled. Silvia slipped her hand into Berty's. "This is my first open Wassail in a long time," she said to him. "I almost forgot how festive it was."

He squeezed. "I'm glad. Ready?"

Smiling, she said, "I'm beat. And full."

They ascended the staircase with feast holdouts. Everyone left to cross a bridge at the landing. They kept climbing. When the staircase ended, they entered a Watching Room. Chairs and a few tables lined the walls of a curved room. Peeking out a window, Berty gazed at the village. Upstairs lights replaced downstairs ones. The Sages' Grove was getting ready to sleep off the abundance of food and drink.

A knock on the door tore him from the window. Entering, Tacitus bowed to them.

"I'll meet you at the stairs," said Silvia before leaving the room.

"Are you ready?" Berty asked him.

"Yes, my Lord," said Tacitus. "It has been an honor serving you, Emperor."

"An honor to have you in our service," Berty replied. He led the former Roman to the steps rising out of the Tree. Cool, late autumn air meandered into the hallway. Silvia handed Tacitus his bags.

Taking them from her, he bowed his head. "Empress."

"Safe journey," she said, then said something in Latin.

He placed his fist over his heart. He and Berty climbed the final staircase. A cold precipitation smell hung in the air. The Cider Master's magic still kept the clouds from releasing it.

Berty and Tacitus stood in the middle of the Star Gazing Platform. "Tong," Berty called to the sky, "Dragon Match, I need your service and counsel."

The men's white cloaks flapped in the wind. Moisture heavy clouds crawled over their heads. The surrounding soft black revealed nothing. Bare branches clacked. Berty's weight shifted from foot to foot. He kept his gaze beyond the railing.

"Emperor," said a voice, "it takes longer to get here than I first anticipated. Would you like me to instill the fear of Dragon into your foes?" A golden mustache floated over a smiling boxy mouth.

"The time will come for that, Tong," said Berty, "but now is not it." Golden eyes, then the rest of his black, boxy head materialized. "Thank you for coming."

"You said something about counsel," said Tong.

"How are our friends?" Berty asked.

"Doing well. Growing stronger."

"Good. You have been traveling the lands," said Berty. "What have you seen?"

"Filth from God Mountain pours into the Dragonlands," said Tong. "The clans are reluctant to do anything about it. A First Council needs to be called. And you or the Empress must call it. Go to Angana and request immediate First Council. The clans will slow the flow. The clanless will follow you, Sorcerer. As Emperor, you have the power to release them."

"I will discuss this with the Empress," Berty said. "In the meantime, we are coordinating with our friends. Would you be able to bring Tacitus to them?"

Tong eyed Tacitus. "We will be stopping the desecration of the blue city," said the Dragon. "Half of it lies within the Dragonlands. Am I included in the strategy?"

Knowing Alvar had not thought of the Dragons, Berty said, "Phase two does. Right now, we must set phase one. For this to be a success, you and any others who join us need the element of surprise."

The Dragon gave Berty a broad smile. "I will gladly take Tacitus to our friends," he said. His long, black body curled around the platform. "Get on," he told Tacitus. "Until we meet again, Emperor, good luck." Once Tacitus sat on the Dragon's back, Tong sped into the clouds.

Standing alone on the platform, Berty watched the dark sky inch. He thought he saw a shimmer of gray holding the rain or snow at bay. Thinking that he would ask Declan about it tomorrow, he returned to his chambers.

He found Silvia sitting on the bed. "Everything go as planned?" she asked.

Undressing, he answered, "Yes and then some." He peeked at Silvia's raised eyebrow through the neck of his shirt. "Tong seems bloodthirsty." He relayed what Tong told him.

"Dragons won't admit that their own bloodlust fueled Dragon slayers," Silvia said. "Stymying their bloodlust was a condition of the binding to the Dragonlands." She sighed. "To win this war, we need the Dragons. Tong is the only one who can fight on our side of the Dragonlands. We may have to chance the bloodlust."

Getting into bed, Berty said, "So we head to the Dragonlands."

"Yes. With Delyth, Declan, and Edwin." She smoothed the covers. "We need a sixth person. I'm just not sure who."

"Obie," said Berty. Although a boy, he had no doubt that he should go.

"Obie," Silvia repeated. She nodded in understanding. "Edwin should prepare him for the journey. We should go there before Pixisle. Goodnight, Berty." She gave him a kiss.

"Night, my love." Berty magically extinguished the lanterns.

Breakfast was a bevy of good-byes. While Berty's family brought their bags to Hope's chambers, Silvia spoke with Edwin. With the help of Jon, Teresa, and Hope, everyone crossed the portal, including Martin, Martha, and Declan.

After many hugs, all but Martin and Martha left the house. While Silvia changed, Berty magically disguised the gold trim on his clothes. He lent Declan a coat. As he fiddled with the zipper, Declan stared at Silvia's modern clothes of jeans and a sweater as she descended the stairs. "We'll follow you," Berty said to Martin.

"My son and grandson will probably be home," Martin said.

Berty led Silvia and Declan to his car parked behind the house. Martin waited in his car on the street. Pulling out of his driveway, he followed Martin's blue sedan.

Martin lived relatively close to the house in which he grew up. Berty pulled up to the curb in front of his editor's house. The normal looking house sat up on a hill. An awkward cement staircase masqueraded as a walk from the street to the front door. Low growing juniper clung to the hill in lieu of a front lawn.

Opening the light blue front door, Martin stood aside, letting everyone else inside his home. Narrow steps hugged the one wall. A narrow hallway ran to the back of the house. Through an arched opening to the right, Martin's son and grandson played videogames on the couch. Eyeing company, his son paused the game.

"Declan," said Martin, "my office." He led the Watcher up the stairs.

Martha brought Berty and Silvia into the living room. "Marty," she said, "this is your cousin, Silvia, and her husband, Berty. Berty writes articles for your father." Martin and Martha agreed to introduce Silvia as Martin's niece rather than his sister to their family because her aging slowed.

"Nice to meet you," said Marty, standing. He shook both of their hands. "My son, Mike." The five of them sat on the couches. Marty stared at Silvia. "I met Aunt Silvia a long time ago. You look a lot like her, from what I remember as a kid."

Smiling, Silvia said, "Yes, I suppose I would."

"I didn't know Aunt Silvia had a daughter. Dad said she moved away after Grandma and Grandpa were killed in the car crash," said Marty.

"Yes," confirmed Silvia. "Most of my life was spent abroad."

Marty nodded as though that answered all his questions.

"Daddy, may I be excused?" asked Mike.

"Go ahead. Just don't bother Grandpa," said Marty. Mike ran through the adjoining dining room.

"Seems like a great kid," said Berty.

"He is." Marty beamed. "And he wants to be in the fencing club so badly. The school let a girl in the grade behind him in the archery club, so he thinks they should let him in the fencing club."

"That may be my fault," Berty said.

Marty raised his eyebrows.

"The girl is my niece. I introduced her to archery."

Marty laughed. "Mike has wanted to fence ever since he found my dad's gear in the basement. He practices down there when he doesn't think anyone's watching." Chuckling, he looked at Martha. "I think Dad has been teaching him." He brushed his reddish brown bangs out of his eyes. "What's your niece's name?"

"Hope. Hope Chase."

"Well, Hope and Mike might be seeing a lot of each other if I can wrangle him into fencing," Marty said. "May I ask about her extenuating circumstances?"

"You would have to ask her parents," said Berty, remembering the attempted abductions.

"Fair enough," said Marty.

"Is he good?" asked Silvia. "At his age."

"He has a natural talent," Marty answered.

Silvia nodded. "That may run in the family. I began fencing at an early age. So did your father, if I remember correctly."

"Telling stories about me already?" Martin asked from the arch.

"Just how your grandson takes after you with fencing," Silvia said.

"Ah." Martin's eyes scanned the room. "He's in the basement, isn't he?"

"I believe so," said Marty. His gaze kept drifting to Declan who stood next to his father.

"Declan, this is my son, Marty," introduce Martin.

Declan gave Marty a nod and kind smile.

"Well, if everything is finished, we should get going," said Silvia.

"So soon?" asked Marty.

"We need to pack," said Silvia. "We're leaving early tomorrow."

"A holiday vacation or business?" Marty asked.

"We're going to see a Dragon," Silvia answered with a smile.

"Are you going to slay it?" Mike asked from under the dining room table.

Silvia and Berty laughed. "Of course not," said Berty.

"Nobody slays Dragons anymore," Silvia added. "We're simply going to talk to the Dragon Council."

Mike crawled out from under the table, careful not to hit his head. "Then what's the use of learning how to use a sword, if not to slay Dragons?"

"Well," said Silvia, "balance, coordination, and self-defense."

"What about Trolls under a bridge or Goblins in a cave?" asked Mike. His brown eyes were wild with excitement.

"They're not doing any harm simply being there," said Silvia.

"Swords are useful against Vindalf," said Berty.

Mike's eyes lit. "What are those?"

"Elves who sell their souls for power," explained Berty.

Mike froze.

"Or," Berty added, "you can always use a sword on regular, run-of-the-mill bad guys who try to hurt people—your family, your friends." By the look on Mike's face, Berty figured he sufficiently petrified the boy.

The boy looked to his father. "But, but," he stammered. "Hope's in archery club. Everyone says she's the best. And she's only in second grade." He found his feet interesting. "I'm not good at anything," he said in a small voice.

Marty knelt at his son's side. "Just because you're not in the fencing club, does not mean you're not good at fencing," he said.

"Then why Hope and not me?" Tears could have escaped from the boy's eyes at any moment as he looked at his father as if he held all the answers of the universe.

Marty's lips moved, but he said nothing.

Berty's heart broke for father and son, but it was not his pace to tell them why. "Marty, if you have a pen and paper, I'll give you my brother's number."

Mike watched Marty grab his phone off the side table. Marty entered the number Berty gave him. "Thanks," said Marty. Mike's head bobbed from Marty to Berty then back again. "Hope has a special circumstance," he told his son."

"I want a special circumstance," Mike said.

"Trust me, Mike," said Berty, "you don't want hers."

Marty smiled at Berty in gratitude.

After saying good-bye, Martin accompanied Berty, Silvia, and Declan to the car. "Are you sure I shouldn't destroy it?" Martin asked.

"The one who imbued it with magic may know," said Declan. "At this point, I think it's best not to let on that you know. The best option might be bringing it to the Empire Tree."

"On my next visit. I don't think anyone else should touch it," said Martin.

"Probably wise."

Shaking Declan's hand, Martin said, "Thank you."

Berty drove away as Martin climbed the steps to his front door.

"Consensus?" asked Silvia.

"The magic in the journal concentrates in the binding," answered Declan. "That's how it reads every page. The way the magic flows though the journal, I'd say that someone has an identical journal—at least magic wise. My summation is that whatever Martin writes in his journal shows up in the other journal. Without taking the journal apart, I cannot tell if it works both ways or just one."

"And you think the other journal would show signs of this one being destroyed?" asked Berty.

"Highly probable." Declan stared out the window. "Until we stop Leif, the best place for the journal is magical item storage."

"Going to see the Dragons should help with that," said Silvia.

The blinker clicked its rhythm while Berty waited for the light. Home was only a few streets away. Brake pedals lifted in front of him. The wheel turned. He hoped Silvia was right.

Chapter Fourteen

A Council of Dragons

Silvia and Berty requested that Alvar meet them in their study. When the Elf arrived, they discussed the Dragons.

"Do you think they'll fight?" asked Alvar.

"Tong practically begged me to join the fight," Berty told him. "He would be a great asset."

"What if any of them join the other side? He can't be the only Dragon without a clan," said Alvar.

"That's why we need to meet with the clans. They keep the clanless in check," said Silvia. "Only an Empress or Emperor has the power to set a Dragon free of the Dragonlands. And only one has ever done so." She glanced at Berty.

Alvar nodded. "I can work Tong into our plans. He can recruit others to fight for us on the Dragonlands side," he said. "If the clans can stop the creatures coming from God Mountain, it could secure our victory."

"Good," said Silvia. "I'm not sure how long we will be, but we expect a report when we return."

"Of course, Empress."

"In the meantime, keep to the schedule regardless of where we are," said Berty.

"Yes, Emperor. Estelle has been watching the stars. We move when she indicates the best timing," Alvar replied.

"Excellent," said Berty.

Alvar bowed his head. "Safe journey." When he left, Berty and Silvia packed.

Setting his full pack on his chair, Berty heard his wind chimes. "Come in," he said.

"Obie is coming with us to the Dragonlands?" Declan stormed into Berty's study. "I protest!"

Berty stared at the flushed face of his sandy-haired friend. "He's the sixth man."

"He's a boy, Berty! A boy! Who has been kidnapped recently."

"He's not just a boy, Declan," Berty said calmly. "He's a Warlock who has been training as an Empire Guard under Edwin and as a healer under you." He watched Declan's ruddiness lessen. "You'll lose him to the Guard soon. How many guardsmen will have experience with Dragons?"

Slowly falling into a chair, Declan looked around the room. "You're right," he conceded. "He'll have a sword, his dagger, and his magic. And at least he'll behave better than Sean."

Berty cracked a wry smile. "Miss him?"

Declan gave him a look that said, "No."

Sitting near Declan, Berty said, "I wouldn't have him come if I didn't believe in him."

Declan nodded. "Guess I'm filling in for Cecil more than I thought."

Understanding that, Berty smiled to himself.

"Where's the Empress?" asked Declan when he noticed the pack on Silvia's desk.

"Library Vault," Berty answered. "Looking up Dragons. When she was an Elder, she felt like she had access to all this knowledge. Now, not so much."

"Magic is strange," mused Declan. His light eyes searched for a place to rest. "The rules seem to be changing or maybe there aren't any rules or maybe they can be bent or broken." He paused for a breath. "Or maybe *we* created the so-called rules. I don't know anymore."

He wished he could give his friend an answer, but magic befuddled him as well. Actually, not magic per se, the more he thought about it, but how magic behaved.

"Well, I better show Obie how to pack as a healer," said Declan. He stood. "Thanks." Lifting his white hood, he strode out the door.

While waiting for Silvia, Berty sat at his desk. He needed to organize his thoughts. Opening a notebook, he lifted his pen, writing another chapter of *The Adventures of Leigh and Marcus*.

Nudging woke Berty. The sun had yet to kiss the horizon. Silvia glided across the room in the lone lantern light. "Time to get up," she said. More lanterns lit the bedroom. Silently groaning, Berty trudged to his bathroom.

Berty and Silvia joined the rest of their group in the Reception Room. Breakfast and provisions waited for them. Under Obie's white cloak, he wore some sort of leather armor and a scabbarded short sword hung on his side. While getting food, Delyth patted Obie on the shoulder. A string secured her dark curls at the nape of her neck. Her ponytail momentarily mesmerized Declan.

After eating, they packed the provisions Theodore provided. Hatcher ran up the steps from the Receiving Room. He stopped at the top step. "The gates are being watched," he said.

"We'll leave another way," said Silvia. "Hatcher, inform Alvar. Do nothing out of the ordinary. Watch them. Before the army leaves, they will need to be taken care of."

"Yes, Empress," said Hatcher. He ran back down the stairs.

Looking at the white cloaks around him, Berty said, "Too bad white cloaks only make us invisible to Whispers."

Silvia extracted her Empire wand from her cloak. "Edwin," she said, holding it towards him, "take it."

The Elf stared at the small piece of wood. His hand slowly reached for it. He held the wand between his thumb and index finger.

"Hold it in your hand like a tree branch and do what you need to go invisible," instructed Silvia.

Edwin raised his eyebrows, but clutched the wand tightly. Delyth gasped. Where the Elf stood, Berty saw a faint shimmer.

"Good," said Silvia. "Now... Declan, touch his arm."

Declan's arm stretched toward the shimmer. "Whoa," he said as he became part of the shimmer.

"Take Delyth's hand," she said.

"Wait a minute," he answered. "My sight is adjusting. Okay." Delyth, too, became a shimmer.

"Obie, take my hand," said Silvia. She held her hand out for him. He grabbed it. Berty held Obie's other hand, then took Delyth's outstretched shimmer. He saw the Reception Room through a light green filter.

"Lead us to the carriage house, Edwin," ordered Silvia.

They shuffled across the bridges to the carriage house. Without letting go of Obie's hand, Silvia touched the wall. It pulsed. "Step through it," she said. "Let's see if we can be quieter than we were on the bridge. Head for the trees, Edwin."

Berty waited to move until he felt Delyth tug on his hand. The sensation of passing through a pencil eraser washed over him. They tiptoed through the clearing between the wall and the forest in slow motion.

The leaves had fallen and the underbrush prepared for the onset of winter. Unless they found evergreens, staying out of sight would prove difficult.

Edwin navigated the forest with ease. Invisible, they sneaked around thorny bushes and potential noisemakers. They stopped in a small ravine, out of view of any onlookers.

Silvia appeared first. She nodded to the others. When Edwin materialized, he gave Silvia back her wand. They rested for a drink. Silently, they kept moving.

The air smelled heavy. "It's going to snow soon," said Declan. Their slow start impeded their progress. They would not reach Portal Road by nightfall. Finding a secure site, they made camp.

Camp consisted of one white tent. The heavy material kept most of the cold outside. "No fire until we're in the Dragonlands," Silvia insisted. Delyth drew a Fairy Ring around the tent for protection. They huddled around the dim lantern for warmth. After eating a cold meal, they slept with Edwin and Declan taking turns on watch.

They awoke to a light snowfall. "This will help," said Edwin. The men packed the tent while Delyth removed the Fairy Ring.

Moving quickly, they tried to make up for lost time. After a few hours, they reached Portal Road. Edwin and Declan scouted before they crossed. "No one's out here," said Declan.

"That's because we're not near a portal," said Berty.

"Or maybe they rely on Whispers," Delyth said. In response, Declan scanned the treetops. He shook his head.

Reaching the Dragonlands, Silvia said, "Let's see how far we can go before we need to make camp."

Quarter sized snowflakes plummeted between the branches. Edwin rolled the shoulder he hurt fighting the Firewalker a few times. The wet cold probably made it ache. Declan walked over to the Elf. Berty could not discern what he said. He watched Edwin shake his head.

"How do we know we're going the right way?" Delyth asked.

"A Dragon will find us," assured Silvia.

The distance between trees widened as they trekked deeper into the Dragonlands. Berty scanned the bare treetops from time to time. He saw nothing through the falling snow. Tong would not be their guide. He had released him from the bond of the Dragonlands. Tong no longer served Cian. "Silvia," he whispered, "I just thought of something. Maybe I'm not the best person to be here. I may jeopardize everything."

"I'm positive they're angry with you," she whispered back. "Precisely why you need to be here now."

He took a deep breath. Silvia was right. If he stayed away, the Empire would look bad and perhaps lose the Dragons' trust. He still felt that perhaps she should do most of the talking.

Nighttime loomed. They found a somewhat sheltered area to erect their tent. Large snowflakes gave way to tiny ones. Outside the tent, Edwin and Obie stacked wood for a small fire.

"Do you think the Dragons have the same problem?" Delyth asked as she pulled her cloak more tightly around her.

"Hmmm," Silvia responded. When she looked at the wood, it caught fire. "That could be. I haven't read anything about it. I guess we'll have to see."

Berty cherished the warm bowl of food resting in his gloved hands. The stew warmed him on the inside.

"Winter wants to arrive early," said Edwin.

"Estelle said it would," said Delyth.

Obie sat near the fire, watching the others converse. It was his first excursion without Hope or Freesia. He bolted off his log, hand on the hilt of his sword.

"What is it?" asked Edwin.

"I hear something," whispered Obie.

Declan scanned the skies. "Dragon," he said. "Do not attack," he warned.

Following Declan's line of sight, Berty noticed a fluid shape descend from the sky. The round potbelly told him the Dragon was not Tong.

A mint green Dragon landed next to the fire. "Who goes there?" it asked.

Silvia stood. "The Empress of all that surrounds us," she said.

The Dragon blinked twice. Berty thought there was something familiar about the Dragon. "Ah, Empress, yes. I see you and your party." It paused to count. "Emperor, you have questions to answer. I do not remember the Fairy nor the boy."

"I see you have been restored, Emdellion," said Berty.

"We all have," said Emdellion. "Angana will wish to see you."

"We wish to see her as well," said Silvia.

"I will fly low so you can follow," Emdellion said.

With a wave of Silvia's hand, the campsite packed itself. Although exhausted, they almost ran to keep pace with the Dragon. When Emdellion finally stopped, Berty's lungs felt heavy in his chest. Each breath hurt in the cold. He thought he heard Delyth wheezing in the frigid night air.

Dragonfire lit woodpiles around the rocky area in which they stood. The fire provided some warmth. However, without trees, the wind whirled the snow and cold throughout the clearing.

A silver Dragon strolled into the clearing. She looked down her snout at the six of them. "Has the Emperor come to face justice for his crime?" she asked.

"And what was the Emperor's crime?" asked Silvia.

"The Emperor has broken the bond of the Dragonlands," accused Angana. Twelve Dragons landed around them. Berty recognized the blue Dragon as Nagend, the First Dragon of the Clan of Mitrah. He noticed Dragons with horns and spikes. Some had potbellies like Angana and Emdellion. Others were long like Tong. Some had muscular, sleek bodies. A tiny rainbow Dragon hovered in the blowing snow like a hummingbird.

"The Emperor should release all of us or face his death," said a Dragon.

"Death?" said Silvia.

"He released his Match," argued another.

The Dragons bickered over one another, ignoring the people standing between them. Berty stopped trying to listen to his supposed fate.

"Fools! All of you!" bellowed a voice. A black Dragon materialized above the clearing.

"How dare you interfere, Tong!" yelled a Dragon.

"You are not of a clan!"

"You give Dragons a bad name!"

"Enough!" Silvia screamed. A pulse of power shot from her. The wind died. The snow blew only outside the rocky clearing. "You have no jurisdiction to decide the Emperor's fate," she said in a clear voice.

"And you are going to stop us?" asked a Dragon with spines for skin.

Thirteen tornados erupted around each First Dragon. "You forget the covenant to which you all agreed," said Silvia. The tornados disappeared. Each Dragon had an icy coating. Panicked Dragons roved their eyes as far as they could move them. "No, you cannot move. No, you cannot speak. You can see. You can hear. And you still have your lives." Silvia stepped towards Angana. "Do not think for a moment that I cannot or will not take any or all of your lives. Now, you will listen. Tong, explain why you were released from your bonds."

As the only Dragon able to move, Tong flew in a few circles around the clearing before landing on snow covered rocks. He breathed fire on the rocks under his feet. "Thank you, Empress, for giving me the opportunity to speak," he said. "My Sorcerer Match, the Emperor of all that surrounds us, called me to God Mountain. He and his rescue party were under attack from creatures that… reside there. We know what kind live there for we put many there ourselves. However, the creatures that roam eternally just beyond our border are being collected. They are being led by what we do not name."

Fear flashed in many of the Dragons' eyes.

Silvia nodded at Angana. The silver snout moved. Angana said, "Are you sure, Tong?"

"I fought beside you, Angana," Tong answered. "I remember what it looked like. If I had not saved the Emperor... Well, I'm sure you can imagine." Tong glanced at the other Dragons.

Silvia nodded again. "I thought it was imprisoned," said Nagend. "That, too, was a condition of our binding."

"Nothing can leave God Mountain without a willing guide," said Silvia.

"Someone has been leading things out of God Mountain," Tong said. "Someone who wishes to bring down the Empire. The Empire of which we Dragons are a part."

"The leading force sits in the blue city," said the tiny Dragon. "We can only attack half of it. The other half must be fought by the Empire's biped forces."

"We?" Nagend laughed. "The Pygmy Clan has never exactly been warriors or fighters of any sort," he said. "Men simply crushed you because they could. Your clan still fears them to this day."

Snowflakes resumed their cascade. The Pygmy plummeted from its hover. Reaching out an arm, Silvia stopped the Dragon's descent. Inches from the ground, the tiny Dragon flapped its wings. It darted toward Silvia. Bowing its head, it said, "I am the First Dragon of the Clan of Pygmies. You may call me Paul."

"It is nice to meet you, Paul," said Silvia. "I am glad you understand our predicament."

Around them, Dragons began discussing the paths the creatures took through the Dragonlands. "What I don't understand," said one, "is why the multiple different routes?"

"So we don't notice," said Nagend. "And we haven't."

"They are trying to hit us from all directions," said Edwin. "They will split our fight. Or they will attack the Empire Tree while we focus on liberating Fairyland."

"Not if they do not reach the Land of Sages," said Angana. "Nagend is the best strategist among us. I'm sure he'd love to eradicate the filth spilling from God Mountain."

The blue Dragon grinned. "Nothing will leave or enter the Dragonlands," he said.

"I have news of an army coming from the Outlands to join the Fairies," Tong announced. "I will escort them through myself."

"Let them know that if they stray, they die," said Nagend.

Tong leapt into the air. "I'll go now."

"Tong, wait," said Berty. The Dragon hovered. "They may not believe you to be friendly. You may need to bring with you someone they trust."

"I know exactly who," Tong answered. "Thank you for your insight, Sorcerer." He disappeared into the dark gray sky.

"The Pygmies would like to help in the blue city, Empress," said Paul, "but we need permission to enter."

"On behalf of my mother and father, Queen Lida and King Elrick of the Fairies, I give the Pygmy Clan permission to enter the walled city of Fairyland for the express purpose of helping the Empire and the Fairies to eliminate the anti-imperialists and any of their willing helpers or sympathizers," Delyth said.

"Thank you, Princess," said Paul.

"Speak with Lieutenant Edwin for specifics and with me for the layout of the city."

All the Dragons disappeared into the night except Angana. She studied her guests. "Shall we get out of the storm?" she said to them.

At Silvia's nod, they followed the Dragon to a shallow, widemouthed cave. Angana breathed on a pile of wood in the back. The blaze immediately warmed the cave.

Angana sat on one side. "You'll be safe here. You're under the protection of Cian," she said. "I apologize for what had to happen. Tong is envied by most." Berty's eyebrows raised. "You might as well make yourselves comfortable, make food, whatever you need. The early winter storms in these parts can be brutal." Declan had Obie help him with a stew. "Tong is one of the old great warriors," Angana said. The rest of them rolled out their beds. "Like I am the only silver Dragon, Tong is the only Dragon with the ability to dematerialize and rematerialize anywhere he wants." Berty sat on his bedroll, listening to Angana. "When we decided to form clans, he chose to remain independent. In time, he became the defacto head of the clanless." She paused to gaze out into the blowing snow. "Of the Seven Ancient Dragons—the ones with deep magic—only he has retained his magic. My luster may have returned after Eirawen's true death, but it is not what it used to be. Many thought it was because of his release, thinking he has access to more magic—being in proximity to the Scepter. That simply having gone to the Empire Tree allowed his magic to stay." She shook her head. "First, he held on to a semblance of his magic even with Eirawen. Second, only two living Dragons have ever been to the Empire Tree—Tong and me. Granted, I visited once before the formation of the Dragonlands, before we bonded ourselves to this world in-between the portals."

The glimpse into the Dragons' history fascinated Berty.

The silver Dragon watched Obie hand bowls to the adults. "Empress," she said finally, "I did not think the bonding gave you power over us."

Silvia placed her bowl on a nearby stone. "It doesn't," she answered the Dragon.

"Then how...?" Angana's eyes widened. "You are of ancient magic. Of course, the Scepter would only choose those with deep magic." She glanced at Berty. "It makes sense to me now. Like attracts like. You have all traveled a long way. Please, sleep. No one will disturb you. Well, Paul might." The Dragon walked out of the cave, muttering, "I still can't believe he changed his name from Sindrin to Paul."

Picking up Silvia's bowl, Berty handed it to her. "I think you scare them," he said. She raised an eyebrow. "You're formidable. And scary."

She laughed, then sipped some stew. "I believe we've given Angana a new respect for people," she said while eating. Placing her spoon into her empty bowl, she whispered, "I'm not getting as worn out anymore. I always had to do more demanding magic in the presence of the Scepter to keep my strength." She stared into the whitening woods. "The wooden protectors are still out there, too." Smiling, she took hers and Berty's bowls to the fire to be cleaned.

Berty awoke to Delyth's scream. Paul hovered over Delyth, carrying six dead rabbits in his talons. Her hands grasped her heaving chest. "It's okay," she said. "Paul just startled me."

"I'm sorry," said Paul. "I did not meant to startle you, Princess. I brought food." He shook the rabbits. "Do bipeds eat rabbits?"

"Yes," she answered, breathing regularly.

"Here," said Declan with an outstretched hand, "I'll take them from you."

His short snout turned to Declan. His eyes narrowed slightly.

"He's the Duke of Fairyland," Delyth told the Dragon.

Paul gave Declan the rabbits. "Why didn't you say so?" he said in a cheerful voice.

"Paul, could you give me some room?" Delyth asked.

The Dragon hovered back a little. "Princess, are you sure he's a duke? He's not of the blue."

Berty glanced where the Dragon stared. Declan and Obie hunched over a stone, preparing the rabbits. All Berty could see was the back of Declan's shirt.

"He has done more for Fairyland than most Fairies."

Paul gave Delyth an expression that Berty could not read.

"What do you need, Paul?" asked Delyth as she laced her boots.

Turning away from the Fairy's conversation with the Dragon, Berty asked Silvia, "How long do you think we should stay?"

"The storm will calm eventually," she answered with a glance at the blowing white outside the cave. "Besides, Angana will not want to keep us here too long."

The aroma of roasting rabbit permeated the cave. Paul hovered over Declan, asking him what he was going to do with the innards.

"He's going to orchestrate reconnaissance," Delyth said to Berty and Silvia.

"Paul?" asked Berty.

"Yes. With the Knownots," answered Delyth. "Should be very helpful. I sent Paul to speak with Edwin, but I think he got sidetracked." She watched Paul flutter around Declan.

"He'll find his way to Edwin," said Silva.

While they ate a rabbit breakfast, Paul chatted with Edwin. The Dragon gave a strange, midair bow to Berty and Silvia before flying out of the cave.

"How does he fly in the snow?" asked Obie.

"He has Dragonfire to melt him a path," Silvia answered.

After everything was packed, they waited in the warm cave. Edwin mostly paced. Declan kept an eye on the snow.

"We should get going," said Edwin.

"I'm pretty sure there is magic protecting the opening," said Declan.

Edwin looked at Declan, but said nothing.

Angana returned when the snow died down a bit. "Patrols have been set along both borders," she said. "We have also organized search parties to comb the forest for anything that may be wandering. Paul says that we will be using Knownots to communicate with the Empire Guard. If you are ready, I will escort you to the border."

Trying not to show his surprise, Berty looked around the cave to make sure they had everything.

"What do you know of Whispers, Angana?" Silvia asked.

"I don't know of what you speak," the Dragon replied.

"Very well," said Silvia. "Then, I guess we're ready."

They followed Angana out of the cave. The Dragon melted a snowless path with her breath as she walked. After a while, she asked, "Empress, what are these Whispers?"

Silvia explained them in basic terms, giving the Dragon an idea without revealing too much. Berty found her to be an expert at conferring just enough information at any given time.

"Oh, I see," replied Angana. "The Pixies would visit the Dragonlands often in the early days. I don't remember when they stopped coming. They just did." The Dragon took a few steps, melting more snow along their path. "I always found the Pixie Priestess to be... strange." Angana did not say more nor did Silvia press her.

The snow slowed as night fell. Angana led them to a sheltered campsite. Leftover rabbit and its bones found its way into a stew. "Would you like some rabbit?" Berty asked Angana.

She tilted her snout. "I ate earlier. But, thank you, Emperor," she said.

"How do you know how to do all this Uncle Declan?" asked Obie.

"Many years of practice," said Declan.

"When you were on your own?"

Declan stared at his nephew for a moment. "Just because you're out in the wilderness, doesn't mean you shouldn't eat well," he said.

Obie's eager eyes wanted to ask more, but his mouth did not comply.

Declan handed his nephew two bowls. He had a way of avoiding talking about his past.

The snow stopped sometime during the night. They rose early and trekked through the Dragonlands by snow light. Angana said nothing as she lumbered ahead of them. Finally, the Dragon stopped. "This is the border," she said. "And as far as I can go. Good luck, Empress, Emperor."

"Thank you for the escort, Angana," said Silvia.

The silver Dragon watched them cross into the Land of Sages. Halfway to Portal Road, Berty heard leathery wings unfurl. He spun to see Angana flying back to her clan.

"Why did she escort us?" Edwin asked, also watching the Dragon.

"She was probably hoping the Empress would free her," said Delyth.

"No," said Silvia. "She was surveying from the ground. Taking us was the only way to do that without letting the others know."

"But why?" asked Edwin.

Shrugging, Silvia replied, "Dragon logic."

They camped closer to Portal Road than the Empire Tree. Declan cooked the last bits of the six rabbits Paul gave them. "Will we be entering the Sages' Grove the same way we left?" asked Delyth.

"Depends on the scouts," said Silvia. "We could just be travelers entering the Sages' Grove."

"We'd need to shed the—" Declan stopped talking to study the woods. "Fairy Ring?" he asked in a whisper.

Delyth nodded.

Both Declan and Edwin had their bows in hand. Only a Fairy could cross a Fairy Ring. They waited in silence.

Berty heard something or someone fall into the cold ground. Silvia fingered her wand while Declan watched the dark sky. Wood creaked. Screams. Thuds.

"Fairy!" yelled Declan. Delyth jumped into flight.

Edwin aimed an arrow outside the circle. Placing a hand on the Elf's arm, Berty said quietly, "If we can shoot out, then they may be able to shoot in." He exchanged his bow for his sword and shield.

Aiming upwards, Declan had both his bow and wand ready.

The wooden protectors restrained the other would be attackers outside the Fairy Ring.

A scream of pain sliced through the night. A female roared above. Declan fired three arrows in close succession. Branches snapped. A dark cloaked Fairy crashed to the ground. Three arrows and a sword pierced it.

"Dust," warned Declan. He raised his wand. Lassoing, his wand caught the bright blue particles that would have rained upon them.

Delyth landed hard, clutching her side. When she swayed, Silvia grabbed her. "She... hit me," the Fairy labored.

"Lay her down," ordered Declan. "Obie, my bag." While Obie scrambled, Declan untucked Delyth's shirt. "Looks like you've been hit with a club," he said. "Does it hurt when you breathe?"

She shook her head.

"Bruised ribs," he said. "Might be cracked."

"Dust water paste," she said.

Nodding, Declan took her velvet pouch. While he made a Fairy Dust paste, Silvia crouched beside the Fairy. "I'm going to get help. Stay within the Ring," she said.

Berty raised his eyebrows.

Showing her wand, she said, "I'm the only one who can pass."

"By yourself?" he asked.

"I'll have my protectors," she said. "I'll be faster alone. I'll return soon."

"Be safe," he said. He watched her cross the Fairy Ring unscathed. When she turned back, Berty blew her a kiss. She ran into the darkness. Her wooden protectors creaked by her side.

Gingerly, Declan smeared the paste over Delyth's ribs. She winced with every touch. After lowering her shirt over her injury, he tipped a little Fairy Dust into her water skin. He brought it to her lips.

Closing her eyes, she sipped. Her lips then mouthed words Berty believed to be ancient Fairy.

"Should you give her something for the pain?" Berty asked Declan.

"Not yet. Let the Fairy Dust do its work first," Declan answered.

Berty nodded. "You seemed to have mastered Fairy Dust," he said.

"I've gotten better with practice," Declan replied. "Mastering may take a lifetime." He knelt next to a writhing Delyth. "No one touch her. The Fairy Dust is working."

"Should I prepare some willow bark, Uncle Declan?" asked Obie.

"Yes."

Delyth sipped more Fairy Dusted water. "Thanks, Dec," she breathed.

Taking her hand, Declan said, "Try to sleep." With their fingers intertwined, she closed her eyes.

Berty walked the inner circumference of the Fairy Ring. Peering into the dark, snowy forest, he found no other disturbances. Nor did he find Silvia. Fallen anti-imperialists dotted the white blanket. A body rolled beside the Fairy Ring. He turned, sword drawn.

Declan squatted at the edge of the Ring. A sword pierced the ground at his side. Looking up, he said to Berty, "Thought Delyth would want her sword back. I confiscated everything important from the body." He held up a dark pouch. "Didn't want the body in here with us."

Nodding, Berty sheathed his sword. He closed his eyes. Silvia ran up the stairs of the Empire Tree. When he opened them, he said, "Silvia made it back."

Twisting, Declan glanced at Delyth sleeping by the fire. He stood. "That Fairy whacked her with a branch," he said. "She is incredible and strong. But how much can one family take?" He sighed. "She'll heal in a couple of weeks. Faster, if Alina can help her."

They sat with Edwin and Obie around the fire. The four of them constantly watched the woods for signs of movement.

Berty's head leaned forward. His eyelids dropped. The wooden protectors carried Silvia and Alina and someone else through the forest. Snapping his eyelids open, he said, "They're coming very quickly."

Berty and Edwin stood at the edge of the campsite. Silvia, Alina, and Freesia stopped on the other side of the Fairy Ring. "Alina needs to setup," said Silvia. "Freesia will escort Delyth out."

While Silvia helped Alina unroll bedrolls and set lanterns, Freesia stepped over the Ring. Declan woke Delyth. "Freesia's going to take you to Alina," he said. With Freesia's aid, she stood.

"Lean on me, Princess," said Freesia. Declan walked with them to the Ring's edge. The two Fairies crossed. Silvia helped Delyth onto a bedroll.

Pulling his cloak more tightly around him, Declan watched Alina work. The girl pulled a book from her bag. In the lantern light, she flipped pages. She tied a scarf around her nose and mouth, then fitted what looked like goggles over her eyes.

After a few minutes of examining, Freesia asked Declan, "Did you give her anything for the pain?"

"Nothing beyond Fairy Dust," he said. "A dressing and a little in her water."

Alina nodded. She began pounding in her mortar and pestle. When she finished, Alina removed the goggles and scarf. "The Princess needs rest, Empress," she reported. "She has three cracked ribs. The magic has already begun mending."

"How much time until we can move her?" asked Silvia.

"Ideally, a couple of hours."

Silvia glanced at Berty and Declan. "Freesia, can you draw a Fairy Ring?"

"No," said the Fairy. "I can remove it, but it will kick up a lot of Dust."

"I should be able to remove and redraw it without any Dust potentially hurting Edwin," said Declan.

"Don't do more than you can," said Silvia. "It's not important to redraw the Fairy Ring."

While Declan used his wand on the Fairy Dust, Berty, Edwin, and Obie gathered the campsite. Once the Fairy Ring broke, Silvia magically moved the campfire. They erected the tent. Alina moved her stuff inside while Berty and Silvia magically carried Delyth into the tent.

Leaving the females and Obie in the tent, Berty checked on the Fairy Ring progress. Declan stumbled away from the Dust. Catching his arm, Berty asked, "Are you okay?"

"That was a lot of Dust," Declan said. "Just need to sit for a moment." Berty brought him next to the fire.

"Nothing seems to be out there except for those wooden things," said Edwin, joining them. "Think the Fairy Ring will work?"

Declan shrugged. "Never drew one before," he said, "but I've watched Delyth do it. Don't think any of us should test it. I am not carrying you back to the Empire Tree."

Laughing, Edwin said, "I'll take first watch."

"No need. Get some sleep," said Silvia. She sat with the men around the fire. "The scouts are either dead or in the dungeon. The wooden guard will protect us tonight."

With a bow of his head to Silvia, Edwin brought his bag into the tent.

"Can you see it?" Declan asked Berty.

"See what?" asked Berty.

"The Fairy Ring—its magic."

"Oh." Berty stared at the perimeter Declan drew.

"There should be a pink haze," explained Declan. "Until the effects of the Dust wear off on me, I can't see a thing."

"Using Fairy Dust affects Hope the same way," said Berty.

"Really?"

Berty looked into the surrounding forest. He closed his eyes. A pink barricade surrounded them. "It's there," he said.

"Couldn't see it without closing your eyes?" asked Declan.

Opening his eyes, he glanced at the invisible barricade then looked at Silvia and Declan. "It's a strong pink, not a haze."

"My first Fairy Ring." Declan smiled. "I'm going to check on Delyth." He retreated to the tent.

Berty slipped his hand around Silvia's. Bringing it to his lips, he kissed the back of her hand.

"What was that for?" she asked.

"Can't a husband love his wife?" he replied with a smile.

"Uh-huh." Laughing a little, she scooted closer to him.

He let her hand drop to his chest as he threw his arm around her. Her head tucked between his shoulder and neck. He inhaled the familiar summer berry pie aroma he loved.

Footsteps startled him. He still held Silvia close and realized he must had fallen asleep. Lifting his head, he saw Edwin approach. "Just checking on you," Edwin said quietly. "It's warmer in the tent."

Berty gave Edwin a nod, then nudged Silvia. "Why don't we get a little sleep in the tent," he suggested when she stirred. He raised her to her feet, then led her to her waiting bedroll.

Awakening after too little sleep, Berty helped pack the campsite. Delyth grimaced whenever she moved. Alina allowed Declan to give her pain medicine. She gingerly removed the Fairy Ring after a small argument with Declan. Declan carried her pack while they walked slowly through the forest.

"I'm sorry I can't go faster," Delyth said when they stopped for a break.

"Nonsense," said Silvia. "You need to heal."

Giving her a weak smile, Delyth stood with assistance. They continued their trek.

"I'll take care of you," Berty overheard Declan whisper.

"I know you will," breathed Delyth.

The archer had not left her side since the campsite.

"Love finds its way," Silvia said in Berty's ear.

She wound her arm in his. "Yes, yes, it does," he said, then gave her a peck on the cheek.

By the time they reached the Sages' Grove, the first wave of Empire Guard had left for Fairyland. Berty saw the village much more empty, but the lack of its usual business still unnerved him. Young men headed to war. He did not want to think of how many might not return. They did not start it, but they would end it. They had to. Berty took a deep breath, then followed the injured Delyth inside the Empire Tree.

"Delyth!" Lida cried.

"Ow," escaped Delyth's lips.

"Be careful, Your Majesty," said Alina.

Lida held Delyth's hand as tears rushed down her cheeks.

"I'll be fine, Mother. I just need to not move for a while." Delyth touched her side.

"Is there anything we can do for you?" asked Elrick. He looked from Alina to Declan.

"Not right now," Delyth breathed.

Watching Delyth make faces, Declan said, "I think it's time for another dose."

"Come, Lida," said Elrick, "Declan and Alina are more than capable of taking care of her." To his daughter, he said, "Get situated. We'll check in on you in a bit."

She gave her parents a smile, then allowed Declan to lead her to her chambers.

Noticing the floor to ceiling fir in the center of the room, Berty said, "Yule is almost upon us."

"The decorations should be up tomorrow," said Silvia. Leaving Berty's side, she walked over to the Fairies.

After a muscle relaxing shower, he and Silvia joined the Advisory Council, Edwin, Obie, and the Fairies in the Roundtable Room for the season's first faðbra. Declan helped Delyth to her seat. They discussed the role the Dragons decided to take in the war.

"With the Dragons and the Trolls, we will have tipped the scales in our favor," said Alvar. "I wish I knew what kind of magic they might throw our way."

"No luck at the Watcher's Guild?" asked Declan.

"They've been helpful," said Alvar.

"But?"

Chapter Fifteen

Trekking to Tren

Alvar made a face. "Nothing specific that we can use. Besides a Warlock, there is no real defense. We have one, young Warlock." He motioned to Obie. "That is simply not enough. Though we do have a special Watcher force led by someone with a locket, Brian, I think."

Declan nodded.

"I'm sorry our research failed you, Alvar," said Delyth.

"No," said Alvar, waving a hand. "I'm frustrated that we as an Empire did not preserve more knowledge."

"We must accept that there are things that we do not know," said Silvia. "All knowledge is not locked in books. Some can only be experienced. We must do the best with what we have and hope we can find our way. Like life, magic cannot be contained in books. Though, I did wish they kept records of what was imprisoned in God Mountain."

"The next wave leaves tomorrow," said Alvar.

"Then we must leave soon for Pixisle," Silvia said. She looked at the faces around the table. "Edwin, I am afraid you cannot come with us."

"I will wait for you at the shoreline," said Edwin.

"No," said Silvia, resolute. "Declan and Obie only." She turned to Berty. "And Hope," she added.

When they returned to their chambers, Berty wrote Jon a note about wanting to speak with him. With a tap of his finger, the note disappeared.

"Berty, what is it?" whispered Jon's voice. "It's late."

"Sorry. Silvia and I are going to come by tomorrow morning," he said to his brother's voice.

"You could have called," said Jon.

"What's the fun in that?"

"Argh. Goodnight."

Although his brother made only an auditory appearance, he could feel Jon's presence leave the room.

Skipping breakfast, Silvia and Berty crossed the portal and dressed in modern clothes. They reached Jon's house in barely under forty minutes. Jon answered the door before they reached the stoop. Hope waited impatiently beside her father.

In the kitchen, the four adults gathered at the table. "What's this about?" asked Teresa.

"Hope needs to come with us to Pixisle," Silvia said.

"I wanna go," said Hope, running through the kitchen. "Pixisle is where the Mother Wood Sprite is."

Jon glanced from Silvia to Berty. "Go now?" he asked. "She'll miss Christmas."

"Possibly," said Berty.

Jon removed his glasses, then rubbed his eyes. "Can't it wait until after?" He replaced his glasses.

"As we speak, men are marching off to war and may never return to their families," said Berty. "All because we don't know how to stop the Whispers." Speaking the words aloud crushed him inside. "We can all have a special Christmas when we come home."

Teresa's eyes glistened. "My uncle didn't," she said in a small voice. "My mom said her family was never the same." She breathed deeply. "I will stay in the Empire Tree with the midwife until Hope and Jon return."

Jon's head snapped to look at his wife.

"Go," she urged. "I will be fine. I can cross the portal by myself if I have to."

"And you can take others while holding hands," said Silvia.

"It won't come to that," Jon said, taking his wife's hand.

Jon and Teresa made a few calls while they packed. Jon's car followed Berty's back to the house. He parked in the back with Berty. Hope skipped into the house.

"Don't go through the portal without us," Teresa called after her.

Upstairs, Hope waited for them by the tapestry portal that led to her chambers. Berty and Silvia quickly changed, then accompanied Hope and her parents through the tapestry.

Inside Hope's playroom, Berty explained, "Jon, you and Teresa have the same chambers as last time. In the wardrobe, you'll find traveling clothes. There will also be a packed bag in the room. Change into those clothes and transfer anything you need into that bag. When you're done, come to our study with your bag." Carrying his and Teresa's bags, he left. "Freesia has a packed bag waiting in

Hope's bedroom," he said to Teresa. "She should also change into what she finds in the wardrobe. We'll meet you in our study."

Donning their plain traveling clothes, Berty and Silvia set their packs near the door. Wind chimes heralded the arrival of Jon, Teresa, and Hope, then Declan and Obie, and finally, Theodore. The Head Tender brought food, provisions, and a package for Jon. "The horses will be ready for you," said Theodore before leaving.

Staring at the long bundle, Jon said, "Horses?"

"We're not walking to the harbor," said Silvia.

"Is that?" Jon asked, pointing at the bundle.

"Eat first," said Berty, steering his brother to the dining table.

Sitting, Teresa asked, "Where's Edwin?"

"He's staying here," answered Silvia.

"It's the four of you and two children?" Teresa asked.

"I planned on having Delyth come with us," said Silvia, "but she needs her rest."

Teresa ate a few bites before asking, "How long will it take to reach the harbor?"

"Depends on the weather," Silvia said. "I'm thinking we'll be gone for about two weeks."

"As long as Hope's winter break from school," said Jon.

When they finished eating, Berty gave Jon the bundle. Unwrapping the cloth, Jon said, "It's a sword."

"It's *your* sword," said Berty.

"Mine." Jon adjusted his glasses. "How do I...?"

Berty showed Jon how to attach it to his belt. He stepped away from his brother to give him room.

"I feel stupid," muttered Jon. He walked around the coffee table. "It just hangs there. Like extra dead weight."

Rolling his eyes, Berty said, "You'll get used to it."

Packs and white cloaks secure, they marched across the bridges to a secluded side of the village. White horses with white saddles and reins waited for them.

Jon stared. "I don't know how to ride," he admitted.

"It's easy, Daddy," said Hope.

Teresa hugged both Hope and Jon. She stood to the side while her husband and daughter mounted their horses.

"Breathe," Declan told Jon. He showed him the basics. "Stay with Berty. I'll be behind you."

They waved to Teresa. Jon blew her a kiss.

Silvia led them between the wall and the village until they slipped out of the gates. Jon's horse followed and kept pace with the other horses. Keeping to the road, they passed no one. The empty road allowed them to keep riding well after dark. Eventually, they chose a campsite with the trees' approval.

The crackling fire provided music by which to eat. Cold swirled around their backs. The smell of frozen water hung in the air. "It's strange traveling without Edwin," said Declan. He prodded the logs of the fire. No one answered. Hope dozed on Jon's lap. Watching Obie stifle a yawn, Declan said, "I'll take first watch."

"Not necessary, Uncle Declan," yawned Hope. "We're protected here."

Jon raised his eyebrows.

"It's part of her gift," said Silvia.

Sitting up, Hope stretched. "Night, Daddy," she said.

"I'll be in soon," Jon said.

"Okay." She hugged her father, then disappeared into the tent.

"When did she start calling you, Uncle Declan?" Jon asked.

Declan bit his lower lip. "Ah… I don't know. It just happened one day."

Laughing, Berty said, "Obie calls me Uncle. So, why wouldn't Hope call Declan Uncle?"

Jon laughed with his brother. Looking around, he asked, "Where is Obie?"

"I'll check to see if he's with the horses," said Declan.

Both Jon and Declan jumped off the ground. While Declan ran to the horses, Jon rushed inside the tent. "He's here," Jon called, poking his head out the flap. Soon, Declan joined him in the tent. When the men emerged, Jon said, "The two of them are asleep, facing each other."

"Probably talking themselves to sleep," said Declan.

Jon's smile contorted. "As long as he doesn't start calling me Dad anytime soon," he muttered.

They lingered around the fire until Silvia extinguished it with magic. Declan laid his bedroll with a good view of the tent's entrance. Pretending she did not notice Declan, Silvia tapped the tent with her wand. Magic pulsed around the tent.

For two more days on the road, they encountered no one. When the road forked and other roads intersected, Declan led. Well-traveled, Declan knew the way to their harbor town destination.

Clouds obscured mountaintops in the distant north. They rode towards them, yet west. The road climbed steadily. Pine mingled with the cold, sharp air. North winds carried the promise of snow.

"It's taken almost a week simply to get here," complained Jon. "How are we to get there and home in only two?"

"Have faith," said Silvia. She returned to eating her stew. The unyielding winds forced them to camp earlier in the day than they wanted.

Jon made a face, then dug his spoon into his bowl. Recognizing the face, Berty chuckled. He had seen his brother use that face on numerous occasions.

"What?" asked Jon.

"You're doing the face," Berty answered.

"What face?"

"The 'I'm exasperated, yet helpless' face."

Sighing, Jon allowed his elbows to drop to his knees.

"You're travel weary. You'll see Teresa soon," assured Berty. "At least she sends messages every day."

"It's not that. I mean, I miss her." He adjusted his glasses. "But, here we are. It's cold. Been traveling for days and we're nowhere."

"And you ache," added Berty. "And you're uncomfortable."

"The pain meds I've been taking aren't working," muttered Jon. "Or maybe they are and I'd be worse without them."

Declan's head turned sharply to stare at Jon.

"I'm not drinking any of that vile stuff," Jon told Declan.

"I wouldn't give you any," said Declan. "You need to feel this pain. It needs to work itself out. Don't take anymore of whatever it is you're taking."

Jon kicked snow into the fire. He reached into a pocket. A small, white plastic bottle emerged with his hand. He tossed the rattling bottle to Declan.

Catching it, Declan read the label. He mouthed the name of the pills. His fingers struggled with the cap. "How do you open this?" he asked.

Hope took the bottle out of Declan's hands. She twisted effortlessly. Handing back the bottle and its cap, she said, "It's childproof." As Declan stared at the plastic in his hands, she explained, "Squeeze here and turn." She showed Declan the trick of the cap.

Berty turned his attention to his brother. "What's really bothering you?" he asked in a low voice.

"Each day, I'm more uneasy and I don't know why," Jon whispered.

Berty patted his bother on the shoulder. "It's the unknown."

Nodding, Jon said nothing.

By morning, the wind calmed. "Move quickly before the wind returns," said Silvia. They pushed the horses as fast as they could go through the snow, avoiding the night wind shaped drifts. Stopping, even to eat, was out of the question.

Finally, the road crested, revealing a winding descent. In the distance, gray sky met gray sea. Color dotted the shoreline. "We're not going that far north," Declan said, observing where Berty gazed. "We can't see Tren from here, but we should reach it tomorrow if we get off this mountain quickly."

A few hours from the top, the winds stayed aloft. The water view remained, and Berty half expected to be able to smell the salty sea air, but none reached the twisting road. Descending further, tall, majestic pines obscured the view of the sea.

The road eventually leveled. A crisp saltiness sprinkled the breezes. The sun plunged behind the trees. "What's that light in the sky?" asked Obie.

They paused to look skyward. Shimmering green ribbons danced across the dark sky. "The Aurora Borealis," said Jon.

"The Winter Lights," answered Declan. "We can travel with its glow." They kicked their horses onward.

"Is it magic?" asked Obie.

"It's essentially caused by the sun's radiation getting caught in the Earth's magnetic field, which is strongest at the poles. Solar flares and sun storms can cause the Lights to travel farther south," Jon explained.

Obie said nothing, but constantly watched the lights ebb and flow with different hues of green and yellow.

"Daddy, how did the sun get trapped in the Earth's sky?" asked Hope.

Jon took a deep breath. Berty held back a chuckle. "Well... Essentially... Gravity," Jon answered. "But it's not just Earth. Other planets have auroras at their poles."

"What is gravity, Mister Chase?" asked Obie.

"Nine point eight—" Jon stopped talking. "It's the force that keeps us on Earth instead of floating with the stars," he explained.

Obie looked up then nodded.

"I have some books you can borrow if you're interested in reading more about it, Obie," said Jon.

"I'd like that very much, Mister Chase. Thank you." Obie stole glances at the sky as they rode.

Fatigue made them stop. Under the shelter of pines, Hope pulled out her velvet pouch of Fairy Dust while the others set up camp. The snowless pine needle carpet softened their steps. "What are you doing, Hope?" Jon asked.

"Constructing a Fairy Dome," Hope answered.

Jon watched her chant in the ancient Fairy language while sprinkling Fairy Dust in a circle around the campsite. "What? Why?" he asked.

"The trees probably told her to make one," said Silvia.

When the circle completed, a shimmering opalescent dome encased the campsite. For the first time, Berty could see outside the glowing dome. It glowed more dimly than he remembered and much more translucent.

"That's bright," said Jon, marveling at his daughter's work. "Aren't people going to see us?"

"It looks different from the outside, Dad," said Hope. "When people look at it, they see nothing."

Jon smiled. "Clever."

While Jon rattled about how the dome achieves invisibility, Declan whispered to Berty, "You can see outside now."

Nodding, Berty whispered, "I can see the dome, too."

"Really?" Declan looked around. "I see a swimming heat haze only. I know where the magical boundaries are, but I don't seem the dome itself or the glow everyone's mentioned." He stoked the fire. "We see differently. It's interesting."

The tent afforded them relative darkness for sleeping. In the morning, Jon sipped a cup of magically brewed coffee. He watched Hope remove the dome. "How is she able to do that?" he asked Silvia. "Will my other daughter be able to as well?"

"Delyth taught her ancient Fairy magic," Silvia answered. "And without wearing Fairystone, no non-Fairy could do what she does."

"We should reach Tren this afternoon," said Declan as he mounted his horse.

Snow from branches danced across the road. The snow blowing breeze carried a hint of fresh salt. A stone wall barricaded the view of the sea.

When the road brought them closer, Jon asked, "Are those spikes in the wall?"

Thin metal protrusions stuck out of the stone at haphazard angles. "Keeps out the Gnomes," said Hope.

"Gnomes?" said Jon.

"Don't think they're the garden variety," said Berty.

Jon pursed his lips while his hands tightened on the reins.

Spiked metal gates swung into the walled area. Lance wielding guards eyed them as they passed. Snow covered fields flanked the road inside the wall. "Must be a terrible threat if they have to protect the farms," said Silvia.

Beyond the farms stood a higher spiked wall. More guards monitored the trickle of traffic in and out of town. A guard raised a hand for them to stop. "Horses are not permitted in Tren," said the guard. "Stable is right inside. They charge five cops a night per horse or you can leave them to the mercy of the fields. This gate closes at sundown."

"Thank you," said Declan. "We'll stable our horses."

The guard nodded them through. A young stable hand met them by the stable door. "Ya horses need bordin' for da night?"

"We should be in town a few nights," Declan told him. Sliding out of the saddle, he said, "We'll pay you for two nights now and the balance when we leave."

The young man glanced behind him. An older man, probably his father, nodded. "Dat will do," said the stable hand.

They removed what they needed from the horses, then paid. The father helped collect the reins and bring them inside the stable.

Narrow streets weaved between tall, half timber buildings. Declan navigated the maze without only a few pauses to get his bearings. The sun began to set, throwing long shadows on the upper floors of the buildings. A chill coursed through the streets. Declan led them to a pub near the waterfront.

The place reeked of stale beer and lingering pipe smoke. Weathered patrons cloistered around wooden tables and clung to the bar like fixtures. Jon grabbed Declan's arm. "Are you sure about this place?" he asked through his teeth.

"Not many public houses are open during Yuletide," Declan answered. After Jon released him, he brought them to an empty round table.

A waitress waded over to them. "What'll it be?" she asked.

"Something hot and filling," answered Declan, sounding weary.

The plump woman cracked a tiny smile. "Be right back."

Declan's light eyes studied the room. Most of the patrons paid them no attention. Some gave them curious looks. Declan nodded to himself as if he agreed that he chose the right establishment. Before Berty could ask Declan what he was thinking, the waitress returned with their food.

"Traveling through?" she asked while setting bowls of steaming stew and pints of frothy beer on the table.

"Visiting some family in Frey," answered Declan.

She placed half pints in front of Hope and Obie. Frowning, Jon removed his glasses as if he did not want to see it. "Still got a long ways ta go," she said. "If ya've got the coin, ya might want to hire a boat ta take ya there. There's a few captains in here ta-night. Plus, we've got a couple-a vacant rooms if ya be needin' beds."

"Thanks for the suggestion," Declan said with a smile. "We'll consider it while we eat."

She gave him a pleasant nod, then tucked her tray under her arm before checking on another table.

"Does my daughter have beer?" Jon asked in a low voice. When his eyes met Silvia's, he quickly looked away and ripped off a chunk of bread.

Berty's eyes roved to look at her, but she only had eyes for her food.

With their food eaten, a woman dressed more like a man sat down with them. "I hear you're looking to hire a boat," she said.

"That depends," said Declan.

"Two lids take you to Frey," she said.

Declan took a long sip of his beer. "How much to go elsewhere?" he asked finally.

"Gotta speak to the Captain for that," she answered.

"Who's your captain?" he asked.

"I am." The voice belonged to a dainty woman clenching a pipe in her teeth and carrying danger in her eyes. Her cascades of brown hair shook when she jerked her head for the other woman to leave. Thick soled boots clomped on the wooden floor as she stepped to the now empty seat. Studying the occupants of the table, she inhaled on her pipe. "Hello again, Declan. It's been awhile," she said.

"Mabe," escaped Declan's lips.

A wicked smile crept across Mabe's face. "What's this about going elsewhere?"

"Pixisle," said Declan.

Mabe almost cackled when she laughed. "Why do you want to go there? And at this time of year?"

"I have business with the Pixies," said Silvia.

Mabe turned her attention to Silvia. Leaning back in the chair, she said, "All right then. I'll take you. Will you be needing a return trip?"

"Yes."

Not taking her eyes off Silvia, Mabe chewed on the end of her pipe. "For five lids I can have us sailing in an hour. An all female crew should not be a problem," she said.

"We will accompany you to your ship and pay you once we board," said Silvia.

"Fair enough," said Mabe, "if you don't mind waiting while we load."

Silvia gave the ship Captain a stern nod. Declan went to the bar to settle their bill.

Outside the pub, Mabe told her crewwoman, "Get it ready to sail." The woman who first spoke to them ran down a side street.

"We're the only ship that sails to Pixisle anymore," Mabe said, leading them to the wharf. "We conduct trade with the Pixies exclusively on behalf of merchants and the like. No one usually wants to go there though."

Moored ships rocked quietly beside the long wooden piers. Multiple gangplanks rubbed against the pier with the bobbing waves. Mabe gestured to cross a gangplank to a wooden monstrosity with a Viking-esque body and several Asian sails.

The wooden gangplank led to the top deck of the ship. "Welcome aboard the Nereida," she said. They watched the flurry of crew heave cargo aboard the different gangplanks. Once all cargo was secure, they pulled in the gangplanks. "Ready to sail, Captain."

Mabe gave the woman a nod, then turned to Silvia. "Payment."

Berty extracted five gold coins from his coin purse. He showed them to Mabe, then handed her two. "You'll get another when we moor on Pixisle and the balance when we return," he said.

Shaking her head, she cracked a smile. "I like you lot," she said.

After turning the two coins over in her hand, she tucked them into a coat pocket.

The Nereida drifted away from the dock. They were given a private cabin with hammocks below deck. When the harbor twinkled in the distance, Silvia touched the tip of her wand to the pointed bow of the ship. White flowed over the brown, across the deck and up the masts and sails.

"What is this sorcery?" Mabe bellowed. "What have you done to my ship?"

Silvia turned to face the storming Mabe. "Open your sails. The wind is coming," she said. Her brown eyes burned into Mabe's. "Everything will go back to normal when our voyage is over."

"I can make that be now," seethed Mabe.

"Open. Your. Sails."

"I don't take orders from nobody."

The wind whipped across the deck—the magical manifestation of Silvia's anger. The two women faced each other. Neither flinched. The wind pinned the crew to the sides of the deck.

"You don't scare me, Sorceress," Mabe defied.

Silvia shrugged. With a flick of her fingers, Mabe turned upside down. The gold coins Berty paid her clinked on the deck.

"What are you doing?" demanded Mabe.

"I don't need you. Just your ship." Silvia smiled at Mabe. The sails opened on their own. She waved her hand and Mabe flew off the side.

"Wait!" Mabe screamed. Fear tinged her voice. She froze over the open water. "These are Sprite infested waters."

"Not my problem," said Silvia.

"What do you want from me?" asked Mabe.

"Speed," said Silvia. "And if the crew isn't willing to help, they will share your fate. Good-bye, Mabe."

"Nooooo!"

The roaring wind cut off all noise. Catching the wind, the Nereida sliced through the water, leaving little wake.

Stunned, Berty wondered whom he married.

Chapter Sixteen

The Nereida

Silvia glared at the crew. "I'm not doing everything myself. Sail this ship," she ordered.

Women hustled to their duties.

"She's locked in a cell in her own hold," Silvia whispered to Berty. "Perception. We're outnumbered in Sprite infested waters." She released a breath. "She'll come around."

Declan looked at her in disbelief.

"We women have a way of understanding one another," she said with a sly smile.

The crew kept a respectable distance from the passengers. Satisfied with the pace, Silvia encouraged the others to sleep. At the door of their cabin, Silvia continued down the hall. "Where are you going?" Berty asked.

"To see our friend." Placing her hand on his arm, she smiled. "Don't worry about me."

He entered the room without her, but she stayed in the forefront of his mind. Hope and Obie climbed into the top bunked hammocks. "Sleep with your bow within arm's reach," Declan warned Hope. Jon's hands paused as he pulled a thin blanket over his daughter. "You can't trust any of them," Declan continued.

Berty laid in a hammock with his leg dangling to the floor. His foot pushed slightly, rocking his hammock. Closing his eyes, he saw Silvia.

She strolled towards a holding cell. Mabe screamed obscenities at the top of her lungs. "No one can hear you," Silvia said. "Your crew believes you're… well… swimming with the Water Sprites."

Mabe stepped away from the bars.

"You can't be heard nor can you be seen," Silvia continued. "But all of that can change. Your crew won't remember you being swept out to sea by the swift winds."

"What do you want?"

"Your cooperation, Mabe." Silvia used a calm, almost friendly tone. "I want to get to Pixisle and back as quickly as possible. And I don't want you to have an issue with me coercing the wind to blow in our favor. The white gives us protection as we travel. You see me as a threat. I am merely helping."

Mabe shifted her weight.

"I'll tell you what. As a token of good faith, I'll give you ten lids right now. And ten more upon our safe return to Tren. There won't be any more surprises—at least on our end. What say you?"

With a breath, Mabe turned her back to Silvia. The women stood in silence. Spinning around, she stepped to the bars. "All right," she said. "I just want you off my ship for good."

Silvia dropped ten gold coins into Mabe's hand, one by one. After Mabe tucked the coins into her coat, the cell door opened. They walked unnoticed through the ship. On the lantern lit upper deck, a woman said, "Captain, if this wind keeps up, we'll reach Pixisle in a day."

"Keep the sails in the wind, girls," Mabe bellowed.

"See you in the morning, *Captain*," said Silvia. She climbed below deck.

When Silvia opened the door, Berty's eyes snapped open. Declan lifted his head off the hammock.

"She won't give us any trouble," she announced.

"Uh-huh," grunted Declan. He lowered his head.

"How do you know Mabe?" asked Berty.

Without lifting his head, Declan said, "After Geraint died, I spent a couple of years in Frey, doing odd jobs—sometimes working as a healer. Frey happens to be one of her ports of call. She has a whispered reputation. I met her through one of my jobs."

"You must have left an impression," said Berty. "She remembers you."

Declan said nothing while Silvia claimed her hammock. "Our paths crossed fairly often," he said finally, "until I received the invitation to the Watcher's Guild."

"If it makes you feel better, the door is locked with magic," said Silvia.

The cargo ship confined when gray blue ebbed and flowed to seemingly nowhere, everywhere. No matter where Berty went, he could not escape the gray meeting gray. Mabe distanced herself from them, as if she respected their privacy. Declan kept his watchful eye on every one and every thing. He constantly fluttered from one area to another. Jon hovered around Hope. During the sunless day, she had two shadows—Jon and Obie.

In-between meals, Berty stared at the bobbing waves. Although he knew the ship moved, he felt static. Silvia wore a calm smile everywhere she roamed on the boat. However, to Berty, the Nereida was not that big. Looking across the top deck to the other railing made him feel claustrophobic. He wanted to disembark.

Closing his eyes, he tried focusing on his parents or Teresa, but he could not see them. He scowled at the clouds as if they blocked his vision.

"Grip the railing any tighter and you're going to get splinters," said Silvia.

Berty let go of the wood. The muscles in his hands hurt. Flexing his hands, he said, "I won't get splinters, I'm wearing gloves."

Silvia laughed just for his ears. "Sea sickness?"

"Ship fever," he answered. "No wonder they have so many activities on cruise ships."

"Should see land tonight," she said. "Relax. We haven't even been at sea that long."

"I'll relax when we're back on land," said Berty.

Silvia nestled her arm in his, then rested her head on his shoulder. Her touch comforted him like always, but he could not shake his uneasiness.

After dinner, Berty unpacked and repacked his bag just for something to do. "I don't like not hearing the trees," Hope said behind him. He turned. His heart broke seeing her sad face.

"You'll hear them soon," Berty told her.

"I know," she said. "I just don't like it. Reminds me of the Frost Giants."

"There aren't any Frost Giants on Pixisle," he reassured. He gave his niece a hug. "Don't worry."

She squeezed him so tightly, he barely heard her say, "I won't. Thanks, Uncle Berty."

"There you are," said Jon. He stood in the doorway. Concern melted from his face. "Are you getting ready for bed, Hope?"

Unlatching from Berty, she said, "No Frost Giants on Pixisle, Daddy."

Jon half smiled. "That's good," he said. While he hugged his daughter, he looked at Berty with question.

Having no intention of explaining to Jon why his daughter feared Frost Giants, Berty shrugged.

"I'm ready for bed now, Daddy," said Hope.

By the time Hope fell asleep, the crew spotted land on the gray horizon. Silvia confined their party to the insides of the ship until morning. She wanted to keep their arrival a surprise.

In the morning, the winds returned to normal. The ship carefully approached a pier jutting out from a cliff face. Women in blue tunics rushed out of a hole in the cliff to meet them. "The Dock Master herself," muttered Mabe, sounding amused.

When the moorings were secure, the Dock Master called, "Captain Mabe, please state your reason for docking today."

"Bringing passengers from the Mainland," Mabe said.

"Who are these passengers?" the Dock Master asked. "We do not permit just anyone ashore."

"The Empress and Emperor of all that surrounds us," Silvia announced, stepping forward.

Gasps and wide eyes surrounded them.

The women on the dock bowed. "Forgive us, Empress. We were not informed of your arrival," the Dock Master said.

"No, you were not," said Silvia. "No messenger could have gotten here any faster."

"I notice there are men in your party, Empress," said the Dock Master. "Men, even the Emperor, are not permitted entry to Pixisle without a copulation agreement. The boy, however, may join you."

Silvia and Berty looked at each other. He gave her a slight nod. Addressing the Dock Master, Silvia said, "We understand. The men will stay aboard the Nereida."

"Thank you for understanding," said the Dock Master. "A guide to take you to the Grand Temple can be found in town."

"Then we best be on our way. Ready, Hope, Obie?" asked Silvia.

"I don't like this," Jon hissed in Berty's ear.

Berty ignored his brother.

"Captain, your crew is free to trade and resupply while you're in dock," the Dock Master said.

Mabe nodded her acknowledgement. "My Lady," she said, "I offer members of my crew for an escort to replace your men."

"Thank you, Captain Mabe. Two would suffice," said Silvia.

Mabe chose two women to accompany Silvia to the temple. Silvia, Hope, and Obie said good-bye to Berty, Jon, and Declan. The men watched the women cross the gangplank to the dock.

"Go. Do business," Mabe said to her crew. "I'll stay aboard with the Emperor and his men."

After the women going ashore disappeared into the hole in the cliff, Mabe said, "Why didn't you tell me who you were?"

"Because during war, secrets and information trade higher than gold," said Berty.

While Mabe gave an agreeing nod, Jon fidgeted with his cloak. "I don't like this," he said. He began to pace. "How long will they be gone?" He stared at Mabe for an answer.

"I don't know. I've never been to the Grand Temple," she said. "It's a large island. If the temple is centrally located and they travel on foot, I'd estimate two or three days."

Jon stopped pacing to sit on a step. Mabe thrust a flask in his face. When he looked at her, she said, "Takes the edge off." He shook his head. "Suit yourself." She unscrewed the cap, then took a long swig. "I'm heading below where it's warmer. You're welcome to join me."

After Mabe left them alone, Declan said, "I agree with Jon. Something feels off."

Chapter Seventeen

Sisterhood

Berty closed his eyes. Silvia and the children followed the Dock Master through a medieval town with narrow streets cutting around tan stone buildings. As the roads steepened to roads with steps, the building facades changed to crumbling stucco, desperately clinging to the hillside. At the top, a lone building was carved out of the rock. The Dock Master pulled a sash that rang a bell deep within the structure. She motioned for all to enter with her. His vision darkened. He could no longer see Silvia. He opened his eyes. "Magic blocks my vision," he told them. His heart skipped a beat.

"They might have entered a temple," Declan said. "All Pixie temples ward against intrusion," he explained.

"And you just happen to know this?" Jon asked.

"The Watcher's Guild teaches about warding," said Declan. "I remember reading about Pixie temples when I was researching other stuff."

Closing his eyes, Berty saw nothing. "Might as well go below deck and keep warmer," he said, opening his eyes.

"Decided to join me, eh?" Mabe said when she spied them. She sat at a table, drinking a hot mug of something. "Mulled mead?" she offered. "Glad you didn't run after them. The dock maybe empty, but, trust me, they're right inside that cliff."

Declan ladled mugs of hot mead. "What do you know about the Pixies, Mabe?" Berty asked while he accepted a mug.

"I don't get involved much," she answered. "They've got their ways and their silly little temples. Not that I'd step foot in one." She plunked her mug on the table. "Life didn't turn out too bad for you, Declan. Emperor's guard. You should thank me for getting you out of Frey."

Declan stopped himself from spitting out his mead. "*Me* thank *you*? The rocking of the waves has addled your memory, Mabe," he said.

Mabe smiled then pulled her mug to her lips.

Noticing Declan's eye roll, Berty asked, "When will your crew return?"

"They'll be in and out all day. A lot of them have made friends in town," she responded.

"Not you?"

"I'm not the friend type," she said.

"No, I suppose not," said Berty.

She chuckled through her nose once. "How about a friendly game of cards while we wait, Emperor?"

"No, thanks," Berty answered. He stared into his mug. He refilled it a few times with hot mead while Declan, Jon, and Mabe carried a civil conversation. Berty hated not knowing where Silvia was and if she and the children were all right. Drinking did not remove his worry, but he kept trying anyway.

Snapping her eyes to the ceiling, Mabe reached for her cutlass. Declan followed her lead and readied an arrow. "My Lord," he warned.

Berty stumbled off the chair and swayed behind Declan. Two women in royal blue cloaks slowly stepped into the room. They held their open hands in front.

"We would've asked permission to board, but no one was on deck," said one of them.

"What do you want?" Mabe asked. Her weapon stayed steady.

"We wish to speak with the Emperor."

Berty took one step to the side. "Speak," he said.

"My Lord," the both said, bowing.

"The Empress is not being taken to the Priestess," one said. "The Priestess is being held captive and we have been unsuccessful so far in freeing her. Her prison is magical and we cannot get inside. We believe that outside help is necessary to free her. We implore you, my Lord, to help us. You and your men, while the imposter is distracted with the Empress."

"I thought men were not allowed ashore," said Jon.

"That was not always the law," said the other woman. "We know how to get you past the guards."

"We only have a small window of opportunity, my Lord," the first woman pressed. "We should leave now."

Her words sunk into his mead induced haze. Silvia could be in trouble. "Lead the way," he said.

The Pixies parked a dingy next to Mabe's ship. Jon, Declan, and Mabe followed Berty into the boat. The craft bobbed in the water. Berty placed his hand over his mouth. Up and down and up and down. His stomach churned. He could feel it rise. Mabe held him close to the edge. The contents of his stomach and then some emptied into the ocean. When he straightened in his seat, Mabe asked, "Feel better?"

"Still could do without all the movement," he said. "You didn't have to come."

"Aye," she replied.

The women dragged the boat on a strip of sandy shoreline. The unmoving ground eased Berty's insides. He took a few deep breaths before rejoining the group. The Pixies led them to a hidden staircase hewn into the cliff. While climbing, Berty noticed how the Pixie women were as tall as he. Mabe looked child sized next to them.

The unforgiving steps ended at a fissure in the cliff. Stone towered over them as they walked single file. Bare trees waited for them when they emerged. A stone ruin clung to the sides of the cliff across from them. Now dormant trees and vines grew over windows and through spires. An iced waterfall cascaded over a roof and down a wall.

"This is Taru," the second woman said. "Legendary entrance to Virva, a place sacred to the Sini." She looked from man to man. "You have no idea what I'm talking about."

The first woman huffed.

"Sini are keepers of Taika," she continued to explain. She swallowed. "My name is Grier. The Priestess is locked away somewhere within there. A magic prohibits women from entering Taru. Virva may or may not still exist. Her lights are tricky, especially if Terhi— never mind. You'll find her. Let Tuulikki be your guide."

The men approached the opening of the ruin. "I don't think I should go with you," Declan said. "Remember what she said in the fire."

Berty recalled the line the Pixie Priestess said to them in the fire in the Outlands, *Only you can free her tie.* "That could pertain to something else," he said.

Shaking his head, Declan said, "I don't think so. I'll wait for you here and find out what Sini and Taika are."

Berty thought Declan held something back, but he did not press it. He simply gave his friend a nod. Leaving Declan by the doorway, he and Jon entered the ruins.

"What was that all about?" Jon asked. He looked around. "It's dark in here."

"Declan's interpretation of what the Priestess said," Berty explained. "He thinks you or I will free her since she only appeared to the both of us." He stood in the middle of the room, turning in a circle. "This used to be one of their temples. I saw Silvia enter something similar." Something on the wall caught his eye. When he examined it, he realized that it was a crystal sconce like the ones in the Scepter Room. It glowed a soft blue at his touch.

"Now, we have to find more of those?" said Jon. He brushed dust off of something, which made him cough.

With a forceful yank, Berty removed the glowing sconce from the wall.

"Berty!"

"You want to fumble around in the dark?" he said. "I'm not sure if I can or want to use my magic in here."

"Couldn't we just light a torch or something?" asked Jon.

"I didn't see any. Besides, the smoke could be dangerous in here." In the soft blue light, cave-ins or something blocked doorways. They only had one path to follow.

"It feels like we're going deeper in the earth," said Jon. "I wish we could see further than just a couple of feet ahead."

The path widened, revealing multiple passages. "Which way?" Berty asked.

"Hello?" Jon called. He stood in front of one of the entranceways. "I think I see light down there."

Berty's cloak fluttered in a slight breeze towards a different doorway. "This way," he told Jon.

"But the lights," Jon protested.

"Ever hear of will-o-wisps? Their lights lead men to their deaths. I'd rather not be one of them," he said.

"But those are just—" Jon said nothing more. He followed his brother down another tunnel. "So, how long has the Priestess been imprisoned?" he asked.

"From some point after she gave the prophecy in the Empire Tree," Berty answered. "I'm not sure how long ago that was."

"Are you sure we're going the right way?" asked Jon after the tunnel had brought them nowhere.

Berty slowed. "I'm following the signs," he said.

"Signs only you can see?"

"You can see them, too."

"If I drink as much as you have?"

Stopping, Berty turned. "Either embrace your magic fully or don't. There is no halfway."

"Magic can't do everything," Jon said. "It doesn't stop one from making mistakes."

"What, so far, has been a mistake?" Berty's tone cut, but he could not hear it.

"Where should I start?" Jon's tone matched his brother's. "How about throwing Mabe overboard?"

"That was necessary."

"Oh?" said Jon. "Your wife is dangerous."

"My wife is in danger."

"So are we, in case you haven't noticed. This," he gestured around them, "is a trap and we're deep in it."

Jon's chest heaved while Berty took a step back. "What?" He shined the blue light on the smooth walls. "Where have we been going?"

"You brought a blue stone," said a woman's voice. "How thoughtful. Very thoughtful."

Berty turned in the direction of the voice. He lifted the blue stone over his head.

"Blink. The deception disappears," she said.

"You're the Pixie Priestess," said Jon. He looked at something Berty could not see.

"I am," she replied.

"I can understand you," said Jon.

"Limitations of my magical prison," she said. "Emperor, if you wish to get out of here, you need to blink."

Berty's eyelids obeyed. Deep wrinkled skin surrounded blue-gray eyes that stared at him. The stone he carried cast a blue hue on silver hair wildly cascading past her bare shoulders. Scraps of leather covered the most private areas of her otherwise naked body.

"Using my magic down here ages me," she said. "I have one tattoo left, then my magic is gone." She threw a ragged silver robe around her sag draped bones. "Blue stones are sacred to the Sini. Since it glows, it retains magic. We must place it," she crossed the dark room, "here. Right under the Pixstone."

Berty set it on the ground where she pointed.

"The Empress is here. I felt her presence with the Sini," she said. "The Sini have not been corrupted by what fuels the movement against the Empire. The others," she paused while circling the stone. "They know about you, Emperor, because of my prophecy years ago. They do not know of the Empress' power." She stopped, facing Berty. "We must break the stone to free us and my people. Communicator," she said to Jon, "tell one of them it is a trap. They are in the Grand Temple above us. Your magic will work. Tell them Trine magic."

Jon inhaled deeply. He closed his eyes. "Say nothing to me, Hope; just listen," he whispered. "It is important that you tell Aunt Silvia to use Trine magic. Uncle Berty and I are imprisoned below with the Pixie Priestess. Be strong, Hope." With his eyes still closed, Jon stumbled. Catching his brother, Berty saw through Jon's eyes and heard through his ears.

Silvia encircled a blue altar rock. "This is beautiful, Farica," she said to a woman in a shimmering blue tunic. "Hope, what is it?"

"Trine magic," Hope said.

"Yes," said Silvia with a nod. She looked in Hope's general direction as if she knew they could see her. "Open your eyes and disconnect. You will need your focus."

"She was talking to us, Jon. It's time you put your faith and trust in my dangerous wife," Berty said. "Can you stand?"

"No matter. He can sit where he is," said the Priestess. "I will sit here. Emperor," she motioned for him to take his place to form a triangle.

Sitting, Berty stared into the blue stone. The Priestess began a chant in a language Berty could not translate, even wearing his red stone pinky ring. Jon joined the chanting. Relaxing his focus on the blue stone, Berty allowed the chant to wash over him. He began chanting words he normally could not pronounce.

The blue stone glowed brighter. Something rumbled. The earth beneath his seat shook. When dirt sprinkled their heads, Berty looked at the Priestess. She did not seem concerned. They continued chanting.

Others' words mingled with theirs somewhere. The magic strengthened. A blue bubble encapsulated them. A flash of white. Two thuds. A loud rumble. The blue glow remained while the magic pulsated through the air.

The Pixie Priestess stood. She ended the chant, then beckoned the brothers to follow. Daylight seeped through a crack. She led them up a packed earth staircase to the surface. With the speed of a much younger woman, she wrapped her arms around the raven haired woman who Silvia called Farica.

"No!" the woman screamed. She tried to wrestle free, but the old woman's arms held firm.

The Priestess whispered something in the woman's ear. A million little lights froze her in place. Farica melted into the old woman who de-aged. Smooth skin lifted off bones as silver dissolved into dark brown waves. Blue designs appeared on her skin. She looked like the woman Berty had seen appear to him in the crystal of the Scepter.

A Pixie next to Hope with similar blue markings knelt in homage. "Rise, Sisko," said the Priestess. "Let it be known that with the help of the Emperor and the Empress and their companions: the Communicator, the Listener, the young Warlock, and the Keeper, the Sini have defeated the invaders."

"Yes, Merja," Sisko said. The woman walked through a side door.

Berty finally examined his surroundings. Swirl designs covered the insides of the blue stone temple. A colorless crystal altar lay broken in half in the center of the room. Silvia's wand perched in the crack.

The Priestess Merja stared at the wand. "Your magic has been exposed, Empress," she said. "Someday, it will know and it will come for you." She turned to a blue dressed attendant at her side. "Bring Grier, the Keeper, and the Captain," she told her. "It is not every day we get such important visitors. Come, let us show you Pixie generosity."

A slight breeze flowed through the temple as if the entire structure needed caulking. With the exception of spirals and crystals, the austere décor gave a sense of devotion to serenity. She led them to a dining area with multiple massive stone hearths running along the walls.

Fires instantly ignited in the fireplaces. "Please, sit, all of you," Merja said. Once seated, she continued, "The sand must have been mixed with Fairy Dust. We know not how it arrived. The magic affected them. I was captured. Many Sini were slaughtered if they didn't pretend to be affected by the magic."

When Declan entered with Mabe and Grier, Merja said, "Please, sit, honored guests. While we wait for our feast, Grier, your report."

"Yes, Merja," said Grier as she sat. "The One is dead. The light clap cured the others. Pixies will want their sons and husbands to return."

"All cannot be the way it was," said Merja. "We were frozen in time. Their husbands and sons... We will find new husbands, have new sons and allow them to stay."

Other painted blue women arrived with the food. After introductions, Berty could not remember all the names. Light conversation flowed with the wine. When the food cleared, many of the women puffed on an odd mixture of herbs that smelled vaguely of Berty's college days.

"Now, tell me, Empress, why have you come to see me?" asked Merja.

"How do we stop a Whisperer?" Silvia asked in return.

Merja closed her eyes as if she did not want to hear such an unpleasant question. The Priestess nodded. Opening her eyes, she said, "One cannot tamper or manipulate Whispers without detriment regardless of free will or magical force. The only way out for a Whisperer who does is death. Grier, form your squad. You leave with the Emperor and Empress in the morning."

"Yes, Merja," Grier answered. She asked Declan a question before leaving the table.

Chapter Eighteen

Garden Variety

After a strong cordial, a blue robed attendant showed them to their suite of rooms. Hope rambled to her father. "I can hear the trees better now. It's like they were shakin' awake. And I spoke the words, too, and did magic, Daddy. And when Aunt Silvia touched the stone with her wand, it broke in two. And light blasted from the wand like a bomb. Boom." Her hands mushroomed over her head.

"What do you know about bombs?" Jon asked.

"I've seen them on tv," she said, "at Cassie's sleepover."

Jon's lips twisted in disgust.

Chuckling, Berty turned to Declan. "What did Grier want?"

"To know if we were traveling on horseback," he said. "I think Mabe got a room to herself. The women she sent are in a different room."

"Closely guarded," said Silvia. "They don't want her sailing off without us."

"The Pixies know her well," muttered Declan.

Once the children fell asleep, the four of them discussed Mabe and the Pixies until they, too, slept.

In the morning, they met Merja by the broken altar stone. Mabe stood off to the side as if she needed to escape. The Priestess' blue robe flowed over her younger body like the ocean. She gave them a pleasant smile of gratitude. Another Sini joined them, carrying a tray. "Accept these warding amulets as a token of our appreciation," said Merja. While the Sini gave each person, including Mabe, a small pewter pendant on a leather cord, Merja continued, "The wards will protect you from magical harm—very ancient magic. Wear them always."

"Will they interfere with doing ancient magic?" asked Silvia.

Merja titled her head slightly. "Not if you are its origin," she replied. "Only if you are the recipient."

"Thank you, Merja," said Silvia. She tied the cord around her neck. The pendent fell behind her shirt. Berty and the others did the same. Jon helped Hope tie hers.

Grier arrived with four other women with blue marking on their faces, dressed for travel. "We are ready," she said.

The Priestess gave her a nod. "Empress, Emperor," said Grier, "allow me to introduce my squad who will be returning with you to the Empire Tree. Aloysia, Verena, Kirsi, and Zelda." Each woman bowed her head when her name was called.

"It will know soon," said Merja. "Go. Speedy journey."

The women fastened white cloaks around their shoulders and raised their hoods. "Follow us back to the ship," said Grier. Only Mabe and her two crewwomen lacked white cloaks gleaming in the sunshine outside the Grand Temple. The Pixies gathered the reins of their white horses and continued walking into a clearing. Shimmering blue discs stood in a circle around the clearing.

"Portals," said Declan.

Raising an eyebrow, Grier explained, "They connect every temple all over the island. This one," she led her horse to one of the blue discs, "leads to the pier temple."

"I don't see anything," Jon whispered Berty's ear.

"Step where I step so you go through the right one," she said to them, then disappeared.

The rest of them followed her footsteps through the portal. They emerged on the hillside near the temple Berty saw Silvia enter. Grier brought them down the hill to the town. As they navigated the narrow streets, Mabe said to one of her crew, "Gather the girls. We leave now."

Within minutes, they entered the tunnel carved through the cliff. The horses whinnied complaints. On the pier, Berty noticed the crew readying the ship for sail. Mabe barked orders while they walked to the docked Nereida.

Crewmembers stabled the horses in the hold. The Pixies stared at the open water while the crew disembarked. Silvia nodded to Mabe before the strong wind caught the sails. One of the Pixies emptied a bottle overboard.

"What was that?" asked Silvia.

"Gift for the Water Sprites," the Pixie answered. "If we're lucky, they'll help us reach the mainland faster."

"It also might appease them," said Grier. "We're not allowed to cross in a Pixie vessel, but we never crossed in another."

Clear skies mocked rough seas. Jon had Hope and Obie clutch ropes tied to the central mast. Crew tangled themselves to the ship.

The rest grabbed onto whatever stationary object was closest to them.

The ship rocked. Berty was glad for the small breakfast. Waves crashed against the hull, spraying everything with a salty mist. Higher waves reached for the deck and sails. Water covered the white wood. Puddles gathered into forms. Silver fish like creatures morphed into people with very light blue-silver skin. The androgynous watery people threatened the crew with long, barbed spears. The one in the middle of the ship spoke in the ancient tongue. "Pixies do not cross." They stepped closer to the Pixies, pointing their spears. "Get off or turn the ship around or everyone sinks to the bottom of the sea."

"We only leave Pixisle to fight the Hobbamok," said Grier.

The one speaking titled its head. "Are you sure?" it asked.

"Yes. It threatens the Empire," Grier answered.

The water people waited in silence as if they listened to the sea. Finally, the spears raised to resting positions. "You five may pass," it said. "Reinforcements must be announced. All who cross the sea must return. Death will be noted." Their lower halves fused into tails. A wave swept them into the sea.

When the seas calmed, Jon asked, "Were those mermaids?"

"Water Sprites," answered Silvia.

"I think I may have had my fill of boats," said Jon.

Berty silently agreed with his brother. While the Nereida sliced through the water, he escaped below deck to see if there was anything hot to drink that was not mulled mead. A strong tea filled a mug around which he hugged his gloved hands. He sat in a chair against the wall until someone spotted land. Most of the ship had come through and, at some point, Jon joined him.

The Chase brothers returned topside as the ship pulled into port. Only the lights of the harbor greeted the Nereida. The rest of Tren's lights darkened hours prior to their arrival. "The gates don't open until dawn," said Mabe. "You're welcome to stay aboard to sleep."

"That is very kind, Captain," said Grier. "But per our agreement with the Water Sprites, we must disembark once the ship has moored. We wish not to test them after they have granted our passage on another's ship."

While the crew secured the ship in the dock, they collected their belongings from the cabin. Before the gangplank touched the pier, Mabe called, "Declan." She held a hand out to shake. He stared at it. "I still owe you for saving my life," she said. "We should end the animosity. Maybe now you'll trust me a little."

"Maybe," said Declan. He shook her hand—briefly.

"Captain," Silvia said, saving Declan. "Your lids." She pressed coins into Mabe's hand.

The Pixies waited for their horses on the pier while the rest of them crossed the gangplank. Stopping, Silvia touched her wand to the white gangplank. The white melted, revealing the sun and sea washed wood. Silvia and Mabe locked gazes before Silvia turned to walk at Berty's side into Tren.

"Shall I find us rooms?" asked Declan.

Grier looked at the half moon high in the night sky. "It's bright enough. I'd rather we press on. Being on that ship has given enough rest. We should move quickly if we want to defeat...," she said without finishing her sentence.

"I thought they kept the gates closed because of Gnome attacks," Jon said.

"Gnomes know better than to come near a Pixie," said Kirsi.

"Our horses are in the stables," said Silvia.

The Pixies walked behind them through the streets. At the stables,

Declan and Obie paid the owner and retrieved their horses. The town gatekeeper anticipated them. Before he opened the gate, he said, "Gnome attacks happen after midnight. Good luck out there."

On the outer side of the inner gate, the snow blanketed farmland screamed serenity. They mounted their horses. Snow filled depressions showed tracks from earlier in the day on the road between the gates. A snow smell lingered in the air. The promise, however, traveled east—ahead of them. Fires from the outer gate danced atop the white smothering mantle.

Two men stood near the fires, keeping warm. Lifting their heads, one said, "Gnome country until you hit the higher elevations. Even your white camouflage won't keep them from smelling you."

"You'd be better staying the night in the fields," said the other.

"We wish to leave now," said Grier.

"We can open the gate for you to leave," said the first. "Know that we cannot open it for you when the Gnomes come nor can anyone come to your aid."

"We understand the implications," said Berty.

They cranked open the gate barely enough for them to fit through on horseback. When the gate clanked shut behind them, Jon said, "I don't think we understand the implications."

Grier dangled a turquoise pendant from her hand. "This way," she said. She led them through the moon glistening night. Atop a snowy knoll, she stopped, watching the pendant swing. "I can't get a reading," she muttered.

"What are you looking for?" asked Declan.

"This place gives me the creeps," mumbled Jon. "Hope, Obie, come closer," he called.

"Haven't you ever seen a portal key?" asked Aloysia.

"We haven't used them for centuries," said Silvia. Aloysia nodded. "Millennia actually, but who's counting?" she added.

"This one finds and opens the portal to Sage Wood," Aloysia explained. "Grier is listening to it."

"I don't understand," Grier said more to herself than the others.

"Gnomes!" Hope screamed.

Dark blights swarmed on the white blanket.

"Fighters," rallied Verena. The Pixies, except Grier, formed a line between them and the Gnomes. The four women drew arrows. "Fire!"

Their arrows pierced the swarm. Berty could see the magic in the arrows try to reach each other, but the dark dots devoured the magic. A few of them popped with magic.

"Hope!" Jon cried. She rode her horse to the Pixie line, then fired her own arrow. Shapes splattered against a shimmering pearlescent wall.

"Fairy Dust," Hope said to the Pixies. "It won't hold them long." The women and Declan tipped their arrows into Hope's velvet bag.

Six dusted arrows paused the onslaught. "Ride," ordered Zelda, "and don't get bit."

"I don't know which way," said Grier. "The Gnomes must be blocking it."

Declan touched his wand to the turquoise. It pointed. "Hurry," he said.

They galloped over the frozen fields. "They're coming," said Hope.

Obie rolled red spheres across the snow. Long, stiletto like teeth sank into the spheres. Obie gasped. One of the Pixies swore. Gnomes who nibbled on the magic exploded with a satisfying pop.

"There's too many," said Obie. "And they have to eat my magic first."

Dragonfire erupted from Berty's palm. Snow melted. The front line of Gnomes ate the fire. Those Gnomes incinerated. Gnomes behind them pushed forward. Stunned, Berty pulled the glove back over his hand.

Claw like hands dug into the snow. Pointed heads reflected the moonlight that dared to peek through the increasing clouds. They pounced from their all fours running crouch with their red beady eyes latched onto the horses' hindquarters. "No!" screamed Jon. He swiped his arm instinctually. Gnomes bowled into each other.

"There," pointed Grier. Berty saw a blue disc shimmer to life. "Can you see it?"

"Yes," said both Berty and Declan.

"Go," she screamed. "I'll be right behind you." She and two other Pixies brandished long blades.

Hope launched two arrows before following Declan and Obie through the portal. A Pixie rode through with Jon and Silvia. The ugliest creatures Berty had ever seen since *Gremlins* clawed at the Fairy Dust barricade. He raced across the portal. The Pixies galloped through. Once Grier crossed, the blue disc disappeared.

"Did it get you, Aloysia?" Kirsi asked.

"No, just scratched my boot," said Aloysia.

"We should camp for the night," said Declan. He looked at Hope.

Hope's head titled as she watched Silvia clutch her wand. Straightening, she said, "Protected clearing over there." She led with Declan riding beside her. If the Pixies thought that following a child peculiar, they did not let it show. After finding the secluded campsite, they lit a fire and erected tents.

Digging into a bowl of warming stew, Jon said, "I'll never look at those little statues the same way again."

"They've never attacked like that," said Kirsi.

Zelda nodded. "Too organized."

"They feared nothing," said Aloysia.

"It's been three hundred years since we've been on the mainland," said Verena. "Things change."

"No," said Grier. "They've been influenced by magic. It confused the portal key. Fairyland must be freed."

"You believe it to be connected?" asked Silvia.

"When the sand came, it only took the women. Those of us who were warded froze in time," Grier explained. "Our husbands, brothers, and sons either fled the island or perished at the hands of their loved ones." She looked into the dark woods for a moment. "We knew the years passed, though those affected didn't. We couldn't stop it. We *were* warned. The Mother Wood Sprite warned us before she went into hibernation. She should awaken in the spring."

Hope smiled into her bowl.

"How did the Priestess—Merja—deliver her prophecies if she's been imprisoned for centuries?" asked Silvia.

"She was bound, then taken to the mainland by people who were not Sini. The prophecies were real although everything else was a scam," said Grier.

Nodding, Silvia said, "Let's get some sleep before morning comes."

Morning arrived with Berty still feeling the night's exhaustion. Mounting their horses, they rode in the direction of the Sages' Grove. Snow and darkness fell by the time they stopped for a hot meal. "I estimate a few more hours of riding at a brisk pace," said Declan.

"Then we should continue after we've rested," said Silvia. "But I don't want to push the horses too much in this cold."

"Berty," whispered Jon, "what happened with the Gnomes?"

"What do you mean?" he asked his brother.

"Who pushed them away?" Jon asked.

"Not I," said Berty. "Must have been you."

"Are you sure it wasn't Silvia?"

Berty shook his head. "Her magic is still recovering from the boat."

He did not think Jon heard him until Jon said, "What about one of the Pixies?"

"Jon—"

"I can't, Berty. I can't," he said. "You have it. I... I wear glasses."

Berty laughed until he realized all heads turned to look. "Jon," he said in a low voice, "what does wearing glasses have to do with anything?"

"If I can do magic, why do I need glasses to see?" Jon asked. He leaned over to speak in Berty's ear. "What am I?"

Berty had no magical answer for him. Finally, he said, "You're my brother. That's all that matters."

When they extinguished the fire and straddled the saddles, Berty did not feel rested. A few more hours, he told himself. A few more hours of riding in the cold, wet snow with the harsh winter wind stinging his face. A few more hours before he could curl up with his wife in their warm, soft bed.

Chapter Nineteen

March

Jon rode close to Hope, distracted. His horse simply followed the others. Obie rode next to Hope, as always, but he kept an eye on Jon as well.

A white cloaked shape slipped off a white horse onto the white forest floor. Berty turned his horse. "Aloysia!" Kirsi yelled.

Declan raced to the fallen Pixie. Verena already pulled off Aloysia's boot when Declan crouched next to her. "She's burning up," he said.

"Gnome bite," said Verena. She looked to Grier.

"There's magic in the wound," said Grier, peering at the foot. "A Wizard lives in a hamlet nearby. Closer than the Sages' Grove."

Shaking his head, Declan said, "That hamlet is nothing but ruins now. Allow me?" Both Grier and Verena nodded.

Obie brought Declan's healer's bag without being asked. Plunking a jar in Obie's hand, Declan said, "Warm some and spread a thin layer on a bandage to cover this." Obie held the jar in both hands. What looked like solidified honey melted. Declan held his wand near the wound. The colors near the bite marks made Berty avert his eyes.

"Your wand is sucking out the magic," said Grier.

"Yes. And the Ogreflower honey should start fighting the infection until we can get her to the future Witch of Rowan," said Declan.

After Declan bandaged the wound, Verena laced Aloysia's boot. The inured Pixie groaned. "Up you get," said Verena. Declan helped the two Pixies drape the third over the saddle.

"I ride," mumbled Aloysia as Verena strapped her to the horse.

"Not fast enough to get you help. Stop being stubborn," said Verena.

Two of the Pixies sandwiched Aloysia as they continued riding. The snow lightened the dark forest. With their white cloaks and horses, they blended with the falling snow.

Tiny flakes stung Berty's eyes. He could no longer feel the reins through his gloves. Eventually, someone had the sense to stop. They lit a sheltered fire under pines. Wrapped in a blanket, Aloysia shuttered next to the fire. Declan checked her foot. "Get warm. We still have a ways to go," he said.

"How are you doing?" Berty asked Silvia.

"Exhausted and cold," she said. He wrapped his arm around her, pulling her into his warmth.

When it was time to ride again, he hated relinquishing her. She gave him a look that promised later.

Aloysia attempted riding upright. Verena and Kirsi agreed to stay with her if she lagged behind.

Riding began to wear on Berty's derriere, if he could feel it. The three Pixies fell back. With a flourish of his hand, Berty send a wisp of magic for them to follow in case they lost their trail.

When they reached the wall of the Sages' Grove, the three Pixies could not be seen. Declan said something to Obie and the gatekeeper. "I'm going back for them," he told Berty and Silvia. "Obie's bringing Alina to the Tree. See you soon."

They rode to the double doors while Declan rode back the way they came. Someone took their horses while they entered the Empire Tree.

The Light of Life Tree shone in its red, blue, and gold decorations. Hope breathed a, "Wow," as Silvia spoke with Theodore. When Obie emerged from the floor below with Alina, both stared at the mighty fir in the center of the room.

"They're probably a half hour behind us," said Silvia. "A Tender will show you to your chambers. Warm up while you wait for them."

"Most gracious, Empress," said Grier with a bow of her head. The two Pixies followed a waiting Tender.

"Did Obie tell you about the Gnome bite, Alina?" asked Silvia.

The girl nodded.

Silvia turned to Jon. "Why don't you let Teresa know you have returned. Freesia will be here soon." Tenders poured warm drinks. As soon as Freesia could be seen on the steps, Jon walked onto the bridge, mug in hand.

Berty sat in a chair, warming his hands around ceramic. After a few sips, the kids used their energy to run around the fir. "I used to sneak in here as a child to look at the decorations at night," said Silvia. "Always found peace in the magical glow." She chuckled. "My Fairy Godmother must have known although she never said anything."

"Because she knew it was important," said Freesia. Her eyes watched the kids play.

Berty watched them, too. "Where do they get the energy?"

"They'll sleep as soon as they walk through the door," said Freesia. "I have beds for all three of them ready in Hope's playroom." The kids sat on the floor between the dais and the tree, mesmerized by the golden glow.

"Just a few more steps," Declan's voice said. Alina sat straight, then ran over to the table.

The Pixies sat Aloysia in a chair with her leg stretched on another. While they removed her boot, Alina opened a book on the table. Kirsi glanced at the child studying her book.

Alina examined the bite. Her nose wrinkled. After consulting her book, she said, "The bite's infected. The Ogreflower honey has helped some." She spoke to a Tender. "We'll apply a new dressing after you wash the foot and leg."

Declan spooned a little of his honey into the bowl Alina gave him. She added items from bottles she pulled from her bag. Stirring it over low coals, she spoke an incantation that sounded like a song. Berty saw a flash of magic swirl into the bowl.

She dabbed the contents of the bowl on the clean wound. Aloysia grimaced. "We'll reapply in a few hours," Alina said. "Sleep sitting up." Another incantation passed through her lips while she bandaged the foot and leg.

Declan sat the swaying Alina on a chair. He repacked her bag while Kirsi and Verena helped Aloysia to her feet. Freesia scooped the little Witch-in-training off the chair, then told Hope and Obie to grab her things. The Fairy brought all three kids upstairs.

The Pixies followed a Tender to the chambers where the others waited. Dropping into a chair, Declan sipped from a steaming mug poured for him. "No matter how well she grounds, her Witch magic is too strong for her to use like that. She's going to be some Witch," he said. He leaned against the back of his chair and closed his eyes.

"We're going to bed," Berty told him as he and Silvia rose.

"Yeah. Me too," muttered Declan without opening his eyes.

Berty trudged up the steps of their private staircase behind Silvia. "Did you know about the portal?" he asked her. "Would have taken us almost another week to get back."

Spinning, she gave him a wry smile. "I had an inkling. Not necessarily about portals, but of someway they travel across the land more quickly than the rest of us."

When they reached their chambers, their warm bed welcomed them.

An uncommon emptiness filled the Reception Room in the morning. Only Edwin, Estelle, Delyth, and Teresa joined the four of them at breakfast. The Pixies had yet to arrive.

"Captain Alvar had to leave," said Edwin. "The King and Queen of the Fairies march with him." The Elf stopped talking when Grier and the other Pixies entered from the bridge.

"We apologize for our tardiness," said Grier with a bow of her head. Aloysia limped to a seat while the others got her food.

"No need to apologize," Silvia said. "Aloysia, how are you feeling?"

"I will only lose a few days to the injury," Aloysia answered. "The Witchling has tended to the bite well. Only some minor discomfort as it heals. Thank you for your concern, my Lady."

Lark sat next to her husband, then said something in his ear.

Silvia introduced the Pixies to those who remained in the Tree. "Many of our number march on Fairyland," she said.

"When will we, Empress?" asked Grier.

"We need to consult our Lieutenant and our Astrologer before we make any decisions," said Silvia.

After breakfast, Berty had Edwin meet with them and the Advisory Council in the Roundtable Room. "We have successfully cut off their supply lines," Edwin reported. "They are trying to find us. According to the Watchers, the Whispers can't see us. They will start to send people out soon. Or creatures. The Dragons are keeping up their end of the bargain. The flood from God Mountain has been reduced to a trickle. Initial reports indicate a lot of magic harbored within Fairyland. Scores of Fairies have been found slaughtered before they could reach protection." Delyth's jaw shuddered, but she said nothing. "The Troll forces should be joining the Captain soon."

"Where is Hatcher?" asked Berty. "And Colvin?"

"Colvin has not yet returned from Grunnan," answered Edwin. "Hatcher took the early shift at the gates."

"Estelle, when is the best time for us to leave for Fairyland?" Silvia asked.

"I shall have a more precise answer later this evening," said Estelle.

With a nod, Silvia said, "Declan, Delyth, Edwin, be ready to go. Obie must be ready as well. Defenses are ready?"

"Yes. Besides Obie and me, no other Empire Guards will be leaving. Hatcher has a lock down plan in place and regulars already have gate passes. Anyone coming in or out must have the proper pass or subject to a search."

Berty's stomach turned at the thought.

"Problem, my Lord?" asked Edwin.

He had to have cringed. "I suppose there is no other way," he said. "Are we well stocked?"

"We are. We can survive a siege without issue," said Edwin. "Lark will be sending a bird at least once a day. She is also keeping abreast of the situation in Calledin."

"What is happening there?" asked Silvia.

"They stormed Calledin Castle last night. More news to come," he said.

"Delyth?" said Silvia.

"I am ready," said the Fairy. "My ribs have healed nicely."

"Good," Silvia said. "If that is all, we will rest." While chairs scraped against the wood, she said to Berty, "I will speak with the Pixies. See what your brother and his family wish to do."

Berty brought Jon and Teresa to his chambers. "Silvia's two week estimate was right on," said Jon. "Hope has two days before school starts again."

"We could leave for Fairyland at any time," said Berty. "We'll know more tonight."

"We?" said Teresa.

"Me, Silvia, Declan, Delyth, Edwin, and Obie."

"Obie too? He's just a boy," Teresa said.

Berty's palms rubbed his knees. "He's a Warlock. The only one on our side. He'll only be used if need be. He'll be in the command tent with us mostly."

"Will you fight?" asked Jon.

"I'll try to keep it to magic only," said Berty.

"Berty, you're a…," Jon said.

"A writer, not a fighter?" finished Berty. "Yeah, I thought that once. Pen is mightier and all that. The sword has its place." He glanced from his brother to his sister-in-law. "So does Dragonfire."

"It does," said Jon. "Um… Do I bring the sword home with me? Should I leave it here?"

"You bring it home," Teresa said before Berty could. "I have to come back at regular intervals to see the midwife. Ask Edwin to have you train with someone when you come with me."

"What about the, uh, the other thing?" Jon asked, pushing his glasses further up his nose.

"Practice your magic, Jon," said Berty. "Would you like some books left in Hope's chambers for you to read?"

"Ah…"

"Yes," said Teresa. "He's been researching on the internet." She rolled her eyes.

"We'll stay until Hope has to go to school," said Jon.

Berty nodded. "The training room is open to use. Just crank a dummy into the training circle. No magic."

"Thanks."

After Jon and Teresa left, Berty wandered to his desk. He had run out of notebook in which to write *The Adventures of Leigh and Marcus*. Stacking a pile of paper in front of him, he penned a few more chapters.

"Colvin's back," Silvia said as she entered their study. "Grunnan's Battalion with other Dwarves wanting to fight are heading to Fairyland using the tunnels."

"Good," he said. He placed his pen on his writing. "What books would be good to leave for Jon to help him understand magic?"

"None," she said in a flat voice. "Hope has most of the basic ones in her study already. I'll augment. In her chambers?"

Berty nodded.

After lunch, Berty helped Silvia choose and carry books to Hope's chambers. Theodore waited for them on the platform when they emerged. He bowed. "Alfred has returned with an Elf army," he said.

They descended to the Reception Room where Edwin and the Advisory Council waited. The Pixies and Berty's family watched from the side.

Alfred led Wystan, the Dominatrix, and Katell to the dais steps where Berty and Silvia stood. White cloaked the four Elves.

"Alfred, welcome home," said Silvia.

"Thank you, Empress, Emperor," said Alfred. "I have arrived safely with the Warriors of Irmingard, the Dominatrix, and her protégé." He stepped to the side.

A handful of white cloaked Warriors stood in the back of the room, watching their Commander approach Berty and Silvia. "Emperor, Empress," said Wystan with a bow, "on behalf of High Elf Avery, Low Elf Kael, the Ørgranden, and the people of Irmingard, I command the Warriors of Irmingard to war against the Enemies of the Empire. We are, in coordination with our Empire brethren, marching to Fairyland. We respectfully request a respite in the Sages' Grove before we continue on our journey north."

"We would be honored to have you and the Warriors rest in the Sages' Grove, Commander," said Berty. "Captain Alvar has already left for Fairyland. Lieutenant Edwin has charge of the Empire Guard in the Sages' Grove. You and your men must confer with the Lieutenant."

"There is room in the barracks," said Edwin. "Allow the Empire Guard to extend our hospitality to the Irmingard Warriors."

"Thank you, Lieutenant," said Wystan. The brothers' eyes smiled at each other. They enjoyed the formal show for the men.

Wystan stepped closer to his men. The Dominatrix and Katell came forward. "My Lord and Lady," the older Elf bowed, revealing white leather armor beneath her cloak, "our intentions follow with Irmingard and its Warriors. I request that you grant me a final stay before my final battle and the next Dominatrix her first."

"Your request is granted," said Silvia.

"Thank you, Empress, Emperor," said the Dominatrix.

Berty and Silvia stepped into the room properly. "We'll have Tenders make up rooms for you both," Silvia told the Elf women.

"Rooms?" said Katell. She immediately bowed her head in reverence. "I'll get our things."

"These old bones thank you," the Dominatrix said, placing her hand on Silvia's.

Edwin and Wystan descended the steps. All but two white cloaked Warriors followed them. Studying the Elves, Berty noticed they did not don the Warrior's metal armor. They wore a mixture of white leather and chainmail.

"Ah," said Alfred, standing next to Berty. "Avery and Vidor send me Blóvǫr for my personal protection."

"After Edwin gets the Warriors situated, speak to him about their placement," said Berty.

"Nice to see that your brother and his family came for Yule," said Alfred.

"Not exactly," said Berty. "After you get settled, I believe we will be calling a meeting."

By the time they could call a meeting, Tenders began to serve dinner. Wystan joined them in the Reception Room to eat. Breaking with formality, Wystan hugged his sister-in-law whom he met for the first time. Estelle left dinner early to consult the stars. After, Berty and Silvia invited the Pixies, Wystan, the Dominatrix, and Katell to join the Advisory Council and Edwin at the Roundtable.

The newcomers gawked at the round room about which many of them only heard. "Thank you for coming," said Silvia. They took the cue to sit. "Estelle will be with us soon with her reading." Chairs in place, all eyes found her. "As some of you know, the Emperor and I traveled to Pixisle for help with the Whispers. The Pixie squad, led by Grier, has the arduous task of finding and neutralizing the Whisperer or Whisperers. The Whisperer somehow controls the Whispers. I expect a Whisperer to be well protected and have access to the outside."

"Captain Alvar has a map of Fairyland drawn by King Elrick, Queen Lida, and Princess Delyth," said Berty. "The map will be available for consultation. They will use magic against us."

"And we will use magic against them," said the Dominatrix. "Every magical item in our stores has been assigned to a Warrior. I expect Vindalf and legendary creatures and those known only to us through myth and lore. We have taken no chances."

"Nor have we," said Silvia. "The Dragons fight with us. One of whom can cross the border."

"How many Giants do we have on our side?" asked Grier.

"None," said Silvia. "Besides the Frost Giants, who tried to kill us, *we* don't know where they are."

"Then we have a lot of magic users," said Grier.

"We won't need an army of magic users," said Estelle from the doorway. She sat in her chair. "The Elves will leave on schedule. We leave the day after—after midday. We will come across that which will turn the tide in our favor."

"We?" asked Delyth.

"Not I," said Estelle. "The Pixies will travel with us."

"Thank you, Estelle," said Silvia. She looked at Wystan.

"Our plans are to move out tomorrow," said Wystan, answering her unasked question. "We are a large force. I wished to speak with the Lieutenant about our best path forward from here."

"We should also consult with Princess Delyth," said Edwin.

"And we should take two separate ways to Fairyland," Delyth suggested. "Both avoiding the road."

"Map it out tonight," said Berty. "Be prepared for anything in Fairyland and on the way to Fairyland."

"They have Watchers," Declan added. "Keep magic to a minimum."

"I thought Watchers could only see magic in constant use," said Katell.

"Assume everything you knew about magic is wrong," said Declan. "We have discovered many magical half-truths and untruths. Be careful."

Berty and Silvia ended the meeting. On the way out, the Dominatrix said, "Princess, I have old maps of Fairyland that date back to when our people warred. Will you look at them with me?"

"Yes, of course," said Delyth.

"I want to try something," Berty said in Silvia's ear. He gave her a kiss on the cheek, then ran downstairs. "Jon," he said, waving his brother over to follow.

"I know this look, Berty. Do I have to?"

"I have an idea."

"That's what I'm afraid of."

"Declan, wait," called Berty. The brothers accompanied Declan and Obie.

When they entered into the box behind the one Sages' Seal in the back of the Receiving Room, Jon asked, "What's this?"

"Magical elevator," said Berty.

They dropped into the roots of the Tree. "I don't like your ideas,

Berty," said Jon. "Just for the record."

"Don't tell me you left your sense of adventure in Pixisle?" said Berty.

When the door opened, Jon adjusted his glasses. They followed Declan to the cavern where they practiced magic. "So, does this idea involve magic perchance?" asked Jon.

"Why, yes, yes, it does."

"Great."

He walked backward a few steps to look at Jon. "Well, me using magic. You can think about it." For some reason Jon did not look nearly as excited as Berty felt about his idea. He explained to the three of them, "I battled a Warlock once. I deflected his spheres, but his stream... We were at a stalemate until Delyth dusted him from above. When I use magic in battle, I merely push people out of the way." Jon's head raised. "Is it enough? Only me, Silvia, and Obie can use magic combatantly."

"You also have Dragonfire," said Declan.

"I can't use it within the city. Burning down Fairyland would be bad," said Berty. "I would like to watch Obie work and perhaps practice a little."

"Okay, Uncle Berty," said Obie.

Obie threw a dozen small blue spheres of light into the cavern. Then, he crafted a yellow disc as wide as his body. Out of his left hand, a stream of green magic hurled at Declan. Declan's wand deflected it back. The yellow disc acted as a shield, absorbing the magic. With each round, the yellow disc moved to shield Obie from the magic.

"Does it absorb the magic because the magic is yours to begin with?" asked Berty.

"I don't know," said Obie. "We haven't been able to use anyone else's magic to try. But I do know that I can't attack—magically or physically—if the shield is completely around me."

"It does protect him from both types of attack," said Declan.

"Can I try shooting magic at you?" said Berty.

Obie nodded.

Berty mimicked Obie's stance. Nothing erupted from his palm. He thought about something magical escaping. Dragonfire burst out of his palm. He promptly stopped. Obie's shield diffused the Dragonfire before it burnt out to nothing. "Sorry," said Berty.

"Good to know," said Declan.

"Maybe I can't shoot anything other than Dragonfire," said Berty. After motioning for them to continue, he leaned against the wall, watching Obie form his magic.

"Trying to figure out how he does it?" asked Jon, leaning next to him.

"Maybe I shouldn't use my hands," said Berty. "Silvia just thinks and magic happens."

"Yeah, but Silvia has the advantage of practicing her magic since she was a girl. You've had a year, at most," said Jon.

He ran his hand through his dark hair. "I know." His eyes followed the magic moving between Obie and Declan. "What if I'm sending them to their deaths?" he said barely above a whisper.

"You're not alone, Berty," said Jon. "Silvia is with you. Besides, you've got Dragons on your side."

Berty clapped Jon on the shoulder. "We leave the day after tomorrow."

"Are you scared?" Jon asked.

"Fear... I...." Words did not want to form in Berty's mouth.

Jon's brown eyes stared at him through his glasses. "Some things you need to fight. When it threatens your life, your family, your home, fear cannot be a factor. Am I afraid? Yes, but our lives depend on it." He gazed out at Declan and Obie. "Their lives. You face it or you die trying, because this fight is worth fighting." He pushed off the cavern wall to stand. "Good talk, Jon. Thanks."

"What *are* brothers for?" Jon said.

The brothers rode the magical elevator back to the Receiving Room while Declan and Obie practiced. "How would you have gotten down there if the magic stopped working?" asked Jon.

"Much more slowly," Berty answered. "How's the midwife?"

"She's nice and knowledgeable," said Jon. "Better than all those books Teresa and I read when she was pregnant with Hope. She's really put Teresa at ease, especially with all the problems in the past. Wish we had her around the first time. We were so scared. We are thinking about bringing our moms over to talk with her."

Berty let out a little chuckle when the doors opened.

"Exactly," said Jon.

They found their wives in Hope's chambers. Silvia poured the men hot drinks as they sat at Hope's table. Hope played on the other side of the room.

"How did your idea go?" asked Silvia.

"It needs work," Berty answered.

"We'll try tomorrow," she said.

When Obie entered soon after, he received a hot mug from Teresa then plopped on one of Hope's colorful poufs. He watched Hope play while he drank. After finishing the drink, he plunked the mug on the side and joined her game.

Reaching for the pot, Berty noticed Teresa wiping her cheeks. He refilled his mug without saying anything.

When Berty and Silvia returned to their chambers, Berty wrapped his arms around his wife. He breathed, "I love you," into her ear, then kissed her. Her arms pulled him closer as the lanterns magically extinguished in their bedroom.

After breakfast, the Elves finished packing their partial camp around the barracks. Berty and Silvia accompanied the current and future Dominatrices into the Sages' Grove. Delyth and Declan stood with them, bidding the Elves farewell, while the rest watched from the balcony. Edwin and Noll stood in rank by the barracks. Elves on horseback and carts of supplies rode through the gates.

Berty tried not to think about that he would leave the next day to face the same fate. Once the Sages' Grove felt empty again, Edwin brought Lieutenant Noll into the Empire Tree to consult with Berty and Silvia.

The Elf entered the Roundtable Room for the first time. His back stayed straighter than the chair in which he sat. "Lieutenant Noll," said Berty, "the final handful of us leaves tomorrow. The protective magic surrounding the Sages' Grove will not wane. We are counting on you and your defensive forces to keep the Sages' Grove, the Empire Tree, and the Scepter safe. Expect tests of our defenses. We know you will not show weakness and defend with honor."

"Four members of the Advisory Council are available to you," said Silvia. "Emergency messages can be sent via the Fairy Godmother, Freesia." Surprise shown on Noll's face before he contained it. "Or via the Emperor's brother, Jon, if he is here. Only the four of us know this information outside of Freesia and Jon."

Noll nodded sharply.

"We must prepare. Good luck, Lieutenant," Silvia dismissed.

"Good luck to you, Empress, Emperor," said Noll. He stood, then gave them a full bow before leaving.

They called Jon and Freesia into the room. After telling them about the messages, Jon wrote a number on a piece of paper. "My new cell number," he said, giving the paper to the Fairy. "Anytime day or night." He looked at Berty. "I will have to tell Teresa."

"On the other side of the portal," said Silvia.

"If she asks," Berty added, "tell her we were discussing evacuation procedures into the house."

Jon nodded.

"Freesia," said Berty, "you are the only one who can cross the portal into the house. Only you can bring everyone through. We have instructed the Rowans to retreat to the Tree if need be. If you must evacuate, call Jon or George."

"Yes, my Lord." Freesia took a deep breath.

Next, they discussed the evacuation plan with the Advisory Council. "How many do we evacuate?" asked Colvin.

"As many as possible through the tunnels," said Silva. "The Rowans and the rest of you through the portal to the house."

"I will go with Colvin in the tunnels," said Hatcher.

"Very well," said Silvia. "Alfred, your guard may accompany you."

Silvia had Jon, Teresa, and Hope join her, Declan, Obie, and Berty in the training cavern. Once Obie released spheres of light, she had Berty do the same. "Jon?" she urged.

"What?" asked Jon.

"Light. Add your spheres."

"I don't know how," he said.

"Sure you do," said Silvia. "Doing magic is less about your ability than your acceptance of that ability. What is magic other than the manipulation of energy? What else do you know that manipulates energy?"

"Science," Jon almost whispered.

"Precisely. You know *how* to do magic. You just need to believe that you can," said Silvia.

Jon swallowed.

She stood in the center. "Obie," she said. He sent a sphere flying towards her. It stopped halfway between them. "Another," she said. That sphere froze in midair as well. "Stream," she ordered. A blue stream of magic erupted from his palms. The stream wound around her like a python. Then, shattered, falling to her feet.

Declan watched Silvia walk to Berty's side. "Feel the connection between your feet and the dirt," she said. "Be a conduit, Obie, and you won't feel as tired. Working magic will wear you out, but less so if you're grounded."

Her words, while directed at Obie, were meant for all of them. Berty mulled while Jon closed his eyes. Declan's wand rearranged the magic in the room. The light spheres spun, creating a disco ball effect. Darkness filled the cavern. "Sorry," said Declan. After a second, he continued, "Ah, I don't know how to put it back."

Berty laughed, then released a sphere of light. Then another floated in the cavern. Jon watched it with a surprised smile on his face. Rubbing Jon's arm, Teresa sat on a nearby rock.

Obie spread his hands apart, creating his shield. The glimmering yellow stretched around him, leaving slits for his arms. He practiced throwing his arms out of the slits. He sucked the shield closer to his body. His hands stayed outside as if he wore a cloak with sleeves. He pulled them inside the sleeves, then pushed them back out, releasing a few spheres.

"He needs his hands to work magic," Silvia said to Berty. "You don't."

"But using my hands increases things," said Berty.

"Yes, sometimes it helps," she conceded.

Berty faced a wall opposite him. As if he were bowling, he threw magic from his hand. A spurt of Dragonfire scorched the wall.

"Hmmm," said Silvia. She imitated Berty. A sphere rolled to the wall.

Jon tried the same thing. A weak something or other traveled a few feet before fizzling. "Cool," he said.

"Very good, Jon," said Silvia. "I think the Dragonfire overrides other magic," she said to Berty.

Berty stared at his upturned palms. "You might be right."

"It was a good idea having them think you were a Warlock," she said.

"Are there any female Warlocks?" he asked.

"I've never heard of any, but that doesn't mean girls aren't born with Warlock magic," she answered. "Enchantresses usually have different magic. No Enchantress births have been recorded in over one hundred fifty years." She addressed Teresa. "Your daughter may be the first in generations."

Instead of practicing his own magic, Berty watched the others. Even Hope used ancient Fairy magic. Berty sat on the rock next to Teresa. "How are you doing?" he asked.

"I wish you didn't have to go," she said. "But... You have to make it a safer world for Hope, for Lily, for Obie, for your children when they come. Being Emperor isn't much different than being a parent I don't think. Tons of responsibly and hard choices to make. You can only hope you make the right ones." She stared into the cavern. "You better come home in one piece, Berty Chase. I don't know what Jon would do without you."

When Teresa looked at him, he had to smile. "Don't worry about me," he said.

After a quiet dinner, they began packing although they had an afternoon departure. Unsure of the length of their campaign, he packed whatever his wardrobe offered. Silvia did the same. With their bags in the study, Berty asked her, "Do you think we will be there long?"

Her fingers rested on his lips. "Let's not think of that right now," she said. "Hold me, Berty."

His arms found her back and waist. Lips met. They wandered back upstairs.

He awoke entangled in Silvia. He did not want to let her go, not yet. They would ride to war... later. Berty wanted to hold on to the moment, to last night, to... softness, to love, to what was good and right in the world. His limbs wound around Silvia more tightly. His lips found her forehead. Her head tilted. Her lips found his.

During breakfast in their chambers, the wind chimes rang. Edwin entered, saying, "I have news of the cart vendor that sold Robert the flask." Berty had Edwin sit at the table. "The man met with no one. We think he was simply a tool—a means to an end. Should we continue to monitor him?"

"No. They would never try the same thing twice," said Berty.

"Have those Guards come home," said Silvia.

"Yes," said Edwin. "The horses will be ready to go when we are."

"If everything is in place, Edwin, you can spend some extra time with Lark," Berty said.

With a nod of his head, the Elf left.

They spent the rest of their morning with Jon and Teresa. Finally,

Estelle announced that they must depart. Jon, Teresa, and Hope met them in the Reception Room.

Hedda waited for them in a plain guard's uniform. She bowed low to Berty and Silvia. Her battle braids did not move. The Captain's wife became an Empire Guard. Berty figured many of the spouses did to add to the defensive numbers. Tenders carried bags to the horses while they secured their white cloaks.

Hope started the hugging when she hugged Berty. She knew where they were going and why. Children understood—too much than Berty wished. She moved down the line, hugging even Edwin, to his surprise. Both Jon and Teresa hugged Berty. Estelle hugged Silvia like old friends. After Silvia, Teresa gave Delyth a hug and admired her intricate battle braids that almost matched Hedda's. Teresa also hugged Obie as if he were her own son going to face the unknown atrocities of war. Letting him go, she turned her head. Berty saw her hand reach her face.

They raised their hoods before following Hedda to the horses. The Pixies mounted first. Berty's heart thumped as his feet shifted in the stirrups.

Chapter Twenty

Pure of Soul

Delyth held her braided head high as she led them and three packhorses out of the Sages' Grove. Once the treed wall disappeared from view, Edwin rode next to the Fairy. "This isn't the way you indicated the other night," he said.

"No." She looked at the Elf. "I trust Wystan, but not the rest of them. I chose an alternate route."

Edwin fell back to let her lead. Before the sun set, she brought them to a campsite. Edwin and a Pixie unpacked tents off the horses. Mid unbuckle, both drew weapons at something Berty could not see.

"Golden Blade Flame Sword or whatever it's called," said a male voice. "Lieutenant Edwin, I presume."

Recognizing the voice, Berty looked at Declan. Declan made a face and shook his head. "Estelle did *not* mean him," Declan grumbled.

"State your business, *Sean*," said Edwin, not lowering his blade.

"I was hoping you'd have some food," Sean's voice said. "I've been fighting these gray skinned Elf things."

"Vindalf," said Edwin.

"Oh, they have a name? Well, turns out they don't do so well with the lightning," said Sean, "but it seems that I've run out of food." Edwin let him enter the campsite. Sean's gray gaze swept over everyone, then he bowed. "Emperor, how nice to see you again."

"Join us, Sean," Silvia invited.

"Thank you, Empress," he said with an extravagant bow.

Declan rolled his eyes while he walked away to help pitch the tents. Silently, he accepted help from Sean who allowed his staff to hover.

Once Delyth constructed the Fairy Dome, all of them gathered around the fire while the food cooked. "How did you start hunting Vindalf?" Edwin asked Sean.

"They attacked my village," Sean replied. "I returned from standing in the lake and being hit by lightning. Lightning still crackled between my fingers and these gray Elf things—Vindalf—leapt over the wall like it was nothing. They sliced through anyone nearby. I shot lightning at them. They incinerated so quickly like they were only empty shells of Elves. Anyway, after killing them all, my village elected me to make sure no more came for us. Been wandering awhile." He studied everyone.

"How come I don't know about the whole cloak thing? Mine turned silver with a hint of light purple if you look at it in the right light." Sean played with his cloak, showing off its sheen. When no one seemed interested in his cloak, he continued, "I came across some of those dark cloaked people. They're, uh, those cloaks are part of some sort of binding. Is that what this is?"

"No," said Silvia. "The white cloaks hide us from the view of Whispers."

"I want a white cloak," said Sean.

"Only if you agree to come with us to free Fairyland," said Berty.

"Just the," he counted, "eleven of you?"

Laughing, Declan said, "Estelle sent everyone in stages."

Sean smoothed his cloak. "If Estelle says…, then okay," he said.

While Silvia walked behind Sean, Berty and Declan exchanged glances before Declan checked on the food. Silvia's wand touched Sean's cloak. Sean watched the white wash over the silver.

While they ate, Grier asked, "Princess, does the dome attract magic diviners?"

"Yes, unlike a Fairy Ring," answered Delyth. "However, they know there's magic here, but they don't know what's inside. Also unlike a Fairy Ring, no one can enter, not even another Fairy. We'll know if anyone is out there."

The dome allowed the cold morning wind to interfere with packing the tents. Sean muttered incoherently. After making sure her saddlebags were secure, Kirsi said to him, "Do you ever have periods of silence?"

"He doesn't," said Declan.

"Sure I do," Sean argued.

"Once, maybe twice," Declan said.

"Collapsing the dome," announced Delyth. In a blur of white, she encircled the former campsite.

Snow crunched under the horses' hooves. Riding one of the supply horses, Sean barricaded his voice inside his mouth. Snow laden branches creaked over their heads. Deep in unfamiliar snowy woods, the horses stepped slowly. "This way," said a whispered voice. They stopped. "This way," it said again. "Hurry."

Edwin rode near a tree. Green eyes stared out of the trunk. "Hello again, Elf." The tree morphed into a tall female form. Her smooth brown skin radiated.

"Miradelle," said Berty.

"The Wood Listener said you'd be coming this way," said Miradelle. "I have found pure of soul. They need your help."

"Lead us," said Edwin.

Her long strides allowed the horses to keep pace as she brought them to a thick grove of pines. "In there," she said before turning into a tree.

Edwin slid off his horse. "Wait," said Zelda. "This could be a trap. The Wood Sprite is not in her proper mind."

"It's only a trap if she's not the Wood Sprite," said Edwin.

"She likes to play games, especially with Elves," Zelda cautioned.

"I know. We've met before," said Edwin. He stepped between the pines. "It's all right. I'm not going to hurt you," Edwin's voice said. "Declan," he called. Declan hurried through the pines. "I'm with the Empire Guard. You're safe now."

Edwin walked out of the grove. "Children," he said. "Mostly Fairies." He stopped Delyth from scrambling off her horse. "No, Princess. You don't want to go in there."

"Why not?" she asked. "There are Fairy children."

Shaking his head, Edwin said, "Let Declan examine them first." Declan returned for his bag, then disappeared again between the pines. "They're covered in filth with no protection from the cold besides these trees. And," the Elf looked around as if he were choosing the right words, "they're so thin. They've been out here a long time… alone."

"Maybe I can help Uncle Declan," said Obie.

"Not yet, Obie. When he calls for you."

Poking his upper body through the pine, Declan said, "Obie, boil snow. Lots of snow."

Dismounting, everyone helped Obie fill pots with snow while Berty and Silvia started two fires.

"How many children?" Silvia asked Edwin.

"I counted six," he answered.

Declan came for a pot of boiled snow, wearing a cloth over his nose and mouth. "Two have been gone awhile," he said through the cloth. "A third…." He shook his head and left.

After a few pots of snow disappeared with Declan, three young children, two boys and one girl, shuffled out of the grove with Declan's old cloak wrapped around the three of them. Their gaunt, emaciated bodies broke Berty's heart. One of the Pixies gasped. Declan followed, carrying a fourth child who looked older than the others. "Obie, make a weak honey tea," he instructed. "Each of them gets a cup." He set the girl down near the others. He wrapped his cloak around her, too.

"Are there any adults?" asked Delyth.

"No," wheezed the older child. "They killed them." She closed her sunken eyes.

Declan lifted a pot of boiled snow. Sean and Verena took the other two into the grove behind Declan. Within minutes, Sean returned and walked some distance away with his staff.

The children slurped the cups Obie gave them. Obie helped the older girl tip the cup to her mouth.

After a few moments, Sean walked back into the pines. He exited with Declan and Verena, who both carried a dead child in their arms. Shriveled periwinkle wings hung from the back of one of the children.

Berty followed Silvia and Delyth who walked to where Sean halted with his staff.

Sean stood behind two child-size graves. The others gathered with each Pixie carrying a child, wrapping him or her with her cloak. Verena lowered her child first, then Declan carefully placed the one he carried into the freshly dug hole.

Tears streaked down Delyth's face. Without wiping away her tears, Delyth stood over the graves. "*Grack gom*," she said. "*Grack gom*, little Fairy. *Grack gom*, little Human." Her voice cracked a little. "*Fro shay grack gom*. May peace find you both."

"Is this the final good-bye?" asked one of the boys.

"Yes." Kirsi put him down in the snow.

His twig like legs stumbled through the snow to Delyth's side. "Thank you for saving us, Blane and Pernilla," he said. His little wings twitched. "We will never forget you." His frail hand slid into Delyth's.

After a few moments of silence, Sean wiggled his fingers. The piled dirt filled the graves. The end of his staff touched two stones. They rose off the ground and landed atop the graves, marking them.

Delyth and the boy led them back to the fires. "These children need the Witchling," Aloysia said to Berty and Silvia.

"They'd never make it," said Declan. "If these four are going to chance at survival, they must come with us."

"We're going to war," Aloysia said.

"Yes. But they will have food and warmth," argued Declan.

"They could die," Aloysia exasperated.

"They might still," said Berty. He glanced at the children sitting next to the fire. "They are woefully malnourished. Declan is a healer. Without magic, it will take longer for them to regain strength. However, none of us can take them back to the Sages' Grove. And Miradelle, while restored, is not equipped to sustain the lives of children."

Aloysia looked from man to man. Her gaze finally fell on Silvia. When she did not refute the men, Aloysia walked away.

"They need to learn that we are equals," Silvia said. "Declan, get the children ready to travel."

Each child rode with an adult. All the Pixies agreed to take a child. The eldest, who could not walk on her own, rode with Declan. Aloysia insisted the one boy ride with her. Verena and Kirsi took the other two.

Delyth led them through the woods. Faint movements in the trees told Berty Miradelle followed. They stopped to give the children honey tea once before reaching the western flank surrounding Fairyland.

Chapter Twenty-one

White Tent City

White tents formed a small city. Fires burned inside special tents only. White cloaked men and women rushed between tents. Silvia surveyed the area from her horse. "Over here," she said. She brought them to a more sparse area. After unpacking the tents, she waved her hand. Five tents pitched themselves. "Grier, Delyth, Edwin, come with us," she said. "We'll meet the rest of you back in the central tent."

The five of them walked through the tent city. They found a tent where a fire flickered inside. Voices raised. Berty ducked though the flap first. A head glanced at them over the fire. "Go away, we're in conference." Berty stared at the broad shouldered man whose white cloak had been cast aside. The others around the fire wore theirs. "Someone will give you an order later," he said. His tone carried resentment.

"We were told to work together," said another. "What about that can't you get through that thick skull of yours?"

"Fat chance of that with this stubborn—" the man stopped mid-sentence when he noticed Silvia and Delyth.

"These people are villagers. They need one leader not a council," said the cloakless man. "Why are you still here?" He glared at them.

"You know you're a villager, right, Gregory?" said a hooded figure standing in the back of the tent.

"Shut up. You can't seem to do what you're told either," said Gregory.

"I'd say that's the mark of a poor leader," retorted the figure.

Gregory stood, brandishing his sword. The hooded figure raised a bow with a readied arrow. The hood fell off his blond head. "Archers," dismissed Gregory. "Completely useless against a blade."

"I can fire two arrows into your chest before you even lift your arm to swing." He reduced the tension in the string. "But, out of respect for the ladies present, I won't. Unless you do something incredibly stupid."

"The enemy is out there," said Berty, pointing towards Fairyland. "Be wise to remember that." Gregory lowered his sword. Taking a step forward, Berty said, "Vander, nice to see you again."

Vander shouldered his bow, then shook Berty's hand with a smile. "Likewise. Was wondering when I'd run into you," said Vander.

"So, it just you, or…?"

"No," said Vander. "I've been elected to represent the Boudonians. The Brotherhood of Archers is here as well as anyone willing to fight. I'm afraid you've walked in on the representatives of different villages' fighting forces trying to get along."

"Yes, I suppose we have," said Berty, looking at the five men and one woman congregated around the fire. "No sergeant or lieutenant has been assigned here?"

"Not as yet," said Vander.

Berty turned to the representatives. "Lieutenant," he said, "how would you recommend everyone get along?"

"I need numbers of able fighters, separated into fighting categories," said Edwin, "from each of you. And specialists or magic users, regardless of age, gender, or race will see me this evening in my command tent not too far to the west of here."

"One Empire Guard uniform wearer out of five just happens to be a lieutenant?" scoffed Gregory.

"I am Edwin of the House of Erland, First Lieutenant of the Empire Guard directly serving the Emperor and Empress of all that surrounds us," stated Edwin. "I require your lists this evening."

"Yes, Lieutenant," said the woman then promptly left the tent.

The rest gave Edwin a nod, before leaving. Gregory exited without looking at any of them. Vander gave Berty and Silvia a bow. "Declan and Obie are with us," Silvia told him.

"Thank you, Empress. We will be there shortly," said Vander. He sat at the small table in the back of the tent.

"Shall we press on?" asked Berty.

When they exited the tent, they continued east. "I am not walking this entire camp in the dark," said Delyth.

After coming across the Troll forces, they spoke with the Head Troll then moved farther east. Dwarves flanked the next command tent. Seeing Edwin, they let them enter. "Is there a message?" someone asked.

"Lieutenant," greeted the low growl of Goscislaw. "My Lady, my Lord, Princess." The Dwarves bowed. "Making the rounds, I see," said Goscislaw.

"We just arrived," said Silvia. "We visited Pixisle. Prince

Goscislaw, please meet Grier, the head of the Pixie special fighters."

"An honor," growled Goscislaw.

"Have you had a chance to consult the map?" Delyth asked.

"What map?" a Dwarf in bronze armor asked.

"Not as yet," said Goscislaw.

"Our tents are west of the Trolls," said Silvia. "We'll be collecting you and your head men later this evening for a meeting with everyone. The moon may be waning, but it is still bright. No lights outside the tents."

"Yes, Empress," said Goscislaw.

They traversed between the rows of tents westward. Hearing the call of the eagle, Berty looked skyward. The eagle he found in God Mountain descended. When it landed on his shoulder, its dark feathers turned white. It stayed perched there while they returned to the tent.

A fire cooked food in the central tent. Berty fed the eagle bits of his food. Strolling around the tent, Delyth stretched her wings. The children stared in awe. One of the boys tried to flap his wings, but they only inched.

"Wait until you have more strength," said Delyth.

"We haven't used our wings in a long time," said the boy. "We were told to hide them."

"By whom?"

"Our mommies," he said in a small voice. "So no one would know we're Fairies."

"You can be Fairies here," said Delyth. "My name is Delyth. What is yours?"

"Quniby," said the boy.

"And you?" she asked the other boy sitting next to Quinby.

"Carr," he answered.

Delyth looked at the young girl. "Malin," the girl said, "but I don't have wings."

"So?" said Delyth.

"You're the Princess," Malin said. She stared into Delyth's violet eyes. "What you said this morning was nice," she said. "Why... Why did you say a Fairy blessing over Blane? He wasn't a Fairy."

"You don't need to be a Fairy to receive such a blessing," explained Delyth.

"That's good. Blane got us out, but got hit with an arrow. He and Pernilla and Sanna," Malin indicated the older girl, "refused to eat so we would. But we ran out of food anyway."

"Excuse me, Lieutenant," said a voice from the tent opening. "I have a list for you."

"Come in," said Edwin. A few, including Gregory, gave lists and left. Two brought others.

A man, who was not a representative, pushed a girl around thirteen forward. She stumbled towards Edwin. "Sorrel, here, has a wand."

"Let's see the wand," said Declan.

"Who are you?" the man behind the girl asked.

Declan showed his wand. "Empire Advisor," he said.

Sorrel froze. "Go on, girl. An Empire Advisor ain't gonna hurt you."

Without turning her head, she peeked at the man prodding her. She flinched a little. Her hand slid into a pocket of the oversized coat she wore. Her hand shook pulling out a thin piece of wood that resembled a twig with its bark peeled and smoothed with handling.

"Hold it in your hand," instructed Declan.

Her feet shuffled forward. She swallowed as Declan's wand touched hers.

"Well?" said the man.

"She needs to stay to be assigned," said Declan. "The Lieutenant has your village's list. You may go."

When the man left, Declan beckoned Sorrel to the side with Berty and Silvia. "Are you afraid of that man?" he asked her.

She stared with wide blue eyes, but said nothing.

"He doesn't know you lied about the wand," said Declan.

She shook her head.

"Why did you lie?" he asked.

She bit her lip.

"Can you see magic?" asked Declan.

She shook her head.

"Can you do magic?" he asked.

She looked at him without saying a word, then glanced at Berty and Silvia.

"I'll take that as a yes," said Declan. "We'll talk again soon. Don't go anywhere."

The other specialists included an elderly Mage, a strong man, two archers—one who vacated once Vander and Cecil arrived, and a man Berty could only think to be a ninja.

While Vander gave Edwin the list, Cecil spent time with Obie. After speaking with Delyth, Cecil ducked out of the tent.

The Mage practiced practical magic. Silvia thought he was best suited to helping in the tent city, like he already did, and aiding in battle from afar. "I can do that, my Lady," said the Mage. "It is an honor to defend the Empire. Princess, we will get your home back."

Delyth gave him a respectful nod.

As tall as Edwin, but triple the girth, the strong man carried himself like an Ogre. "We will find a place for you, Fisk," said Edwin. "Possibly breaking down doors or through the gate."

Fisk grunted.

The archer explained how she hunted with a longbow. Edwin told her that she will have a place as well.

The "ninja" displayed his agility and swiftness with multiple short blades. After Grier said something in Edwin's ear, he said, "Tarmo, the Pixies would like you to accompany them through the city."

When the four left, Cecil returned with Geraldine, Leon, and another woman. Sorrel hungrily watched the women fuss over the emaciated children. "Want to tell me what's going on?" Silvia asked her quietly.

"What happened to them?" Sorrel asked.

"Lost without food," said Silvia. "All because their homes were taken from them."

"Will they be all right?"

"Only time will tell," answered Silvia.

Sorrel fingered her wand. "I made the wand myself," she admitted. "It was the only way." She paused to watch the kids smile at Geraldine. "My uncle stopped when he knew I had a wand."

"Do you have magic?" Silvia asked.

"I needed a wand," she said. "Only wand carriers have magic."

"That's not true," said Silvia.

Sorrel's eyes snapped to look at Silvia.

"What can you do?" Silvia asked.

"In front of everyone?" she asked in return.

"Something simple," said Silvia.

Sorrel's hands faced each other. A pink sphere sparked to life between them—not perfectly spherical like Obie's. Sparks from her fingertips jumped to the sphere and back.

"You're a Warlock, Sorrel," said Silvia.

"What does that mean?" Sorrel collapsed her sphere.

"The term, Warlock, means breaker," Silvia explained. "It's destructive magic best used in war."

Sorrel brightened. "Where do I go? What do I do?" she asked.

"Gather your things and bring them to this tent," said Silvia. "If we're not here when you return, wait for us. If anyone gives you a hard time, tell them it's at the request of the Empress."

"Thank you, my Lady." She ran out of the tent.

"So?" Cecil asked his mother and the other woman.

"We can get clothes made for these kids by tomorrow morning, the latest," the woman answered.

"Thanks, Edie," said Cecil.

"Spend time with your grandson, Geraldine," said Edie. "I'll take care of everything."

After Edie left, Declan said, "Mom, Dad, why are you both here?"

"Well, someone has to make sure people eat," said Geraldine.

"And I wasn't staying home," Leon said. "Besides, I can still use a bow, too, you know. Not that I'm going to fight, but I can defend the tents."

Sean edged closer to Declan's family, trying to be included in the conversation while Edwin scrutinized the lists. After the Elf gave Silvia a nod, she said, "Geraldine, Leon, I'm sorry, but we must attend a meeting. And we have to take Obie with us. Would you two be able to keep an eye on the children?"

"Of course," said Geraldine.

Delyth folded her wings. "Who is going?" Sean asked.

"You as well," said Silvia, "and all the Pixies." Silvia spoke privately with Declan's family while hoods raised.

They stepped into the night. A waning quarter moon gave them all the light they needed to see walking through the tent city. They stopped to gather the Head Troll and Goscislaw and his General.

Clouds covered the night sky in the west when they arrived at the central command tent. Edwin entered first. "Lieutenant," said Alvar's voice, "does that mean?"

Alvar studied those entering the tent. "Emperor, Empress," he said with a bow of his head. Lida and Elrick stood on the other side of a table. "Get the others," he said to a guard.

While they waited, all of them studied the three-dimensional map of Fairyland. Elrick, Lida, and Delyth answered questions mainly asked by the Troll and Dwarves.

Wystan and the Dominatrices entered the tent. "New arrivals, Captain," said the guard. "Prince Telor and Colonel Gwron of the Fairies." Lida cried, running to her son. "And Ojore and the Outlander of the Ghost Tribe in the Outlands."

A large white cat entered beside the proud woman who shouldered a rifle. "Ojore, Akia," said Berty, "we are honored to have you here."

"When the Colonel came to us for healing, we pledged our help to the Fairies," said Ojore. "Fighting for the Empire is our duty." Ojore and Berty grasped each other's forearms in greeting. "All our fighters and the Shaman are here."

"Is it here?" Berty overheard Delyth ask Telor.

Not hearing Telor's response, Berty said to Ojore and Akia, "Let's gather around the map and discuss strategies."

Telor stood between his mother and father. A hard determination shone in his green eyes. "We came out here," said Telor, indicating an unmarked place on the map.

"Do you think we can get back inside that way?" asked Delyth.

"I don't know," he said. "One thing I have learned is to have faith in the ancient magic. Everyone who found the way to the ruins has learned it. Some are more skilled than others, but we trust in it. We must for the future of Fairyland."

Delyth nodded, then glanced at Declan.

"The Pygmy Dragons and the Knownots have the Dragonlands side of Fairyland covered," said Alvar.

"With the encouragement of the Dragon, Tong," said Telor, "the clanless have protected us. They escorted us and the Ghost Tribe through the Dragonlands. They await the order to attack."

"The question is, do we attack them, or do we wait for them to come to us?" asked Goscislaw.

"If we attack, they will retreat to the castle, which is protected by ancient magic," said Elrick.

"Unless we use the old ways to get inside first," said Delyth. "Being the former Historian, Millicent will know certain things. But she can't know everything. The Dominatrix showed me some maps of the original city."

"I have them here," said the Elf. She pulled a few parchments out of a bag and handed them to the Fairy.

Delyth chose an old, battered parchment to hold to her nose. "I thought so," said Delyth. "This map is Fairy made." She handed the others back to the Elf.

Opening the parchment, Delyth rubbed Fairy Dust on the drawing. As she whispered words in the ancient Fairy language, a three-dimensional drawing popped out of the paper. She threw it over the map on the table. With a final ancient word, it aligned itself with the other map, superimposing itself on the three-D world as the ruins they became.

"*That* is impressive," said Sean.

Delyth pointed. "This is the tunnel you used," she said. Unfolding her wings, she jumped into the air. Delyth hover-bobbed over the map. After a few minutes of study, she said, "Here. We'll enter from here."

"Surely not everyone," said Wystan.

"Delyth will choose her infiltrators," said Silvia. "The rest of us will attack. Mixed forces, except the Dragons."

As Delyth touched ground, Alvar said, "Fairyland has five gates, two of which are in the Dragonlands. The Dragons will handle those. We will focus on these three and the two walls between them. Five forces led by Commander Wystan, General Dwarf Conall, Colonel Gwron, Head Troll Gunther, and me. We have seven Watchers besides Declan. A Watcher will be assigned to each force. Two will stay behind."

"How do we get past that green dome that sits atop the wall?" asked Wystan.

"I've contemplated the dome for months," said Telor. "I think I know how to defeat it."

Alvar nodded. "Princess, have you chosen?" he asked.

"Declan, Edwin, Verena, Zelda, some Knownots, a Guardian Troll who has not yet enlarged, and a Dwarf skilled in close combat," she replied.

"I know who will go with you, Princess," said the Dwarf General.

"Do we attack before the snow, after the snow, or with the snow?" Katell asked.

"With the snow," answered Silvia. "We attack once Telor destroys the dome. While the five of you concentrate on enemy forces, Grier will lead the search for the Whisperer. The Emperor and I will take a team inside to look for Leif."

"Sean, Obie, Ojore, Akia, Cecil, Vander, and Fisk," said Berty.

"The Dominatrices and Sorrel," added Silvia. "We will fight our way in and meet Delyth and the rest inside the castle."

"I am leaving at first light," Delyth told the Troll and the Dwarf.

Edwin stayed to discuss the western flank fighters with Alvar while Berty and the others returned to their tent. During their walk under increasingly cloudy skies, the Pixies interrogated Delyth about Fairyland.

Inside their command tent, the children slept around the fire with the watchful eyes of the Firths nearby. Sorrel kept to herself off to one side with her bags. "Where's Vander?" Declan asked Cecil.

"With Jordis. He's smitten," said Cecil.

Silvia approached Sorrel. The girl stood. "You fight with us tomorrow," Silvia told the girl. "Northeast tent. Choose a cot and get some sleep."

Obediently, Sorrel picked up her bags and left.

"What about the children?" Aloysia asked.

"We'll split them among us," said Declan.

"Excuse me," said a heavily accented voice.

"Come in, Shaman," said Silvia.

A white cloak covered all the bones draped around his neck and cascading to his bellybutton. Only the bone piercing his nose showed. "I was told about children," he said.

Silvia motioned to the fire.

He crouched next to one, placing his hand on her head. "Shh, go back to sleep," he said. He removed his hand. "She needs the most attention." He stared at her. "She does not walk?"

"No," said Declan.

Standing, he glanced at the others. "I will return shortly," he said. "Do not move them yet."

"Is he a Wizard?" asked Aloysia.

"Yes," said Declan. "He is very good at what he does."

"Excuse me, Aloysia," said Delyth. "Declan, it's time."

He looked at the Fairy. "Time for what?" he asked. "I thought we were leaving in the morning."

"Time for you to learn ancient Fairy," she told him.

"But, I'm not good with the ancient tongues," he said, taking a few steps away from her.

"Magic, Declan, like with Hope." She walked towards him.

His hands barricaded her from him as he continued to step back.

"I'm not going to hurt you," she said. She stopped her advance. "No Fairy Dust. Just a few words and a tap of my hand on your forehead."

"I—"

"You're the Duke of Fairyland, Declan," she admonished.

"I know," he said.

"You're afraid," she breathed.

"What if it takes away my ability to see?" he asked quietly.

"That's redicu—oh." Her fingers covered her mouth. "I don't think it works that way."

"I'd have to talk to Hope first," he said. "I'm sorry, Delyth."

Delyth gave him a slight nod. She retreated to the other side of the tent.

The tent flap moved. Edwin entered, saying, "I spoke with the Knownots." He glanced from Delyth to Declan. "They will be here."

He shifted his focus to a bag near the perimeter of the tent. "I took the liberty of having armor made for you. Not as heavy as Guard armor, but crafted from the same leather." He removed cuirasses from the bag. "My Lady," he said, handing her a female version of his armor. "My Lord." He gave Berty supple, yet stiff, leather armor that would cover his front and back. Edwin handed Delyth and Declan theirs as well. "I have none for you, Sean. I did not expect us to meet again."

Sean shrugged. "Which tent do I sleep in?" he asked.

The Shaman returned with a bottle of something for the children. Each of the younger children received a one teaspoon dose while Sanna swallowed two. "It will work while they sleep," he said. "I will check on them for as long as we're here."

"Thank you," said Berty.

They separated themselves and the children in each of the four tents. Declan's family returned to theirs.

Before the sun lightened the heavy clouded sky, they huddled around the fire in the central tent, eating. The four of them wore the leather armor Edwin gave them. With ties and straps, the Sages' Seal embossed leather fit well. Berty moved easily in it. By the time the Troll and Dwarf entered their tent, wearing the armor felt normal.

"The Knownots are waiting outside," Edwin told Delyth.

She nodded. "The sky lightens," she said. "Are we ready?"

Her chosen group raised their hoods in response. Raising her own, she said to Silvia and Berty, "See you on the inside." Delyth led her group out of the tent.

When Edie and others arrived with clothes for the children, Aloysia helped Carr dress. The Shaman returned to administer more doses. Those unfamiliar with him stared at the bone through his nose. Most of those dressing the children hastened back to their tents.

Vander entered the tent, searching. "Where's Declan?" he asked.

"Gone already," said Berty.

"Oh." His face fell.

"Pardon me, Emperor," said an Empire Guard through the flap. "Prince Telor will be ready in an hour. The Captain wishes everyone to begin lining up for our march on Fairyland in a half hour."

"Thank you," said Berty. Everyone in the tent froze for a second. "Vander, alert the village forces."

After giving a sharp nod, Vander exited the tent.

The Shaman scooped Sanna into his arms. "Hold hands," he told the other children. He held his free hand out for a child to take. "We're going on an adventure." A tiny, bony hand held onto his. He pulled them out of the tent.

Silvia said, "You all know what to do. Aloysia, Kirsi, Grier, if your hunt takes you out of this battle, let us know somehow when it has been completed."

"We will, Empress," said Grier.

Outside the tent, the rest of Berty and Silvia's chosen met them. As they walked to their places behind the force, passersby gave the leopard a wide berth. The group stayed close to the tents while Berty and Silvia parted the troops to the front line.

"Fighters of the Empire," addressed Silvia. "Today, we fight to defend our Empire, our homes, our families, and ourselves. We fight to liberate Fairyland. Lives have been lost. Families broken. Security shattered. We descend upon the walled city to trounce the invaders and curtail their destructive advance across these lands. Some of you already know atrocities at the hands of the anti-imperialists. Today, it ends."

"Do not expect a fair fight," said Berty. "They will use magic against us. They will use creatures. They may even resort to dishonorable tactics. Be ready for anything. Use your instincts. Fight with honor. Take back Fairyland. Restore our peace—our very lives. Today, your Empress and Emperor fight beside you. For you. *You* are the Empire. *You* are who we defend. Together, we save our home."

"For the Empire!" someone shouted.

"For the Empire!" a chorus of voices responded.

"Keep your eyes on Fairyland," said Alvar, riding along the flank. "When the dome disappears, attack! Begin your march. Keep your hoods raised."

Berty and Silvia returned to the others while the front line marched forward. The mix of Troll, Elf, Fairy, Dwarf, and Human moved haphazardly. It took a few minutes to find a rhythm. To the eagle on his shoulder, Berty said, "Go." A gentle pressure told him that the white bird pushed off to fly into the white snow.

Chapter Twenty-two

The Battle for Fairyland

Thickly falling snow obscured the view of the blue walls protecting Fairyland. An advancing army could easily be spotted crossing the fields from the lookouts on any other day. The snow and white cloaks protected them.

Green replaced white while the eagle lent Berty its sight. Telor streaked across the dome, spreading Fairy Dust. After crisscrossing the green, the Fairy stopped at the crest of the dome. His lips moved, but the wind carried away his words. Blue glowed against the green. Cracks appeared in the dome, giving it a crackled glass effect. Telor's head drooped.

"Telor's having problems removing the dome," said Berty.

"It needs a spark," Sean said. He raised the crystal topped Staff of Lightning. A crack of lightning shot from the crystal.

The eagle pushed Telor back. Lightning struck the crest of the dome. Blue sizzled through the green. Shattered green shards rained upon the multicolored city. Telor and a team of Fairy Guards zoomed inside, firing arrows at will.

Dark cloaked figures scrambled. Arrows whistled through the cold air over the wall. Shouts mobilized the invaders.

A long, black shape materialized over Fairyland. Tong opened his mouth. Dragonfire singed the backs of hairy creatures from God Mountain. He swooped between broken buildings. All four of his claws crushed then dropped dark shapes. His roar reached the forests beyond Fairyland. Roars of other Dragons in the trees answered his.

The eagle showed Berty the different colored lights of Knownots creating havoc. Pygmy Dragons zipped through the city, hunting anti-imperialists in teams. Fairies in dark cloaks made it safely to the snowy sky before meeting their white cloaked counterparts. Anti-imperialists waited in formations at each gate.

"That gate," said Silvia, indicating a scrolled metal gate arrows could not penetrate.

Sorrel produced a sparking ball.

"Not yet," said Berty. "Fairy magic flows through the metal." A faint pulse wove through the gate and wall. "Sean, what if you hit it?"

"Hmmm." Sean studied the gate from their distance. His staff moved as if determining the best spot.

The pulsing ceased. "Wait," said Berty. "Sorrel, send your sphere."

The sparking sphere soared over the armies. When it connected with metal, the gate exploded. White cloaks pushed inside.

"Awesome," said Sorrel.

Metal clanged beyond the walls. The Dominatrix freed her long sword. It glimmered with magic. Katell unsheathed her non-magical sword. "We fight together," the Dominatrix told her protégé. "We are the Dominatrix." The younger Elf gave her a stern nod.

Sean held the Staff of Lightning in one hand and his sword in another. After drawing his sword, Obie popped his yellow shield around his body. Both Cecil and Vander kept their bows ready. Ojore separated his bone spear to make two—one for each hand. Akia raised her gun while her leopard trotted by her side.

When both Berty and Silvia unsheathed their swords, worry crossed Sorrel's face. She had no weapon. Even Fisk clenched his fights, ready to pound. "Keep your magic at your fingertips," Silvia suggested. Sorrel lifted her hands. Sparks jumped from finger to finger.

They rushed inside the mangled metal gates. The Pixies chose a different route through the city with their ninja companion. As Silvia led them through winding streets, battles enveloped Fairyland. The Dominatrix decapitated Vindalf fighting from the shadows. Both Obie and Sorrel let their magic fly. Sean electrocuted anti-imperialists shooting from rooftops. The rifle's gunshot crack surprised fighters from both sides. Halfway to the castle, the enemy ignored their advance through the city.

Silvia stopped beside the last building before the road widened in front of the castle. "Shoot the lookouts," she ordered. Katell changed to a bow, joining Declan's brothers shooting at figures posted on the tops of the towers.

"There's one behind a window," said Katell.

"Show me," said Akia. Katell pointed. A gunshot echoed. Glass broke. "Taken care of."

"Berty, magic on the castle door?" asked Silvia.

Peeking at the blue on blue, he searched for some sort of movement in the walls. "None that I can see," he answered.

"Fisk, get the door," Silvia said.

They followed the brawny man to the ornate, blue metal castle doors. Fisk's mighty hands pushed against the metal. The center of the double doors buckled inward. As he pressed, the gap between the doors widened.

When they could pass through the opening, Akia scratched the white leopard's head. It skulked between the doors first. Tearing and slashing could barely be heard over half screams. Thuds. Then the cat meowed. "All clear," said Akia.

Inside, the castle interior threw a gray cast on their white cloaks. Four mutilated bodies spilled blood across the stone floor. Berty expected more resistance, more people defending the castle itself.

"Should we split up?" asked Sean. A ball of magic hurled towards them. Obie deflected it with one of his own. Sean's sword blocked an attack. "I think that's a no," he said. Tall figures enclosed them.

"Vindalf," Katell breathed.

Berty's sword met another's. In addition to being strong, the Vindalf he fought had a quickness Berty could not match. Berty pushed a couple of flames of Dragonfire out of his palm. The Vindalf stumbled back. His torso caught fire. The fire spread quickly. By the time he dropped to the ground, it consumed him. Berty recalled the flames before the blaze incinerated the carpet or tapestries.

Only Sean did not use his magic to dispel the attacking soulless Elves. Lightning probably would do the same or worse than Dragonfire in the enclosed space of the castle corridors. Leaving dead Vindalf, they continued toward the Throne Room.

Attacks sprung from side corridors and other rooms. Silvia dispatched an attacker with a few quick strokes of her sword. The leopard took detours, mauling anyone it crossed. Ojore's bone spears killed with efficiency. Cecil and Vander shot at targets out of sword's reach.

Eventually, the attacks ended. Beyond their footsteps on the stone, a battle raged. Muffled clanging, explosions, and roars permeated the castle corridor. Beautifully carved wooden doors waited only a few yards away. "The Throne Room," said Berty.

"Why isn't it guarded?" said Ojore.

"Because we weren't supposed to make it this far inside the castle," said Sean.

"Could be a trap," said the Dominatrix.

Sean tried the doors. "Locked. Perhaps barred on the inside."

Fisk threw his shoulders into the double doors. With each pound, wood splintered. Akia tucked the butt of her rifle into the crook of her shoulder. Her finger rested on the trigger. Vander and Cecil nocked arrows.

The door shattered. Chunks of wood clunked to the stone floor. Fisk fell backward into the hall. A quiver-full of arrows stuck into his broad chest. Gunfire reverberated off the stone. The leopard sprung into the room. Claws dug into the waiting dark cloaked army.

The brothers volleyed arrows into the room from an angle beside the doorway. Obie and Sorrel released spheres and streams into the Throne Room. Lightning escaped Sean's staff. When sections of ceiling fell, it ceased. He charged, sword first. The rest ran behind him. The Dominatrix and Katell fought back to back, slicing through the dark cloaks.

Berty released spurts of Dragonfire at the decreasing army. The Staff of Lighting blocked like any old staff, but of its own accord while Sean slashed with a sword in each hand. Ojore spun, stabbing with precision.

The Throne Room transformed into forest. Silvia's Wood Guard joined the battle. As the dark cloaks' numbers dwindled, a female voice screamed, "No!" Berty glimpsed a shining gown moving between the trees. "You need the Scepter for that magic," the woman squeaked.

"Think what you wish," said Silvia, "Millicent." Her sworded opponent fell at her feet.

Berty slammed a few into trees with a wave of his hand. The strawberry blonde Fairy launched into the air. Neon blue sprinkled over Silvia. "Old Fairy Dust," warned Berty. Silvia covered her head with her cloak. The Throne Room returned and the wooden protectors disappeared with the forest.

"*Crem dum bine!*" yelled another voice. The Dust froze in midair.

Declan, Edwin, a Troll, and a Dwarf emerged from a translucent wall behind Delyth. Silvia rolled out from under the frozen Fairy Dust. More dark cloaks poured through the battered door. The Troll grew to its club wielding Guardian size. It barged through the dark cloaks, batting them aside like gnats.

Declan fired his arrows faster than both of his brothers. Edwin cut a line through the cloaks to Berty and Silvia. The Dwarf brutally cut down everyone in his way. Delyth fought in flight.

Magic exploded, shaking the room. Berty spun as glass pelted his back. Snow streamed through the broken windows. A dark shape slithered past. The Dragon's roar rattled the remaining glass.

Millicent cackled as she spewed Fairy Dust that Delyth froze. A scream pierced Berty's eardrums. A white shape crumpled to the floor. Her long sword rang against the stone. The Dominatrix lay on her side, eyes staring nowhere. Katell stumbled. She retrieved the long sword from where it fell. Magic filled her. Katell became the new

Dominatrix. She danced around the Throne Room. Anti-imperialists suffered the rage of her blade.

"Follow me," Silvia said to Berty. Snow whipped throughout the golden Throne Room. Silvia stood in the center, Berty at her back. "Gather," she ordered the others. White cloaks and a leopard fought to her side.

Magic blasted from her epicenter. Dark figures dominoed to the stone floor. Squealing, Millicent flew out a window. Silvia crumpled to the floor.

"Don't let her escape," Berty said.

Sword in hand, Delyth sped after her.

"Secure the castle," Berty commanded. "Find Leif. Employ the Knownots if need be." Everyone scrambled.

Berty knelt beside Silvia. "Are you okay?"

"Fairy magic drains," she said. "So strong. Fights mine."

"Like that Sethbravin ruins place."

"Yes."

"I'll carry you out." He lifted her off the floor.

Carrying her through the corridors, Berty brought Silvia to the grounds behind the castle. A tall, bright green cloaked figure struggled through the deep snow. "Leif," said Silvia.

Berty used magic to trip him. The old man fell face first into the snow.

"I can walk," Silvia said.

After setting her on her feet, Berty ran to the form pushing himself out of the snow. "Hello again, Leif," he said. The point of Berty's sword hovered inches from Leif's chest.

The former scholar shot Berty a disdainful stare. "Get away from me, you usurper," he said. Invisible hands pulled Leif out of the snow.

He floated a couple of feet above the white. Silvia approached. "Empress," he breathed. Fear flashed in his eyes.

Millicent circled above them. She sprinkled neon blue Fairy Dust. Berty stepped back. When the Dust hit Leif, he crashed to the ground.

A blur zoomed overhead. A streak of metal sliced Millicent's arm as she flew closer to the trees.

"That was for my father," said Delyth. She lunged, but Millicent dodged.

Millicent covered a part of her arm while bobbing over the edge of the forest. "I heard he walks with a cane. Too bad the Fairy Eater didn't finish the job," she taunted. "All my efforts to find that beast. Well, all the beasts. Years of planning." Slowly, the Fairies circled each other. "Searching for the Prime Stone. Experimenting with old Fairy Dust. Bending Leif to my will." Her laugh suggested her mind plunged into somewhere. "All the Dust I've fed him over the years. Only the Dust Master can help him now. That's if the Dust Master is still alive." She laughed again.

Enraged, Delyth pushed the circling faster until they were both blurs against the snow.

Declan stopped next to Berty. "She's been behind it all?" he asked.

"Seems that way," said Silvia.

Raising his bow, Declan poised to shoot. He lowered it again, saying, "I can't. I may hit Delyth."

Red blood blemished the white snow.

"For my mother," said Delyth, still a blur of the lightest lavender.

Blue blood dropped alongside the red.

"For my brother," they heard Delyth say.

The lavender cut across straight. Millicent spiraled out of the blurry circle. The snow carried her screams. They died with a crack and a squelch.

Delyth hovered near a tree bordering the castle grounds. Blood stained the pointed top of a trunk that snapped during a storm. Dangling a few feet from the top… dainty hands and feet, periwinkle wings, strawberry blonde waves—dancing with the snowflakes.

"For me, Fairyland, and the Empire," said Delyth. After a moment of staring, she landed beside Leif lying in the snow. Examining him, she shook her head.

"What?" asked Silvia.

"Fairy Dust poisoning," Delyth answered. "Stand back and avert your eyes."

"What are you doing?" asked Declan.

"I must remove the Dust, but that may not restore his health," Delyth told Silvia.

"Could the Dust Master—?" began Declan. He stopped when she raised her hand.

"*I* am the Dust Mistress," said Delyth. "Just a few steps back will be fine."

Chapter Twenty-three

For the Betterment of the Empire

They stepped closer to the castle then turned to face it. White piled on the blue turrets and ramparts. A murmur of the ancient Fairy language filled the spaces between the snowflakes. The peace of winter washed over Berty. "How are you feeling, Silvia?" he asked.

"Better," she said. "There was no ground in there. It was all Fairy magic."

"The old Fairy stronghold the city had been built upon is extensive," said Declan. "There are rivers of magic down there. Delyth tapped into one to remove the defenses."

"Okay," called Delyth.

Turning, they walked towards Leif who seemed resigned to not move. He groaned. "My Lady," he labored, "forgive me."

Telor landed with a few guards. "Delyth," he said, hugging his sister. "I saw...," he said into her braids.

"Is the castle secure?" asked Berty.

Releasing his sister, Telor said, "Yes. The Dragons have been… incinerating escapees. Commander Wystan and Captain Alvar are taking care of the prisoners. General Conall and Head Troll Gunther are helping Gwron secure the city. The Dominatrix and Lieutenant Edwin control the castle. I believe I saw the Pixies chase someone or something into the Dragonlands." He looked at Leif. "What shall we do with this one?"

"Help him stand," said Silvia. Two of the Fairies helped him up by the arms. "Leif," she said, standing squarely in front of him, "you are hereby charged with the following crimes against the Empire: treason, conspiracy to commit murder, empricide, abduction, attempted abduction, and murder. This list may be incomplete and may change during the course of our investigation."

"I was under Millicent's control," he said in a weak voice.

"Crown Prince Telor," Silvia continued, "Leif needs a guarded room in which he will give a full account of his crimes under the influence of Millicent and where the Wizard will attend him."

"Of course, Empress," said Telor. "We will take him now." The guards lifted Leif off the snowy ground, then followed Telor inside the castle.

Delyth's gaze kept wandering to the tree impaled Millicent. Taking her hand, Declan pulled her towards the castle. Without saying a word, the four of them returned to the Throne Room. Clear of all bodies but one, shattered glass sparkled on the floor in the brief passing of sunlight.

Two Irmingard Warriors stood by the broken doors. Katell carefully straightened the former Dominatrix's body. The older Elf laid on a narrow cart resembling a gurney. When the younger Elf was satisfied, she placed a white sheet over the body. A horn decorated the funeral shroud. Katell stood to her full height. She gave the Warriors a nod. They rolled the cart out of the room. "The High Elf must inter a Dominatrix," she said. "I need to prepare to honor the fallen Warriors. The Outlander has taken my mantle as castle protector."

As the Elf strode away, a Pygmy Dragon darted through a broken window. "Princess, we have cleared our section of the city of anti-imperialist scum."

"Thank you, Paul," she said. "We could not have done it without you."

"Is there anything else you need us to do?" he asked.

"Rest for now." Delyth's voice sounded robotic. "The King and Queen will want to thank you personally. I must fetch them."

"Very good," he said. He glanced over Delyth's shoulder.

She turned. "Paul, please meet my brother, Crown Prince Telor," Delyth said. "Telor, this is the First Dragon of the Pygmy Clan."

Telor nodded his head to the Dragon. "Leif is secure. We need patrols in the city while residents return and provide order during the clean-up," he said.

"We can patrol the Dragonlands side," piped Paul.

"That would be much appreciated, Paul. Thank you." After giving a strange bow of sorts, the Dragon zipped through a window. "We need to assess so we can plan for the survival of the rest of winter and the rebuilding of the city. I will set-up in the Dining Hall." He took a few steps towards the broken door. "If anyone can be spared, please send them to me." He walked into the hall.

"I need to collect my parents," Delyth said. She opened the golden doors to the balcony behind the throne. Without closing the doors, she leapt into the sky.

The three of them walked to the bent castle doors. "I should tend to the wounded," said Declan. "My full bag is in the tent. I only brought emergency supplies."

Edwin and Akia guarded the inside of the doors. Through the opening, Berty saw the leopard keeping guard. "We found horses," said Edwin. "I sent Obie, Sean, and Declan's brothers to retrieve our stuff. Ojore rode to gather the Shaman."

"Thanks," said Declan. "Tell Obie where to bring my healer bag. See you later." He ducked through the bent doors.

"When Sean returns, tell him that Prince Telor could use his assistance," Berty told Edwin. "He's in the Dining Hall if you need him."

"We will be interrogating Leif," Silvia said. She and Berty climbed the stone steps.

They eventually found the guarded room. The guards opened the door and closed it behind them. Leif sat propped on the bed. His eyelids fluttered open to stare at them. White overtook all remaining vestiges of red in his wild mane. His skin had a bluish hue, probably from the Fairy Dust. Berty decided not to look at him. Instead, he placed two chairs at the foot of the bed.

Once they both sat, Silvia said, "You may begin."

Leif only looked at Silvia while he spoke. "When Millicent arrived at the Empire Tree as Historian, she asked me if I could show her the Advisor Vaults. While we were down there, she blew Fairy Dust in my face. I was hers ever since. She wanted to be Empress, to have the power of the Scepter at her fingertips. She said there was a terrible injustice—an imbalance of magic and power in the world. She had to correct it. She wanted to make a better world.

"We schemed. Made alliances with Watchers in the Guild. Hired men to spread our magic propaganda. People believed what we fed them. Then, we fanned the flames.

"Once free of the Empire Tree, we gathered followers. She can be... very persuasive without having to use Fairy Dust. We latched on to the Fairy underground movement. I think she had contacts there from before her Historianship.

"We came across a Whisperer who used the Whispers to play pranks on people and spy. He learned about Vindalf, the Faematask and found the locations of creatures and how to open their prisons. With his help, we collected sympathizers and magic users. He made them take oaths, which darkened their cloaks. In a matter of months, we amassed an army.

"We needed to house the army and having a headquarters near the Dragonlands made sense. The plans to grab Fairyland came together quickly. Millicent had some sort of personal vendetta against the Fairy royal family, but I do know not what it was. I do think that influenced her zeal in taking Fairyland."

Leif stared out the lead glass windows. "I believe you know the rest," he said. His eyes found Silvia again. "Will I die a prisoner?"

Silvia said nothing for a moment. "Yes," she finally answered. "You jockeyed for power within a council of equals. You coveted an ancient magical object no one could have. Before Millicent arrived, you approached the Watcher's Guild. You spoke with the Guild Master, trying to change the course of the prophecy. There is pre-Millicent evidence of correspondence with the Fairy anti-royal movement and with family houses of Irmingard known for their contempt of the Empire."

Leif's eyes widened and nose flared before he regained composure. "I was merely obtaining information about Fairy Dust and magical weaponry for the betterment of the Empire."

"Why not correspond with the Dust Master or the Dominatrix?" Silvia countered.

Anger filled his lined face. "You have allowed this man, the outsider, to cloud your judgment," said Leif.

"I've heard enough. You do not accuse the Scepter's chosen. It is your judgment which has been clouded," said Silvia. She looked to Berty. "Emperor?"

Berty stood. "Leif, I find you guilty of conspiracy against the Empire and the Empress, treason, and dereliction of duty as a member of the Empire's Advisory Council," he said.

"Without an audience and witnesses?" asked Leif.

Silvia stood next to her husband. "We're saving the fanfare for the Fairies. We are in Fairyland, after all," she said. "A Wizard will be in to see you shortly."

"There are no Wizards in the Land of Sages," said Leif.

"There is today." She and Berty left the room.

Cecil waited for them in the hall. "We have your things," he said. "Edwin told us to see the Prince. Vander ended up assisting him with Sean. The King and Queen arrived a few minutes after we did. Before the Prince could assign me somewhere, Delyth had me find you."

Entering the Dining Hall, Berty overheard Lida say, "Geraldine, you are the mother of a Fairy noble. You will not cook in the castle kitchens."

"I will supervise," said Geraldine.

Lida pursed her lips.

"It's cold. People will need something to warm them," Geraldine said. "Not one fireplace in the castle is lit. The best warmth comes from the inside."

"There might not be anything," said Lida. "Because of the siege."

"Don't worry," Geraldine said with a smile. "We'll come up with something. Hunters are already out there." When Lida gave her a nod, she left.

"We will need wood for now and for the rest of the winter. I have made an arrangement with Prince Goscislaw for some coal, but it won't be enough to last," said Telor, lifting his head from shuffling his papers.

"I'll take care of it," offered Cecil.

Lida's eyes found Berty and Silvia. "A full castle is a warm castle," she said. "Elrick and Leon are supervising clean-up. I will make sure people have plans to sleep. Emperor, Empress, you have been so accommodating in our time of need. I don't know how we can ever thank you."

Lida assigned them a room to where they brought their entire group's belongings. After, they greeted the Shaman at the bent castle doors. "Where are the children?" Berty asked while they walked to Leif's room.

"Fairy Godmother Guild," said the Shaman. "They are taking in any and all children that need to be watched, fed, or otherwise taken care of while Fairyland rebuilds."

The guards opened the door for the Shaman. Berty and Silvia waited outside. After mere seconds, the Shaman returned to the hall.

"He has taken his own life," the Shaman stated.

"What?" Silvia pushed past him into the room. Berty ran after her.

Leif hung from the canopy above the footboard. Twisted bed curtains wrapped around his neck.

Tearing her eyes away from the painful defiance on his face, Silvia turned to the Shaman who stood in the doorway. "How long has he been dead?"

"He hanged himself before I passed through the gates of Fairy-land," he answered. "His neck broke. Death was instantaneous."

She nodded. "Coward," she muttered, facing the body.

"Put him with the dead," Berty told the guards. He placed his arm around Silvia, steering her out of the room.

Silvia busied herself helping Lida place people in castle rooms. Berty found himself back inside the breezy Throne Room. Snow collected on the windowsills and floor. Behind the thrones, Elrick stood on the balcony. Joining him, Berty finally saw the damage Fairyland sustained since the invasion. Cracks and holes decorated the sparkling, colorful buildings. Sections of the city smoldered. The white cloaked dead gathered in the square and the streets radiating from it. The dark cloaked dead lined lesser streets and alleys.

"The price of war," said Elrick. "The city can be rebuilt. Lives..." His gloved hands tightened around the railing. "They attacked the defenseless, farming communities, villages where half the population were away working." The Fairy paused to watch Tong encircle the city. "No matter how justifiable, even in the defense of your own, there is always a price to pay. Sometimes, it would be easier if the price were only blood. Every man, woman, and child this war touched are changed forever." He let out a breath. "We must be strong for them."

"Your Majesty?" Leon stood just inside the doorway.

Elrick turned. "Call me Elrick," he said.

"Elrick," said Leon, "I found some wood we can reclaim to cover the door. Should keep the majority of the cold out of the castle from this room. I'm going to need some help carrying it."

"I can carry," said Berty.

"My Lord?" said Leon.

"I'm Emperor, not an invalid," Berty said. "I can also use some tools. Just don't let my father know I admitted that."

Elrick laughed a little. "I'll help, too."

The three of them carried panels of wood, some carved, some plain, from obscure places in the castle to the Throne Room door. Leon also scrounged hammers and nails or nail-like metal. Elrick and hammers did not get along well. The Fairy was relegated to holding the wood in place or handing the other two nails while they hammered. Berty could hear mumblings of, "Is that the King?" and, "That's the Emperor," as people passed.

When they had finished, the men stood back to admire the patchwork doors. Berty's shoulders ached. "Dad," said Declan, who approached looking as weary as Berty felt.

"How are the injured?" asked Elrick.

"We addressed all the major injuries," said Declan. "Four healers and the Shaman made a world of difference."

The Fairy nodded. "Let's get ourselves to the Dining Hall."

A washbasin by the door allowed them to wash their hands. People crammed around the room-filling table, eating a self-serve, simple stew. The men filled bowls and joined the table.

Every type of guard patrolled the city as Fairies trickled back to their homes, if they still had homes to which to return. Those who needed food or fuel or clothing or shelter found it from neighbors, strangers, or the castle.

Tong helped carry dead anti-imperialists outside the city. Leif's and Millicent's bodies rested on the top of the pile. Millicent's wings stood impaled on the tree trunk in the center of the square. Silvia and

Berty watched Tong burn the bodies. A small crowd gathered beside them, most hoping that the "funeral" would give them closure.

While the anti-imperialists burned, villagers, the Dwarves, and the Trolls brought their dead home. Before the Dwarves left, Goscislaw promised to send metalworkers to fix the doors and gates.

Katell, the new Dominatrix, presided over fallen Warriors' funerals. Her dark hair and white dress blew in snow-filled wind. She spoke in the ancient Elf language. It sounded similar to the words Avery used for his mother's. In lieu of proper pyres, the dead held sticks to symbolize the Elf's connection to the trees. Tong, again, provided the fire under the Dominatrix's instructions.

The Fairies made a new cemetery for burying their dead as well as those not burned or brought home for private funerals. Sean magically dug the graves in the frozen dirt. Elrick and Lida gave the interred the Fairy blessings.

Alvar oversaw the makeshift pyres for the Empire Guards. Both Berty and Tong used their Dragonfire to light the pyres. Silvia said a few words in the ancient tongue. All Berty heard was Elrick's words from the balcony: *the price of war.*

The Boudonian Woodsmen made sure every fireplace had a supply of wood. Warmth kept to the castle bedrooms. Drafts haunted the remainder of the castle, forcing castle dwellers to wear cloaks everywhere. Hunters and expert foragers provided food for larders and root cellars. After a few days, most of the non-Fairies returned home. Declan's family stayed at Elrick and Lida's request. Alvar kept an Empire Guard escort behind for Berty, Silvia, and Declan as well as for Declan's family. Their escort would report to the Outpost near Boudon. Sorrel accepted an offer to join the Empire Guard. After thanking Silvia and Declan for giving her a chance, she left with them to start her training in the Sages' Grove.

The Outlanders left after one night huddled in a few rooms in the castle. Fairyland's winter did not agree with their hotter climate's temperance. When each faction readied to leave, both Berty and Silvia and Lida and Elrick personally thanked the leaders.

It took the better part of a week to try and convict all the anti-imperial prisoners. Fairyland carried out swift justice. Elrick devoted a room in the castle to collect all the stuff they left behind. From weapons and armor to wands and clothing to books and papers that belonged to the anti-imperialists found a place there. Declan and his fellow Watchers sorted for magical items. The Dominatrix searched for legendary weaponry and armor. Others poured over papers, cataloguing plans, and information. They recycled every bit until the room was empty.

"It wasn't there," Declan reported to Berty and Silvia. "Leif had plenty of journals, but none like the one Martin has."

"Maybe he destroyed it," said Berty.

"Maybe," repeated Silvia. She stared out a window in the little study they commandeered. "Or it may still be out there somewhere. Anyone could use it and not realize what they have." Stepping away from the window, she sat at the desk. "Whatever happened to it, Martin will deliver it to the Vault as soon as we return."

The Head Mistress of the Godmother Guild personally delivered the children they found to the castle. They almost regained a healthy weight. Sanna walked with the assistance of two crutches. While the children gawked at the Dining Hall, the Head Mistress said, "Quinby still has family, however, they have yet to return to Fairyland. The rest are orphans without any family still alive that we have found. Malin is special. Fairy born without wings."

"Where's Aloysia?" Carr asked Delyth.

"Her mission isn't over yet," Delyth told him.

His eyes drooped.

"The Guild is not equipped to house children long term," the Head Mistress stated. "We can find them suitable homes."

"In the meantime, they will stay in the castle," said Lida.

"Shall I send a Godmother to them?"

"That would be wise, Head Mistress. Thank you."

"One will arrive later today," she said. As she left, the Pixies entered.

"Aloysia!" Carr cried. He ran to her.

She scooped him into her arms. "You've gotten so big," she said with a smile. Aloysia held him while Grier reported.

"The Whisperer is dead," Grier announced. "We wish to remain on the mainland to search for other Whisperers. If any are found, they will be sent to Pixisle for training. This can never happen again."

"Very well," said Silvia. "Thank you." She extracted her wand and touched the tip to her white cloak. The white faded from everything whitened by tree magic. All the original colors returned. "It's time we leave for home," she said to Elrick and Lida.

That evening, the Fairies served an extra special stew. "Elrick and I have come to a decision," Lida said. She smiled at her guests.

Elrick and Lida stood. Elrick said, "We wish to announce the engagement of our daughter, Princess Delyth of Fairyland to Duke Declan Firth of Fairyland."

Delyth gasped, then smiled. She grabbed Declan's hand.

"We're hoping for a spring wedding once the Throne Room has been restored." Lida raised her glass. "Blessings to the happy couple."

Chapter Twenty-four

Peace

Declan invited both Berty's and Matt's families to his wedding. They were his only personal guests. Since Lida bonded with Kate, she loved their addition to the guest list. Silvia made sure they all had appropriate dress before they took the carriage to Fairyland.

Upon their arrival, they discovered that most of Boudon traveled to Fairyland to celebrate their only noble son's marriage to a Princess. None of whom would witness the wedding.

Flowers decorated the Throne Room. Many sprays disguised in progress renovations. Berty and Silvia sat in their gold trimmed finery in the front row with the Advisory Council. Across the aisle sat the Heads of the Empire. Edwin, Lark, and Berty's family filled the rows behind them. Teresa sat herself on the outside of the row, so she could leave quickly if need be. Lily was due to arrive soon. Her midwife had a room in the castle, although not a seat in the Throne Room. The Fairy Court occupied the remaining chairs.

On the dais, the thrones rested against the back wall. Empty chairs waited closer the front—three on one side and seven on the other.

Wedding guests stood. Elrick, Lida, and Telor processed down the center aisle. They waited, standing on the dais for Declan's family. Leon and Geraldine led Cecil, Vander, Julie and Matt, and Obie to Delyth's family. After the Fairies received the Firths, the families sat on their respective sides.

Two doors opened, one behind each family. Delyth and Declan entered the dais from their family's doors. Delyth wore a silver gown, trimmed with deep purple. Her wings reflected the twinkle of her dress. Flowers wove through her dark curls. Declan's rich red wedding tunic had a silver archer crest on its chest, though the Bow of the Moon did not have a place on his back. His smile stretched from ear to ear when he saw her. When they reached the center of the dais, they joined hands.

"Declan, Duke of Fairyland," said Delyth, "I bind myself to thee."

"Delyth, Princess of Fairyland," said Declan, "I bind myself to thee."

In unison, they said, "I accept your binding from this day to the end of all." Sill holding hands, they kissed.

The families stood. Behind the couple, the families hugged one another. They parted to let Declan and Delyth walk to the balcony. As they lifted their joined hands, cheers echoed in the square and beyond. When the cheering died down, the newlyweds led their guests to the Dining Hall for the wedding feast.

Eating and dancing intermingled. Elrick could dance without the aid of his cane. As the feast wound down, younger members of the Fairy Court joined the street parties. "Someone has to spread the gossip," said Lida. "Might as well be them." Whoever remained in the castle retired to their rooms. Berty gave Declan a congratulatory smile before leaving with Silvia.

The food and wine weighed Berty's stomach down as they walked back to their room. "They're going to be happy together," he said to Silvia. "Like we are."

"Yes, they will," said Silvia smiling. "Maybe not quite as happy."

"Why not?"

"Because, Berty Chase, love of my life, you're going to be a father."

He stopped midstride. Smiling, he placed his hand on her abdomen. His hands then slid around her waist. Kissing her, he could not wait to get home and prepare to welcome a new life to their now peaceful world.

The World In-between Series

will continue…

Book 5: Hope

Coming 2016

Book 6: Dreamweaver

Coming 2017

About the Author

IE Castellano is an American author and poet living in the Eastern United States. Falling in love with the mechanics of the English language at an early age, she started writing poetry before venturing into fiction. She loves history (especially ancient), mythology, archeology, and anthropology. Anything IE reads, sees, or does could wind up in one of her books in some manner. With her propensity to ask, what if, she writes speculative fiction—authoring the dystopian sci-fi novel, *Tricentennial*, and the contemporary epic fantasy series, *The World In-between*.

For news and a current list of her writings, visit her blog: IECastellano.blogspot.com. Contact IE at IECastellano@zoho.com. Connect with her on Google+ and Twitter.

Also by IE Castellano

The World In-between Series:

    The World In-between (The World In-between, 1)

    Bow of the Moon (The World In-between, 2)

    Secrets of the Sages (The World In-between, 3)

    Yuletide Magic (A World In-between Short Story)

    The Dragonlands (A World In-between Short Story)

Short Stories:

    The Hunt (Moon Shadows)

    Sector Three-three (Across the Karman Line)

    All That Lies (Disturbance)

Other Novels:

    Tricentennial

    Where Pirates Go to Die

www.ingramcontent.com/pod-product-compliance
Lightning Source LLC
Chambersburg PA
CBHW051524250626
47156CB00001B/217